THINGS
INVISIBLE

A NEBRASKA MYSTERY

William J. Reynolds

G. P. PUTNAM'S SONS NEW YORK

G. P. Putnam's Sons
Publishers Since 1838
200 Madison Avenue
New York, NY 10016

Library of Congress Cataloging-in-Publication Data

Reynolds, William J.
Things invisible: a Nebraska mystery/William J. Reynolds.—

1st American ed.
p. cm.
I. Title.
PS3568.E93T47 1989   88-28797 CIP
813'.54—dc19
ISBN 0-399-13448-4

Printed in the United States of America
1 2 3 4 5 6 7 8 9 10

This one is for
JIM CARNEY,
because he ought to have a book dedicated to him;
and for
PEG,
because everything is for her.

chapter

1

"Days like this remind you that you're going to die."

I looked from the cup and saucer in the woman's lap to her eyes, which were focused, or unfocused, on the window, past the window, on something beyond the moisture-spotted pane. I looked, and knew what she meant. It was one of those gray, drizzly, blustery days, the kind that descend on the Midwest in late September and remind us that the bright, balmy days will, like everything, pass away and be replaced by the cold, bleak landscape of winter. And there's nothing anyone can do about it.

On this particular Monday morning the world, or that portion of it occupied by Omaha, Nebraska, was the color of lead. The air had been replaced with some thick, wet substance that carried the subtle but definite aroma of fish. The skies, heavy and close, couldn't decide whether or not to rain, so until a consensus could be reached they just hung there, gray and misty. The bullet wound in my left arm, a nearly healed leftover from an escapade earlier that summer, ached dully from the damp.

The woman was definitely more interesting than the weather, so I looked at her again.

She was, I suppose, a few years older than me—mid- to late-forties, make it—dark-haired, olive-skinned. Small-boned, a little plump by modern standards. But mine are not modern standards. When you grow up with Hollywood proffering the likes of Jane Russell and Sophia Loren, Marilyn Monroe and Senta Berger and Elke Sommer as the epitome of feminine beauty, it's hard to get too worked up over the slender, even emaciated look that's been in vogue—and for all I know *Glamour* and *Cosmopolitan* and

Mademoiselle too—far too long. The pendulum was past due for its return swing.

I said, "Mrs. Berens, about your daughter . . ."

Donna Berens turned away from the window and fiddled with the cup in her lap, dipping a silver teaspoon in and out, in and out of the beige liquid. Her fingers were long and delicate and ended in well-tended nails that were painted a pale, pearly pink. That one of them was chewed down to nothing was the only clue that they were her own and not Lee Press-On Nails. That a few strands of hair glinted silver under the unflattering blue-gray light from outside indicated that the color was hers and not Lady Clairol's. That a dark puddle had gathered below her left eye proved that her long, dark lashes were a gift from Max Factor and not Ma Nature, but what the hell.

"I'm sorry," she said and her voice was cool and smooth, like silk on glass. "I just . . ." She looked at me, straightened her backbone and lifted her chin. "What can I tell you, Mr. Nebraska?"

"You tell me." I smiled winningly. "I'm smiling winningly, incidentally. I learned it from watching Spenser on TV."

She smiled, sort of. "You really are the oddest man."

"Now we're getting somewhere." I sipped coffee from a china cup so delicate I was almost afraid to touch it. "Let's see if I have the facts straight." I consulted the little wire-bound pad on my knee, but there was no need: The story was easy enough to remember. "You spoke with your daughter, Meredith, on the telephone yesterday afternoon." Donna Berens nodded. "You tried to call her again last night and there was no answer." She nodded. "You tried again several times—"

"Four times."

"—during the evening, still with no answer." More nodding. "You tried twice more after midnight—"

"If Meredith had gone out—and she hadn't, or she'd have told me—but if she had she would have been home by midnight. She had to work today. She was *supposed* to work today . . ."

"—with no answer. You tried again twice this morning, same result."

"And Meredith didn't show up for work this morning," Donna Berens said. "I talked with her employer. She didn't call in sick, she gave no indication that she wouldn't be in today. She simply didn't arrive."

All of which occupied less than one of those stingy little notepad pages.

I said, "What about friends? Relatives? Someone Meredith might have gone to stay with."

This time the dark head moved in a negative wag. "There's no one, really. Meredith is . . . Meredith has always been something of a loner. Perhaps that's my fault. Her father and I separated twelve years ago, when Meredith was only thirteen. Meredith and I moved back here and I suppose she was somewhat . . . isolated. It's hard to make new friends at that age. The girls at Duschene were awfully cliquish." Duschene was and is a girls' high school. "Not that Meredith is . . . *abnormal* in any way," she added, the words almost rushing out. Her eyes darted, swept the sterile little room as if seeking some flaw. Her voice was stiff, perhaps even defensive, as if she was afraid that I or someone else might accuse her of disloyalty to her daughter. "She's a perfectly normal girl. A beautiful girl. She has friends." As if I had said she hadn't. "Just not the sort she would up and go stay with. Certainly not without telling someone. Telling me."

"Perhaps she tried to and you were out."

"I wasn't. I went to Mass yesterday morning *before* I talked to Meredith, and then I was home all day. In any event, I have an answering machine. She would have left a message."

I carefully positioned my cup in its circle in the saucer and let my eyes wander the living room.

The private-eye books all begin with the hard-boiled hero in his down-at-heels office, sitting behind his battered wooden desk, leaning back in his creaky swivel chair, his feet up (which explains how the desk came to be so battered), a glass of whiskey in his hand, a half-empty bottle on the blotter. Half-full, if you're an optimist. Across the desk from him sits the client: female, of course; attractive, of course; disapproving, natch. She's having a hard time getting to the point, and our hero is doing his macho best to ignore her, focusing his attention on the spinning of a spider in a corner of the ceiling or the buzzing of a blue-bottle fly against the dirty window. Eventually the flinty-eyed protagonist will (a) get the client sufficiently ticked off to tell him what she's there for or (b) get the client sufficiently ticked off to leave. Doesn't matter; the case will come back around to him one way or the other. Trouble Follows Me, and so on.

It's a good scene, but even when I was in the PI business full-time, and had the requisite down-at-heels office downtown in the Condemned Building, I preferred to hold the preliminary meeting on the potential client's turf. You get a better idea what sort of person you're apt to be dealing with when you see him or her in the natural environment. Since quitting the business, to the extent I have quit, and taking up the equally low-paying life of a free-lance writer, preference has become necessity. My "office" is a desk shoved into a corner of the bedroom of my apartment on Decatur Street. Put me, a client, and a blue-bottle fly in that room and you've exceeded the legal occupancy.

Donna Berens's townhouse apartment was small, too, but she gave it the illusion of spaciousness by underfurnishing it. In the living room, white wicker furniture perched prissily on golden-oak floors, while a few small, pale watercolors watched from white metal frames on the walls. The walls were blue, but only barely, and the woodwork was white. A narrow oak étagère held a peach-colored vase of dusky silk flowers, a couple of small photographs in large, wide frames, some tasteful, forgettable bric-a-brac, and not much else. The room was as empty of personality as it was of furnishings, loaded with all the warmth and charm of a model unit. And yet it was vaguely familiar—not the room, but the atmosphere of it, the flavor of it. I sat gingerly on a white wicker love seat and wondered about people who seem to have no *feeling* for a home, who decorate from a magazine instead of from the heart. God knows, my joint is done up in a combination of Early Mismatch and Clutter Provincial but at least you know it was thrown together by a human being.

Donna Berens sat erect in a tall-backed chair at the far corner of my loveseat, waiting with something like expectation on her face. "Relatives?" I repeated.

She shook her head, and a dark curl that had escaped the shell of hairspray holding the rest of her coif bobbed and tickled her right cheekbone. She had well-defined cheekbones and an ex-pressive mouth that was almost too small for the teeth in it. When her lips stretched across her teeth her mouth was pulled into an involuntary smile. She reached up and tucked the lock behind her ear and everything was nice and neat again. "Nobody."

"What about Meredith's father?"

"He doesn't live in Omaha."

"Where does he live?"

She stirred her coffee some more. By now the cream in it must have been well on the way to becoming butter. "Wilmette. Illinois." So I wouldn't confuse it with all the other Wilmettes in the country. "It doesn't matter. We haven't had any contact with him for more than ten years."

"*You* haven't," I corrected gently. "You don't know about Meredith."

Donna Berens looked at me long. "Yes," she said. "I do."

I shrugged. "Your daughter lives on her own, Mrs. Berens. You don't screen her calls, you don't open her mail, you don't know who she sees or where she goes . . . obviously." Her chin came up at a dangerous angle. "It's not impossible that she may have had some contact with her father without your knowing."

"You don't know Meredith," she said stonily. It was true. "If Meredith were fifteen, or sixteen, or seventeen, I would say, yes, you have a point. But she hasn't so much as set eyes on her father in over ten years. He's not a part of our lives and we're not a part of his. She would have no reason to go to him."

None except biology, I thought. Heredity. History. Call it what you will. It struck me as entirely possible—I didn't know any of these people, you understand—but it struck me as entirely possible that a young woman, living on her own, et cetera, might develop an interest in reestablishing a relationship with a father she hadn't seen in more than a decade. And since the Berenses' obviously was not an amicable parting, it further struck me as likely that the girl would not mention this interest to her mother. For all we knew, Meredith Berens may have been in contact with her father for months, or longer. For all we knew, the father might be able to provide some helpful information. Or not. The point is, in any investigation you like to turn over as many stones as you can, even if your client thinks her ex-husband might be living under one of them. Still, I let it go. For one thing, she wasn't any client, not yet, not until I had determined that there was a case worth investigating and she had crossed my palm with silver—or check, money order, stamps, or major credit card. For another, how hard could it be to find a guy named Berens in Wilmette, Illinois? How many could there be?

I said, "I don't blame you for being concerned, Mrs. Berens. But if you want my advice, I'd hold off hiring an investigator to look for your daughter. You're better off contacting the police."

"I'd rather not. Besides, don't the police make you wait several days before they'll take a missing-person report?"

"There's a reason for that, and the reason is that most missing persons aren't missing at all; they turn up in a day or two all by themselves."

"I don't want to wait a day or two. I don't want to sit here doing nothing, worrying. I want to find my daughter. I want *you* to find my daughter. If you won't take the job, perhaps you'd be so kind as to recommend someone who will."

I drank some coffee. It was very good: strong and yet smooth, the way coffee should be. There was the slightest hint of amaretto to it, an aftertaste more than anything else. "I didn't say I wouldn't take the job, Mrs. Berens. I only said that I would wait, if I were you. I was trying to save you an unnecessary expense."

"Well, you're not me," she said tartly; then she visibly softened. "I'm sorry. I understand what you're saying, and I appreciate it. But I won't wait. I can't. And as for the expense—I have money. Don't worry."

"I won't, then. Let's get back to your daughter. I assume you went by her place?"

"Yes. She has an apartment on Dupont Street. I stopped by there this morning, after I tried calling her at work and found out that she hadn't come in today."

"She works where?"

"Castelli and Company, a little public-relations firm on St. Marys. I don't know the address . . ."

I was writing. "I can get it. Who's in charge there, do you know?"

"Dianna Castelli. She owns the company."

I could probably have guessed at that.

"All right. What happened at Meredith's?"

"Well . . . she wasn't home, of course. I knocked on the door but there was no answer."

"Did you go in?"

She seemed not to understand me. She frowned, and cast around her, a flash of something—worry, fear, something—springing to life in her dark eyes as she looked for someone who could translate my question into a language she understood. "I told you," she said unsteadily, "there was no answer at the door."

"You don't have a key?"

She shook her head.

"Did you find the manager or landlord and ask to be let in? Under the circumstances I'm sure they would have let you."

She kept on shaking her head, harder and faster now. "I . . . I guess I just didn't think of it. My first thought . . . well, I suppose you could say I panicked. That's when I called you. I came straight home and called you. It was the only thing I could think to do."

Odd, I thought. Most people would call the police *ages* before even thinking of calling a private investigator.

Donna Berens still held the twisted napkin between her slender fingers. Now she wound the pink rope around her left index finger. "I'm sorry," she mumbled.

"It doesn't really matter," I said, and it didn't really matter. What would we have gained if Donna Berens had entered the apartment? Excepting obvious and unlikely possibilities, such as finding Meredith dead or stoned or sharing the place with an all-midget orchestra, Donna Berens would have noticed nothing. Nothing except that what she was looking for was not there: her daughter. I couldn't expect her to have been able reliably to report what shape the apartment had been in, whether anything appeared to be missing, whether her daughter's clothes, makeup, jewelry and so on were all there. No, even though Donna Berens had not gone into her daughter's apartment, I would still have to go and see for myself.

"How could I be so stupid," the woman was saying, mostly to herself. "Why didn't I find the manager . . ."

"It doesn't matter at all," I repeated. "Does anyone have a key to Meredith's apartment, do you know?"

The query threw her. She was trying to stay sane, and it took all of her concentration.

"A key to Meredith's apartment," I said. "I'll want to have a look for myself. Begin at the beginning, as the poet has it."

Again the woman looked around the room, uncertainly, as if the apartment was as strange to her as it was to me. "I don't . . . Who would Meredith give a key to if not me?"

A neighbor, a boyfriend, a coworker, but what was the point of going into it? Donna Berens was fading fast.

"Won't the apartment manager or whoever have a . . . a pass-key or something?" she wondered, frowning.

"Almost certainly," I said in a chipper tone, although I wouldn't put too much money on even my ability to convince an apartment manager to let me into one of the tenants' apartments. Give me a peek, sure, if only to see that the tenant wasn't lying dead in the middle of the living room floor; but not let me conduct the kind of search that I would want to undertake. Having a key would make life so much easier. I could have taken Donna Berens with me, I guess. A mother's plight might soften even a landlord's minuscule heart. But us down-these-mean-streets guys work best solo. Besides, there was no telling what I might find when I got there, and Mrs. Berens was already wound as tight as her little napkin. I didn't need the aggravation. Neither did she.

There was a pause, the kind novelists like to call "pregnant," although "awkward" is more accurate. Then she said, "If there should be any, you know, any trouble, I'll back you up. With the police, I mean. I'll tell them you had my permission."

And that plus thirty-five cents would buy me a copy of the *Omaha World-Herald.* "Thanks for the sentiment, but I'm afraid it wouldn't do me any good. You have no more to say about my entering Meredith's apartment than a bum sleeping under the North Freeway overpass."

"But I'm her *mother.*"

"Doesn't matter. If I have trouble with the police, you don't back me up: You don't know what I'm doing, all right? You hired me to look for your daughter and beyond that you don't have the foggiest notion what I'm up to. Right?"

"All . . . all right." Her hands gripped the arms of her chair until her knuckles were the same color as the wicker. The strain had a cumulative effect on her, an effect that was accelerating before my eyes. It was obvious she wouldn't hold up much longer, and I couldn't blame her. I hurried up and put together some more questions.

"Mrs. Berens, do you have any other children?"

"No. No. Only Meredith." She started to say more but her voice caught and she stopped, tearing one hand from the arm of her chair and pressing her fingers to her lips.

"Is Meredith seeing anyone? Does she have a boyfriend? Or boyfriends?"

She moved her hand from her mouth to her throat. Her eyes were trained not on me but on some point over my left shoulder. They did not seem quite focused.

"Boyfriends?" I repeated.

It startled her. "I—I told you. Meredith keeps to herself a great deal."

"What about you?"

I might have thrown a glass of ice water in her face, the way she reacted. "What *about* me?"

"Do you have, for want of a better word, a boyfriend?"

Donna Berens stood, suddenly—so suddenly that I thought for an instant I had somehow offended her and she was about to show me the door. She moved to the étagère, regarded its contents for the span of a heartbeat, then returned to her chair, her high heels tapping imperatively on the wood underfoot. She didn't seat herself, but rather moved behind the chair, resting her nervous hands on its high back. She might have been posing for a portrait. Or she might have been using the white wicker as a shield. A shield against me. "What can that possibly have to do with anything?" she said, and her voice trembled. The untamed curl of hair jumped from behind her right ear, bobbed and swayed. Her slender fingers flexed on the wicker, tightening and loosening, tightening and loosening their grip.

"I haven't the faintest idea," I said truthfully. "None, maybe. Probably. But you never know. I'm trying to think of reasons that Meredith might have disappeared; often, the reasons give us a good idea of where the person disappeared *to*. Family tensions are a pretty common reason."

"I see." Her body was stiff and unreceptive. She turned her back to me and looked out the window. "No," she said to her watery reflection in the glass. Her voice was both regretful and proud. "I'm not seeing anyone. No one . . ."

I believed her. I had no reason not to. But you wonder about the ones who get so worked up about personal questions. Do they simply value their privacy? Or do they have something to hide?

"Did you and Meredith argue Sunday afternoon?"

She shook her head.

"Have you argued recently? Say, in the past week or so?"

For a while I thought she must not have heard me. Then she said, to the glass, "What if Meredith hasn't disappeared?"

"I beg your pardon?"

Mrs. Berens turned, very slowly, and faced me. Her small body was taut, her cheeks sucked in, accentuating the infrastructure of her face even more than usual. I had the impression that she was biting the inside of her mouth and, when she spoke, I had the impression that there was blood on her tongue. "You talk as if Meredith has gone away, voluntarily. What if she hasn't? What if something has happened to her?"

She looked at me in a kind of numb panic, as if I was supposed to have the words that would disprove the horrible thought she had forced herself to voice. As if I had the words that would make the hideous fear an impossibility.

I hadn't. If I had, I would surely have spoken them.

But all I had to say was, "We'll deal with that if and when we come to it, Mrs. Berens."

Her face relaxed then, but not her body. Suddenly tears washed over the dam of mascara below her left eye, sending a bluish stream over the rounded swell of her cheek. She moved back to her chair, to the coffee table between it and my chair, and took one of the small, square paper napkins to stanch the flow. She had it under control again, just that fast. The air fairly hummed with the energy it took for Donna Berens to keep her concern, her panic, in check. But she did it.

"Then you will help me, Mr. Nebraska?" she said after a long moment. Her voice was thick and husky, but steady. She twisted the new napkin between her fingers, winding it into a tight, little pink licorice stick.

"If I can. I'll need some things from you—a recent photograph of your daughter, color would be best. Her address. Her place of work we already know. The kind of car she drives, license plate number, if you know it. The name of her bank. Any close friends, coworkers, people she might confide in."

She nodded rapidly, taking it all in, welcoming any little distraction from what was so heavy on her mind. "I can get you most of that," she said. "I don't know the license number, but everything else." She smiled, then, and it was a real smile, not the illusion caused by the high cheekbones and the wide, full mouth. "I . . . Well, thank you. There's no one else I can turn to. If you hadn't helped me . . . But I knew you wouldn't let me down."

"Really?" I smiled. "I've been wondering how you happened to call me, Mrs. Berens." I don't exactly maintain a high profile, even if I still keep my line listing in the Yellow Pages.

Donna Berens retrieved her cup from the glass-topped table and sipped for a moment before answering. "You did a favor for a friend of mine, Mr. Nebraska. A good friend of mine. Several years ago."

"Did I?" I said with bland politeness. It would come when it would come. I had spent enough years trying to get things out of people—years as a newspaperman, years in army intelligence, years as a private investigator—to know that you can't really get anything out of someone who doesn't want to give. Short of relying on rubber hoses and electric prods and chemical injections, that is; but using them, especially on potential clients, is considered bad form in the detective biz, and anyways I was fresh out of sodium pentathol. "Who would that have been?"

"It was a long time ago."

"I'm sure I'd remember; I don't do that many favors."

"It's not important. I take it you don't do a lot of detective work anymore . . ."

She took it right. I had been tapering off for several years now, reasoning that while free-lance writers are paid even worse than private investigators, the job is on the whole a lot less strenuous and, if properly undertaken, requires almost no bullet-dodging. However, a couple of small magazines that I had been writing for pretty regularly had gone the way of the dodo, and my checking account and I sorely missed even their niggardly and invariably tardy contributions. I had long since squandered the advance for The Book, my epic detective novel, on food and drink and rent, and I was still a couple of months away from finishing the pulse-pounding sequel. And it had been a couple of months since my last assignment. So, not to put too fine a point on it, I wasn't turning my nose up at any investigations work that happened along. Or at least I wasn't turning it up as far as usual.

In fact, with time and a friend of mine who happens to be a psychologist, I had come to accept and even enjoy the schizo-phrenic nature of my work life. Where is it written that a guy has to be just one thing? Variety is the spice of life—I think that's in the Bible, or maybe the Bill of Rights—and if variety spices up the bank account, too, so much the better.

But Donna Berens didn't need to hear all of this. I merely said, "No, but I manage to keep my hand in," and let it go at that. She wasn't the only one in the room who could be evasive.

My coffee was gone now, and it was time for me to imitate it. I didn't particularly like the idea of heading into this investigation feeling that I didn't know everything I should—about Meredith Berens, about her mother, about the relationship between mother and daughter. I wasn't even sure *what* it was that I didn't know enough about, just that there was something, something in Donna Berens's evasiveness that didn't sit right. Nevertheless, I couldn't see what harm it would do to at least have a quick look-see at Meredith's apartment. No telling what that might reveal. Or not.

There was a time when I'd have kicked up more of a fuss with Donna Berens, when I'd have pushed her hard to let the police handle the matter—they're good at stuff like missing persons, the police: it's sort of like a specialty of theirs—when I'd have bullied her for answers to the unanswered questions. Eventually, though, I'd have probably taken her money anyway. For one thing, most people who have their hearts set on hiring a private detective aren't soon talked out of it, and they may as well give their dough to me as to someone who'll just rip them off, right? For another thing, if Donna Berens had it in mind to evade my questions, she'd probably only lie if I pushed her. A lie can be worse than nothing at all, in investigations and life in general.

And for a third thing, perhaps most important, I was interested. I'd done a lot of missing persons, a ton of runaways. None was quite like this one sounded. I'd had cases where the subject plain up and disappeared like a puddle on a sunny day: Usually they were men, and usually they were leaving an unhappy domestic situation, or maybe just a boring one. I'd had cases where women made themselves scarce, usually for the same reasons; but typically they gave some indication of their intentions, even if you didn't recognize it as such until after the fact. Women tend to tie up loose ends. Dumb stuff: canceling the paper, that type of thing. Men figure the hell with it, but women will usually take care of them. It's the same with suicides, a lot of the time.

But man, woman, or child, the disappearee was almost invariably abandoning a no-win relationship. Teenagers—good God, teenagers don't split for any reason *except* family. Meredith Berens, however . . . If she had lived under her mother's roof, I might have put more stock in the possibility that the women had fought and Meredith had split. But she hadn't; she lived alone. And she didn't seem to have anything to run from.

To run *to*? Perhaps. There was the old man back in Wilmette, the ex-husband that Donna Berens didn't want to talk or think about. And there was the possibility that Meredith had a boyfriend that Donna didn't know about, or didn't want to know about, or wouldn't talk about, and the two had run off together.

A lot of unanswered questions. I like to try to put answers to unanswered questions. Nature abhors a vacuum, or something like that. As I've stumbled through my life trying to figure out what I want to be when I grow up, I have always been drawn to endeavors that seek to answer unanswered questions.

I stood up.

"Are you taking the case?" I hadn't noticed her eyes anxiously studying me.

I nodded.

"When will you start?"

"I've already started." I tapped my temple. "Now give me some money and I'll go away."

chapter
2

Fifty years ago, the house must have been magnificent. It must have stood tall against the sky, narrow and long on a gentle bump of green yard that also was narrow and long. That was before someone had the bright idea of carving it up into apartments, before someone had the bright idea of selling off half of the backyard so that someone else could build another house, far too big for its lot, facing the cross-street, and before someone had the bright idea of paving the south yard with lumpy blacktop to fashion a four-car parking lot. Now the place was just a big old house on too little land off of Dupont Street, not far from Hanscom Park. Old houses, old trees, narrow shady streets. The house sat under a colossal maple that dribbled water and tree-litter onto the roof and sidewalk.

I climbed out of my crate and grabbed my windbreaker from the backseat. The morning, though wet and cool, was too humid for the jacket, but I needed it for another purpose and slipped it on, already starting to stew in my own juices. I locked the car and rummaged through the trunk. Then I closed it up and looked both ways before crossing the street, and didn't see another living creature except for a pair of robins hunting in the tall grass in front of the house. According to the adenoids on the car radio, the afternoon was supposed to be cloudy but dry. It wouldn't be—dry, that is. When you see birds out having brunch in the rain, it's a safe bet that you're in for an all-day wet. Otherwise the birds would wait until later. Your average bird is smarter than your average disk jockey.

The front door was locked. A sun-yellowed card Scotch-taped

inside the storm door said, in faint blue spidery script, that it must ever be so. An uneven, tree-littered sidewalk went around the south side of the building to the back, and so did I. A glance at the little parking lot to my right was all I needed to determine that Meredith's car—a dark blue Mazda, her mother had told me— was not parked there. I hadn't noticed it on the street, either.

The flimsy storm door at the rear of the house opened at a touch; the heavy old slab of wood beyond it required some hip action, but eventually agreed to admit me to a small landing. Three steps down, three up. Meredith Berens's apartment was first-floor, front, according to her mother. I made myself upwardly mobile on the appropriate stairs and put a little more wear on a well-worn runner down a long, bare hallway, smugly certain that Nero Wolfe could not have accommodated himself to its narrowness.

The hall obviously had been constructed when the house was subdivided into flats; it doglegged twice before ending at the front door. Along the way I passed four numbered doors spaced at irregular intervals. Three of the doors were very old, suggesting that they were original issue, doors to rooms that had been there when the house was a house. The fourth was newer, added during the remodeling—or, as the preservationists would have it, "re-muddling."

Meredith Berens's door, across from the stairs just inside the front door, was new. Her apartment must have been the house's living room, or part of it, judging by the tall, wide windows I had observed from the street. I wondered what the house's original owners would have thought if they could see the place now.

I knocked lightly at the door. Politeness is one of the lesser known tenets of the Private Eye Code. Besides, with my luck, it would turn out that the girl had simply dropped out of sight for a couple days' R and R and got home safe and sound mere minutes before your intrepid hero came busting in like Eliot Ness.

Such was not the case. At least, there was no answer.

Having tried the door and found it locked, and having inspected the lock as thoroughly as possible from the hallway side, I toddled off in search of the apartment manager—no easy feat, inasmuch as the building's residents didn't go in for signs, labels, or other such traveler's aids. As it was, the manager—a faded, wizened old thing in plastic hair curlers and a flowered housecoat that exposed her flabby, pale upper arms, and thin, birdy lower legs, and very little else—found me. She came out of the apartment at the rear of the building, near the back door, and confronted me with that unlikely mix of arrogance and anxiety that only old women can manage. "Can I help you," she said challengingly. Her mouth was a thin, bloodless gash in a hard, pointed face that might have been molded of wax. The gash moved more than was necessary to produce the tremulous words.

I smiled that old winning smile and asked if she was the manager. She put a thin hand to her hair, dull reddish hair spun tight around the curlers, and admitted to it. "I'm Mrs. Schneiders." She pronounced it with a long *e*. "There are no apartments open," Mrs. Schneiders added. Somewhat smugly, it seemed to me.

"Oh, I'm not looking for an apartment, Mrs. Schneiders; I'm looking for one of your tenants." I hauled out the ID. She took it in her bony, short-nailed fingers and studied it closely, her colorless eyes moving rapidly in their watery sockets behind the lenses of her glasses. The lenses were thick and somewhat bulbous. "My name is Nebraska," I said charmingly. "I'm a private investigator." "Investigator" sounds so much more official, and upstanding, than "detective." I use "investigator" the way lawyers use "attorney" and doctors use "physician"—to make myself sound more than I really am. "I've been retained by Mrs. Donna Berens to look for her daughter, Meredith." "Retained" is another good word, for the same reason.

Behind the little windows, the eyes came up to my face. "Is Meredith in some kind of trouble? Mrs. Hunsberger—she owns the building, you know—Mrs. Hunsberger doesn't stand for any trouble with her tenants."

"That's a good policy." I took back my paper. "No, Meredith's not in any trouble—at least, we hope not. It's just that no one's seen her or heard from her since yesterday afternoon, and her mother's worried. She asked me to come by here and check."

The old woman sniffed. "Why didn't she come herself?"

"She did. There was no answer at Meredith's door. She got worried and called me. I suggested that the apartment manager certainly would let me have a peek inside, just to make sure Meredith's not in there, sick or hurt." I turned up the rheostat on the smile. But only a bit. Too much more wattage and Mrs. Schneiders would have to go back to her apartment for a pair of sunglasses.

The woman's mouth worked aimlessly as she considered my request. "Well . . . I'd have to go in with you."

"Of course," I said immediately. "We'll just pop our heads in the door and see that everything's as it should be."

"I haven't seen Miss Berens for a couple of days myself," she said as if to herself. "But then, I'm not a nosy Nellie, you understand. The people here all mind their own business and nobody causes anybody any trouble. That's how Mrs. Hunsberger likes it."

If I had to smile much longer or harder my ears were going to drop off.

"You wait here," Mrs. Schneiders said testily, which seemed to be her normal tone. She shuffled back into her apartment and returned a few moments later clutching a small set of keys attached to a cross-stitched square the size of a slice of bread. She wore ancient scuffs that *clack-clack-clacked* against her heels as she led me back down the hall to the front of the house. The clacks echoed faintly in the poorly lighted corridor.

The lock worked like they're supposed to work. Mrs. Schneiders opened the door slowly, an inch at a time, one hand on the doorknob and the other tapping sharply at the door as it swung inward. "Miss Berens? It's Mrs. Schneiders. Are you here . . . ?"

She was not. It was instantly evident: The apartment was one square room with a bath and no good hiding places. Mrs. Schneiders scuffed three feet into the room and stopped, peering around the gloomy, cluttered space. I stayed in the doorway.

The lock, as I had guessed from my brief inspection of it, was a standard spring lock. You pushed in and turned a button set in the inside doorknob, and the door locked automatically when you closed it after you. There was no deadbolt, just a chain to set when you were home.

The moment Mrs. Schneiders's back was toward me, I reached inside my windbreaker and silently peeled away the small square of duct tape I had lightly affixed there. The tape was from the roll I carry in the trunk of my car, an ancient Impala whose ever-increasing unreliability necessitates an ever-growing emergency-supplies kit. I slapped the patch of tape over the latch bolt, that spring-activated wedge that pops into the opening in the strike plate on the doorjamb to hold the door closed. When the old woman turned back to me, I was standing between her and the door, blocking her view of my handiwork.

"She's not here," Mrs. Schneiders said unnecessarily.

"No, she's not," I said, equally unnecessarily. "Well, okay, I guess I'd better report back to her mother. Thanks so much for your help, Mrs. Schneiders. We really appreciate it."

During the speech I was gallantly holding the door for her, ushering her out into the hall. Then I made a small show of depressing the lock button and swinging the door closed—quickly, before she noticed the tape. The door fit snugly enough to stay closed with no help from the latch bolt, if you didn't put much pressure against it. Tugging the knob toward me slightly, I twisted it a few times to prove that it was locked, which, as far as the lockset was concerned, it was.

"Safe and sound," I assured Mrs. Schneiders, beamingly.

She was convinced. I escorted her back down the hall. She remained outside her apartment door and watched me go down the three steps to the back door. I paused at the threshold and looked back. "Thanks again." More smile. "Good-bye."

There are few certainties in this imperfect world, but one of them was that Mrs. Schneiders was already shuffling toward the front of the building to make sure I was leaving. So I did. I went out to the Impala and, without a backward glance, got behind the wheel and drove off.

I explored the neighborhood for five or six minutes, then headed back toward the old house, coming around from the back way and parking a block away on the cross-street.

I came up on the building from the south side, the side opposite the Schneiders woman's apartment. I bumped open the back door as quietly as possible, quickly ascended the three steps to the first floor and then, without pausing, went on up to the top floor, where I stopped at the top of the stairs.

Below me a door opened. I heard the shuffle and clack of scuffs on threadbare carpet and in my mind's eye saw the emaciated woman peering down at the back door. More shuffling. She turned and peered down the corridor. I heard a thready voice: "Hello . . . ?" I stayed put. There was no sound from downstairs for the longest time, then the scuffs dragged across the carpeting and the door closed again. I waited until I heard the scrape and rattle of the chain in its plate, then set off down the hall.

The upper floor was a duplicate of the lower, except that the hallway was straight until it reached the front of the house. I assumed that was because the hallway was part of the upper floor's original design instead of an add-on, as it was downstairs. The carpet was in no better shape here than below, however. I moved down it slowly, mindful of vocal floorboards. There were none, none of any significance, at any rate. Toward the front of the house the hallway ended in a largish, high-ceilinged space at the top of the front stairs. At the bottom of the stairs was Meredith Berens's apartment.

My trick with the duct tape had worked. I pushed open the door, peeled away the tape, closed the door, and locked it after me.

And resumed breathing.

The apartment, as I said, was one large room—the house's original living or sitting room. I'm sure the tiny apartment was very pleasant on a sunny day. This was not a sunny day. At first glance, the place seemed a bit of a mess. Second glance confirmed this. Oh, not your call-the-board-of-health kind of mess, but something more than your ordinary day-in-the-life clutter. Odd, I thought, given the cold, sterile precision of Meredith's mother's home. Who was it said the apple falls not far from the tree? Probably the same DJ who insisted it was going to be dry this afternoon.

I checked my watch. It was twelve past one. I wanted to be out of there by one-thirty, one forty-five at the latest. In and out—it lessens the chances of being caught where you oughtn't be.

Meredith Berens had a lot of clothes, and most of them were in plain sight, draped over furniture, piled on an unmade bed, spilling out of a wardrobe that was weighted down with stacks of more clothes. I gave the room the once-over and decided it hadn't been tossed; this was just the way it was. Then I stepped into the middle of the apartment and surveyed it more carefully.

The door opened into the living area: a sofa, a floor lamp, and two low-backed easy chairs under the tall front windows. A black metal trunk, serving as coffee table, supported a portable television set in a pink plastic cabinet. The phone hung on the wall next to the door. Below it, a cheaply made two-legged table was bolted to the wall. Directly opposite the windows, against the east wall, were a twin bed, a dresser with mirror, and the oak-veneer wardrobe, its doors standing open, its innards crammed full of clothes and shoes. The shoes tumbled out of the wardrobe and lay scattered on the thin indoor-outdoor carpet. The clothes marched out of the wardrobe and hung huddled over the doors. A yellow refrigerator stood guard over the bed. Next to the fridge was a junior-sized gas range, also yellow. Two saucepans and one skillet were nested on a back burner. Against the wall opposite the door, under another set of windows smaller than the front windows, was a kitchen counter and stainless-steel double sink. A drying rack piled high with dishes, a toaster, a twist-tied loaf of Wonder Bread, a couple of coffee cups, a stainless-steel percolator and a dirty table knife filled most of the available counter space. A small dining table and chairs were shoved up against the front wall, south of the windows. The table was piled with clothes and other possessions, including a steam iron. The bathroom was a tiny room created in the back corner of the place, near the foot of the bed. Stool, sink, shower—no tub—and your standard mirrored medicine cabinet.

Every investigator has a different way of going about the searching of a place. Me, I like to spend a moment soaking up the ambience. Is anything upset or out of place? Or carelessly set straight after having been out of place? Is something missing? Is something there that shouldn't be? Has someone been here before me? In the case of a place like Meredith Berens's—namely, an unholy mess—it's hard to form definite answers to those questions. But as near as I could tell, as near as I could *feel,* the answer to all of them was no.

After taking inventory for a couple of minutes, I went to work.

The wardrobe, as I've indicated, was full of wardrobe—more than full. Blouses, jackets, pants, and skirts hung from the single rod and the tops of the two doors. Shoe boxes were piled three deep on the floor, more shoes were stacked atop the boxes, with fellow shoes strewn here and there on the carpet. On top of the wardrobe, clear plastic boxes stacked halfway to the ceiling held folded sweaters and sweatshirts, a couple of purses. Empty. Empty, that is, of anything important or especially useful: They contained the usual assortment of crumpled Kleenexes, loose change, aspirin tins, lip balm, and other minutiae that women almost invariably leave in a purse when they "empty" it.

A yellow Samsonite suitcase hid under the bed, along with a dozen old, forgotten newspapers, three months' worth of *Savvy* magazine, *My Secret Garden* in paperback, and some dust mice hunched on the hard, thin, industrial-strength carpet. In keeping with the decorating philosophy evidenced by the rest of the apartment, there wasn't much unused space under the bed—certainly not enough to have once contained a second suitcase, now missing. Not a good sign, I thought, though not necessarily a bad one.

The dresser held more clothes. Top drawer: underwear, hose, and a small, black-velvet-covered jewelry box containing a few pieces of good jewelry, gold and white-gold, some passably decent costume stuff, and, oddly, a chintzy gumball-machine ring whose plastic "chrome" had flaked away almost completely. I wondered what significance the ring could have for its owner. In the shallow chamber under a false bottom in the box I found Meredith's passport, some old wallet-size graduation pictures of people I didn't know, a crumpled thousand-lire note. Also a tiny yellow key on a piece of blue yarn.

I opened the passport. It had been issued in 1981, the year Meredith had gone to Italy, according to the blurred stamps. The passport photo showed a plain-featured, brown-haired girl staring glassy-eyed at the camera. Mug shots are more flattering. The photograph that Meredith's mother had given me was far better. It was Meredith's high school graduation picture, but Donna Berens insisted that her daughter still looked *exactly* the same. Which is just the sort of thing a mother would say. The picture in my pocket showed a quiet-looking, long-haired brunette with wide, dark eyes, a small, pouting mouth, and a long, angular face.

Second drawer: socks, T-shirts, sweatshirts, shorts, two pairs of sweatpants, two one-piece bathing suits, one black, one fuchsia with mint-green flowers across the midriff. Under the bathing suits there was a small book with pink leatherette covers and a ridiculous little phony-brass-plated lock on the right-hand side. I went back into the first drawer, into the jewelry box, and fished out the yellow key. It fit the diary lock. The book's pages were blank.

Why would you separate your diary and its key—*hide* the key, even, albeit pretty halfheartedly—if your diary was empty?

I flipped through the book again, seeing only white pages with faint gray rulings. Then I examined the top edge of the book. Half a dozen pages had been painstakingly razored out of the front, so close to the binding that you could see it only by looking down at the top of the book, near the spine, and observing the sixteenth-of-an-inch gap.

The first page in the book—the first page *left* in the book—was blank and smooth. No impression left by the writing on the previous page. Only TV detectives get that kind of luck.

I put the diary and the key back where I had found them.

Third drawer: towels and sheets. Towels to the left, crammed up against the side and back of the drawer. Sheets to the right.

Bottom drawer: miscellany. Cancelled checks, check blanks, and a savings-account passbook showing a balance of eight hundred fourteen dollars and thirty-nine cents; wrapping paper; greeting cards received and to be sent; note paper; an orange plastic flashlight; a lidless box of unlabeled keys; a sticky-paper lint picker-upper; and a box that said it contained one dozen blue-ink Bic roller pens but in fact contained three pens and forty-eight U.S. cents.

The top of the dresser was protected by a thin lace runner on which sat a collection of commonplace junk. I sorted through some more loose change, a miniature porcelain birdbath that contained, in addition to a miniature porcelain bird, a collection of straight pins and rubber bands; three small bottles of inexpensive perfume; a pair of folding scissors; and a framed five-by-seven portrait of Donna Berens. I slipped the photo out of the dime-store frame, but there was nothing behind it but corrugated cardboard.

Another photograph, a four-by-six snapshot, was tucked between the dresser mirror and one of the four brass-plated clips that fastened the glass to the metal railings that supported it. Mother and daughter this time, captured slightly out of focus against a green and leafy tree. Donna Berens smiled toothily at whoever was behind the camera. Meredith did not. I left the picture untouched and leaned in close to peer at another brass-plated fastener, identical to the first, under which something else had been tucked and then removed, leaving a scrap of paper barely visible behind the clip. Using the nail file on my money clip, I freed the torn scrap.

This, too, had been a photograph—the paper had that slick, emulsified finish to it. The bit that remained was a triangle, half an inch on two sides with the third side a jagged, cockeyed tear.

If Meredith had valued the photograph, she would have removed it carefully from its place. If she hadn't valued it, she wouldn't have displayed it where she would see it every day. *Ergo,* Meredith had once valued it but no longer did.

Or still did, but had removed it hurriedly, for whatever reason.

Or someone besides Meredith removed it.

Whatever its history, the scrap was by itself useless to me. I saw what might have been the arm, possibly the leg, of a Caucasian of undeterminable gender, and, just above that, a bit of navy blue that could have been a short sleeve or the leg of a pair of short pants. From this Sherlock Holmes would be able to deduce the subject's height, age, school, regiment, wife's mother's maiden name, and political affiliation—not just the subject's, but also the subject's wife's mother—but I found it considerably less helpful. I pocketed the scrap and turned my attention to wastebaskets.

There was only one in the main room—the place was hardly big enough to require more than one—a tall, brown plastic kitchen wastebasket that stood at the end of the kitchen counter. I popped off the swing-lid assembly and peered into the white plastic liner-bag, holding my breath. When I used to do this kind of thing full-time—snooping, I mean, to earn what I facetiously referred to as my living, not prowling through people's garbage—I kept a box of rubber dissecting gloves in my car. You can get them at any college bookstore. They're perfect for sifting through other people's garbage, or your own, for that matter, I suppose, although I doubt that's what the manufacturers have in mind. However, the heyday of my garbage-sifting career had passed, and so had the necessity to carry rubber gloves, or rubber anything else, everywhere I went. I took a quick tour through Meredith Berens's kitchen cupboards and drawers—there were two of each—and came up with nothing worth mentioning except a plastic Ziploc storage bag that I slipped over my right hand when I went through the garbage.

Luckily for my favorite private detective, Meredith had emptied the trash recently, and what lay in the bottom of the white bag wasn't unreasonably stomach-turning: three damp tea bags (Lipton Flo-Thru variety, if you care) and the red and yellow box in which they and ninety-seven of their brethren had arrived; curled, dried scraps of orange peel; a thin flimsy paper box that a tube of mascara had come in; a small brown bag that contained the receipt for the makeup, dated a week earlier; half a dozen pieces of junk mail, all opened; and a white business-size envelope addressed to Meredith in a solid, masculine hand.

The envelope was good quality, not the kind you pick up at the supermarket in boxes of twenty-five. The exterior had a texture to it, a subtle grain; the interior was patterned to protect the contents from prying eyes.

The contents, incidentally, were missing.

I sifted through the trash again, even going so far as to open all of the junk mail, whose glossy come-ons Meredith Berens had conscientiously reinserted in the envelopes before tossing. Nothing.

Moisture from the tea bags had smeared the address on the white envelope, although it was still perfectly legible. There was nothing noteworthy about the hand in which the address had been penned in blue felt-tip ink: small, squarish characters, all caps, marching crookedly across the middle of the envelope, evidently leaning into a strong wind. Appropriately enough, the postmark was the Windy City, the date on it a little more than a week back.

There was no return address.

That was it for the garbage. The wastebasket did not contain the rest of the picture whose torn corner was in my shirt pocket.

I trashed the Ziploc bag and returned the wastebasket, which I had set up on the dining table, to its rightful place on the floor. I gave the little room another looking-over. There were a couple of nondescript, generic pictures on the wall: I would check behind them. There were half a dozen book-club hardcovers on a crooked wall-mount shelf over one of the easy chairs; I would go through them. There were sofa and chair cushions; I would look under and behind them. Looking for . . . whatever might be there.

Which was nothing. Except for eleven cents under the sofa cushions. I figured the woman had to have fourteen-hundred dollars lying around the place, here and there, in small change.

There were three pennies on one of the two glass shelves in the bathroom medicine cabinet. Also a tube of Crest, a blue Reach toothbrush, a vial of Secret roll-on antiperspirant, a bottle of Pepto-Bismol, a bottle of Robitussin, a bottle of aspirin, a digital thermometer, a Massengill box, a bottle of Cutex, a jar of Noxzema, a jar of Vaseline, half a bag of cotton balls, some Q-Tips in a chipped ceramic mug, and a couple throwaway razors. On the lid of the toilet sat a low basket that contained makeup supplies, an emery board, a long comb, and two hairbrushes. Not to mention seven cents in loose change. Next to the basket were balanced a portable blow-dryer and a curling wand. The blow-dryer was plugged into the single outlet in the light fixture above the mirrored cabinet doors.

In short, the bathroom contained just about everything that the average American twenty-five-year-old woman would take with her if she were going away for a day or two.

If she had *planned* to go away, that is.

I wandered back into the main room, a gnawing feeling of unease working at my guts. It wasn't looking good, not good at all. I had expected—half-expected, say; the other half was hope—to find some kind of evidence that Meredith had simply decided to take a day or two off and, for whatever reason, had failed to notify anybody. But it obviously was not so. The suitcase, the quantities of clothing, the bathroom artifacts all said otherwise. So there were three possibilities.

One: Meredith had gone away for a few days—her car wasn't around—but hadn't packed, deciding to buy everything she needed when she got where she was going. Highly unlikely.

Two: Meredith had dropped out of sight for a few days, but hadn't left the Big O. Her car was missing because she had gone to the movies, gone shopping, gone to have her hair done, or whatever twenty-five-year-old women do with a day off. Not as unlikely as the previous possibility, but not exactly in the "Eureka!" category either. Why wouldn't she have picked up the phone, called her boss, and said, "I need a couple of days off"?

Three: Meredith's mother was right, and something *had* happened to the girl. An accident—an auto accident would explain the missing car. But surely the police would have notified Donna Berens by now, for surely Meredith would be carrying identification. It was the most likely possibility—indeed, the *only* likely one—but even it seemed unlikely.

Something had happened to the girl, all right. But not a car wreck.

I was interrupted by a faint, tentative rapping from the other side of the main door, the bare brushing of knuckles on wood, the kind of a knock you undertake when you're afraid someone might actually be home. I froze. Had Mrs. Schneiders heard me moving around the apartment? I doubted it: My efforts weren't big noise-generators and, in any case, I had been taking pains to work quietly. Plus I was certain I would hear her shuffling and clacking down the hallway long before she reached the door.

I ignored the door and concentrated on inventing some kind of brilliant next move.

And was standing in the middle of the dinky apartment, mulling over the nonexistent alternatives, when a key scraped in the lock and the door swung inward.

chapter

3

We hard-boiled private-eye types have an instinctive reaction to situations like this: We look for someplace to hide. In a small, square, closetless room there aren't too many such someplaces. I suppose I could have hopped into bed and pulled the covers up over my head, but that seemed a little inefficient. I settled instead for dropping into one of the low-backed chairs, the one that faced the door, and affecting nonchalance. It's what Simon Templar would do.

The door opened and the door closed, and when it was through with all of that I no longer had the place to myself. I had been joined by a pale, platinum-blond woman who was just a little "too"—too made-up, too bejewelled, too old for the too-gaudy clothes that were just a little too small on her. She wasn't much younger than me, which meant she was breathing hard and hot down the neck of the mighty four-oh, and, like most of us aging postwar baby-boomers, she could have stood the loss of ten or fifteen pounds. Nevertheless she had begun the day by wriggling her way into one of those shapeless dresses that's little more than a knee-length sweatshirt. On her, the shapeless dress got a shape, at least a hip and bust, both of which were generous. The dress was a color that you might have called green, although a shade not to be found in nature, festooned with yellow geometric shapes in an abstract, asymmetrical patttern. She also wore yellow hose and white ankle-boots, and I've already hinted at the makeup that earned her a line on Mary Kay's permanent Christmas card list.

She had been scanning the room in an unfocused, uncertain fashion—I recognized it because it was exactly what I had been doing until she interrupted me. Now she spotted me, sitting motionless in my chair, and jumped a little. "Who the hell are you?"

"No fair. Since I was here first, I should get first dibs on the questions. Who the hell are *you?*"

The pale-haired woman hesitated for the thinnest shaving of a second, if that much. Then she stepped farther into the room and dumped her oversized canvas bag into the unoccupied chair as if she owned the joint. Which was exactly the intended effect.

"My name's Meredith Berens, if it's any of your business," she said with almost—*almost*—the right amount of indignation. "This is my apartment, and if you're not out of it in just about five seconds I'm gonna—"

"Call a cop. All the good lines have been said to death, haven't they?" I slipped two fingers into my shirt pocket and extracted Meredith Berens's graduation photo. The woman watched me closely as I pretended to examine the picture.

"What's that?" she wondered suspiciously.

I turned it so she could see it. "Your graduation picture, Meredith. If you don't mind my saying so, these past six or seven years must've been pretty tough. I mean, I don't think your own mother would recognize you."

"Where'd you get that?"

"Your own mother. More accurately, *Meredith's* own mother. The one who hired me to look for"—I tapped the picture—"her. The one who gave me the key to this place. The one who—ah, well, I've made my point. How 'bout you? You want to have another go at the who-are-you question? Tell you what—I'll give you a hint: Try Dianna Castelli."

Her head came up as if she'd been hit from behind. "How'd you know my name?" Her voice trod the middle ground between anxiety and indignation.

"I'm a detective; I deduced it. Process of elimination. You aren't Meredith Berens and you aren't her mother, and the only other female-type name that's been kicked around so far belongs to Meredith's boss. Dianna Castelli. Okay, so it's more of a guess than a deduction; it's right, isn't it?"

She said nothing, which was as good as saying yes. She shoved her bag into a corner of the easy chair, leaving enough room to plant herself in, which she did. She combed her hair with her long-nailed fingers. The hair was the color of cotton wool, short on the sides, longer and almost spiky on top, still longer in back, delicate tendrils tracing down her neck.

"Detective, huhn?" she said, making a good job of trying to sound unimpressed. "Your parents give you a name?"

"A couple of them. The one I use most is Nebraska. You can use it too."

Dianna Castelli's eyebrows—which, incidentally, were considerably darker than her hair—went up. "Peculiar name. For a person, I mean."

You get used to it after the first thirty or thirty-five years.

"From the Osage word *nibthacka*," I said, "which means 'flat water' and probably was a reference to the Platte River." The Platte cuts a lazy, meandering path across the state and empties into the Missouri River, the boundary between Nebraska and Iowa, south of Omaha.

"Really?" said the Castelli woman. "Are you a Native American?"

"There are no *native* Americans; everyone here came from somewhere else originally."

"And you came from . . ."

"Decatur Street."

"Uh-huh." She hooked a heel on the edge of the trunk that was pretending to be a coffee table and hoisted her other leg up over the first. It was a nice leg—they both were, in fact, being a matched set and all, and I didn't in the least mind having a closer look at them, yellow-wrapped though they may have been. "Well, detective from Decatur Street, here we are."

"So it would seem."

"What have you detected so far?"

"No Meredith Berens here."

"No fooling," Dianna Castelli said drily. "Tell me, how much does Donna Berens have to pay for that news flash?"

"You knew Meredith wasn't here, eh? Then why'd you knock on the door before busting in?"

"I . . . Oh, hell—touché, already. I *knew* she wouldn't be here but I knocked anyway. Partly out of habit, like closing the bathroom door when you're the only one home. And partly because . . . well, for all I knew maybe she *was* here, sick or something, and I didn't want to just come barging in."

"Too sick to call in to work? Too sick to let her mother know?

That's pretty sick, especially for someone who was apparently in good health Sunday afternoon, the last time Donna Berens spoke with Meredith."

Dianna Castelli shrugged, an odd sort of shrug, right shoulder coming up and head tilting as if to meet it. "People get sick."

"You don't believe that."

"I've known people who got sick. I've been sick myself."

I frowned. "Sick or well, Meredith Berens is decidedly not here."

"No fooling," she repeated, no less sarcastically this time around. "Any idea where she might be?"

"Not a one. I had hoped that having a look-see at the place might provide some inspiration. Clues, you know, like the guys in the books are always tripping over."

"And . . . ?"

"And the only kind I find are the kind I'd just as soon not find. Meredith Berens isn't here. Obviously. But her suitcase and her clothes and all of the sorts of things you would take with you if you were going away *are* here."

The Castelli woman frowned. "Meaning she hasn't gone away?"

"Meaning she didn't *plan* to go away. Or something happened."

"Something as in an accident."

"Possibly," I said. "It's hard to say for sure. I'm guessing it's unlike Meredith to simply disappear like this, without saying anything."

"*Completely* unlike her." She noticed the apartment, as if for the first time. "This is how you found the place?"

"This is how I found it, and this is how Meredith left it—most of the time, by the look of it. Incidentally, how did you get in here?"

"Amazing." She was referring to the state of the apartment. "At the office, her desk is always so tidy. You can find anything in her files." She looked at me. "It's called a key, I believe. Handy little things."

"I can imagine. Meredith gave you a key?"

"No, I took a wax impression of it one day at the office when she was in the ladies' room. Of *course* she gave it to me. She took a couple days' vacation back in June. I offered to water the plants. She said she didn't have any plants—she didn't lie; what could live here?—but she thought it'd maybe be a good idea for someone to have a key, in case of emergency. Today's the first time I ever used it. It seemed like an emergency to me, sort of."

"Don't you think it's a little peculiar that Meredith would give a key to you and not her mother?"

"I didn't know that Donna didn't have a key to this place, but I'm not surprised. This is where Meredith came to be *free* of that woman. She gives her a key, the freedom's gone."

"They didn't get along, Meredith and her mother?"

Dianna Castelli sighed, recrossed her legs in the other direction, which was just as good a view as the first, and folded her arms beneath her ample bosom. "I don't know . . ." She stopped, frowned, and tried again. "It's tricky, because Meredith and her mother don't *fight* as such. It takes two to fight, and Meredith won't. She buckles, every time. You'd think the girl was five, not twenty-five. It was everything I could do just to get her to move out of the deep freeze."

I smiled. "You've been to Donna Berens's home, then."

She pantomimed a shiver. Or perhaps it wasn't an act. "I was there—to help Meredith move out, and I hope it's the last time."

"Moving out was your idea, not Meredith's?"

She shook her head. The medium-length spiky hair on top swayed. "No, it was Meredith's idea, all right. She'd been talking about it for more than two years, ever since she started working for me, in fact. But that's just it: All she did was *talk*. I finally told her to put up or shut up, and just to make sure she didn't chicken out— for the umpteenth time—I threw her into the car and we went apartment hunting, and then I helped her pack and got her moved in here." Again she surveyed the room. "Geez, it looked a lot nicer last winter."

"When did Meredith move in?"

"January first—second, really. Liberation Day, we called it."

"And up until then she lived at home?"

Dianna Castelli nodded. A couple of things were starting to come into focus, on the edges at least. Moving out, not giving her mother a key to this apartment, keeping the apartment in a state of clutter bordering on mess. In a sneaky, passive kind of way, Meredith was rebelling against Donna Berens. The first two acts were perhaps obvious; the third less so. But by keeping her apartment chaotic, cluttered, wasn't Meredith making a statement, albeit a private one, against the orderly, underfurnished, even sterile home she had grown up in? Like the actor hawking cold medication on TV, I'm not a doctor, but I'd spent quite a bit of the past nine or ten months playing doctor with a very good local psychologist, and I was willing to bet money she would agree with my guess.

"Is there animosity between Meredith and her mother?" I asked.

"I wouldn't say that. I think Donna overprotected Meredith to the point of suffocation. And I think, the last couple years, being out in the 'real world' and everything, Meredith has begun to realize how sheltered a life she's been forced to live. I suppose she must resent that at least a little—wouldn't you?—but I wouldn't say there was any real *animosity* or anything. Why? You don't think—"

"I'm just trying to get an idea of whom I'm dealing with here. I barely know Donna Berens, and I don't know Meredith at all. But as I told Donna, if we assume Meredith went away, and if we can guess at *why* she went, we may get an idea of *where*."

"But you said Meredith didn't go away."

I wagged my head. "I said Meredith didn't take the sorts of things you would expect her to take if she went away. And I said that makes me think she didn't plan to go away. That doesn't mean that something didn't come up suddenly to cause her to leave."

"Like what?"

"Like I don't know—that's why I keep asking *you* questions."

She blew out a disgusted breath and crossed her arms even tighter, hugging herself, digging her chin into her chest. "And I'm not much help, am I?"

"That's not your fault. What about Meredith's father?"

"What about him?"

"Did she ever talk about him?"

She paused, and her face took on that expressionless, abstract, let-me-see look. "No-o . . ." she said slowly. "Not really. I knew that her parents were divorced, of course, but I guess I didn't know one way or another if her father was alive."

"He is. Apparently. Donna Berens wasn't of much help on that score. I gather the parting was not amicable."

Dianna nodded. "I have the same impression," she said, "mainly from the way Meredith never spoke of it. I mean, after two years of working together we've gotten to be pretty good friends, yet she never would talk about her father. Kind of strange, I always thought. But in another way it kind of all added up, too. The way

Donna sort of kept Meredith under wraps, protecting her from the big bad world and all the big bad people in it—like loud-mouthed blonds." She laughed at herself. "I kind of figured that the divorce had been a mess, and that in her own cockeyed way Donna figured she was doing the kid a favor. Does Meredith's father live around here?" she wondered, suddenly hopeful. "You don't suppose she—"

"It's a nice thought," I agreed, "so hang onto it. Evidently the old man lives in Illinois. Wilmette. Donna says they haven't been in contact since this state was admitted to the Union. That's about all the useful information she supplied, if you call that useful."

"Not very." She tossed her head, indicating the wall behind her. "There's the phone."

I shrugged, got up, went over to the wall phone, and called directory assistance for Area Code 312.

"Strike one," I said to Dianna Castelli as I replaced the receiver. "There's no listing for anyone named Berens in Wilmette."

"Crap." She thought a minute. "Wilmette—is that around Chicago?" I nodded. "Well, maybe his mailing address is Wilmette but the telephone exchange or whatever you call it is for some other suburb. Haven't you ever gotten a phone bill that you think is wrong because it lists a call to a city you never called, and then you find out you did call, but you thought you were calling somewhere else because of the address?"

I looked at her hard. "I *almost* know what you're talking about."

She sighed. "I have an aunt who lives in Eden Prairie, Minnesota, but whenever I call her the bill says Minneapolis, not Eden Prairie. See?"

"Where the heck is Eden Prairie, Minnesota?" I said.

"Well, it's just south of— Look, that's not the point. The point is—"

I laughed. "I take your point, but I think you're wrong. I might call Wilmette and see Chicago on my bill, but if a guy lives in Wilmette and I call directory for Wilmette, they're going to show a listing. *If* he's in Wilmette and *if* he's listed."

"What if he's moved away? What if he's not listed?"

I moved back to my chair. "Then the job becomes a little harder, but not impossible. I know some people in Chicago. Besides, Meredith's father isn't our only possibility, or even our best: If Meredith had gone to visit him, wouldn't she have called in to let you know? Wouldn't she have packed a bag?"

The woman jumped up and paced the room, what paceable space there was, her arms still wrapped around her. "You know, Mr. Nebraska, you're a whole *hell* of a lot better at asking questions than you are at answering them."

"We're not to the answering part yet, Ms. Castelli. I've found you pretty much always have to go through the asking portion first. And, yes, I am good at asking questions. You don't know the right questions, you don't get the right answers."

She stopped and looked at me, managed a shrug and a smile, both of them half hearted. "I apologize. I know you're only trying to help."

"Fine. Back to Meredith. Is there anyone you know of who's especially close to her? Someone she might have confided in, told something to that could be of use to us? Her mother indicated that Meredith was pretty much a loner."

Dianna turned down the corners of her mouth. "Two days ago I would have told you that *I'm* close to Meredith. At least, I thought so. But I guess there are things she's kept to herself." She shook off the self-pity and looked directly at me again. "You've talked to Thomas."

"Thomas?"

She frowned. "Thomas Wayne."

I frowned. "Thomas Wayne?"

Her frown continued for some time, but not as long as mine did. Mine was still in place when she began laughing and dropped onto the short sofa near the chairs.

"Perfect," she managed between guffaws. "Just perfect."

"I do my best," I said, "but isn't 'perfect' a little strong?"

She wiped at one eye and successfully smeared her mascara. "Perfect in terms of the whatever-you-want-to-call-it between Meredith and her mother, I mean. It's absolutely perfect that Meredith wouldn't tell her mother about her engagement."

The frown on my face vanished; more correctly, it did an about-face and my eyebrows headed for the high ground. "Engagement?" I echoed. "Donna Berens told me Meredith didn't even have a boyfriend, much less a fiancé."

The woman, still smiling, spread her green-and-yellow arms. "What'd I tell you? Perfect. I wonder if she's ever going to tell Donna, or if she'll just let her see the wedding picture in the paper."

I rubbed my forehead. Heavy, close weather of the kind we'd

been having lately gives me a headache anyhow, and this business with Meredith Berens wasn't helping. "What's the story of this Thomas Wayne?" I said. "Besides the fact he has two first names."

Dianna Castelli shrugged and rearranged herself on the sofa, tucking her legs under her. "What's to tell? He's a nice guy, good-looking, about my age—late twenties."

I had gotten up and gone into the little bathroom for aspirin. Now I leaned out the doorway and looked at Dianna.

"All right, all right—late thirties. *Early* late thirties. Anyhow, he runs Midlands Realty and Development. You've heard of them."

I swallowed three aspirin, scooped water from the tap into my mouth, and reemerged daubing my lips with my handkerchief. "Commercial property, aren't they?" I said. "They're big."

"*Pretty* big. Thomas's dad, Alexander Wayne, started the business. He's Midlands' chairman, I think, but it's Thomas who handles the day-to-day."

I sat again, in the armchair that Dianna had occupied. "So there's money there."

She nodded. "Not oodles and oodles, but, yeah, I'd say they're doing all right. Why?"

"Merely an observation. Money changes everything, as the song says. This engagement—how long ago was it announced?"

"Not long. They haven't *known* each other long. They only met last February, at my Doldrums party—I have a Winter Doldrums party every February, sort of to carry us through that long dry spell between New Year's Eve and Saint Patrick's Day—so, anyhow, I was pretty surprised here a couple of months ago when Meredith announced they were getting married." She shook her head. "I guess it happens."

"I guess so. Have they set a date?"

"No. Meredith said they were thinking of next year sometime. She joked that maybe they'd hold it to coincide with the Doldrums party next February." She laughed. "*That* would liven things up. Why are you looking that way?"

"The word *elopement* is flashing across my brain like a stock-market quote."

Dianna's eyes widened. The mascara smudge gave her face a lopsided, off-center look. "Holy cow," she said reverently. Then the wide-eyed look disappeared and was replaced by one of resolution. "Nope. Impossible. Meredith would *never* do something like this without telling me. Without telling her mother, sure; me, never. She knows I'd kill her, and then I'd fire her."

"Maybe it was a spur-of-the-moment kind of decision."

"You don't know Meredith," she said with certainty. "And anyhow, Thomas would never go for it. If he's going to get married, he's the big church type. Tuxedos and ice carvings and hot-and-cold-running champagne—all that traditional stuff."

It sounded like Dianna Castelli knew Thomas Wayne rather well, and I said as much.

"Oh, no, I'm not falling into *that* again. I thought I knew Meredith Berens pretty well, too. But seriously, I don't know how well I know Thomas, but I've known him a long time, at least five or six years, I suppose. We know a lot of people in common."

"That's it?"

She looked at me and pursed her lips. "We dated two, three times. Nothing serious. That was a long time ago."

"That's it?"

"That's it."

"The parting was friendly?"

"There wasn't any *parting* per se. We just didn't go out together anymore. We still saw each other—here and there, at friends' houses, at parties. Thomas handled the negotiations for my office space. I invited him to the Doldrums. We're friends."

"So it didn't bother you when he and Meredith became friends."

Dianna laughed, but in an incredulous, not amused way. "I think I'm supposed to resent that, but what the hell. No, it didn't bother me. I *encouraged* it, if you must know—and I guess you must. Ask Thomas. Ask Meredith. Donna Berens steered you right on one thing: Meredith *didn't* have any boyfriends, or any close friends at all. I could see that Thomas was interested in her at the Doldrums. When she told me he had asked her out I practically *insisted* she accept. Thomas is a great catch—geez, is that sexist or what? But he is. Good-looking, successful in business . . . there's even talk of a political career for him."

It seemed a little to me that Meredith had traded a smothering, overprotective mother—Donna—for a bold, overbearing one—Dianna—but it wasn't anything to me. My only interest was getting a line on the girl; how she conducted her life, or let it be conducted, after she got found was no concern of mine. It's been my experience that fiancés usually have at least a general idea of the whereabouts of their fiancées, so an interview with Thomas Wayne rocketed to the top of my list of things to do.

"When was the last time you spoke with Meredith?"

"Friday evening," she answered promptly. "We stopped off for a drink after work—Meredith and I and Steve, Steve Lehman, my account exec."

"How did Meredith seem to you then?"

"Fine. Perfectly fine."

"Did she mention any plans she had for the weekend?"

She chewed away some of the paint on her lower lip. "I don't think so."

"Was she going to see Thomas?"

"I don't know. I don't think she mentioned it, but I suppose she would see him. I mean, after all, they *are* engaged."

"Why were you surprised when Meredith told you about the engagement? Hadn't you known they were seeing each other?"

"Sure. Meredith had kept me pretty much up to date on it, I think. But, like I said, they hadn't known each other very long . . ."

"No, there's more to it than that. You said, if Thomas were to get married, he'd prefer a traditional church ceremony. *If.* Why *if?*"

Dianna put a hand behind her head, catching tendrils of hair between the scissors formed by the first and second fingers of her hand, twirling them into ringlets. "Well . . . to be honest, I was *partly* surprised about the engagement, partly because I knew they hadn't known each other very long, and partly because I never figured Thomas had much interest in marrying *anybody*. He's dated some, sure—he dated *me*—but he never seemed interested in getting too serious with anybody. I just assumed that he was more interested in his career, his business and civic organizations, and maybe this political thing. I remember warning Meredith—I knew she was real starry-eyed about Thomas, and knowing what I thought I knew about him, I didn't want her getting hurt. She laughed it off, said that Thomas loved her as much as she loved him and this was the real thing." She shrugged. "I guess I was wrong and she was right—Ms. Right, for Thomas Wayne."

I said, "Who else was surprised by news of the engagement?"

"Well, Donna Berens will be surprised, I bet," she said with a certain malicious glee.

I smiled tolerantly. "I'm thinking more along the line of friends of Meredith—acquaintances, coworkers . . ."

"Well, you know, Meredith really did keep to herself pretty much. Outside of Thomas and those of us at the office, I don't think that she knew very many people. And at the office, well, there's only me, Steve Lehman, the receptionist, and a production artist. And Meredith, of course, my copywriter."

"What's a production artist?"

"Someone who specs copy for typesetting, then keylines it when it comes back—cuts it up and pastes it down on a board that the printer shoots to make plates. There's more to it than that, but not much more. Anyhow, that's the gang, and I don't think Meredith really associated with anyone but me and Steve. Kelly, the receptionist, is only eighteen: Even a twenty-five-year old doesn't speak her language. Don, the production artist, is about Meredith's age—twenty-seven, I think—but he's married, and that puts people into a different mindset, too, socializing-wise. Steve was probably a little surprised—I mean, we all were—but I think maybe Steve had a little bit of a crush on Meredith." She smiled fondly. "There are days when I wish I could afford to hire adults."

I said, "Meredith was pretty taken with this Wayne fellow, huh?"

She said, "It's what usually happens to people before they decide to get married."

"I meant before that even. Was everything between the lovebirds on an even keel, as far as you know?"

She made a face that said the same thing her mouth did a second later "Sure. Why? You think they had a lovers' quarrel and Meredith took a powder?"

"It wouldn't be an original idea. Think about it: Young love nose-dives into the crapper. The dream of a lifetime, shot between the eyes. What's Meredith going to do? Where's she going to go? Home to mama? Hardly. That would be the final, the ultimate humiliation. 'See, baby, this is what mommy told you would happen if you didn't do what mommy said, so let's pack up now and you can move back with mommy where you belong.' I don't think so, not after what you've told me."

Dianna pursed her lips. "Well," she said a little poutingly, "she *could* have come to me. She knows that."

"Does she? No offense, Dianna; I know you're deeply concerned about Meredith. You wouldn't be here if you weren't; we wouldn't be having this conversation. But think about it—you warned Meredith. You told me so yourself. You told her to be careful of Thomas and she laughed you off. Now, say, it turns out you were right. Thomas says, 'You're a nice kid and all, Meredith, but I'm not ready for the old ball and chain.' Is Meredith any more likely to come boo-hooing on your shoulder than her mother's? I doubt it. The girl must have *some* pride."

Dianna sighed. "You're right, of course. I should stop thinking of myself and think of Meredith. Love's tough at her age."

"What's age got to do with it?" I said. "What's the line in that Paul Simon song—the only time love's an easy game is when other people are playing."

"Ain't *that* the truth," she agreed fervently. "But, Nebraska—if Meredith and Thomas did split up, and Meredith couldn't turn to me or her mother, why wouldn't she just come *here* and be alone?"

"Alone? With her mother calling every thirty seconds and private detectives and worried bosses letting themselves in? You can be more alone at the airport."

"Well, wouldn't she at least come home, pack a bag, and call to tell me she wouldn't be in today?"

"You'd question her, you'd want to know if everything was okay, and she wouldn't want to talk about it. She and Thomas have their falling out, she's very upset, she needs to get away . . . she gets into her car and *goes*."

"Goes where?"

"Wherever the freeway takes her. Wilmette. I don't know. I'm guessing, all down the line. Given a little time, I probably could come up with two or three other story lines that *seem* to fit the situation . . . and which would be of exactly as much use to us as the one I'm playing with now. We don't know that Thomas or Meredith had a row. We don't even know whether they saw each other over the weekend. I'll find out when I talk to Wayne."

"You want me to talk to him? Like I said, I know him pretty well."

"Thanks," I said, "but I had better do it myself. And—I'm sure I don't have to mention this—but this all stays on the qt, hmm?"

"Of course," she said with an offhand kind of gesture. "I just wish there was something I could do . . ."

"You've done a lot, believe me. You've provided a lot of information."

Dianna Castelli straightened her legs, worked her way off of the sofa, and came over toward me to retrieve her bag. "I'd better get going. My girl can't go to lunch till I get back." She looked at her watch and *tch*ed disapprovingly. "Two-thirty already. I might have to fire me for taking these lunches. You'll let me know if there's anything I can do to help?"

"Of course."

"And you'll let me know what's going on? What you find out?"

"Sure," I said. "As far as I can."

She nodded, hefted the huge bag onto her shoulder, and trudged toward the door. There she paused. "Nebraska," she said.

I turned in the chair to look at her.

"She's all right, Nebraska. Isn't she?"

According to the Code, that great body of regulations promulgated by the International Federation of Private Detectives and adhered to religiously by anyone who seeks eventual admission to the Private Eye Hall of Fame, I was supposed to say something inane. Such as, "I'm sure she is, Dianna," or, "Don't torture yourself, Dianna. Don't give up hope." In the clinch, however, I blanked out and couldn't come up with any of the union-approved, hard-boiled-type platitudes.

All I could think of was, "I don't know."

chapter

4

We of the Midwest do not properly value our history—perhaps because, in terms of much of the rest of the country, and certainly of the world, our history is short. The pioneer spirit here on the flatland is still strong within us. That is both good and bad. Good for all of the hackneyed, platitudinous reasons—we're hard workers, we're God-fearing family people, we're trustworthy, honest, brave, clean, and reverent, and so on. Bad because the pioneers of necessity led a lifestyle that can perhaps best be described as temporary. Except for the land itself, nothing was permanent— certainly no human invention or structure. Their sod houses were designed to carry them through the long, cruel winter; come spring, something better could be built. The attitude has lasted more than a hundred years, indeed, it has hardened, ossified, into today's almost unshakeable belief that that which was built yesterday is temporary and therefore without value; first chance we get, we'll pull it down and throw up something newer and, naturally, better.

"Throw up" is the operative phrase there. The glass-and-steel boxes that pass for improvements on the local skyline are enough to make you puke. Especially if you remember the buildings that were razed to make room for these modern monstrosities. Of all the cities of the Midwest—the *real* Midwest, from the Great Lakes to the Rockies, not the Eastern states that the TV weathermen mistakenly think constitute the Midwest—only Chicago is well in touch with its architectural heritage. The so-called Twin Cities, Minneapolis and St. Paul, have gotten on the bandwagon in recent years. Omaha, except for the ubiquitous small pocket of preservationists and historians and other wrong-thinkers, is far behind. In fifty years, we'll wake up. By which time, of course, it will be too late.

Not that I'm that much of a historic-preservation buff. I don't believe in hanging onto anything simply because it's old. But I know that a lot of the charm, if you will, a lot of the soul, has been hacked out of Omaha, especially downtown Omaha, in the past twenty or twenty-five years. In the process, we are destroying our own bridges to the past.

Which is perhaps the long way around to saying I didn't think much of the big square gray box in which Midlands Realty and Development Corporation was located. But, as usual, nobody asked me.

It was a five-story building—we also don't go in for height in a big way around these parts, having got a lot of width and depth to fill—that had a nice view of the telephone company headquarters. Midlands occupied most of the fourth floor, according to the directory in the lobby. The elevators were conspicuously convenient, but I sought and found the stairs, physical-fitness buff that I am.

Nothing too overwhelming about the offices, from what I could see from the reception area. Lots of glass. Lots of oak. Thick, mauve carpet, green leafy plants in oversized woven containers. Textured wall coverings, generic prints in brass frames. Your basic late-twentieth-century office, right out of the catalogue. Hey, Murray, send up a number seventy-two.

The young woman who helped me—there were two behind the big oak-and-red-granite reception desk—was very pleasant, very professional. She asked if she could help me. I said I wanted to speak to Thomas Wayne. She asked if I had an appointment. I said I did not. She asked if she could ask what it was in regard to. I said she could ask, but that it was personal. She said Mr. Wayne was out of the office and she didn't know when he would be back. I said why did we have to play twenty questions, then.

The police station was only a few blocks away. I hoofed it. The physical-fitness thing again. Unlike Travis McGee, I don't own a houseboat on whose deck I can do eleventy-six sit-ups every morning. Unlike Spenser, I don't belong to a seedy gym where I can box and lift weights and rub shoulders with the kind of people who leave something on you when you rub shoulders with them. My idea of a morning workout is bending down to pick up the newspaper at the door. And I have the paunch to prove it.

I was only slightly soaked by the time I plopped down in the uncomfortable green chair next to Kim Banner's desk. Kim Banner was not at her desk. The sergeant up front said she was meeting with "the boss" and would be available soon. He knows me, by sight at least, so he gave me a visitor's badge and admission to the sanctum sanctorum rather than making me wait up front with the great unwashed. I drank piss-warm gritty brown water from a Styrofoam cup and waited.

The wait wasn't long. Banner edged into the three-walled cubicle—the cubicle was small; edging was the only way to get in—and plopped into a well-worn swivel chair that squealed alarmingly when plopped into.

"Well, then, Sherlock," she said with an attempt at levity that didn't quite come off. "What's news?"

"Not much. Is this a bad time?"

"Of course." She tossed her dark-blond head in the general direction of her lieutenant's office. "*He's* being his usual pain-in-the-ass self."

"I *heard* that, detective," came a male voice from somewhere in the maze of cubicles.

"You were *supposed* to, Giannini."

Banner faced me with a look that could melt titanium and scrubbed a hand through her short mop of hair. She's a compact woman, Kim Banner, with small, sharp features and a throaty rasp of a voice and an easy, sure confidence in herself and her abilities. That last quality makes her easy to work with. Competent people always are easy to work with, since competence means not only technical proficiency but also a consuming interest in getting the job done and done well. The guy who's "good at what he does but impossible to get along with" is, ipso facto, *not* good at what he does.

I said, "I'll just say what I have to say, then get out of Dodge, as Marshal Dillon always said."

"Maybe a good idea," Banner said, the steam still rising off her.

I filled her in fast about Donna Berens and the missing Meredith. Banner is a good cop; I didn't need to connect all of the dots for her to see the picture. I'd known her for less than a year, but we had had occasion to work together two or three times, and we'd seen each other socially, as the saying goes, two or three times, and we were pretty much on the same wavelength. Which helps.

"Tell the mom to come in tomorrow and file an MP," Banner advised.

"She won't. She doesn't want the police involved."

"I guess that explains what you're doing here."

"You know how it is. Mom's writing the checks, but it's the kid who needs the help. Probably. I told Donna Berens that I wouldn't go against her wishes as far as OPD is concerned—but I meant *officially*."

"And I guess that explains why you're talking to a homicide cop about a missing person."

"I need to know about any Jane Does. Would've turned up last night or today. Cauc, twenty-five, brown hair, brown eyes, five-six or five-eight, say a hundred and ten. Here." I handed over the picture of Meredith Berens.

"Cute kid. Hang on a sec."

She lifted the handset on the black desk phone and punched in two digits. "Leroy? Kim Banner. Not too bad. Listen, Leroy, I need a Jane Doe from yesterday or today." She repeated the telegraphic description I had given her. "Uh-huh. Anything from the hospitals?" Her gray eyes came to me. "He's checking. How's the literary life? I shouldn't say so, but when you show up here it's usually a sign that you're stalled out. Or broke."

"Or both. Lately it's the checking account that's been dry. The writing's okay, but it always takes longer than you'd like, and you don't get paid until you finish. If then."

"So grow up and get a real job. —Yeah, Leroy, I'm still here. Okay, thanks much." She cradled the phone and leaned across the desk to hand back the photograph. "No match," she said. "They found her under the overpass off of Seventh, by the river. It's where she lived."

"Yeah, well, those people will be a lot better off when the Strategic Defense Initiative is in place."

Banner laughed. "Riiiight. Is that it?"

I could almost taste her impatience to get me out of there and get herself back to whatever it was that her boss was unhappy about. I said, "I was interested in knowing whether the girl's car had been picked up. But I can check up fron—"

"Cut it out," she said gruffly, grabbing the phone again and stabbing out the two-figure number. "You know the number?"

"Of course not." I gave her the description of Meredith Berens's two-year-old Mazda and she repeated it into the phone. Less than a minute passed before she thanked whoever was on the other end and hung up.

"We're oh-for-two," Banner said. "Want to try for three?"

"Pass. It would have made fast work of the job if the girl were in the care of the coroner's people, but sometimes you'd just as soon the job not be wrapped up quite that fast, quite that way."

"You know," Banner said cagily, "the mom isn't the only one who could file an MP."

"I thought of that," I said. "*I* couldn't do it—I'm only *stretching* my promise to my client by talking with you off the record; to file a report would be to break it—but I bet I know someone who *would* be willing, even eager to sign the papers. That would certainly up the odds of the kid getting found."

"What's the mom's problem anyway? Doesn't she like cops?"

"Some people, huh? La Donna's a queer case—I haven't got her pegged yet. Cold as a mackerel on the one hand, all worked up about her kid on the other. Both at the same time. First she says she'd rather not contact the police. Then she says her reason is that she doesn't want to wait until you'll let her make the report. There is more there than meets the eye, as Cyclops said, but I'm damned if I know what."

"Do you care?"

"Not enormously. Only to the extent it may or may not affect my search for the kid. If it doesn't . . . fine, let her be a woman of mystery. If it does . . . well, we'll worry about that when it's time to worry about that. Meanwhile, I said I wouldn't take much of your time, so . . ." I stood up.

So did Banner. "I'll walk up front with you. I want to run off a copy of that picture. In case something—some*one*—turns up."

"Good idea." I handed it over and followed her to the over-lighted little room where the copying machines and the Teletype and all the other officey machinery was kept.

"Really I just like using this color Xerox machine," Banner confessed.

"How do those things work?"

"Well, you put the picture here and you push this button and it makes you a copy."

"This isn't a police station, it's a comedy club." The copy floated out into the tray. "That's not too bad," I said.

"No, it does all right," she agreed, taking the photocopy from me and handing back the original. "I made it enlarge the picture a little because the copier has trouble with smaller pictures. The colors sort of bunch together. This isn't good enough to put in a photo album, but it'll be more than sufficient to help with a pre-liminary ID, if anyone turns up matching the general description."

I pocketed the picture. "I'll appreciate hearing from you if some-one does."

Banner smiled. It takes her whole face for her to smile, and she can barely keep her eyes open when she does. "What else are we here for?" she said.

It was late and I was hungry—it's funny how even sixteen or seventeen cups of coffee really don't stick with you more than, say, eight hours or so. I swung down to the Old Market and shoved my heap into a parking space down the block from M's Pub. Parking was easy; the Market was deserted. The tourist season, such as it is here in this Florence of the Farm Belt, had passed, and the drizzly, unreliable weather took care of any stragglers. The low, dark brick buildings looked forlorn in the grayness. The brick pavement was wet and slick underfoot. I figured the shop-keepers and restaurateurs were having a boring time of it today. I wondered if it wasn't something of a relief every now and then.

Business was light at M's. I conned a waitress into fixing me a cold sandwich from the leftovers of lunch, and made it and two Harps disappear in record time. I was working on the third beer when Koosje came through the door at five-oh-eight. Her office is just down and across the street, over the bakery. She spotted me at my back table and came back, peeling off her pale-green raincoat as she did. She was perfectly professional in a black suit with gray pinstripes, a gray bow tie, and a blouse the color of bone. There were pearls on her wrists, at her throat, and in her ear lobes. Her makeup, what little there was, was light and flawless. Her lips were very pink. She slid in next to me and pecked me perfunctorily on the cheek.

Things had not been just right between me and Koosje Van der Beek, Ph.D. We were out of step, somehow, out of synch, and had been since earlier that summer. It was my fault, too, which only made it worse. While ours was not a relationship of pledges and promises and exclusivity, it had at its foundation a bedrock of trust and an implicit understanding which I had violated. Not to put too fine a point on it, I hopped into the sack with another woman, an old flame who had come back into my life after a twenty-year hiatus. I nearly got my head blown off as a result, but that didn't seem to mollify Koosje much. Not that she was angry— or hurt, or accusatory, or sullen, or *anything,* really. She was just . . . different. Or maybe I was. Or maybe the whole relationship was. Koosje may have understood where my head was at when I went to bed with Carolyn Longo—in fact, I'm *sure* she understood: Her reputation in the professional community is not based solely upon her great legs—but I guess there's a considerable difference between understanding and acceptance.

Koosje ordered a vodka and tonic and said to me, "Are you working?"

I lifted my glass an inch from the table. "On my third one."

She rolled her eyes. "On a case, I mean. The one you mentioned this morning."

"Oh, *that.*" I swallowed some beer. "Yes, I took the job. Rent's due."

Koosje smiled tolerantly. "You like to pretend to be mercenary. I think we both know there's more do-gooder than mercenary in you, Nebraska."

"Well, don't let it get around." I told her a little about the case and she listened with close, professional interest. Koosje is Dutch by birth, although by now she has spent most of her life in this country. Still, there's something inexplicably European about the set of her mouth, the intensity of her green eyes. Her accent, while usually so faint as to be unnoticeable, comes on strong in moments of stress or emotion. Her name doesn't quite transliterate into English pronunciation, either. *KOHshuh VANderbeck* is pretty close, though.

"You may have something on the mother-daughter conflict," she said when I had finished my synopsis and she had taken a sip of her drink. "It's hard to say without knowing the personalities, but there's nothing at all unusual about people making a conscious break from the beliefs, traditions, and habits of their parents. As we go about ordering our lives, most of us decide, consciously or unconsciously, either to imitate our parents' behavior or depart from it. Some of each, most frequently. Your Meredith Berens may have opted for the latter to a great extent, probably consciously."

"Because she resents her mother? Because she wants to be as unlike her as possible?"

"Mm," Koosje said. "That's as good a guess as any. Another good one would be that there's no resentfulness as such, but that Meredith has observed her mother's life and has decided that she doesn't want *her* life to be like it. How to prevent that? Change, radically, the external things. It doesn't work, of course, or rather it doesn't *necessarily* work, but people still do it."

I sipped some of my Irish beer and considered it.

"Does the girl have any brothers or sisters? It would be interesting to see how they conduct their lives. It could provide clues about the extent to which Meredith's lifestyle may be a conscious rebellion against her mother's."

"No siblings," I said.

"Mm. It doesn't matter. Some of the other things you've told me about Meredith's behavior toward her mother—not telling her mother about her engagement, especially—lead me to suspect you're probably right about some bottled-up resentments in the girl. 'Lead me to suspect you're probably right,' " she echoed, shaking her head in mild disbelief. "Can you spot the psychologist in this picture?"

The bar trade was beginning to pick up with after-fivers straggling in from the drizzle. The noise level had increased slightly but noticeably. I slid a little closer to Koosje and said, "Let's stick with the resentment bit for a minute, with Meredith's kind of sneaky rebellion against her mother. Do you think it would prompt her to establish contact with her father, a man whom Donna Berens obviously would prefer to pretend doesn't exist?"

Koosje downed a little vodka and pursed her lips and gave it some consideration. "Maybe," she said at length.

"Well, there you have it: It always pays to ask."

She laughed. "Diagnosis is a tricky art at best, Nebraska; these long-distance diagnoses you're always pumping me for make me nervous. The correct answer to your question is 'maybe.' Maybe Meredith's feelings toward her mother are such that she figures, 'If Mother doesn't like the man, he must be okay.' Maybe she thinks initiating a relationship with her father will get her mother's goat when she finds out, as she almost certainly will. And maybe the idea of contacting her father never entered her head—the man has been out of her life for, what, ten years or better."

"Perhaps not entirely." I reached into my pocket and brought out the envelope I had found in Meredith Berens's wastebasket. "I realize a lot of people live in and around Chicago, but I have this sneaking suspicion that this might have come from Meredith's father."

"Mm." She took the envelope and studied it. "You're one of the most suspicious people I've ever met," she said, "which means you've gotten good enough at suspicion that your suspicions are usually fairly accurate. Of course, her father writing to her is no guarantee that Meredith has reciprocated."

"She read the letter, at least. Witness ye that the envelope has been opened, the contents removed."

"Did you find the letter elsewhere in the apartment?"

"No," I said. "I didn't give the place as thorough a going-over as I might have if Dianna Castelli hadn't interrupted me, but no. I had already learned what was at the top of my list—whether or not Meredith had packed for a brief vacation—and I think what Castelli had to tell me is worth more than anything I might have gleaned by going through every shoebox in the closet."

Koosje handed back the envelope. "Will you have to go to Chicago?"

"I hope not. It'd be a waste of time. I've spent a little time in that big-shouldered town, but I really don't know my way around worth a damn. I've got a friend there, an old army buddy—guy's you knew in the army are always 'old' and they're always 'buddies,' have you ever noticed?—who's also in 'the life.' He's with the district attorney's office. I think I'll put him to work on finding the old man. He owes me a favor."

"You saved his life at Omaha Beach?"

"How old do you think I am? Actually, I saved his life *from* Omaha, by backing up some cockamamie story he had told his wife about how he was out all night because *I* had—"

"Never mind, never mind." She turned serious. "What do you really think has happened to the girl?"

I sighed and finished my beer. "I wish to Christ I knew," I said. "My track record with little girls lost isn't the greatest."

"You saved Kate Castelar. In two or three senses of the word."

"How is Kate?"

"We've cut back to two sessions a week for her, but I'm still keeping Amy at three." Amy was Kate's sister. The Castelar busi-

ness—Kate and Amy's old man had been done in, Kate was missing, and it looked like Kate's boyfriend was responsible for both
the murder and the disappearance—had brought Koosje and me
together, nearly ten months ago. Koosje was right: I had saved
Kate; I had saved her *life,* although there was no way to save her
from the scars that were reluctant to heal even under Koosje's
capable treatment. The younger sister, Amy, was even worse off;
Koosje's professional guarded optimism these past months hadn't
fooled me.

Before the sisters there was Adrian Mallory, now dead; after
them was Carolyn Longo, also dead. And stretching back into the
swirlings mists were others, men, women, and children—the lost,
the hapless, the victims. I saved some of them, too. I lost some.
Some of them wouldn't be saved and some of them saved themselves.

Meredith Berens. A name, a face in a stiffly posed graduation
photograph, and a collection of contradictions. That was Meredith
Berens. That was all I knew about her. Would she be saved? Would
she save herself? Or would she be a victim—was she already a
victim, of somebody or something? At first blush she certainly
appeared a victim: held back by a smothering, overprotective par-
ent; then running to a somewhat overbearing employer, adopting
her—or being adopted by her—as a second mother; now, perhaps,
running again. But I had labeled people victims before and seen
them turn, seen them stand their ground and fight back. Perhaps
Meredith would prove one of them. I hoped so. I hoped so, and
I didn't even know her.

I looked at Koosje, who was looking at her wristwatch. "It's
late," she said. "I should get home."

"It's early," I said. "Let's hit Gorat's for a little dinner."

"You can't get a 'little' dinner at Gorat's. And it *is* late if you
have a lot of work to do, which I have." She lifted her purse from
next to her on the booth seat.

I said, "Gotta eat sometime."

Koosje paused, and looked at me, and smiled. "Don't let's do
this, all right? You *know* what. Don't push, Nebraska. Not now.
Not like this."

I gripped my empty glass with both hands and stared hard at it.

"I don't know what's going on," I said. "I don't know how to
act. I don't know what to say or do or not say or *not* do."

"It's no different for me."

"*Why*, dammit?" I lowered my voice. "What is it you want?"

"I don't *want* anything." There was an edge there now. Anger.

"I've told you I regret it. I've said I never wanted to do anything to hurt you, and I meant it. It's still true."

She looked away. "I know that."

"Then what?"

"I trusted you, dammit," she said with a sudden, startling vehemence. "*Trusted.* Do you have any idea what that means? What it means to me, I mean? Stop thinking of yourself, for a change. That's all you've done. Your old girlfriend appears from out of nowhere and you have the opportunity to—I don't know, prove something, make some kind of statement."

"Look, lady, I didn't—"

"Like hell." The Dutch accent was strong now. "You bedded her, then you bragged about it to me, then you told her there was nothing between the two of you. Are you sure you weren't showing her? Are you sure you hadn't decided that this time *you* were going to break things off?"

All of a sudden I wasn't sure of anything. I kept quiet.

"What was it you said to me before you slept with her?" Koosje's voice was calmer now, quieter, more controlled, almost reminiscent. "That you wanted to have her and then wake up the next morning and find it had never happened. Have her, and yet have none of the responsibility. Typical adolescent fantasy. Well, I'm sorry, I can't go along with your scenario. I can't pretend it didn't happen. I can't pretend it doesn't hurt. It *did* happen—it *does* hurt."

Nothing was said for the longest time. Then I spoke: "I know it hurts, Koosje. I may have wished that I could sleep with Carolyn and have had it never happen. Now I wish that it had never happened at all. But, as you say, it *did* happen. There's nothing I can do about that. What can I do about *this?*" I put my hand over hers.

She left it there for a while, then gently pulled hers away, gathered her things, and stood. Her eyes shone with tears. I suspect mine may have too.

"Give it time," she said softly. "Just give it time."

I stayed for a few more hours after that. I drank a few more beers, but they didn't dull the pain, didn't dull the world's hard, sharp edges quite as much or as fast as I would have liked. Eventually I pulled crumpled bills from my pocket and left them on the table, and headed for the door.

No rain, but moisture hung in the air, waiting for the right moment. It gathered around the street lamps in little haloes of haze. I got behind the wheel of my ancient Impala and headed for Decatur Street. The apartment was dark and cold. Damp. And empty. I left the lights out and my jacket on and sat in the big chair by the sliding glass doors, bathed in the lifeless blue light of the night. Outside, on the little balcony, water dripped in a slow, irregular beat from the balcony overhead. At the end of the block, traffic whispered past on the Radial Highway.

Eventually the flavor of beer on the back of my tongue grew oppressive, so I stood and peeled off the jacket and raided the fridge for a fresh beer. I drank it in the dark at the little square dining table shoved into a corner of the kitchenette. At ten I flipped on the idiot box to see what was going on in the great wide wonderful world. There was talk of our former governor, the one who used to date Debra Winger, running for senate. The president said he didn't trust the Soviets much. A television evangelist stood accused of having once behaved unholier-than-thou. The weather was going to stay the same. The Royals were in the cellar.

Another day.

I turned off the tube and sat and listened to the water and the traffic some more. So far I hadn't put a strain on a single light bulb, except the one in the fridge, and it seemed a shame to start now. I dozed a bit in the big chair. Later I awoke, cold and cramped, and staggered to bed. Alone.

chapter 5

It wasn't easy getting up the next morning, but I managed it and was downtown in Midlands Realty's overdone offices a little before ten. I hadn't been entirely slothful up until then, you understand. I rolled out of the sack and went running—what a less imaginative citizen would call brisk walking—for an hour, then cleaned up and ate a low-cholesterol breakfast and called Meredith's bank and called Chicago.

You might think that this mad exercise regimen I had adopted— using the stairs, walking several blocks when a perfectly serviceable automobile was available, running in the morning drizzle—was a typically middle-aged thing to do. You might think, Here's a guy rushing headlong at the forty-year mark. Suddenly he realizes that the actuarial tables all agree that more than half of his life is over. So, in an effort to prove them wrong and stave off the inevitable, he plunges into exactly the kind of crazed activity I have just described. You might think that. And you might be right.

In any event, I ate a low-cholesterol breakfast of whole wheat toast and peanut butter that I ground myself from fresh dry-roasted peanuts—no sugar, no hydrogenated oil, no salt—and called the bank whose name had appeared on the blank checks and savings-account passbook I found in Meredith's apartment. They put me on hold three times before palming me off on the VP who ran the branch. After a little cajoling in both directions, he decided he could at least tell me whether Meredith Berens had made any large withdrawals or closed out an account late last week. He checked. She hadn't.

I called Chicago and caught Elmo Lammers just as he was reaching his desk.

Elmo Lammers, my old army buddy, is an almost completely nondescript black man of about my age. We met in Southeast Asia, where we witnessed and endured the kinds of things that frequently forge an invisible link between men, a bond of friendship and something beyond friendship, a covenant that continues, unweakened by time, even if the individuals never set eyes on each other again.

As it was, I had seen Elmo half a dozen times in the years since then, when business had taken me to Chicago, and had spoken with him perhaps twice as frequently. He greeted me warmly and, over the wire, I heard the soft click of his battered gold lighter as he thumbed it to life and fired up one of the long brown cigarettes he favored.

Elmo Lammers was a good investigator. Not only was he utterly inconspicuous—like most detectives, he looked like your next-door neighbor, not like Tom Selleck; he had a regulation family, a house and a mortgage, and a second-hand car that was rusting out underneath—he also was smart and tenacious and stricken with a total inability to let anything alone until he was completely satisfied he had done everything he could. Sometimes even that wasn't enough for him.

We shot some breeze for a few minutes, since it had been five or six months since we'd touched base, and then I got down to cases.

"I need a line on a guy who lives or recently lived 'round those parts," I said. "Wilmette."

Elmo chuckled into the phone. "Nice neighborhood."

"If you say so. The name's Berens." I spelled it.

"First name? Or is he like you and only's got one?"

"I've got more than one," I said. "I just *use* only one. I assume Berens has more than one, too, but I don't know what they might be."

"Uh-huh. You got anything *hard* you want me to do in my spare time?"

"I called directory in Wilmette; they didn't have a listing."

"They wouldn't show one if he was unlisted," Elmo said. "*Nonpublished,* they say these days. The phone company's got two kinds of unlisted numbers these days, y'know? One of them they won't put in the book, but they'll give it out through directory assistance. One of them they won't give out at all."

"Unless you know who to ask. And how."

"And *how,*" Lammers agreed, chuckling. "Anyhow, the place to check is with the utilities—power, gas, *and* phone. Between 'em they know more about what's going on than the FBI, CIA, and YWCA put together."

"And what *does* that spell?" I wondered.

"I'll check with the electric company first," Lammers said, talking mostly to himself. "If there's anyone in Wilmette name of Berens, and if he's got lights, they'll have a record of him. If he's moved, they'll have that, too. If he never was there, well, then, that gets hairy. How far you want me to go on this?"

"Don't put a whole lot into it. Try Wilmette—we know for a fact he *did* at one time live there—and take it back five years. If you don't turn him up, give me a call and we'll plan from there."

"You don't want to hear from me if I *do* turn him up?"

"Thanks, Elmo."

"Bye, guy."

And I was downtown in Midlands Realty's overdone offices a little before ten.

The young woman I had spoken with the day before—secretary, receptionist, whatever the official handle was—was occupied with a tall, ruddy-faced old gentleman in what I always think of as golf clothes: knit sport shirt, high-rise plaid pants, and bucks. When she had completed her business with him she looked over, recognized me, and smiled in a kind of lamentful way. "I'm sorry," she said before I could speak, "but Mr. Wayne isn't in and I don't know when he'll be back. Are you *sure* you don't want to just leave a message? I'll make certain he gets it."

The old gent, who had aimlessly wandered a few feet from the reception desk, caught up in the handful of papers he had been discussing with the receptionist, looked up and said, "Can I help?"

The woman said, "This gentleman needs to see your son, Mr. Wayne, but you know how difficult that can be to arrange sometimes."

The man smiled, closed the short distance between us, and extended a large, blunt-fingered hand. "Yes indeed," he said jovially. "Well, maybe I *can* help, sir. I'm the chairman of this company, or at least that's my title." He canted his head slightly and winked at the receptionist, who smiled and shook her head and went back to her business. "Alexander Wayne," the white-haired man continued. "Mister . . ."

"Nebraska."

"Ne . . ."

"Yes, like the state." After nearly four decades, I'm used, almost, to the momentary bewilderment. I don't understand it—if the name was England or Ireland or France, even Montana, there would be no glimmer—but I'm used to it. Every so often I feel obliged to explain that it's the monicker the patriarch hit upon when he emigrated to the States and discovered that he had only enough money to carry him half the distance from Ellis Island to California. As I get older and crankier, I find myself less willing to go into the story. Though, as ever, I'm eternally grateful that the old boy ended up in Nebraska and not, say, Xocotepec de Juárez or someplace with as many consonants as his original name had had. "Can we talk in private, I wonder?"

He indicated the space beyond the reception area, past the half-wall cubicles of the rank-and-file worker bees. "They still let me have an office," he said pleasantly.

They did indeed. Alexander Wayne's was big and plush, heavy, with rough, rustic paneling on the walls, good wildlife prints and landscape paintings on the paneling, and very little paperwork on the desk, a slab of wood big enough for Huck and Jim to take down the Mississippi. Three soft, low-backed chairs were lined up in front of the desk. Alexander Wayne motioned me into one and sank into another.

"Get you anything? Coffee?"

"No, thanks; I'm trying to cut back to just thirty cups a day."

He chuckled politely. I guesstimated his age at early- to mid-sixties. He had the puffy, soft look that a lot of good-looking men acquire when age and the good life catch up to them. Wayne's features were still good, the gray eyes bright and quick-moving, the teeth white in a weather-beaten face. But the hair looked worn out and there was too little of it to quite cover his pink scalp, and loose fat hung beneath his chin and across his chest and over his belt. He would be one of those guys, I decided, who hits a little white ball with a stick, gets into a cart and drives after it, hits it again and so on for eighteen or twenty-seven or thirty-six holes, then brags about what a great workout he got. The flab under his chin gyrated when he laughed and when he said, "Well, then, Mr., eh, Nebraska. What can I do you for?"

"I really do need to speak with your son," I said, reaching for my wallet, "but perhaps you can help me, too." I showed him the permit. "Mr. Wayne, I'm a private investigator. I've been hired by Donna Berens to look for her daughter, who has been missing since Sunday evening."

The white-haired man looked from the ID to me; his gray eyes darted in confusion. "I don't . . . Meredith is missing? What happened?"

"Nobody knows. Apparently." I took back the paper. "Her mother spoke with her Sunday afternoon. Sunday evening and Sunday night she didn't answer her phone. Yesterday morning she didn't show up for work."

"Maybe . . . maybe she's sick."

"Perhaps, but she's not at home. I checked it myself. She seems to have vanished, though, of course, people don't simply vanish. She hasn't been in touch with her mother or her friends at work. Has she been in touch with your son, Mr. Wayne?"

He wasn't with me; his eyes were focused on an invisible point on the desktop.

"Mr. Wayne?"

He looked up, startled. "What?"

"Your son. Do you know if he's heard from Meredith Berens in the last couple of days?"

"No. No, I don't. Listen . . ." He leaned forward and laced his broad fingers, his hands hanging loosely between his knees. "Meredith isn't . . . well, that is, they don't think anything's *happened* to her, do they?"

" 'They,' Mr. Wayne?"

"The police."

"So far, this isn't a police matter. They know the girl's missing, although no official report has been made yet, and they know that I'm looking for her. The assumption I'm working on is that, for reasons known only to her, Meredith took off for parts unknown Sunday evening. Her car is missing, too, you see."

"An accident, perhaps? An auto accident?"

That would explain why Meredith hadn't packed a bag or taken any of life's little necessities with her—who packs just to go for a drive?—but it wouldn't explain her absence of nearly two days. Even if she had had a wreck and been killed on the most remote highway in the state, she'd have been found by now. Cars are easily traced. We would know. Whether she was alive or dead, we would know.

I shook my head slowly. "I don't think so. Mr. Wayne, I understand your son was—"

"Wait a minute." He got up slowly and went around to the business side of the great desk, where he lifted the telephone receiver and punched a button on the console. "Joanie, get ahold of Thomas. I know. It doesn't matter, just *get* him, please, and get him down here. This is an emergency." He put down the phone and leaned heavily on the desk, his white-haired arms braced to support himself. He looked at me. "No point your asking me a bunch of questions I can't answer. We'll get my son in here and you can ask him direct."

"I appreciate that."

He sat behind the desk and leaned back and studied a framed print on the adjacent wall. It was one of those warm, woodsy scenes, the kind they put on the L.L. Bean catalogue covers. "Missing," Wayne said ruminatively. "Missing. Funny word. Nobody goes *missing* these days, do they, Mr. Nebraska." He glanced at me. "My God, how do you escape *that* thing?" He waved a hand at the mute phone on his desk. "Cordless phones, car phones, briefcase phones, cellular phones, pocket pagers, answering services, answering machines . . . Arthur C. Clarke—you ever read him?"

"Some."

"Clarke talks about giving everyone some kind of two-way wrist-radio thingummybob, like Dick Tracy's, that could bounce signals off of satellites and guarantee that no one would ever be lost again."

"Unless they wanted to be lost," I said.

He looked at me. "Poor little Meredith."

"You know her well?" It was becoming increasingly difficult to not refer to Meredith in the past tense. But I was not allowing myself to slip into it.

"Oh, no, not really. You know. She was by the house a few times, Thomas told me a little about her . . . that's about it."

"What did Thomas tell you about her?"

He frowned, his pale white brows nearly meeting above the bridge of his nose. "Well, that's an odd sort of question," he said. "What do you mean, 'what'? He told me her name, of course, and how he met her, what she did, where they were going when they went out—that sort of thing. You don't have kids, do you, Mr. Nebraska?"

I admitted it.

"Well, then, I guess you wouldn't know how it is when your kid's dating someone, the way they kind of tell you this and that but can't really *tell* you anything, if you understand me."

"I'm not sure . . ."

"See, it's like they're on their own wavelength, kind of, and the things they do they do in private, even when they're out in public, and that's the way it should be, isn't it? Alone together? And if they open up about it too much, well, that only spoils things."

"You seem very . . . wise about Young Love."

He laughed. "I'm not as old as I—well, no, I guess I *am* as old as I look, but my memory's still okay. And Thomas, let's see, he's thirty-nine, so I guess we've been going through this dating business for—God, twenty-some years now."

"Thomas never married?"

"No." The quick eyes shifted away from me, then back. "Go ahead."

"I'm sorry?"

He smiled, one of those big good-buddy smiles. "Go ahead and ask why. Everyone does. Man's thirty-nine years old, never married, still lives at home. Why?"

"There's a word for it," I said. "Bachelorhood."

"Still, people wonder. People ask."

"I wasn't going to. It doesn't have anything to do with anything. Does it? Besides, I'm under the impression that he's going to be married."

The white eyebrows went up, ever so slightly. "Oh? Ah—you mean Meredith. Well, who knows?"

"Meredith, for one. She's discussed it at some length with her employer."

Wayne performed a gesture that was half a shrug, half a shake of his head. "I think it's been discussed—it's *probably* been discussed—but I don't . . ."

"According to Dianna Castelli, Meredith's boss, Meredith has used the word 'fiancé' in reference to your son, and has discussed wedding plans with her—in a sort of general way, I guess, since a date hasn't yet been set."

He frowned. "There's some mistake. Thomas has said nothing to me about any engagement. And he would have."

I thought about Donna Berens's being in the dark about her

daughter's impending nuptials, but said nothing. Nothing except, "What do you think of Meredith?"

"*Think* of her?" he said, as if the word was unfamiliar to him. "Why—I don't know. She seemed to be a very nice young woman, very pleasant."

"*Seems,*" I corrected. "She's not dead. As far as we know."

Wayne smiled sheepishly. "Of course. A figure of speech . . ."

"When's the last time you saw her, Mr. Wayne?"

"Oh, I don't know . . ." He scratched the flesh under his chin in a lazy, backhanded manner. "A couple of weeks ago, I guess. She and Thomas had gone out but they stopped by the house on the way from somewhere to somewhere, or something. Thomas will remember. He'll be here shortly, I'm sure."

"A busy man, your son."

The big man grew slightly bigger. "He's running the place," he said with an expansive gesture that took in the whole company. "I still have the title, but everyone knows I'm all but retired. Thomas is really moving the place forward. Development, speculation, commercial properties . . . far removed from the little one-man residential real-estate office I opened ten years ago in Lincoln."

"That's the ancestral home? Lincoln?"

He shook his white head. "No, we've been all over, all over the Midwest, at least. I was transferred to Lincoln from Indiana a little more than twelve years ago by the finance company I was working for. Studied for my real estate license at night, got it, sold houses part-time for a local office, then hung up my own shingle. I moved into commercial space in Lincoln, and moved here in seventy-nine to get in on the boom." He spread his arms, indicating our current surroundings. "The rest is history."

There were two gold-framed photographs on the desk. I noticed them for the first time. One was a professionally done portrait of a young man who I assumed was Thomas Wayne. The other was an enlarged snapshot of the same young man and the older man now seated across the desk from me. I reached across and picked up the former. "Nice picture," I said. "Thomas?"

Wayne nodded.

The image was of a young dark-haired man, staring off into space, as commercial photographers will have it, his smile fixed and a little wooden, the backdrop the typical bluish-gray mottling that every photographer on the planet uses. His thick brown hair was parted high, just left of center, and blow-dried to artful perfection. He wore a well-trimmed brown mustache that formed an upside-down V over his thin-lipped mouth.

I set down the photograph and lifted the other one. "You and Mrs. Wayne have just the one child?"

Wayne smiled briefly. "*Had* just one. My wife died when Thomas was very small."

"I'm sorry," I said, although it was exactly the information I was shooting for; it just seemed indelicate to say, "Hey, how's come there's no broad in this pitcher?" I put the second photo back where it belonged.

"That's all right," Alexander Wayne said easily. "It was a long time ago . . . I sometimes wonder if that's why Thomas hasn't married. Perhaps I should have remarried. He was just a boy, maybe he needed a mother more than I thought he did. But I didn't. At the time I couldn't. And now . . . well, now is now." He stood, and looked out one of the two narrow windows that flanked his desk.

At that moment the office door banged open and a man dashed into the room, the same man as in the photographs on the desk. Thomas Wayne.

"Dad, are you all right? Joanie said—" He caught sight of me, realized his father was perfectly fine, and slowed to a halt in the middle of the plush carpet. "She said it was an emergency."

Alexander Wayne had turned away from the window. "It is, Thomas, in a way. Thomas, this gentleman is a private investigator." I stood, introduced myself, and shook hands with the bewildered young man. I keep referring to him as a young man largely because I know he and I were about the same age.

"A private investigator?" Thomas Wayne repeated blankly, taking one of the chairs on my side of the desk. "I don't understand. What's wrong?"

"I've been hired by Donna Berens, Mr. Wayne. Your fiancée has been missing for a couple of days."

"My fi—" Wayne *fils* stopped and glanced at his father, who was gazing steadily at him. The younger man took a deep breath, smoothed a hand over his impeccable hair, and said, "Meredith is *not* my fiancée, Mr. . . . ."

"Nebraska. I understand she told the people at Castelli otherwise."

"I can't *help* what she—" he said vehemently.

"What's going on here, son?" Wayne *père* said. He looked as perplexed as I felt.

Thomas Wayne looked at each of us in turn, then loosened his tie and sat back, slouching, into the chair.

"Meredith has the wrong idea, Dad, that's all. We've been going out, we've had some fun, and that's all there is to it. But somehow, in her head, she's turned it into . . . something a lot more. All of a sudden she was talking wedding. I told her to forget about it—nicely, of course, as nicely as I could—but no good."

"You mean you never were engaged to the girl?" his father pressed.

Thomas looked long at him. "Of course not, Dad. I'd have told you."

I said, "When did you set Meredith straight, Mr. Wayne?"

"Two, three weeks ago, I guess. I explained to her that she was a great kid and I like her a lot, but that I'm not in the market for marriage, not to her or anybody."

Almost exactly what Dianna Castelli had said.

"What was her reaction?"

"Fine, I thought. She heard me out, and then she said something like, 'All right, let's not talk about it anymore.' But she didn't mean it the way I thought she did."

"Not, 'Let's forget about it,' but rather, 'I don't want to hear about it'?"

"Exactly!" he said animatedly. "And when I realized that, I broke off with her." I asked him when that was. He turned his eyes toward the ceiling, thinking, and stroked the back of his neck. "Let's see—what's today? Tuesday? A week ago yesterday."

"And that's the last you saw Meredith?"

He nodded. "But not the last I talked to her. She called me again a couple days later. She wanted to know what we were going to do that weekend. I explained to her again that we weren't going to be seeing each other anymore. And her reaction was about the same. She said it was all right, she had things to do that weekend, and hung up before I could point out that I meant we weren't going to be seeing each other anymore *ever*."

"What did you do then?"

He looked down at the wing tips on his feet, buffed to a high gloss. "The wrong thing, I think. I didn't know what to do, so I left it alone. And she called me *again*, on Friday, and we went through it all again, with about the same results. And then she called me on Sunday and said didn't I think we had better think about setting a date, because her friends were wondering!"

"Sunday as in the day before yesterday?"

"That's right."

The elder Wayne and I exchanged glances.

"And what happened on Sunday?"

"Well, I'm afraid I blew up. You have to understand, Mr. Nebraska. I didn't want to hurt Meredith. I really do like her a lot. Or did, before all of this *engagement* nonsense came up . . ." He looked at me earnestly. "I think . . . I think there's something wrong with her, you know . . ." He tapped his temple gently.

I wondered if he wasn't right. It could put a whole new light on the disappearance. A lot of things that don't make sense—going on vacation without any luggage, for one; not telling anyone you're going, for another—are somewhat more understandable in light of a mental aberration. I said, "Is there anything besides the non-engagement that makes you say that?"

"No. Not really. Like I said, we had a lot of fun. In every other way, Meredith's a great girl. Why?" He looked at his father, who met his eyes. "What's this about Meredith being missing?"

His old man and I exchanged looks again. I didn't know what his meant. I didn't know what mine meant.

"She's been missing since sometime Sunday afternoon or evening. When did you and she talk?"

"What do you mean, 'missing'?"

"I mean, nobody seems to know where she is. Not her mother, not Dianna Castelli or anyone else at the agency, certainly not me. Do you?"

He pulled in his head as if I had taken a poke at him. "Of *course* not. Where could she have gone? Why didn't she tell anyone?"

"Good questions. Here's another good one. When did you speak to her? What time?"

Wayne massaged his forehead with an open palm. "I don't know . . . One o'clock. Maybe two."

"That early? You're certain?"

"I didn't write it down!" he snapped.

"Look, Mr. Nebraska," his father butted in, "just what is it you're getting at?"

I considered my answer, aware of young Wayne's hot eyes on

me and his father's cooler gray ones looking at me hard. I said, "Nothing, necessarily. We know about when Meredith vanished— at least, we know about when her mother last spoke to her and when she tried to phone her again later. Meredith was around in the late afternoon, not around in the evening. It's important to know whether anyone spoke to Meredith after the last time her mother did. It's important to know what was said, what Meredith said, how she seemed." I looked at Wayne the younger.

"Fine," he said tightly. "She seemed fine. Except, of course, for the fact that she was still completely deluded about this engagement."

"Not the least upset or distraught by your anger?"

"No. Perfectly calm. Just as before."

I nodded. "And how did you leave things?"

"We—Well, to be honest, I exploded, I told her off, and I hung up."

"Then you can't *really* say how she took it?"

He worked his jaw muscles. "No," he squeezed out between clenched teeth. "If it matters."

"Does it?" Alexander Wayne.

I turned up a palm. "Could. Let's say Meredith was upset. Understandable enough, but if she was as you say"—I nodded to Thomas Wayne—"deluded about the engagement, her emotional and mental distress could be all the greater. Although she doesn't let on to her mother when they speak a couple of hours later. I think it's interesting that she told the people at Castelli that she was engaged, but never seemed to mention it to her mother. She never mentioned you to her at all, for that matter. In any event, go back to Sunday. She's upset. There's no telling what's going on in her mind, no telling what kind of turmoil." And, I thought sourly, no telling what she might have done.

Alexander Wayne seemed to read my thoughts. "She wouldn't . . . well, not suicide?"

I didn't have an answer for that.

Turning back to the younger man, I said, "Did Meredith ever mention her father to you?"

"Her father? I don't think so. I was under the impression that she hadn't seen him in years, not since her parents' divorce when she was a young girl. Why do you ask?"

"There's a possibility that Meredith may have been in touch

with him, on the qt. It would make life simple all the way around if Meredith, upset about what she may have seen as a broken engagement, or perhaps catching some glimpse of the delusion she had created for herself, fled to her father."

"But she'd have *told* someone," Thomas Wayne insisted. "Dianna Castelli, at least, if not her mother."

Maybe, maybe not. If Meredith Berens wasn't quite all together, she might not. It's hard to say what a girl who had dreamed up a whole engagement may or may not do. And if she had suddenly woken from her dream, perhaps shocked into lucidness by Wayne's outburst on Sunday, she may well have been so upset, or embarrassed, or scared that she wouldn't want to face anyone, wouldn't want anyone to know what she had done, would want simply to disappear.

Disappear how thoroughly, though? Until Alexander Wayne mentioned the word, I hadn't thought—hadn't *allowed* myself to think—in terms of suicide. It had to be considered a possibility. But what they say on all the crime shows is true. Suicides usually do leave notes, and Meredith Berens hadn't. Not one that had been found, at any rate.

"Do you know if Meredith kept a diary?"

He shook his head. "Why?"

I wondered about the razored-out pages in the diary I had found at her place. What had she written on them and then thought better of? Had it been about Thomas, loving comments she had penned and then destroyed when her dreams were destroyed? Had it been about her father? Or something else—something completely unrelated to her disappearance?

Of course, there was another angle to be considered.

"I've heard your name mentioned in connection with political office, Mr. Wayne," I said casually to the dark-haired man. "Sounds like you have quite a bright future."

He regarded me with narrowed eyes. "Meaning what?"

"Be careful what you say here, Nebraska," his father warned. The jovial, hail-fellow-well-met voice was taut now, almost guttural.

"I will," I assured him, and turned back to his son. "But I'll be frank, Mr. Wayne, because that's how the police will be, and, unless Meredith turns up pretty quickly, the police *will* be involved."

"Are you threatening me?"

"If I were, you wouldn't have to ask. I'm just telling you how it might look. Up-and-coming young businessman, civic leader, potential politician—all that Man of the Year stuff. Nice-looking, well-heeled, and an eligible bachelor into the bargain. But then there's a hitch: a girlfriend who's suddenly gotten serious, very serious. Maybe she's a little unbalanced, maybe she isn't. It doesn't matter that much. What matters is she's suddenly a liability. A threat, even. If she *is* a bit unstable, that only makes it worse, because there's not only a potentially embarrassing situation developing, there is also the matter of the maybe-candidate's judgment. Guilt by association; name a political figure who hasn't been tarred with the same brush used on a—ah—questionable friend or associate?"

"*Look,* you—"

"People will talk, Mr. Wayne, and this is what they'll say: She got in the way, she caused trouble. You promised to marry her, you led her to expect marriage, or she invented the whole thing in her head—as I said, it doesn't matter. What *does* matter is that she suddenly disappeared, never to be heard from again. Makes a guy think, doesn't it?"

Apparently not—there was no time for thought between my closing my big fat mouth and Thomas Wayne leaping from his chair to help push my front teeth down my throat.

The attack was unexpected—by me, at least, which is what matters—but ineffective. The low-backed chair's center of gravity was too low for it to tip over, and its brass casters meant that when Wayne lit into me, or tried to, the chair slid away from him before I could so much as react, leaving him on his hands and knees when I jumped from the runaway chair to defend myself. By then, too, the white-haired man had jumped from his own chair and circled the desk and gotten his arms around his boy, half-comforting him, half-holding him back from doing anything stupid. Anything *else* stupid. He looked up at me and his gray eyes were cold.

"I think you had better get out of here, Nebraska," he said curtly.

"If you say so—it's your joint—but the police won't be so easy to get rid of, and I can just about guarantee they *will* be by."

"So what? I don't have anything to hide." Young Wayne got to his feet and shook off his father's help. Or restraint.

"I hope not. I really do, Mr. Wayne, not just for your sake but also Meredith's. I'm sorry to have upset you two gentlemen, but it's my job to consider possibilities and the scenario I just sketched *is* a possibility. You had best be prepared for it, if worse comes to worst. And I don't mean be prepared to pop anyone who theorizes it. That sort of behavior doesn't go a long way toward convincing someone that what he's just said about you *isn't* true."

I went for the door.

chapter

Castelli and Company occupied a squat, square brick building on St. Marys, across from the Catholic bookstore. I pulled into a white-gravel lot west of the building and went in.

The building had not originally been intended as office space. I could dimly recall its having been a corner grocery or a corner barbershop, maybe both, although not simultaneously, when I was a kid. The front door opened into a main room that was set up as a bullpen: a small steel desk near the door, two ordinary steel office desks, a drawing table with a supplies cart, and another steel desk with an extra-large plastic-laminate top, the kind that juts out eight inches beyond the front of the desk.

Behind the latter desk sat Dianna Castelli. She beckoned me over before the extremely young-looking woman at the guard post could finish asking if she could help.

I took a pew opposite Dianna's desk. The other two desks were vacant; the drawing table was propping up a thin, sandy-haired fellow with a dark beard, who looked at me as I crossed the room, smiled briefly when our eyes met, and went back to his board.

"I'm surprised to see you," Dianna admitted. "Any news?"

"Non-news, mostly," I said. "I checked with the police—"

"I thought Donna didn't want you to."

"She didn't. There's no unidentified women in the morgue or any public-hospital bed who matches Meredith's description."

"That's good news, isn't it?"

"It might be; it's too soon to tell. Her car hasn't turned up in an impound lot yet, either. That could be good news, too. At the moment, however, they're just facts, neither good nor bad."

Dianna frowned and thought about it and chewed her lower lip a little. Today, I could see when she stood up behind the desk to greet me, she wore a black cowl-neck sweater with black slacks and a lavender jacket with three-quarter sleeves. Lavender on eyelids and lips. Lots of gold. The pale hair was as it had been yesterday.

"Like they always say, not knowing is the worst," she said. "I mean, I don't want anything bad to happen—or *have* happened—to Meredith, but, geez, at least you can deal with that. This way you're just . . . hanging."

"At least it can't last indefinitely."

"Some consolation there," she said. "How's Thomas taking it?"

"I just finished with him. Or he with me." I gave her the *Cliffs Notes* version of my meeting with Waynes *père et fils*.

"Well," she said, "you can hardly blame him for being upset." She shook her head. "Poor Meredith. I had no idea she was so . . ." She spread her hands. "Whatever. Lonely. Mixed-up. I don't know. I guess it was a mistake to push her at Thomas."

" 'Push her at'?" I echoed. "Yesterday it was 'They met at a party I gave,' today it's 'Push her at'?"

Dianna shrugged and grinned sheepishly. "Well, let's say I introduced them *real good.*" The grin vanished the way your fist vanishes when you open your hand. "I guess it'll be a long time before I play matchmaker again."

"Don't blame yourself. There's no reason to think it would have been any different with anyone else, or if Meredith and Thomas Wayne had met under different circumstances. And anyhow, we have only Wayne's say-so that the situation really was as outlined."

She frowned perplexedly and toyed with a long black stapler next to her desk blotter. "You mean Thomas just wants you to *think* Meredith . . . imagined the whole engagement?"

"I mean there's no one to contradict him. Meredith told you they're engaged. He told me they never were. He told me he had several conversations with her on the subject, trying to straighten her out. She's not here to say one way or the other." I shrugged. "I found a diary at her place yesterday. It was blank, but some pages had been sliced out. Any idea what might have been on them?"

"I didn't even know Meredith kept a diary. Do you think it has anything to do with her being missing?"

"Oh, who can say? Maybe she'd written wonderful things about Thomas and ripped them out when he broke off the engagement. If there ever was one."

Dianna looked hard at me, her eyes narrow and shrewd. "You think Thomas did something with Meredith."

"If I weren't so clean-thinking and morally upright I would say something unbelievably crude about what sort of somethings young Wayne may or may not have done with Meredith Berens. But I am, so skip that. Instead, let's define our *somethings* here. There are two possibilities. Meredith did something with herself or someone did something *to* her. Of the former, there are two possibilities. She's hidden herself away or she's killed herself."

Dianna gasped as if I'd dumped a pitcher of lemonade down her pants.

I said, "Sorry to be indelicate, but there are indelicate possibilities that must be faced. As time passes, it becomes more important to face them. And they become more and more indelicate. Of the two, the former is more likely. I can't help but think that if she'd killed herself we'd know by now."

"What if she went away somewhere to . . . to do it?"

"Could be. Suicides usually die in familiar surroundings—home, workplace, the home of a friend or loved one—but not always. Some check into hotels. But a maid would have found her long before now, and at the very least we'd have a Jane Doe, which we do not."

"What if she went out of town?"

"Now we're reaching. But even if she did, there are registers to be signed, arrangements for payment to be made . . . She'd have a car with Nebraska plates; that could be easily checked. Again, we'd know by now."

Dianna's face brightened. "Then she's alive."

"Then she didn't commit suicide," I corrected. "There's still the second possibility—that someone did something to her. Under that heading there are again two possibilities: Purposely or accidentally. I rule out the latter for the same reason I rule out suicide: If Meredith had been accidentally hurt or killed, we would know by now."

Dianna jumped on it. "Not if she had gone out of—Oh. The car. The license plates."

I nodded. "All kinds of ways to identify someone. On *Perry*

Mason, of course, innocent people were forever spiriting away the corpses of people they'd accidentally killed, or been made to believe they had; but in real life it hardly ever happens. Would *you* know what to do with the body of someone you'd accidentally killed? Not to mention his car?"

"Put 'em with the trash in back of this place," she said promptly. "It never gets collected."

"So we're left with someone *willfully* doing something to or with Meredith. And the way I look at it—"

"There are two possibilities," Dianna supplied.

"Very well put. And the possibilities, which are not mutually exclusive, are kidnaping and murder."

Again she recoiled, but less so than the previous time.

"I'm sorry," I said again, "but I think enough time's been spent thinking happy thoughts. It's time to consider all possibilities and just hope that the nastier ones prove wrong."

She waved it off impatiently. "I'm all right. I—Well, *why* would anyone want to kidnap Meredith?"

"I've asked myself the same question. And I've hoped that you would have a better answer than I have, which is none at all."

"Well, there's no money there. Donna's well enough off, I think, but she's certainly not wealthy. At least, Meredith sure never gave—*gives*—any indication of having come from a lot of money. Plus, there's been no ransom note or anything, right?"

"Not as far as we know."

She looked at me quizzically.

I said, "There's still this mysterious father of hers."

Dianna's eyes and mouth opened in a silent *Ah-ha.*

"For all we know, the old man's an eccentric billionaire recluse. Howard, we'll call him. Someone snatches Howard's kid; naturally they'd present their demands to him, not his estranged wife."

"Holy balls," Dianna breathed, "do you think so?"

"I would if we were on *Falcon Crest;* in real life, all the good eccentric billionaire recluses are dead, it seems. In any case, I want to know more about the old man before I commit myself to *that* theory."

"Then that leaves murder." She did a good job of saying it matter-of-factly. "But why would anyone murder Meredith?"

"Here's a fairy tale I tried out on Thomas Wayne. See what you think of it. Let's say there's a young up-and-comer who finds himself involved with a young woman who has become a liability.

Maybe she hasn't got enough stuffing in her Oreos. He tries to shoo her off but she won't be shooed. She doesn't even hear him. His political future and possibly even his business career are turning dark before his eyes. What does he do?"

Dianna stared at me. "You *cannot* be serious."

"Wayne's reaction was much the same, albeit more emphatic." I scratched beneath my chin. "I'm *not* serious. Very. It could turn out to be that way, but not necessarily. Mostly I just tossed it out to see what would happen. And what happened is, Thomas Wayne pounced on it. Or me, more accurately."

Her eyes were still on me but now they were narrowed, disgusted. "Can you blame him?"

"We're not to the blame stage yet," I said. "Right now I'm just interested in reactions, and his was . . . well, interesting."

She shook her head. "Not Thomas," she insisted stolidly. "Not a chance."

"You could be right," I said lightly. It infuriates the hell out of people, being open-minded like that. Leo Buscaglia tells a funny story about agreeing with people in order to defuse arguments and, on one occasion, frustrating his would-be opponent to the point where the poor fellow blurted, "But—but I could be *wrong!*"

It didn't get quite that far with us. Dianna shook her head a couple more times, to underscore her resolve, then said, "What does Donna think of all this?"

"I haven't spoken with her today. I wanted to talk with Wayne first. I don't really know anything of substance yet, and what little I do know I know from talking to the cops—exactly what Donna *didn't* want me to do. Speaking of cops, they mentioned something to me that we should tuck away in a tickler file with tomorrow's date on it, in case we don't know anything concrete by then: Donna Berens isn't the only one who's allowed to put in a missing-person report."

Dianna's eyes grew. "What do you mean?"

"I couldn't file, because that would be going against my client's wishes even more than I have already. But I don't see why a concerned employer—"

"And friend."

"—and friend couldn't."

"That's *great!*" She reached under the desk and jumped up holding the enormous bag. "You wanna drive?"

"I would, but we'd have to hang around the station until tomorrow, and the coffee there is lousy. They have a thirty-six-hour rule down there, and as of this moment Meredith's not been missing even twenty-four hours yet. We'll do it tomorrow afternoon, if we haven't learned anything helpful by then."

"Well, crap." Dianna threw the bag on the floor. "You bring any other balloons to pop?"

I laughed. "That's the last one. I really stopped by to check out Meredith's desk, if that's all right with you, and also to chat with this Steve Lehman fellow you mentioned yesterday. Although it doesn't look like he's around . . ."

"He's on a call, I think." She raised her voice and sent it over my head. "Hey, Kelly." I turned as the young blond receptionist looked up from her work. "When's Steve gonna be back?"

The girl consulted a spiral-bound appointment book on the desk. "He had to go out to Traveso's, I think . . . Yeah." She looked up. "It doesn't say when he'll be back, but he's supposed to meet Tom Flanagan for lunch at twelve-thirty."

I looked at my watch. It wasn't quite ten-thirty. "Traveso's the restaurant-supply people? What do they need with public relations? They don't deal with the public."

Dianna shrugged. "The big guys can afford to pick and choose and stick with straight PR, lobbying, that kind of thing. Us little guys, we take whatever we can get. The line between PR and advertising gets kind of blurry now and then anyhow, and if someone asks us to put together a brochure or an ad slick for them, we don't squeak. We're doing catalogue sheets for Traveso's. The things their salesman would have in a loose-leaf binder to show you, if you were a restaurant. I think Steve went and picked up some press proofs to show them. It's not public relations; it's advertising, but I won't tell them if you won't."

"Don't worry, I don't know the difference either."

She leaned back in her chair and laced her fingers over her stomach. "Well, let's say you've written a book—"

"I *have* written a book."

"Really? What kind of book?"

"Private-eye thing, of course. A mystery."

"Really? I *love* mysteries."

Everybody says that. And everybody asks whether it's been published and what the title is and where they can find it and whether it's available in paperback. If everybody who said that to me actually went out and bought a copy of The Book, even in paperback, I'd have more money than Paul McCartney.

Anyhow, I gave her all the gory details and she wrote them down and said, "Well, if you came to me and said, 'Let's do a PR number on this book,' we'd get in touch with the papers, the TV stations, the bookstores. We'd send out releases, we'd follow up with phone calls, we'd set up interviews and signings, try and come up with some sort of promotional angle—you know, arrange a donation to the community chest for every copy sold, something like that. That's public relations. Promotion, if you prefer. *Advertising* is more straightforward. Instead of calling the newspaper and saying, 'You should do a story about this guy,' we design an eye-catching ad and buy space in the paper. Or we do a direct-mail campaign, which, more and more, is working out to be the best way to target a market. Have you thought of doing any advertising for your book? I'd think there'd be a real strong local angle . . . not too many professional novelists living in little old Oma-har."

"Not a bad idea. You'd be willing to work on a contingency basis, wouldn't you, taking a commission for every book sold through your efforts?"

"Well, it's been *real* nice talking to you . . ."

"Yeah, right." I looked at my watch. "Since Lehman probably won't be back until after lunch, I might as well take a peek at Meredith's desk and get out of your hair."

"Sure. It's that one in front of the window." She pointed at a desk positioned in front of the big picture window that looked out on the wet intersection. The big window pointed to the fact that this space was originally retail, not office. "What do you want Steve for anyway?"

I looked at her. "From what you told me yesterday, you and Steve Lehman are Meredith's only friends here—and outside of here she doesn't appear to have any friends. Meredith may have said something to Lehman, or within his earshot, that might be helpful. Or he might have some insight to offer. That's all. Put away your gloves."

She laughed. "So I'm a mother hen, so sue me. Meredith's desk is unlocked. What are you hoping to find?"

I stood up and so did she. "I'm *hoping* to find the name and telephone number of the resort she's vacationing at in Baja. I doubt I will, however. Meanwhile, I'll take whatever I can get."

We were at the desk in question by then. I sat in the armless swivel chair and surveyed the desktop. In contrast with Meredith's apartment, it was as tidy as a dowager's parlor. However, there was one similarity to Meredith's home, in the same oddly impersonal air: There were no photographs, no coffee mug with funny sayings, no plants, no knickknacks, no *personality* of any kind. There were the In and Out baskets, stacked, filled with work. A black Merlin telephone. A Rolodex, the kind that sits in the little plastic tray. A pencil cup containing three black pens. A white ashtray filled with paper clips. A small appointment calendar on a plastic pedestal. A blue IBM Selectric sat on the return, the little built-in typing stand that jutted from the left side of the desk.

I checked the calendar. It still showed last Friday's page, and last Friday's entries, penciled in a neat, light script: *St. Joe* was on the eleven-o'clock line. *O'Sullivan* was on the one-o'clock line. *Ofc. mtg.* was on the four-o'clock line. I looked at Dianna.

"We're doing some work for St. Joe's Hospital; the preliminary copy deadline was Friday. O'Sullivan is another client. We ghosted a speech he's delivering at some convention or something. Meredith gave it to him on Friday."

"Here or there?"

"He came here. Geez, you're suspicious. Anyhow, Meredith was on hand for the weekly office meeting—*that*"—she pointed at the four-o'clock entry with a lavender fingernail—"at four. And we went out for a drink afterward, Meredith and Steve and I."

"Yes," I said distractedly, "I remember your mentioning it."

I flipped forward in the calendar. Nothing on the single Saturday-Sunday page. Nothing on Monday's. Today's page showed *GP Hosp.* against the eleven-o'clock mark.

"Great Plains Hospital," Dianna explained. "A pitch. I had to handle it solo."

That was about it for the calendar. I flipped quickly both forward and back, covering a month or so in each direction. Nothing caught my eye.

"If she planned her vanishing act," I said, as much to myself as to Dianna, "she didn't jot herself any convenient reminders." I looked at Dianna. "Take a look through the stuff in that stack and the baskets, will you? Also her Rolodex. I'm interested in anything—anything—that isn't business."

She nodded and went to work.

I slid back in Meredith's swivel chair and pulled open the center drawer. Pens and pencils, scissors, stapler, staple remover, loose change—more loose change!—Liquid Paper, rubber bands, that kind of junk. I closed it. There were no left-hand drawers, thanks to the return, and only three right-hand drawers. The top right-hand drawer was almost as exciting as the center drawer. She had *The American Heritage Dictionary, Bartlett's Familiar Quotations,* and *The Elements of Style* in their paperback editions, as well as a supply of paper: yellow, plain white, and letterhead. The middle-right drawer held a stack of professional magazines and newsletters and a bottle of Bayer aspirin. Bottom-right contained a slim stack of manila folders—current files, by the look of them. I flipped through them. Nothing of note caught my eye. In the back of the drawer was the box in which her Rolodex thingy had come. It was empty.

I slid this last drawer shut and looked at the woman. She had made a stack that included a woman's mail-order clothing catalogue, a magazine-subscription offer, and four cards from the Rolodex. "Her doctor," Dianna said, sliding the first card at me, "her dentist, the service station around the corner, and this."

"This" was a slotted Rolodex card, empty except for a telephone number penciled in the same light hand.

The telephone number was preceded by a 312 Area Code. Chicago region.

I met Dianna's eyes. "Mind if I use your phone?"

"Please do." She handed me the receiver and I punched out the eleven digits. When the little musical selection ended there was dead air for a space, then the metallic clunking and clacking of a toll call, then, at last, a distant ringing.

"Is it ringing?" Dianna asked eagerly. I nodded.

When there was no pickup after the sixth ring, I went to hang up—just as the receiver was lifted on the other end of the line and a deep, male voice said, "Yes?"

I brought the phone back to my ear, fast. "Uh . . . hi," I said with all the rapier-like wit at my command. "Uh, is Meredith Berens there?"

There was a long pause on the end of the line that was in Chicagoland.

"Who is this?" the male voice said. There was nothing to be read in the voice. It was neither hostile nor friendly, neither suspicious nor helpful.

"I'm calling from her office," I said, which was true. "Who is this?"

Another pause, somewhat briefer than the first.

"Who did you say you wanted?"

"Meredith Berens. We're a little concerned about her. We haven't seen her for a couple of days. No one seems to have heard of her. No one knows where she's gone to. We're hoping she's there. Is this Meredith's father, by any chance?"

Again with the pause. This time, though, just as I finished speaking, I thought I detected a noise on the wire, a faint, hollow little *poonk*. As if I was being put on hold for those few seconds between exchanges with the man. I closed my eyes and held my breath and concentrated on listening to the open line. There was just a little static, a steady hiss way down in the background, and a little bit of crosstalk, too faint to make out. Dianna Castelli tried to find out what I was doing, but I cut her off with an impatient chop of my left hand.

Yes, the *poonk* sound definitely occurred milliseconds before the deep-voiced man spoke again. "Sorry," he said smoothly. "You've got the wrong number."

"Well, is this Area Code three-one-t— Hello? Hello?"

"What happened?" Dianna wondered anxiously.

"Hello," I said again into the phone, which was very, very dead. I cradled the receiver, pensively.

"What *happened?*" Dianna persisted.

I tapped the desktop lightly with a corner of the Rolodex card. "Something peculiar," I said.

chapter

7

Traveso's Restaurant Supply, Inc., occupied a big, ugly steel barn south of 480 at about 110th Street. The building looked like one of those prefab numbers—corrugated blue-green steel, low-pitched roof, no windows except those in the little stone-façade VISITORS' ENTRANCE tacked onto the front of the building. Four parking spaces in front of the entrance were marked for company. Two of the spaces were filled, one with a little blue Ford pickup, the other with a little red Honda CRX.

Account executives, even those associated with tiny local PR firms, don't drive Ford pickups. Still, you don't have to be an account exec to drive a sporty car.

I swung out of the lot and trailed down the frontage road, parallel to the Interstate, until I found a pay phone in front of a convenience store. I sank change into the box and dialed Traveso's. It was answered on the second ring by a flat, nasal Iowa twang. I imitated it.

"Hi, there," I said brightly. "How'y'doin' today? Say, I'm supposed to have lunch with Steve Lehman from Castelli, but I'm darned if I can remember where! Can you tell me if he's left there yet?"

"No," Iowa said. "I think he's still with Mr. Pinkowski. I can transfer you . . ."

I hung up the moment she put me on hold.

Back in the lot of Traveso's, I swung around to the south of the little stone addition, putting myself out of the line of sight of any interested parties behind the windows, but leaving myself a good view of the two cars in the visitors' spaces.

After ten minutes, a tall, balding, gray-haired fellow with a gut that stretched the limits of his green coveralls emerged from the building, climbed into the Ford, and drove off. Obviously not young Lehman. I would have patted myself on the back, but there wasn't enough room in the front seat of my old Impala.

Another twenty minutes went by. I listened to the radio, watched the mist bead up on the windshield, and played with the temperature dial on the car heater's "vent" setting, trying to find something comfortable. It was pointless. I wished Lehman would hurry up and finish his business and come out of the building. Every passing minute eroded my confidence in the CRX being Lehman's car—but it had to be. I checked my wristwatch for the ninetieth time. I wanted to get hold of Elmo Lammers, give him the 312 number I had called from Castelli and Company, and see what fun he could have with it. Before leaving Castelli, I had called 312 directory assistance to see if I could buy the name and address that belonged to that number. I couldn't. Northwestern Bell, before uglifying its name to U S West Communications (no periods; it must not stand for anything), used to sell the service for fifty cents a name or something, but a federal judge determined it was too convenient for people and put the kibosh on it. If Illinois Bell ever offered the service, it didn't now. That didn't mean it was impossible to get the name that went with the number. The various dial-tone suppliers are usually pretty good about cooperating with licensed investigators, but I didn't know anyone in security at Illinois Bell. Elmo Lammers certainly would. I had a sneaking suspicion that the number on Meredith's Rolodex would prove to be unlisted, which always makes the data-gathering process trickier, but there are ways and there are ways, and I knew Elmo would know one or two that are not open to the general public.

I had the distinct feeling that whoever I was talking with at that number—and I also had the distinct feeling that it was *not* Meredith Berens's father—was taking direction or instructions from someone else on his end of the line. The way he would put me on hold or mute or whatever for those few seconds between our exchanges, as if he needed to consult someone, privately, before addressing me.

Odd.

Whom was he consulting? Meredith's father? Why wouldn't he come on the line himself? Presumably he would care about his missing daughter. Was she *there?* Well, then why the elaborate minuet? Why not simply say she's there but she doesn't want to talk? At least we could all quit worrying. Was the unheard party Meredith herself? In that case, the same question arises: Why the game?

Or was my wild shot-in-the-dark fantasy about Meredith's having been kidnaped something close to the truth?

Clearly, though, I had not reached a wrong number. Whomever I was speaking with knew *something,* and whomever *he* was speaking with didn't want him sharing that or any other information with me.

Very odd.

I half-wondered whether a junket to Chicago was in my future after all. But there were still a couple of bases to be covered locally, and my pal Elmo was more than competent. Which didn't make the waiting much easier.

Finally the glass door on the west end of the building swung open and a red-haired young man strode out. He carried a three-ring binder under one arm and a flat leatherette portfolio case in the other hand. While he fumbled with his accessories and his car keys, I hauled myself out of the Chevy and covered the distance between our cars.

"Hey, Steve."

He looked up. He was a tall, solidly built kid whose reddish hair was already beginning the steady retreat up his forehead. He had flat, roundish features and a fleshy, pouty mouth and fingernails chewed to the quick. He wore a blue suit with a red tie and black wing tips, and, like a good salesman, he responded to my greeting in a hearty but nonspecific way while his brain shifted into high gear to try to place me.

"Save the sweat, kid," I said, not unkindly. "You don't know me, but I know you. I just left your boss." I showed him the ID and sketched him the background. "Let's go somewhere and drink some coffee."

We settled on a Denny's on Eighty-fourth, just off the Interstate, and were seated in a booth there within ten minutes despite the heavy lunch trade. Lehman was young and earnest, likeable and outgoing, if a bit high-strung, and apparently willing to help. I decided the half-hour wait in Traveso's lot wasn't a waste after all: Lehman's openness would have been blunted by Dianna Castelli's protectiveness if I had arranged to interview him at the agency.

"Dianna told me Meredith's mother had hired a detective to look for her. But what do you want *me* for?"

"You're a friend of Meredith's. One of her *few* friends."

"I suppose so . . ." He played with his spoon, pressing down on the bowl and letting the long end come up from the plastic tabletop and drop back again. And again and again and again.

"Her and me and Dianna. We stopped off for a couple of drinks, a few laughs, and et cetera."

I cringed inwardly and thought to say something, and thought better of it. The world is full of people who say "and et cetera" and "between you and I" and "very unique." Many of them consider themselves well-educated. Going around correcting them would be a full-time job, and could lead to the rearrangement of one's nose. "How did she act then?"

"Meredith?" He thought about it. "Fine, I guess. I mean, I didn't notice anything weird, and I can't think of anything now, so she must have been acting normal. Right?"

Probably. I watched him gnaw a nonexistent fingernail for a moment, then said, "I have got the idea that you would have liked to be *more* than just friends with Meredith."

He looked at me with some surprise. "Where'd you get an idea like that? Me and Meredith, we just work together. We're friends."

The phrase came easily to the tongue. It always does. "That's what you *are*. I'm talking about what you would have liked to *be*. I have it on the best authority."

Lehman stared at me for a few moments, then, with wry disgust, muttered, "Thank you, Dianna. Okay, I suppose it's true. I asked Meredith out once, but she said she was too involved with Thomas Wayne and et cetera, and . . . well, and that was it." He shrugged, perhaps just a little too nonchalantly, and fiddled with the salt and pepper shakers.

I took them away from him and replaced them in their wire rack, but just then our coffee came and he had an excuse to dink with the sugar caddy instead.

"That was it, huh?" I said.

He nodded, stirring a packet of sugar into his coffee. The spoon clinked against the inside of his coffee mug twice per stir—once left, once right. "She wasn't interested. She made that pretty clear." Again with the shrug.

I sipped some coffee. Not bad, for restaurant brew. Probably a fresh batch for the lunchers. "Do you know Wayne?"

"I met him, once. At a party at Dianna's."

"Like him?"

Steve Lehman tasted his coffee, frowned, and tore open another packet of sugar. More stirring, more clinking. "I don't know," he said. "I only met him for a second, you know? He seemed all right. Nice guy, I guess. Pretty friendly. Meredith likes him. A lot, I guess—pretty obvious, huh?"

"Did she ever talk to you about him?"

He had done enough stirring. I took the spoon from him and set it among my flatware.

"No, not really. When I asked her out that time she told me that she would except she was involved—that was the word she used—with Wayne. Then, later, of course, she told me about the engagement."

"How did she break the news to you?"

Lehman looked around the table, as if hunting for something else to play with. But I had taken away all his toys. He attacked his savaged fingernails instead. I said, "I read somewhere once that fingernail-biters are closet masochists. Self-mutilation, something like that."

He gave me a look. "Yeah, my mom's read the same stuff. So?"

I laughed. "So how did Meredith tell you about her engagement to Thomas Wayne?"

"Well . . ." He turned his head and spit invisible flecks of fingernail. "She didn't, really. She told Dianna and Dianna told me—" He looked up. "It wasn't a secret or anything. So she told Dianna and Dianna told me, and I went over to Meredith and, you know, told her I thought it was great."

"And did you?"

Lehman shrugged. "Sure. I guess so. Like I said, I didn't even know the guy, so how do I know whether marrying him's a good idea or not? But that's not what you tell somebody when they get engaged."

"Were you surprised when you heard about the engagement?"

"Sort of. And sort of not. I knew that Meredith was really nuts about this guy—"

"How?"

"I just did, that's all. You know, from stuff around the office.

I didn't know they were thinking about getting married. But there's no reason I would, I guess. Look, what is it you want from me?"

"Just to talk."

Lehman frowned. His reddish eyebrows were so light and thin as to be invisible. "You think something's happened to Meredith?"

"I think she's missing, without any explanation. Why?"

He horsed around with the white ceramic mug until he slopped sweet coffee over the side. He mopped it with his napkin. "The kind of questions you're asking," he said, "they're kind of half like you wonder where Meredith has gone to—like going away was her idea—and then they're kind of half like you wonder if someone *did* something to Meredith."

"Like what?"

"Like hurt her. Kidnaped her." He acted almost embarrassed to say it, and why not? It does sound melodramatic. How many people do you know who have been kidnaped?

"Like who?"

He looked at me. "Like me. Like Thomas Wayne. Him and me, we're the ones you keep asking me about."

"Who else should I be asking about? Who are Meredith's friends?"

He shrugged. "No one you don't know about already, probably."

"Don't be so sure." Even Donna Berens didn't know about her daughter's intended.

Lehman thought, worrying the fingernail some more. "Well . . . I suppose Dianna's probably her closest friend. She gets along okay with the rest of the guys at the office, but Dianna's the only one she's, like, *close* to. I guess she must have friends outside the agency. But I don't know any of them."

I asked whether Meredith ever talked to Lehman about her father.

"Just her mother. Is her father still alive?"

"Apparently he lives around Chicago somewhere. Has Meredith ever mentioned Chicago to you? Has she ever visited there, to your knowledge?"

"No, I don't think so—both questions." He gulped coffee in a quick, nervous gesture. "Look, Mr., uh, Nebraska, I really want to help—because I really care about Meredith, you know—but I don't think I know anything that can help you, and anyway I'm late for a luncheon appointment with a client."

I considered him for a long moment before I said, "Then you

better get going. For a small agency, Castelli seems to have plenty of clients."

He smiled, and made a noise that might have been laughter or exasperation. "Tell that to Dianna, okay? The problem is, most of our clients are one-shots—no ongoing stuff—so we're always scrambling for work. We need more clients like Methodist Hospital. We do a quarterly newsletter for them. In fact, that's where I'm supposed to be right now, so . . ."

"I won't keep you. Thanks for your help."

"I wish I could *really* help."

"Give me your card, will you, in case I need to get hold of you later."

"Sure." He pulled a small leather case from his pocket, extracted a card, and handed it over. It was a textured pale-gray paper bearing the Castelli logo in hot-pink foil and, beneath it, in black, Lehman's name and title.

"Great. How 'bout your home number too?"

He gave it to me, and I wrote it on back of the card. Then he stood and hesitated awkwardly.

"Something?" I said.

"I—Well, I hope you find Meredith, that's all."

"That's all I hope, too, Steve," I said.

Steve Lehman left the Denny's lot and headed up Eighty-fourth to Center. He took Center east to the cloverleaf that put him onto Seventy-second, heading north. At Dodge Street, near the newly facelifted Crossroads shopping center, he made the left turn and steamed up the hill to Nebraska Methodist Hospital, off of Dodge in the Indian Hills district.

I know because I followed him. He was an easy tail. The only time I was in danger of losing him was at the left-turn arrow at Seventy-second and Dodge. Fortunately, like most Omahans, I drive like a maniac, and little things like extinguished left-turn arrows don't bother me any.

Steve Lehman parked his little Honda and went into the big dark-glass building. Remember when Hondas were motorcycles, not cars—which are getting bigger every year, I think—and lawn mowers and whatnot? I think Honda moved in to scoop up the ball dropped by Volkswagen in the seventies, but I also think they're following the same road to ruin, going for sex and splash rather than good, dependable, boring little cars. It might work for a while, but how much good have you heard about VW since they axed the Beetle?

I farted around in the parking lot for a few minutes, thinking automotive thoughts, long enough to make sure that Lehman wasn't coming straight out again. I didn't get where I am today by accepting too much at face value. Then I left my car and, surveying the terrain, ankled toward the Honda.

The driver's side door was unlocked. I popped it and slid in behind the wheel. Nice car. Or it had been when Lehman took delivery. Since then he had filled the front seat with cassette tapes, pens, and coffee cups; the backseat with the paper and plastic remnants of carry-out meals long gone. Whatever I was looking for wasn't there. And the trouble with these hatchbacks is there's no trunk in which to hide who knows what. Or who.

I went back to my own jalopy, fired it up, and moved out.

There was a lot of traffic on Dodge, which is one of the town's main east-west drags, if not *the*. Like most midwestern cities, Omaha's freeway system leaves something to be desired. A freeway system, for instance. What we have is the Interstate, which I'm sure is real swell, but all it really does is circle the city; there is no crosstown freeway. Dodge Street, through good planning or good luck—probably the latter—is the only major thoroughfare that provides a straight, no-detours shot from end to end. That means it carries a lot of traffic. At the noon hour on that particular Tuesday, I would have been willing to testify that only one of Omaha's three-hundred-and-some-thousand souls was *not* on Dodge: Steve Lehman, and only because I had seen him go into the hospital.

Why all the hoo-ha with Lehman? I don't know. He probably was just a nice, high-strung kid. And there's nothing at all odd about someone being jumpy when he's being questioned by a cop, private or otherwise, and *especially* when it's about a coworker who's disappeared without, as the saying goes, a trace. That Lehman had tried to get something going with Meredith and had been rebuffed would only add to his nervousness. It was just the kind of tidbit a crime novelist would make something of.

In my off hours I'm a crime novelist.

I didn't really think Steve Lehman had kidnaped Meredith Berens, you understand, or done her any other kind of violence. Not really. I mean, how often does it happen that the jilted lover nabs his unrequited and locks her up somewhere until she agrees to marry him? *Except* in the old movies. Still, a guy never knows. I had had one case that year that, on the surface, at least, bore a strange resemblance to the little melodrama I just sketched. It's the things *beneath* the surface that'll bite you every time. The odds were that Steve Lehman was exactly what he appeared to be: a nice guy. But I've seen plenty of things that worked out to be the exact opposite of what they appeared. And I've seen plenty of nice guys do plenty of not-nice things. Until you have reason to do otherwise, your best tack is to follow Inspector Clouseau's line: *I suspect everybody . . . and nobody.*

Cut to the benediction: I found a phone book, matched Lehman's home number against the Lehmans listed—there was a baker's dozen, not counting the Lehmanns and Laymans the book suggested, erroneously, I might want to try. Steve Lehman was listed as, simply, LEHMAN STEVE, which meant I hadn't needed to be as clever as I had been about getting his home number, but I didn't know that then.

The apartment was in one of the huge complexes whose stout backs you see from I-680 on the extreme west end of town—the ones with the big banners telling where to call for rental information. They were glowering, dark buildings, each three-stories high and half-again as wide, with low eaves and shake-shingles and security foyers. I found Lehman's building and waited.

There are perhaps eleven or twelve quick-and-dirty ways to get into a security building. Not counting having someone inside buzz you in, that is. I used Number Seven, which requires only a little patience—in this case, about four minutes' worth. I waited in the car until I saw a young woman approach the building. Definitely a resident: She lugged two bulging brown grocery bags from Hinky Dinky, and from her right hand dangled a set of keys attached to a yellow plastic sunflower. I got out of the car and timed my arrival at the front door so as to be just seconds behind her.

Her key was already in the lock of the heavy security door when I stepped into the foyer.

"Here, let me give you a hand," I said. But by then, of course, the hard part was already over: She had the door unlocked and open an inch. I reached over her head and opened the door further, and she ducked under my arm with her packages, laughing her thanks.

She went upstairs and I went down, where I did an about-face, as soon as I was sure I was alone, and headed back to the foyer. It was small enough that I could lean through the self-locking door and read the names on the mailboxes while still keeping a foot in the doorway. Lehman's was apartment 312. "Three-twelve again," I breathed to myself as I hot-footed up the carpeted stairs. "This week's magic number."

I found the apartment and knocked. On the end of the third rap it occurred to me that Lehman might have a roommate. Well, that would be okay.

If there was a roommate, he or she didn't answer. I put my ear against the door. It was thick—the door, not my ear—but not that thick. When I depressed the doorbell button I could hear the bell in the apartment easily if not exactly clearly.

There was not a sound in the apartment, other than the bell when I plied the button a couple more times. No TV or stereo. No furtive movements. No muffled pleas for help.

The lock looked sturdy enough, but not too formidable. Still, I wasn't in the mood for breaking and entering. There was no concrete reason to suspect Steve Lehman of anything except closet masochism. Certainly nothing here had given me cause. It would have been nice if Lehman had been keeping Meredith a prisoner in his apartment until she agreed to lose Thomas Wayne and marry him, but the chances looked a little slim. We won't even *talk* about probability.

I left the place with equal parts disappointment and relief.

The mailbox was full of past-due notices and the answering machine was full of messages back at Decatur Street. I dumped the former on the kitchen counter and rewound the tape on the latter while I rummaged in the fridge to see what I might scrape up for lunch. There was no bread, so I cut some Colby into small, square slices and arranged them on saltines spread with mustard. The apples in the vegetable bin weren't too unreasonably mealy yet, so I quartered two and ringed the edge of the plate with them. There was a squat bottle of Schmidt in the door. I grabbed it, kicked the icebox shut, and ate my lunch at the coffee table while I listened to the machine.

It's the world's cheapest answering machine, in quality if not price, and what it lacks in features it more than makes up for in inconvenience. It's a single-cassette gadget, which means you have to record your greeting, then leave thirty seconds' worth of space for a message, then record your greeting, then, leave thirty seconds, and so on for half an hour's worth of tape. Then, of course, when you listen to your messages, you have to listen to your inane greeting each time too. The machine's supposed to be smart enough to handle the sandwiching of incoming messages between outgoing greetings, but I'd discovered that if there are more than eight or ten messages piled up, the machine gets confused and starts recording when it should be playing and vice versa. The wonders of technology.

There were two hanger-uppers; then a message from the bank that handles my VISA card; then a message from Kim Banner at OPD; then a hanger-upper; then a message from Dianna Castelli; then a message from my publisher; then a week-old message that told me it was time to shut off the answering machine.

I checked the clock on the stove. Calls to New York must be carefully timed so that the bulk of long-distance expense is borne by my publisher, as God intended, and not by me. It was nearly two-fifteen in New York. The chances were good, though narrowing by the minute, that my editor wouldn't be back from lunch yet. If he was back, I was on the hook for a toll charge for upward of half an hour on the wire, prime-time rates. If he wasn't back, I'd get stung for a minute or two at most. Fifty-six cents, on average.

I placed the call. And left word with his assistant. And was off the line inside of ninety seconds.

In this manner my editor and I could avoid direct communication for days on end.

Kim Banner was out on a call. It was nice to see there was more to her career than paperwork. Dianna Castelli picked up no more than twelve seconds after I gave my name to her receptionist. There was an excited quality to her voice.

"Someone called here for Meredith a little while after you left."

"Anybody interesting?"

I heard the rustle of paper. "She just said her name was Jahna. Not Janet—Jahna. I had her spell it for me." Dianna spelled it for me, and I wrote it down.

"Taking your own calls these days?"

"Kelly insists that I have to let her go to lunch at least once a day. Usually Meredith covers the phones when she's out. Here's the number."

I made a note of it. "No last name? Did she say why she wanted to talk to Meredith?"

"No. To both. She asked for Meredith, I said she wasn't in today and could I take a message. She said, 'Just tell her Jahna called.' I asked what it was in regard to, and she said she was just a friend."

"Did Meredith ever mention a friend named Jahna?"

"No," Dianna said with conviction. "I'm positive. I'd remember a name like that."

It seemed that Meredith Berens did a good job of keeping her life nicely compartmentalized. The people at her office knew precious little about her family life and background; her mother knew nothing about her fiancé, her maybe-fiancé, and the fact, or the strong possibility, that Meredith had been in touch with her father; now this unknown, never-before-mentioned friend pops out of the woodwork. Dianna Castelli had never heard of the woman. I wondered if Donna Berens ever had.

"Is Steve Lehman there?" I asked.

"No. He should be back any time now, though. Want me to have him call you? I know you want to talk with him . . ."

"I already talked to him," I admitted. "I was just thinking it'd be interesting to know if he had ever heard Meredith mention this Jahna person. You can ask him yourself when he gets in, if you think of it."

"I will." There was a pause, and faint sounds of static and swirling electronic noises filled the break. Finally she said, "When did you talk to Steve?"

"After I left your shop. You had said he was at Traveso's. I went out there and caught up with him as he was leaving."

"That was kind of sneaky."

"Not really. I told him who I was and what I wanted. We had a nice chat. What's bugging you?"

"You could have mentioned you were going to do that. He *does* work for me, you know."

"Yeah, but I didn't know he was your kid. Listen, Dianna, I understand your maternal feelings toward your employees. I'm sure it's much better than working for a faceless corporation. But I don't think I need to clear it with you first if I'm going to talk to any of them in the course of my investigation. Or in any other context, for that matter."

She sighed heavily into the phone—it came out harsh and hard and buzzy on my end—and said, "You're right. I apologize. I'm on edge. You know that. This business with Meredith and . . . Well, I guess I'm feeling kind of, I don't know, jealous or something. I thought that Meredith and I were close friends. I mean, there's almost fifteen years' difference between our ages, but even so I thought we had a real good rapport. I thought she told me things, confided in me, the way she would with a girlfriend or an older sister. Now I'm finding out there are all kinds of things she never even hinted at—whole parts of her life that she shielded from me, from everybody. It hurts. If that sounds stupid, or petty, I can't help it."

"I don't think it sounds stupid," I lied. "But Dianna—did *you* tell Meredith everything?"

"No, but—"

"But nothing. The fact is, *nobody* tells *everything,* not even to their closest friend, their spouse, or their lover. We're privacy-loving animals. I doubt we could tell everything even if we wanted to; we're just not put together that way. And it looks like Meredith was a bit more compulsive in that regard than most people. Maybe because Donna had her nose in every aspect of Meredith's life for all those years. I don't know. It doesn't matter. All I'm getting at is, I don't think it has anything to do with you. It has to do with Meredith. The whole thing has to do with Meredith."

"You're right," she said heavily. "I keep feeling sorry for myself when it's Meredith who's important here. Okay." She made a visible, or I should say *audible* effort to throw off the self-pity. "Enough of that. Was Steve any help?"

"Not much, I'm afraid."

"Yeah, he can be like that around here, too. Anything else going on?"

I told her no. There was no point mentioning the call from Banner, certainly not until I knew what it was about.

"All right, then. Well, back to the grind."

I hit the disconnect button on the one-piece phone and dialed Banner. Still out.

I dialed the number Dianna had given me for Meredith's friend Jahna. No answer.

Then I called the security department at the phone company and got the name and address that went to that number. It gave me a feeling of accomplishment out of all proportion to the feat

itself, but it was about the first thing I'd tackled and achieved
without being thwarted once or twice first, and I felt downright
smug about it, if you must know.

The listing was held by one Jahna Johansen—surely there could
be only one—and the address was an apartment on Leavenworth
near Fifty-second. At the moment it was useless information, but
I felt better for having it.

I sat in the living room, listening to the refrigerator hum and
thinking great thoughts, for however long it took me to finish a
second beer. Then I picked up the phone to call my client. Then
I set down the phone and told myself I was being a coward. Then
I got up and brushed my teeth and went out again into the damp.

Donna Berens was as cool and reserved, as collected as she had
been the day before. I suspected she was never otherwise. People
like that, the ones who are always on an even keel, what are they
like in a crisis? In an emergency? In bed? The same? Or do they
disintegrate into very small pieces that you have to glue back
together later?

She invited me in politely though not warmly, slipped me a cup
of coffee—no china, this time: I had graduated, or descended, to
a plain white ceramic mug with a thin strip of gold at the lip; we
were in the kitchen today, too, at a tiny white ice-cream table in
a corner of the white-and-blue room—and waited calmly for me
to speak. Ordinarily I don't get the opening line: The client is far
too eager for information. Not that I was exactly brimming with
data. I admitted it straight out: "First of all, Mrs. Berens, I don't
know what's become of your daughter. I checked her apartment.
There's no sign of a struggle or any of what they call 'foul play'
in the movies. Nor is there any sign that Meredith packed a bag
or made any of the arrangements a person ordinarily would make
if she were going away for a few days. I checked with the
police—"

Donna Berens drew in her breath, as if to speak, but held her
tongue.

"—and learned that there are no unidentified women fitting
Meredith's description in the local hospitals. Or morgue."

She looked at me steadily. "I didn't want the police involved."

"They aren't involved. They merely gave me some information.
However, by this time tomorrow they *will* be involved."

She asked the question with her dark, liquid eyes.

"Dianna Castelli intends to file a missing-person report tomorrow if we don't know anything definite by then."

There was a flash of lightning behind the expressionless eyes, a glint of something hot and defiant. "She has no *right!*"

"She does, and she will do it." There seemed no point in telling where Castelli got the idea in the first place. "And it *should* be done, Mrs. Berens. Your daughter has been missing—without a trace—for going on three days now."

Donna Berens got to her feet and crossed the room, stopping in front of the electric range, regarding her reflection in the black door to the microwave at eye level. "I'm aware of that, Mr. Nebraska," she said icily. "You infer that Dianna Castelli is more concerned about my daughter's welfare than I am. That isn't true."

"I don't infer," I said. *"You* infer; *I* imply—and I *don't* imply. I simply say that it's time to bring in the police. They have the manpower and resources—I told you all this yesterday."

"Yes," she said wearily. "Yes, you did. And I told you I didn't want the police involved. I still don't. I want you to talk the Castelli woman out of this . . . this harebrained idea. It would be . . . not good to have the police in on this."

" 'Not good'?" I said angrily. "What the hell does 'not good' mean?"

She hadn't turned, hadn't budged. "The publicity . . ." she told her reflection in the oven door.

"Ah, the publicity," I said. I stood up and walked across the room and stood very close to her, my mouth very near her right ear. It was small and pink and shell-like, and I said into it, "Fuck the publicity, Mrs. Berens. We are talking about your *daughter.*"

She said nothing.

I said, "Or *are* we?"

It got her to look at me, at least.

"It's not the publicity per se you're worried about," I ad-libbed. "It's something that would *come* of the publicity, something you want to avoid."

"Don't be ridiculous." She pushed past me.

"I always try, but sometimes it can't be avoided. Let's see, then—is it something to do with you? Some deep dark secret? Did you used to be a stripper, Mrs. Berens?"

She stopped and turned and looked at me. Her face was no more nor any less composed than it had ever been, but small hotspots had developed above each of the prominent cheekbones. "You are a disgusting, dirty-minded little man, Mr. Nebraska."

"I'm a product of my environment. But enough about me; let's talk about your husband."

No response. No reaction.

I moved closer. "Is *he* the issue here, Mrs. Berens? Is he somebody important? Somebody famous? Somebody infamous? Or are you hiding from him and don't want him to know where you're living? If you tell me, I can help."

She spat a laugh that was hard and harsh and ugly. "You *can*," she said sarcastically. *"You.* I know you, Mr. Nebraska, I know all about you—enough about you. I know you've failed at nearly everything you've ever tried. You've had more jobs than most people have had hot meals, but you don't have what it takes to keep at them. You fancy yourself a writer now, but you're still crawling around doing penny-ante keyhole-peeping because you're no more a success at writing than at anything else. Your wife walked out on you and you haven't got balls enough or brains enough to divorce her. You *let* things happen. And *you're* going to *help* me?" She stretched a smile that was a sneer across her broad, full mouth and shook her head. "Thanks for the offer."

I looked at her hard. The blood sounded dully in my ears and the back of my neck was hot, but my voice sounded relatively steady when I said, "You're remarkably well informed. *How* did you say you'd come by my name?"

The smile-sneer stayed put. "You did a friend a favor—by *not* doing anything, which I'd say is typical of you. It doesn't matter." She turned away from me and suddenly her voice was weary, played out. "It doesn't matter," she repeated. "I don't . . ."

I took her by an upper arm and forced her to look at me. "Who are you?"

"It doesn't matter," she said after a long moment.

"It matters to me."

Her dark eyes held mine for a long time. Then she shook her head, gently, almost sadly, and pulled away from me with equal gentleness. "I want you to go now," she said. "Just go. Send me a bill for what I owe you. I'll pay it."

"Mrs. Berens—"

She left the room. I followed, followed her into the living room, where she stood holding open the door.

I can take a hint.

chapter

A block from the Presbyterian church at Fiftieth and Leavenworth, on an anemic bump of scruffy lawn, a pale-brick apartment building sat hunched on a long, narrow lot that was much too small for it. The building was similar in construction to my Decatur Street digs; that is, it was Early Motel, every apartment opening to the great outdoors rather than a central hallway or lobby. Like the Decatur Street building, it sat sideways to the street that gave it its address— my building undeniably faces not Decatur Street but Forty-fifth Street, or what would be Forty-fifth if Forty-fifth cut through that block. To the untrained eye, then, the building faces the Northwest Radial Highway, although the post office insists the address is Decatur Street.

There could be no such confusion with this place, however. Situated as it was in the middle of the block, it faced only the small stone-fronted house to its south, turning its broad back on an almost identical house to the north. I suspected that at one time there were three like houses situated there, but some ill fortune had befallen the middle house and, by extension, its two neighbors.

The building held only six units, one-third Decatur Street's tally. It also lacked our charming little balconies, which, under the proper conditions, could hold two adults in something roughly approximate to comfort. The mailboxes were your typical gray-steel lockboxes, set into the brickwork near apartment number one. Although the phone company had helpfully provided me with an apartment number, I double-checked at the mailboxes anyway. Jahna Johansen's name, in weathered blue ballpoint-pen ink, was written on a strip of white card tucked into the slot on the door of box number six.

Apartment number six was on the top level, nearest the street. The bell was answered almost immediately by a not-young, not-old woman in pale pink sweats and white Reeboks and wavy blond hair whose shock of white over the left ear was perhaps just too artful to be natural. The woman opened the door wearing a smile that changed character immediately, albeit subtly. It was the smile of someone expecting someone else at the door. I put on one to match it, and hastily turned up the flame under the old charm. Just because Donna Berens had flung me out on my ear, figuratively speaking, didn't mean I didn't still have what it takes. I hoped.

"Hi, there," I boomed good-naturedly. "Are you Jahna?"

Her smile widened and she laughed a little, in that half-embarrassed, self-conscious little way that people often have, as she admitted the fact.

"Sorry to drop by like this without calling, Jahna, but—well, truth is, I *did* try calling earlier but there was no answer and, as I was in the neighborhood just now anyway, I figured I'd take a chance and just stop on up."

"Why, I'm glad you did." To my surprise, she stepped to one side and gestured me into the apartment. I'm good, maybe, but not *that* good.

I stepped in and she shut the door, slipping the little brass chain into place. The living room was small and fussy, with lots of this and that here and there and too much dainty yet overly ornate furniture. The walls held small, anonymous paintings in big fili-greed frames that were badly done in fake gold leaf, the type of paintings you have to go down to the Holiday Inn to buy at "special discount prices" for one weekend only.

I shrugged out of my windbreaker and she took it and hung it over one of the pegs on the wall near the door and said, "I'm sorry, but I can't for the life of me remember your name . . ."

There was, I thought, a very good reason for that. But on the very first page of the private-eye manual, although it is in a foot-note, it says play along. So I played: "Ned," I supplied helpfully.

"Ned . . ."

"Brazda. Ned Brazda." I read in a Travis McGee novel once that you should always select a phony name that sounds something like your real name. That way, when you're prowling around one of the exotic places McGee prowls around, under your assumed name, you won't fail to react when someone calls you by it. It'll be close enough to your real name that you'll at least give a glimmer of a response. Well, hell, it *sounds* good, and I knew a couple of guys in town named Brazda, and it was better than the first name that popped into my head, which was Leonard Elmore.

"Ned!" Jahna Johansen said triumphantly. "Sure. And we met . . ."

I could see this getting out of hand real fast—what a tangled web we weave, and so on. "To tell you the truth," I said laughingly, "I don't remember either." I spread my hands and grinned. "You know how it goes."

Evidently so, for she laughed and said yes, she did, and indicated a sofa that she seemed to think I should sit on and offered to get me a drink.

"If you had a beer collecting dust somewhere I'd take it," I said easily, affecting the lazy, twangy, aw-shucks tone and cadence that seems to come naturally, and which seems to come in handy, in situations like this. "But I don't want to take up any of your time, Jahna. I really stopped by to see if you'd seen Meredith lately."

As in my place, the kitchen was a barely disguised extension of the living room, and Jahna had ambled into it and into the fridge and back into the living room with two squat brown bottles, no glasses, in about the time it took me to speak those sentences. "Oh," she said, perching on an armless chair nearby, "are you a friend of Meredith's?"

I twisted the cap from the bottle and said I was. Jahna deposited her bottle cap in a huge orange-glass ashtray on the coffee table, so I did likewise.

"Well, I haven't seen Meredith in just *ages*," the woman said. I guessed that she was several years younger than me—thirty-three to thirty-five, perhaps—although there was something wise and weary about the way she held her pale eyes, the set of her small pouting mouth. She had a very pale skin, smooth and delicate, which indicated that the hair was at least partly natural in color. Her teeth, when she smiled, were small and unnaturally white and somehow feral. Her voice was a high-pitched, breathy little-girl voice. The childlike character of the voice was contradicted by the long-legged and very womanly body wrapped in pink fleecewear. "In fact, I was trying to reach her just this morning. To tell her about a . . . party tonight." The pale, almost colorless eyes turned shrewd as they sized me up for however long it took her to take a pull on the beer bottle and make it seem like a sexual act. "How 'bout you, Ned . . . what would you say to a little party later on tonight?"

My first impulse was to sidestep the question and get back on the subject of Meredith; but it was superseded almost simultaneously by a second impulse that said to keep playing along, that said there might be more to learn, about Meredith and other things, via the indirect route.

"I'd say . . . 'Hello, ol' buddy!' " She laughed and I laughed— just a couple of fun-lovin' friends who couldn't remember each other—and I took a drink and said, "What kinda party you got goin', Jahna?"

"Oh, you know," she said lightly. "Usual kind."

"Uh-huh. Who's gonna be there? Anyone I know?"

Again she laughed. Her laugh was even higher and more silvery than her speaking voice. "How would *I* know who you know?"

I laughed too, forcing it, and tipped some beer.

"Naw," she said when she was tired of laughing at her wit, "there's some guys from Kansas City up for some kind of meeting or convention or something. I don't know—*you* know how it is."

I grinned. "Boy, *do* I," I said wolfishly, playing the part—and beginning, just *beginning* to feel that maybe I was reaching the point where I wasn't merely playing along, the point where the scene and my role in it came into sharp focus.

"We're getting together at their hotel later on," Jahna continued. "There'll be some other girls, plenty to drink. It'll be a lot of fun."

It sure sounded like it. I said, "It sure sounds like it. Won't these guys—won't they mind your inviting strangers to their party?"

She might have been annoyed; with the Shirley Temple voice it was hard to tell. But her thin, pale little eyebrows came down and met over the bridge of her nose and she said, snippily, "It's *my* party too." Then just as fast the mood evaporated. "Anyhow, no one'll mind. There'll be plenty for everyone. Just bring a bottle, if there's something special you like."

"Is Meredith going to be there?"

Jahna grinned the sort of grin that my mother always told me nice girls don't grin. *"That's* the 'something special' you like, huh?" she said in good-natured accusation. I smiled and shrugged in a way that I hoped would seem embarrassed enough. It was the response called for by the moment. "Well, your guess is as good as mine," Jahna continued. "I've been trying to get her for two days with no luck. No answer at her place, so I finally called her work and she wasn't in there either."

"Huh," I said, making my voice sound perplexed and making my face match my voice. "Where could she have gone to?"

"Beats hell out of me." She took a swig.

I said, "Well, what about family? She got any people around she might be spending a couple'a days with?"

"Beats me," she repeated. "You know how it is, Ned. Someone doesn't volunteer it, you don't ask it."

"Sure," I said hastily.

"I don't know from nothin' about Meredith except she likes to do these parties."

"Do you guys do a lot of these parties?"

She made a sound that was a shrug, and accompanied it with a real shrug. "I do, I guess, and some of the other girls. Sometimes Meredith calls me, when she's short of cash, I think, but mainly I call her when there's a real good one coming up. Like tonight's. She's gonna hate to miss it."

In my mind it had been fifty-fifty whether Jahna and her crowd were prostitutes or merely fun-loving girls. Now the coin came to rest, and it was definitely heads. Meredith, too, obviously, if only part-time. If I was shocked or surprised—and I was—the effect lasted mere seconds. By now I was becoming almost used to the contradictory, compartmentalized nature of Meredith Berens's existence, the many roles she played and the skill, or cunning, by which she kept the various facets of her multifaceted life hidden from those who belonged in other areas of it. Somehow it all had to do with the passive rebellion that seemed to characterize her life. Rebellion against Donna—that much was obvious. Rebellion against Dianna—less obvious, but nevertheless there, evidenced by nothing more or less than the way Meredith kept her at arm's length, too, kept her in the dark about the real nature of her life. Whatever the *real* nature was.

Give the girl credit, though: There was little overlap. The only common denominator, in fact, was that nobody in any of the corridors of Meredith Berens's life knew where the hell she was.

"You don't know where she's been keeping herself, Ned, do you?"

I was momentarily lost in thought, and it must have showed.

"No, Jahna," I said. "That's what I stopped by to ask *you*, remember?"

She laughed. "That's right. Wonder where the girl's got to. By the way, Ned, how did you say you got my address?"

If you weren't looking for it, waiting for it, you might have missed the slight tone of suspicion that had crept into the thready little voice. It was barely there, but there. In her voice, in the way she held herself, in the steadiness of the almost colorless eyes. Too many questions about Meredith from a guy who maybe wasn't the good-time Charlie he tried to act.

"From Meredith," I said casually. "There was one of your parties back, I don't know, a few months ago. Anyhow, you know, I kind of see Meredith off and on and she told me about this party and I said who's gonna be there and she mentioned your name and later she pointed you out at the party. That's probably when you and me met, Jahna. Meredith spoke very highly of you."

"Really?" The woman tried to sound flattered, succeeded only in sounding unconvinced. "And then she told you where I lived."

She wasn't buying into it.

"Of *course* not." I tried to make it sound like the very idea was ridiculous . . . which, of course, it was. "But she told me your name, naturally, and it stuck in my head. Jahna Johansen. It's a very unusual name . . ."

"Thanks," she purred. "I made it up. The Jahna part, I mean. It used to be just Janet, but I think Jahna sounds more special, don't you?"

"I sure do. That's why I remembered the name, because it's special." Good God, the things I have to put up with. "So when I tried to get hold of Meredith here the last couple of days, with no luck, I said to myself, 'Now, who would know where that girl's got to?' And I thought of Jahna Johansen. And I looked you up in the book. Not too many Jahna Johansens in the White Pages, Jahna." I drank some more beer and smiled innocently.

She smiled back, and I fancied that some of the slight tension went out of her.

"Well, Ned, I'm afraid I can't help you. What are you looking for her for anyway?"

I grinned a doggy grin. "What do *you* think."

Jahna laughed. "Sorry I can't help you, then," she said. "But there *is* that party tonight."

She gave me the details and I wrote them down. If Meredith Berens hadn't turned up in the meantime, I might drop by and see if by chance Jahna Johansen had succeeded where I had failed.

When I got down to the car, a white OPD cruiser was parked behind it. When I approached my Impala, the driver's side door of the cruiser opened and the cop who had been sitting behind the wheel edged out, one foot on the floorboard, the other on the wet pavement.

"Nebraska," he said.

The afternoon was cold and the seemingly limitless mist had congealed into a fine drizzle that was designed to discourage conversation alfresco. Nevertheless, I zipped up my nylon jacket and stuck my hands into my pants pockets and wandered over to the patrol car.

I hadn't recognized the cop at first, but I did now. He was a big blond kid named Nowaczyk. It was to get away from names like that that my forefathers came to America. "I was writing you a note," Nowaczyk said. "Sergeant Banner's been looking for you."

"I know. She left a couple of messages on my machine. Must be pretty important if she has prowl cars combing the streets for me."

The blond cop laughed around a wad of gum he was working on. He was one of those big, blunt, somehow incomplete kids you probably knew in school. Athletic, but never a star. Okay scholastically, but no genius. Looked like he belonged two grade-levels ahead of everyone else, acted like he belonged two behind. I gave him maybe five years before the muscle turned to fat and the blond hair, now as light and full and fluffy as meringue, became thin and flat and the big blond kid began to wonder what was going on. Or maybe not. Maybe he was smart enough to realize that eight years of second-string football wouldn't carry him forever, that the muscle was probably already well-marbled with fat and when it was completely saturated the fat would be stored subcutaneously, where it would show, and maybe he would even be smart enough to do something about it before he became just another big fat cop. Every so often you do come across one like that.

He said, "That isn't it. I was passing by—this is one of my streets—and I recognized your car." I followed his gaze. More and more, eleven-year-old red Impalas were becoming noticeable cars. "I knew the sergeant and you had been playing telephone tag, so I thought I'd let you know she was back at the station now and really anxious to see you about something."

"It's hell being so popular," I said, scrunching further into my thin jacket. "I'll head straight over there. Thanks for the word, Nowaczyk."

"No prob," he said, sliding back into the police car.

I went and unlocked the Impala. On impulse, I looked back over my shoulder as I opened the door, up to the second floor of the pale-brick building, up to the window that probably belonged to Jahna Johansen's bedroom. If anyone was watching from there, I couldn't see him or her through the thin, white curtains covering the glass. If anyone had seen me in conference with the cop, there wasn't much I could do about it now.

I went downtown—that's private-eye talk—and stashed the car in a ramp and went into the police building and asked for Sergeant Banner. The civilian behind the desk picked up her phone and spoke into it and, to my surprise, instead of issuing me credentials and sending me on my merry way, pleasantly informed me that Banner would be out in a minute.

It took slightly less time than that, and she had a long tan raincoat with her when she came.

"Hey, Sam Spade," she said by way of greeting. "Let's take a walk."

Don't ask me why, but I didn't need to ask her where.

chapter

The morgue isn't the kind of grim, creepy place that it always is in old movies. Sometimes I think it'd be easier on people if it were. After all, that's what they expect. That's what they've braced themselves for. Then they're taken into these well-lighted, antiseptic surroundings, rather like a hospital or a large clinic, a place of healing rather than of death. Not cheerful, exactly, but not scary either. Professional. And, in its own antiseptic way, distinctly unnerving—probably the last thing people need when they've been called down to the morgue. Perhaps we *need* the stone walls and the bad lighting and the cold, echoing corridors. Meet the grim expectation. Feed the psychic need.

Maybe not.

Their Jane Doe was unquestionably Meredith Berens. "She matched the general description," Banner said, "but I wasn't at all sure until they got her cleaned up. Even then . . . well, I wanted you to have a look before we contacted her mother."

I knew what she was getting at. When I first glanced at the cold, gray body under the harsh milk-white lights, I was annoyed at Banner. Why did she have me come all the way down here to look at a woman who obviously was *not* Meredith Berens, who obviously *couldn't be* Meredith? But then I took out the graduation picture and began to look at details, at specific features, and then the broad outlines, the contours, and then at how the former and the latter conspired to form the whole person, and then I came to realize, with a sinking heart, that behind the broken nose and the dislocated jaw and beneath the scratches and bruises in the sunken, lifeless face, that this was Meredith Berens. Had been Meredith Berens.

I said, "Who did this to her?"

"That's high up on *my* list of questions, too," Banner said with some emotion. She gave the attendant a secret sign and he draped the body. I turned away.

Banner said, "Let's get some air," but there wasn't any to be had; just the same cold, oppressive drizzle, trapping the fumes of downtown traffic. The sky was muslin: hazy, foggy in the distance. The cold air felt good, although not exactly refreshing. I took a deep breath of it and said, "You know how many missing persons I've done in my life?" She said nothing. "Lots and lots. Maybe a hundred; maybe even more. Back when I was first starting out, back before the Civil War, I had some good luck with a couple of runaways, back-to-back, and so I kind of got the reputation for being an 'expert' at tracking down disillusioned teenagers. That's how you get to be an expert, you know: You get a lot of people to think you're an expert."

We were walking. The traffic made sharp swishing noises as it passed us, or we it.

"For the next I don't know how many years, that's all I did. Track runaways. And I was pretty good at it. Not an 'expert,' maybe, but pretty damn good. There were some who wouldn't be found and some who wouldn't come home when they were found— that wasn't any of my affair: I told the parents I was a bloodhound, not a kidnaper—and there were some who came home and left again and some who came home and lived happily ever after." I stopped on the pavement and looked at her, and something very much like rage bubbled up my throat and burned my mouth, burned my eyes and my ears and the skin on the back of my neck. "But none of them ever got killed on me," I said furiously. *"None* of them. *Ever."*

Banner ran a hand through the dark-blond mop of her hair. "So what're you going to *do* about it?"

"Find the son of a bitch."

"Sherlock," she said gently. "Why don't you leave it to the experts?"

"I'm the expert, remember? I'm so fucking expert that I can't find one missing girl until I trip over her in the goddamn morgue."

"That doesn't do anybody any good," Banner shot back, her voice sharp and loud. "You want to feel sorry for yourself, fine. But do it on your own time. Oh, and try not to get all teary-eyed about your client and her dead daughter, huh? You leave them to me, O Great Detective, while you go cry in your soup because some sadistic son of a bitch queered your perfect record. And most of all, get outta my face. I don't have *time* for you, Nebraska. I've got a killer to catch."

She turned abruptly and moved up the sidewalk. I stood there a moment or two, half-stunned. Then I swore under my breath and followed the cop down the rain-slick sidewalk.

"First of all, we don't *know* anything to speak of," Banner said. We were in a coffee shop around the corner, huddled over mugs of, for me, coffee and, for Banner, tea. It was the kind of place I like—*would* like, under different circumstances. Cramped and overheated and thoroughly, but thoroughly unknowing and un-caring what passed for décor in the plastic franchise restaurants that are dominating the country. It was a long and narrow room, the short-order counter straight back, four turquoise booths lined up along one wall, three two-top tables crammed into the space by the window in front, a low lunch counter with turquoise-topped stools running back to the short-order counter. A man in a white shirt and a white paper cap stood behind the grill, drinking from an amber water glass. A woman in a peach-colored uniform and a silly little peach cap stood behind the counter, on a folding chair, rearranging the white letters on the black-felt board near the ceil-ing. That was it for population, until we crossed the threshold. It was a long while after lunch and a short while before office workers' afternoon coffee break, and there weren't the same armies of downtown shoppers that probably had sustained the place in times gone by. The woman on the chair looked down on us with studied disinterest as we slid into the booth nearest the door. She climbed down slowly, bracing herself on a soft-drink dispenser, an old, bulbous, red monstrosity that said "Enjoy Coca-Cola," as if it was an order. It stood next to a stainless-steel milk-shake machine and a clear-plastic cake keeper and a row of little individual-sized boxes of Kellogg's cereals, the kind you never see anybody eating from. The woman filled two amber glasses and brought them to us and said, "Menus?" and we said no, and told her what we wanted, and, in time, she brought it.

Banner had her notepad open on the Formica between us. I had my notepad open, too, writing down what she read from hers. She didn't have to do a lot of reading and I didn't have to do a lot of writing.

"The doc's guess is that she died Sunday night or Monday morning, as a result of the beating. Trauma to the head, he thinks. Perhaps other internal injuries. Perhaps both. We'll know after the autopsy, which will be sometime after we notify her mother."

"I'll take care of that, incidentally," I said.

Banner looked up and so did I.

I said, "You need her to come down for a positive ID and to sign papers and so on, right? I'll bring her. She's still my client. Client of record at least. She threw me out of her place and off the job today, but you know how I am about little things like that."

"I know," she agreed. "Sometimes it seems to me that you don't really get going on a job until you've been fired from it."

"It does seem to work out that way more than it should, maybe. In any event, the job's over. Donna Berens was just a few hours early taking me off it. Or a few hours late, you might say."

Banner made abstract designs on her open pad with the blunt end of her pen. "What made her decide to give you the old heave-ho? Keep in mind I have to get back to the office before quitting time."

"Ho-ho," I said, "that's rich." I told her about my trying to pry information about Meredith's old man out of Donna Berens, and Donna's not wanting to be pried. "I don't understand what the big dark secret is."

"You're not *supposed* to understand it," Banner said. "Obviously. You think it has anything to do with anything?"

I sighed, and switched my attention from coffee cup to water glass. "Not anymore," I said, swallowing. "If I ever did. I half-entertained the notion that Meredith had taken off to be with her old man. Obviously not. I half-entertained the notion that Meredith had been kidnaped by someone wanting to get at—or get something from—her old man. Also obviously not. But obviously Meredith was murdered. Obviously she was the *target,* not just the unlucky victim of a robbery or an assault."

"You know something we don't, boy?" Banner said noncommittally.

"Was she raped?"

"No. No indication of sexual assault."

"Was she robbed?"

"Her purse is missing, and she wasn't wearing a watch, but there's a plain gold ring on her right hand that no one even tried to remove."

"Not robbery, then."

Banner shrugged and sipped tea. A light lemon scent drifted toward me. "Maybe an interrupted one. We don't know. The body was found north of Fontenelle Forest, on the Omaha side—Mandan Park, actually. Near the river. Off the beaten path. It's unclear whether the beating took place there or whether she was killed elsewhere and dumped. It's possible there was more than one assault, one somewhere else and then the final, fatal one in Fontenelle."

"It's been awfully damp lately," I said. "Tire tracks?"

"They're still looking. I was up there earlier—when you returned my call, in fact. They hadn't found anything yet."

"When and if they do, they'll probably match the tires on Meredith's car."

"There you go again. Do you have inside information, or are you just psychic?"

I looked at her. "Did the killer use a weapon or his bare hands?"

"A weapon. For most of it, at any rate. Judging from the size and shape and severity of the bruises, we're looking at something round and hard—a broom handle, say, or a fat dowel."

"There you have it. This was no blind attack. Meredith was murdered. Despite the savagery, the killer was collected enough to use a stick, not his bare hands. A beating like that, his hands would be as bruised and bloody as she is. Hard to explain away—especially if he had to do his explaining to the cops. And if he was that shrewd going into it, when you'd expect him to be ruled by his emotions, then you had better believe he didn't use his own car. He used hers, or another that can't be connected to her, and wherever he abandoned it he made damn sure there's nothing to be traced back to him."

"You sound pretty sure of all this."

"I'm a pessimist. It's part of my charm."

"We only have your word on that," Banner said, and went back to the book. "That about covers it. The body was found late this morning by forest workers. They probably trampled any physical evidence there was to find." She flipped shut the notepad and shrugged. "You know the drill. We'll talk to her mother, her

employer, her friends, her neighbors. We'll get her telephone record from the phone company. We'll see if we can't find out whether
she had an appointment to meet someone Sunday night—and who
that someone might have been. We'll find the car." She regarded
me for a long moment, sipping tea, thinking. "You've been at this
a couple of days now, Sherlock," she said at last. "I'm just getting
started. Want to bring me up to speed?"

"You assume *I'm* up to speed. I don't know where to start," I
said, and I didn't. So I began at the beginning, as wise men say.
Donna Berens and the refrigerated townhouse she calls home. Her
reluctance to involve the police. Her reluctance—no, refusal—to
discuss Meredith's father, to even give me his name. Then Meredith's apartment and the utter chaos that passed for housekeep-
ing. How that struck me as a kind of sneaky, childish rebellion
against her mother, and how Koosje Van der Beek agreed that
that was one possible explanation. Dianna Castelli and her rather
overpowering concern for Meredith. Meredith's engagement, of
which her mother was ignorant. Meredith's fiancé, Thomas Wayne,
of whose very existence Donna Berens was ignorant. Wayne's
insistence that the "engagement" was a figment of Meredith's ov-
erwrought imagination, despite his efforts to set her straight. Steve
Lehman, the would-be boyfriend who never got to bat, let alone
first base. Finally, Jahna Johansen and my near-certainty that,
through her, Meredith picked up spending money as a quasi-
professional party-goer. "There again," I said, "I sense an element
of secret rebellion, of someone doing something to 'get back' at
someone, but being so sneaky about it that the someone in question
doesn't even know about it."

"Complicated girl," Banner noted grimly.

"I wish I could have got her and Koosje together. I don't think
Meredith was schizophrenic, exactly, but there was certainly a
distinct . . . I don't know, *division* of her personality. Koosje could
use all the right words, I'm sure."

Banner transferred some hot water from the stainless-steel caddy
at her elbow into the short white mug. "I suppose everybody's
personality is made up of lots of different elements—dozens, maybe
hundreds. There are those we only show to people we're close to,
and there are those we don't show anybody. Like that old Billy
Joel song, 'The Stranger.' And whether we show them or not, all
these components, if you like, fit together to make up our complete

personalities. And maybe how well or poorly we're adjusted is determined by how smoothly the components work together. Your friend the shrink would know. But in Meredith's case—Jesus, it's like she had three or four really well developed personalities going there, all leading separate little lives . . . and yet all still Meredith. As you said, she wasn't schizo. Maybe only a step removed, but, always, still Meredith. Weird."

I agreed.

"Well," she said heavily, referring to the notes she had made during my recitation, "we'll need to talk to the mother, of course, but I'm going to put that off until tomorrow. The bereaved are no damn use for the first twelve to twenty-four hours at least. Then the Castelli woman and this Wayne fellow. What about Lehman?"

I considered it. "Can't see it," I said.

"Okay. We'll rattle his cage a little anyway, though. It's the drill. It'll keep him honest. This Johansen character bears looking at."

"She is easy on the eyes."

"*God,* I hate that expression. That and 'feast your eyes.' What a stupid thing to say—both of them." She tapped her pen on the pad. "The old man, Meredith's dad, in Chicago or wherever. I don't think it's worth a tumble. We'll have to notify him, of course, but there doesn't seem to be any connection."

"You're probably right. *I* sure didn't get anywhere with it, so I can't tell you one way or another whether you'd be wasting your time."

"Yeah." She thought about it. "Well, let's see what the mom gives us. People will surprise you when they're confronted with the fact of human mortality. Sometimes they even do decent things."

"Only when they're still in shock."

"Well, of *course.*"

I drained my mug and chased it with a mouthful of water. "You need anything else from me?"

"Can't think of it." She smoothed the dark-blond hair across her forehead, the long, thick wave that wanted to hang down into her eyes. "Thanks for doing so much groundwork for us."

"All part of the service." I stood up and reached for the check. "I'd better quit stalling and go see my client."

She looked up at me with something very much like concern in her gray eyes. "You're sure you want to do this?" she said.

"I'm sure I would rather swim in shark-infested waters with a side of beef strapped to my back. But I owe it. Not to Donna Berens. I'm interested in seeing her reaction, but I don't really care. I owe it to Meredith. Donna may have been my client, but Meredith was who I was doing the job for. You've been a cop for ten years, Banner, you know what I'm talking about."

She nodded.

"Well, this little chore's for Meredith, too, I guess."

I suspect there are people who actually enjoy the kind of "little chore" I had set for myself. I suspect it because I suspect I have met several of them over the years. They are not the rubbernecking ghouls you see hovering around automobile accidents. They are not the misnamed sadists who get their kicks from seeing blood and carnage and the misery of fellow human beings, or other animal life. They are not the deeply disturbed souls who seek out the supposedly factual videotaped records of people meeting their grisly ends. They are, rather, people with an overwhelming, almost palpable need to be needed. They are decent people, for the most part; sensitive people. Maybe too sensitive. I've known them as soldiers and cops and ambulance attendants, emergency room doctors and nurses and paramedics, and waitresses, cab drivers, and civil engineers, too. They are not necessarily drawn to an occupation or vocation because it gives them ample opportunity to be needed, to be leaned on, to be turned to. Whatever their occupation, they somehow manage to be where they need to be when it's time to be needed. They are on hand to console a friend when bad news comes. They are in the next aisle over in the market when someone keels over from a heart attack; naturally, they've taken CPR. They are home to receive the call when someone needs someplace to park the kids because dad's been taken to the hospital. And while they would protest, and honestly so, the assertion that they "enjoy" a task such as the one I had undertaken— breaking the dread news to Donna Berens—I am positive they would approach the assignment more resolutely, more determinedly than I was able to.

Nevertheless, there it was. And there I was, on Donna Berens's doorstep, having set no new land speed record getting there.

She was dressed as she had been a few hours earlier: plum slacks, billowy ivory blouse, taupe high heels. Her hair was perfect and her makeup was perfect and if she was the least little bit surprised or annoyed at seeing me when she opened the door, she didn't show it.

"Mr. Nebraska," she said.

"Mrs. Berens." I paused. Stalled, more accurately. "I have some bad news, Mrs. Berens."

Her turn to pause, though only a moment. "I see," she said softly. Then she stepped aside to let me in. I took a few steps into the cold, almost barren room, turned, and faced her. She had closed the door and had her back against it, her arms at her sides, her palms flat against the wood. "It's Meredith," she said. Not a question. Not a guess. A statement of something she knew, inside, was a certainty.

"Yes."

"She's . . . dead." The eyes met mine. They were . . . what? Defiant? Studying me, scrutinizing me, looking to see if *I* was looking for fissures, cracks in the façade? And resolving to show me no such cracks? Who can say? Everyone handles everything differently. It's a mistake to judge someone's innermost feelings or thoughts based on how we *think* they should externalize them. A mistake we commit every day, all of us, but a mistake nonetheless.

Whatever went on in back of Donna Berens's eyes stayed back there. She nodded, perhaps a bit jerkily, as if confirming something she had privately suspected. Her eyes left my face, then returned. "You're—you're quite positive?"

"Yes. However, the police will want you to identify her. If you're up to it."

Again she nodded. She left me. I found myself in front of the windows, studying the communal backyard, green-gray under the fading light of that gloomy day. Birds in the yard, making short work of the worms and insects brought to the surface by the suffocating wetness.

Mrs. Berens returned in what seemed only a short time, although the room was noticeably darker than it had been. The days were growing shorter. "Days like this remind you that you're going to die," she had said. I rubbed the still-healing injury to my left arm, the dull-aching reminder of a day I almost died.

She had changed into a simple gray dress, wide at the shoulders, narrow at the hip, short enough to be fashionable but long enough to be acceptable on a woman her age. Dark stockings. Black heels.

She brought with her the subtle, almost subliminal scent of flowers.

"I'm ready," she said, fumbling with a black leather handbag.

"You'll want a jacket."

She looked around the room. As before, it was as if she didn't understand the sentence, as if she needed a translator. "I—The closet," she said, a trifle breathlessly.

It was near the door. I found a navy-blue raincoat cut like a trenchcoat and held it for her. Then she turned and looked at me.

"I don't know—What's expected of me? What do I have to do? Is there some kind of . . . format? Some procedure I have to follow?"

"No. They'll take you to see Meredith. It won't be . . . She won't look the way you'll want to remember her looking, Mrs. Berens."

She might not have heard me. She made no sign.

"You'll identify her as your daughter. They'll have some papers for you to sign. Then I'll bring you home."

"Will they want to question me?"

"Perhaps later. Not today."

She nodded and turned toward the door. I followed her. She opened it and stopped and asked me, without looking back at me. "She was killed, wasn't she? My little girl was murdered."

There was nothing to say but yes, but I couldn't locate the word. Donna Berens stepped through the doorway and I went after her, closing the door behind me.

She didn't ask me who the killer was.

We went and she identified the body. She studied the battered face for a long time, saying nothing, betraying no emotion except a kind of mute fascination, a seriousness that was almost detached, almost professional. Finally she turned to Banner and said, "This is my daughter."

Banner led us into a small block room, a kind of lounge, where Mrs. Berens could sit and sign the papers, where Banner asked her a couple of questions in a soft, almost conversational way— "Do you have any idea who could have done this to your daughter, Mrs. Berens?" "Did your daughter ever talk about someone threatening her or abusing her?" "Was there anyone your daughter was afraid of?" "Did your daughter have a boyfriend or boyfriends, someone she saw, or had been seeing, on a regular basis?" Donna Berens's barely audible answer to the last one—"No," as it had been to the others—prompted a raised-eyebrow glance from Banner to me.

It was over quickly, almost too quickly, and we were in my old clunker again. The afternoon was a deep gray. Traffic was heavy. My client, or ex-client, said nothing; it had been the same on the drive in. I parked in the little blacktop lot in front of her building, got out, opened her door, escorted her to her front step. She found her keys, found the keyhole. Her hands trembled. The lock gave and she opened the door several inches. Then she looked at me.

"I can't be alone just now," she said. "Help me."

She entered the house and so did I. The room was cold and nearly dark, and she made no effort to address either of those conditions. She dropped her bag onto the wicker love seat that I had sat in at our first meeting, covered the bag with her raincoat, and moved toward a high, narrow table set against the far wall. The table supported three cut-glass decanters and six or eight stout glasses. She turned two glasses right side up, filled each to the halfway point, and turned. I was out of my jacket by then. I took the glass she offered, sniffed it before I drank. Gin. I detest gin. But I drank some. The perfect guest.

"There's ice in the refrigerator," she said, indicating an archway through which lay the kitchen. Nothing can save gin, so I didn't bother with ice.

She sat in the high-backed white wicker chair she had occupied the other day. I sat on the love seat, next to the coats. She drank quickly and silently. I made mine last, which was no trick. Only a few minutes passed before she stood and walked past me to replenish her glass. I caught the powdery, floral scent from her.

"Do they know who did this to my little girl?" she said quietly, from the drinks table.

"Not yet."

"Do you?"

"No."

She turned, glass in hand, and drank, and said, "But you suspect."

"Suspicion doesn't count for anything."

"Who do you suspect? Whom."

Everyone and no one. I said, "There are things that Meredith kept from you, Mrs. Berens. Things she kept from her friends at work."

"Things."

"Things pertaining to her private life, her *very* private life. Do you know a man named Thomas Wayne?"

"No." She drank. "Should I?"

I shrugged, but in the darkness that had enveloped the room in the past minutes, it had no significance. "According to Meredith, he was her fiancé."

"What do you mean, 'According to Meredith'?"

"Wayne disputes it. They dated, fairly often, I gather. There's no question about that."

"Impossible," she said quietly, as if to herself.

"They met at a party last winter. Dianna Castelli introduced them."

"I should have known." She drank. The faint light from the windows at the end of the room glinted on the glass in her hands. "I never liked that woman. I never trusted her. I told Meredith as much. She was always giving Meredith ideas. Meredith wouldn't have moved out of her home, here, with me, except for that woman insisting, badgering, coming between us, getting her worked up. She said it was time for Meredith to make her own way. Go out into the world, she said. Well, she did. My little girl went out into the world, and the world killed her."

As it does all of us, I thought.

There was movement on Donna Berens's side of the room, followed by the scrape of the glass stopper being lifted from a decanter.

"That's unfair," I said gently. "I don't know about Meredith's moving out. There does come a time, I think, when it's important for people to take responsibility for themselves. But Meredith's death . . . you can't put that on the Castelli woman."

"No?" The voice was simultaneously silk and acid. Her heels tapped the oak underfoot; her smooth legs brushed mine as she brailled her way back to her chair. "Dianna Castelli introduced Meredith to this Wayne whoever?"

"Thomas Wayne. Yes."

"And Meredith never told me about him. She never told me she was seeing him, much less engaged to him—which I doubt she was, by the way." The words, spoken low, were coming fast, propelled by bottled-up emotion, lubricated by alcohol.

"As I said, there are many things that Meredith apparently kept from many people . . ."

"I'm her *mother,"* she said, as if that alone proved something. "She would have told me . . . naturally. But she didn't. Why? Because she didn't want me to know about this young man. Is he young?"

"Youngish," I said. "Older than Meredith. About my age."

"This young man. Why not? Because there was something to hide. Something she was ashamed of. Something she was afraid of. You've met this Wayne person?"

"Thomas Wayne," I repeated. "I've met him. He seems pleasant enough."

She laughed. Not because she was amused. *"Pleasant* doesn't count for anything," she said. "I've known *lots* of pleasant men— family men—churchgoing men—pleasant, pleasant men with pleasant, pleasant wives and pleasant, pleasant kids. My husband is a pleasant man. Was. Ex-husban—The hell with it." She drank. She was getting noisy at it. "The hell with them all."

I figured we were fast reaching the point where there was no use my trying to carry on a one-sided rational conversation. I kept still.

"Whatsee do?"

"Wayne? Real estate. Commercial property, mostly."

She made a noise. "Lotsa pleasant men in real estate. What kindsa name Wayne?"

"What kind? I don't know. English, maybe. Irish, maybe. What's the difference?"

She got to her feet, heading for the drinks table again. Whether owing to the darkness or the drink, or both, she stumbled, and caught herself on the arm of the love seat.

"You all right?"

She said nothing and continued on her mission.

"My husban' was a pleasant man," she said again, apropos of nothing. She followed it with a long pause. The pause begged to be filled, so I said, "Mm-hmm?" I heard her turn and, in the gloom, sensed her eyes on me. "Pleasant," she said. "Thoughtful." Another pause. "When he beat me up he always made sure the bruises didn't show."

I was silent.

"He never hit my face," she went on, softly, almost reminiscently. "I could never wear backless dresses, and sometimes I had to wear long sleeves in the summer, and I wore a lot of ankle-length skirts. But never my face. Not like . . . My little girl. My poor little girl.''

A minute passed. Then, her voice low and steady, she said, "An animal beat my little girl to death, Mr. Nebraska. Only an animal could do something like that to a beautiful girl."

There was nothing there that I could disagree with.

"An animal like that deserves to die the same way," she said matter-of-factly. "Beaten to death. Slowly."

I heard the heels on the floor again and pulled my legs in to give her room to pass. She wasn't as good at it as the other times. She stumbled and nearly ended up in my lap. I had parked my drink on the glass-topped table nearby, so both hands were free to catch her. Her face was near mine. I felt her breath, smelled the flowers she was scented with, and both smelled, and felt the liquor as a small amount of it ended up on my arm.

"Mrs. Berens, are you all right?"

"I'm a little drunk," she said, her breath heavy with liquor.

Then she was deadweight in my arms.

chapter

10

I hung around awhile. The mother hen instinct. Donna Berens had had a lot to drink in a short while and on no dinner. I wanted to make sure she was all right. It was the least I could do for her. It was the least I could do for Meredith.

With neither help nor resistance from the unconscious woman, I wrangled her into what appeared to be the master bedroom. The archway off of the living room was set perpendicular to a corridor that led, on the left, to the kitchen, and, on the right, the bathroom and two bedrooms. One of the bedrooms, the first along the hall, was frilly and fussy and populated by stuffed animals and dolls and filigreed pillows. The second bedroom was larger and more remote, its stark, black-lacquered furniture vaguely oriental in a modern, off-putting way. Donna Berens's room without a doubt. I deposited her on the bed and pried off the high-heeled shoes and surveyed the lay of the land. At this point in the detective books, the hardboiled hero is supposed to peel off the distressed client's clothing and roll her between the sheets. All in the name of chivalry, of course. He's to provide commentary on the acceptability of the client's warm and available body, too, but only for local color, since the next step is to haul the covers over her and depart with not so much as a dent in his shining armor.

There was no denying that Donna Berens had a nice body. The gray sheath she wore was close-fitting enough to evidence that, and the way it had marched up her dark-stockinged legs when I let her down onto the bed verified it. I tugged at the hem but the cloth was bunched up behind and under her and wouldn't budge. I loosened the buttons at her throat and wrists and relieved her of the little bit of jewelry she wore. Chivalry or no, I wouldn't have minded following the formula and getting her out of her clothes. I've played the scene before, I know all the moves, and I'm honest enough to say my motivation hasn't always and entirely been the prevention of wrinkles in women's clothing. But, looking at the unconscious woman sprawled across the bed, I knew, or sensed, that this would be different. Not good clean dirty little boy-girl horseplay, the kind that may or may not develop into something later, but an invasion, an obscene invasion of a very private woman. Private, and very much alone.

I put the jewelry on a low, long dresser, put the shoes on the hardwood alongside the dresser, and looked at their owner again. After some consideration I rolled her onto her side, propping her into place with a rolled-up pillow. She murmured a protest when I manhandled her, but put up no fight. The only movement she made was to draw her legs toward her belly, a half-fetal position. I evaluated my work. I didn't know what kind of a drinker she was, and if she'd drunk enough that I had to worry about her throwing up without regaining consciousness, but I figured with her in that position the results would be messy but nonfatal. Then I took the edge of the spread from the far side of the bed and pulled it over her, like folding an omelet. I put out the light and left the door open and felt my way down the near-dark corridor.

Meredith's room, as I've said, was the next door along. The light switch was one of those illuminated jobs, glowing softly against the wall like a feeble light in the window for someone who would never come home. Flipping it ignited pale yellow light behind a frosted-glass square hanging from the ceiling.

It was a little-girl room, loaded with plush, too-cute artifacts that girls collect because, I suspect, they're trained to. I surveyed the dolls and the bears and the pillows and the little sachets without touching them, as if they were museum pieces. In a way they were. The room was as perfect and clean and uninviting as the worst museums. And, now, it was something in the way of a memorial to a dead race. A race of one.

The dresser, a long, low, six-drawer chest with a tall mirror, was loaded with pictures, both portraits and framed snapshots. Most of them were of Meredith and her mother. They had the stiff, posed, unnatural look of tourist photographs snapped by strangers pressed into temporary duty. I recognized some of the backgrounds. The plaza at the United Nations. The lobby of the Empire

State Building. The Golden Gate Bridge and the entrance to San Francisco's Chinatown. The monorail at Peony Park in Omaha.

The pictures covered a span of I don't know how many years. In the earliest of them, I guessed, Meredith was perhaps twelve. She was a skinny, gangly kid with a wary, self-conscious smile. In later photographs she was taller than her mother, and beginning to fill out, the gangliness being erased by the smooth layer of fat that makes girls look like women. Finally she was a young woman, in shorts and a halter at a picnic table, in slacks and a fuzzy sweater in front of the Christmas tree, in her graduation portrait. She looked healthy and strong and well-made. The smile was still guarded, but now, with Meredith's budding maturity, its self-consciousness had developed into a kind of sly modesty that was attractive in its own way. She would be described as a quiet girl. Shy, maybe; maybe not—such designations, like beauty, depend on the prejudices of the observer.

I picked up the graduation picture, an eight by ten of the same shot Donna Berens had provided me, and studied the face. It was a longish though well-proportioned face, framed by Meredith's long dark hair. Her eyes were bright and smiling. Her lips gleamed softly with a pale-pink gloss. Her facial structure was not as pronounced as her mother's but, like Donna, Meredith seemed to have too many teeth for her mouth. A pretty girl. Even allowing for the photographer's artifice—the slightly soft focus that erased any flaw in the skin, the backlight that highlighted the long hair, the kick light that illuminated her eyes—she was a pretty girl.

The image in my hand suddenly was replaced by the image I had seen in the morgue, the bruised and broken flesh, the blood, the shattered bone, the torn and matted hair. I felt a little light-headed and, replacing the picture, leaned against the dresser for a long minute, studying myself in the mirror, until the giddiness passed.

I looked in on Donna Berens. She appeared to be resting comfortably, as the MDs say. As comfortably as you can rest with a bellyful of gin. She was as I had left her: on her stomach, her face near the edge of the mattress, turned toward the door.

An hour should do it, I figured, based on no knowledge or expertise in particular. Within an hour the contents of her stomach either would no longer be in her stomach or they would be there for the duration.

I collected our glasses from the living room and rinsed them in the kitchen sink. I raided her refrigerator, hoping to find something to take the taste of gin out of my mouth and gut. There was no beer, so I made do with a glass of grapefruit juice and an apple. Not a combination I'd recommend. There was a little pastel-colored black-and-white television set on the round kitchen table. I turned it to a newscast, the volume low although I was certain it would take more than a weathercaster to wake Donna Berens. By the warm glow of the range light I watched the news and a rerun of *Barney Miller* and ate another apple and checked Donna Berens three times. She was fine. So was the show. It was the one where the Twelfth Precinct has an apparent visitor from the future, and the resident gay couple has snatched the less sissified one's kid from the schoolyard. I had seen it probably half a dozen times and it was still funny, which is the mark of a truly well done production. That I didn't do much laughing was my fault, not its. After the program was over I checked Donna one last time and let myself out of the townhouse, making sure the spring lock secured the door after me.

The little six-car lot on the north side of the building on Decatur was full, so I drove up the hill and made a U-turn in the next intersection and parked against the curb across and up from my place. I buttoned up the car and trudged across the cold, wet street, my hands jammed into the pockets of a jacket that had grown too thin and too light since I had left home that morning.

The wet pavement did me a favor. It was the sound of rubber on water, not the sound of the engine, that alerted me.

I looked up, startled, and the monster was there. A big car—a Cadillac, maybe, maybe a Lincoln; in the momentary paralysis of panic I didn't register which—bearing down on me, headlights dead, grille gleaming in the street lights like a vicious maw.

My seeing it seemed to enrage it, because suddenly it growled and surged forward.

Instinctively, I lunged toward the building, toward home. The car swerved, as if locked onto me. I scrambled up the back bumper and across the trunk and onto the roof of a Camaro parked in the little lot. The car was wet and slick with the damp; I slipped on the low-pitched roof and went down on one knee as I tried to turn and get a look at my attacker.

The big car avoided a collision—obviously, or I would undoubtedly have been flung off of the Camaro. By the time I got my footing and got turned around, the monster had disappeared, no doubt having jumped the light at the corner, the intersection of Decatur and the Radial. If he wasn't worried about little things like traffic lights, the driver of the big car had four choices: left, north up the Radial, opening into the north and northwest ends of the city; right, down the Radial and into central Omaha or onto the Interstate; straight ahead up Decatur and into the Benson district; or straight ahead through the intersection, bearing left onto Happy Hollow Boulevard and into the Dundee neighborhood.

Four ways to disappear fast, in other words, and four good reasons for me to not bother trying to follow him.

I climbed down from the Camaro, a good deal more slowly and less surely than I had clambered up it, and made my way upstairs.

I spent perhaps thirty seconds telling myself that my near-miss was just a dumb accident—almost-accident. A drunk. An idiot. A kid playing hot-rod games. By then the tall neat bourbon I had poured for myself was gone and my heartbeat was down to only three digits and my hands were almost steady enough that I could use just one hand to pour the second drink. I spent the next ten seconds assuring myself that the arguments presented in the previous thirty seconds were too fat-headed for even me to buy. Then I added some ice to the shorter drink I had poured, cranked up the heat a notch, and moved into the living room to do some thinking.

A guy in my line makes enemies. Down these mean streets, et cetera. I hadn't sent too many crime warlords up the river or exposed more than my share of corrupt kingmakers or toppled an unreasonable number of drug empires. But I had gone out of my way to be annoying to a great many people over the past ten or fifteen years. Some of them were petty and some of them were powerful, and some day I may open my door and find one of them standing on the other side of it with a nasty surprise for me. But this, the monster car, wasn't it. It didn't feel right. The event lacked the memorable, instructive nature of a mob action: It would be too easily dismissed as an accident rather than an act of retribution. Nor did it have the grim, personalized air of a small-timer's vengeance: It was too anonymous, and the instrument of revenge was all wrong. Being hit by a car, even a big car, is no guarantee of death.

The conclusion, then, was that the driver didn't *necessarily* want to kill me.

Reassuring as hell.

Suppose his game had been to scare me. He succeeded. But what was his point? What was he trying to scare me away from—because no one ever tries to scare you *toward* something; it just isn't done—and why?

Well, if I knew the *what* I'd probably know the *why,* and I might have a decent stab at guessing the *who.*

Clearly a three-drink problem. I polished off the second one and was heading for the kitchen to fix a replacement when the doorbell rang. I checked my watch. Only seven-thirty. These sunless days, and the fact that they were getting noticeably shorter, played tricks with the old internal clock.

Quickly, and quietly, I moved through the living room and down the hall and into my bedroom-office. There's a file drawer in the desk. I've got one of those hanging-file racks in the drawer, with the file folders held in heavy green paper slings rather than merely being crammed into the drawer. That leaves a little bit of wasted space between the bottom of the slings and the bottom of the drawer. Enough space to conceal a .38 police revolver and a box of bullets.

I reached down between the green slings and hauled out the gun, peeling it out of the rag I keep it in, throwing the rag into the bathroom as I passed it on the way to the front door. I keep the gun loaded. It soothes my paranoia, which at the moment was running high. I was ninety-nine percent sure that my bad-driver friend had had nonfatal intentions. But there was still that one percent or so that said, *What if he* didn't *miss on purpose, and has come back for another crack at it?*

From inside the apartment, the door opens left to right—which made it awkward to open left-handed, but I managed it, keeping the revolver behind the door, out of sight—but not so far behind or out that I couldn't bring it into play quickly if called upon.

The light in the brick wall just outside my door is dim and yellow, but it was enough to make Alexander Wayne's blunt, ruddy features recognizable. I undid the useless latch on the aluminum storm door and let him in.

"Mr. Nebraska." His voice was the same hearty boom it had been on our first meeting, but there was none of the heavy jolliness he had displayed then. He stepped onto the square of linoleum just inside the door. "Look, Nebraska, I need to—" He had caught sight of the gun, which I made no effort to hide as I closed, and locked, the door. "Er . . . is this a bad time?"

I looked at the weapon in my hand. "No."

He frowned, perplexed, and glanced around the room as if to reassure himself that it was safe.

"What can I do for you, Mr. Wayne?"

"Well . . ." He unzipped his brown-leather car coat. "Would you mind if I sat down?"

"Not much. I was going to have a drink. Want one?"

His eyes were on the gun in my right hand. My hand was at my side, but it's funny: A gun doesn't actually have to be pointing at you to get your attention.

"Fine," he said in a tone that said he didn't really think it was fine at all but that he didn't want to get into it with a lunatic who walked around his apartment all by himself heavily armed.

"Fine," I said, and wandered into the little kitchen. I set the gun on the counter by the fridge. "Bourbon's all I got."

"Fine."

"Ice?"

"Whatever you're having. Don't go to any trouble."

"No trouble." I went about the chore and surreptitiously eyed Wayne under the cupboards that separated the two rooms. He was certainly jumpy enough to have just come from trying to turn my best friend into roadkill on Decatur Street. Or was it just the gun? Or was it something else? If Alexander Wayne had been the anonymous driver, and if his intent had been murder, then I would have opened the door to the type of unpleasant surprise I was talking about a little bit ago. Wouldn't I? But if he was trying to scare me away from something—say, investigating his son and his son's relationship with Meredith Berens, of whose death Alexander Wayne may or may not now know—he might have decided to circle back and see how I was doing, scared-offwise.

If Wayne wasn't my automotive friend . . . Well, then what was he doing here?

I slid the revolver into my back pocket and carried our drinks into the other room.

"Thanks." Wayne sucked half an inch off the top of the glass, sat back against the sofa, and sighed. "Christ, what a night."

"No argument here." I wetted my beak, but only just, and the drink was more tap water and ice than liquor. The two drinks I had already taken care of had done a swell job of smoothing out my nerves and I didn't want them to start working on my wits. "I don't mind the company, Mr. Wayne, but you can get lousy liquor almost anywhere."

He grinned lopsidedly. "Do you know what I've been doing for the past"—he looked at his watch—"hour or so? Answering questions from the police. The po*lice!* And Thomas!"

"What sort of questions did your son have?"

The lopsided grin stayed fixed. "You know what I mean. They questioned my boy, too—and pretty intensely, from what he tells me."

"Huh," I said impassively. "What about, I wonder."

The grin grew ragged. "You know *that,* too," he said, pulling on the drink. "Meredith, Meredith Berens. She's dead."

"You're right; I did know that. But thanks anyway for stopping by with the news."

"You like to annoy people, don't you? You like to pretend to be obtuse." The grin was gone entirely, as was the overblown heartiness.

"Not especially," I said. "What I like better is people getting to the point."

"Fine." He got rid of some more liquor. "Meredith is dead and the police were questioning my son—and me, for that matter— about his relationship with her, this 'engagement' business, and so on."

"Uh-huh."

"From some of their questions—well, your name was mentioned. I got the impression that you may have spoken with them first."

There didn't seem to be any good reason to pretend otherwise. "With one of them, to be exact."

He nodded, as if I had confirmed something. "That . . . assertive woman. Banner, I think her name was. And just what did you tell her to make her think my Thomas killed that girl?" There was something very similar to anger bubbling just beneath the surface.

"The cops arrested your son?"

"No. But from the questions they asked me about Thomas and Meredith, and from what Thomas told me about their questioning of him, I think there's little doubt but that they suspect him. Strongly. And I think there's little doubt but that you had something to do with that, *Mr.* Nebraska."

"Don't flatter me. Of course I told the police everything I know about Meredith Berens." Banner knew I was investigating Meredith's disappearance, and there was no point pretending otherwise, even if I wanted to. Which I didn't. The only private investigators who play cutesy with the cops on a murder investigation—or any other kind, for that matter—are the ones on TV. Or real-life ones who aren't fond of their permits. "Naturally I told the cops about my meeting with you and your son this morning—about his side of 'this engagement business,' as you put it—and about his violent outburst."

"You were *provoking* him," Wayne shot back.

"Absolutely. I was provoking him to see what sort of a reaction I'd get. I saw."

"Bah!" He didn't really say "Bah," of course. No one does, except perhaps in an affected, self-conscious way. But he made a disgusted sound, a disgruntled, frustrated kind of noise that amounted to about the same thing as "Bah." And he drained his glass in an angry gesture. "This is pointless."

"I'm inclined to agree. Look, Mr. Wayne, I can understand your being upset about the police questioning your son, but that's a helluva lot better than what Meredith Berens went through, and anyway he's not under arrest. Whether or not I tried to bias the cops against him, I'm afraid my opinion doesn't really swing that much weight with them. They'll conduct their own investigation and they'll reach their own conclusions. Right now, they're coming from the same place I was coming from this morning—a place from which they can see an awful lot of, shall we say, unusual factors in your son's relationship with Meredith Berens."

" 'This engagement business,' you mean?" He was a little cooler now.

I nodded. "She says yes, he says no. Odd, to say the least, and she's no longer in a position to hold up her side of the debate."

"Oh, come *on*. If Thomas *were* engaged, don't you think he'd tell me? I *am* his father."

Donna Berens had said almost exactly the same thing, in almost exactly the same tone of voice. The statement hadn't proved anything then, as far as I was concerned, and it didn't now.

"I don't know what your son may or may not do, Mr. Wayne. That's sort of the point, isn't it? I do know that Meredith Berens told Dianna Castelli that she was engaged to your son. I understand the Castelli woman is a friend of your son. It was she who introduced them in the first place. For what it's worth, she doesn't think Thomas killed Meredith, and she knows your son better than I do. Anyhow, whether there in fact was an engagement may be secondary."

"Meaning what?"

"As I said this morning, if Meredith *acted* as if there was an engagement and refused to be dissuaded . . . well, her unintentional intended might have felt boxed-in, cornered, with only one way out."

"Bah," he didn't say again, this time less vehemently. "That's utterly ridiculous. The problem with people like you, and the cops, is all you deal with day in and day out is *scum*. Garbage, human garbage. So you begin to think the way human garbage thinks, and you begin to think *everyone* thinks that way, and that *everyone,* given the opportunity, is capable of murder or worse."

"Everyone *is*. Capable, at least."

"*No,* sir. Everyone is *not*. Most people have had the opportunity to kill someone. Most people have even had the motive. But most people do *not* commit cold-blooded murder. How do you explain that?"

"Restraint. Good breeding. Religion. Fear. There are probably two-dozen different reasons for every individual on the planet, Mr. Wayne. The fact that I've never chosen to murder someone doesn't mean I'm incapable of it. It just means I haven't had a strong enough motivation. Or I haven't been pushed hard enough."

"And Meredith Berens pushed my son 'hard enough,' is that it?"

"That *could* be it. Or not. I don't know. Neither do the police. That's why they have to ask questions, and why I had to provoke your son this morning. We don't know. But we *want* to know. And I have the feeling we will."

He held my eyes for a long time. Then he looked away, looked at the empty glass between his big, fleshy hands, and carefully set the glass on the coffee table in front of him. "My son is all I have, Nebraska," he said quietly but strongly. "Everything I've ever done has been for him." He looked at me again. "Everything. I don't want to see his life ruined by this."

"If he's innocent—"

"I'm not as old and senile as I might look," he cut me off. "Whether or not he's innocent doesn't matter, does it? Being under suspicion, and being charged and tried, if it should come to it, is more than enough to ruin him, innocent or not. Being close to it, losing someone he was fond of, has been hard, very hard. A long time ago . . ." He paused.

"A long time ago?"

"I was thinking about Thomas's mother. Her loss was extremely hard on him. He was very young. I think losing a friend, a girl-friend, like this is going to be doubly hard on him, because of that. And to be questioned about her death, grilled by the police . . ." He shook his head.

"All of Meredith's friends are being questioned, Mr. Wayne, or will be. What makes your son special?"

"He's *my son,*" the big man roared. "And I *won't* let him be crucified by you *or* the police, or that silly little girl who called herself his fiancée. Do we understand each other, Nebraska?" His features were twisted into a grotesque parody of his other, palsy-walsy, somebody's-uncle face. Its ruddiness was now blood-red, white in the deep creases around his mouth and across his forehead.

"Take it up with the cops," I said. "It's their party."

"They know my feelings. Now I'm talking to *you*—and you can carry it back to your client, too. I *will not* have Thomas dragged through the mud. You find out how much it'll take for the girl's mother to keep her nose out of it. Hers, *and* yours. And then you go to your little girlfriend on the police force and you tell her you were *wrong,* about Thomas and the girl, about *everything.* You tell her there is no way my son had *anything* to do with that little bitch's death."

I fought to keep my voice, and my dander, down. "I told you, Wayne: The cops don't dance to my tune."

"You sicced them on my boy," he insisted. "Now you can call them *off.* Understand? You get hold of that broad, whatever her name is, and *you call her off! Do* you understand?"

I understood very clearly, or thought I did.

chapter
11

As it happened, Dianna Castelli lived not far from me, in a narrow, old two-story in Dundee. After Alexander Wayne had left—in an older, which is to say bigger, LTD that may or may not have been the car that nearly had me as a hood ornament—I had sat in my chair and nursed my weak drink and thought and got nowhere. I picked up the phone and dialed Koosje's number, hitting the disconnect button with my thumb before the call went through. *What would be the point?* I asked myself. Small talk is easy when things are easy between two people, hard when things are hard. Things were hard between me and Koosje just now, no denying that. And I didn't have the vaguest idea of where to begin to get things back on track.

That was the one good thing about my relationship with Jennifer, my sort-of wife: I knew and always had known just exactly how things stood with us. I knew that we could have a marriage in more than just name if I would give up my residency here in this Paris of the Plains and join her in her endless quest to be in the "in" place with the "in" people doing the "in" thing.

Trouble is, "in" doesn't *stay* "in" very long, and I don't have the kind of energy it takes to keep after it.

I looked up Dianna Castelli in the book and dialed her number.

It occurred to me that, if the police hadn't gotten around to talking with her yet, as they surely would, Dianna might not yet know about Meredith. And even if it turned out that she did know, it was a good excuse for my calling. Because, not to put too fine a point on it, after the events of the day—the scene in the morgue, the scene after the morgue, my nearly becoming just another spot on the pavement, and Alexander Wayne's odd visitation—I needed someone to talk to.

Dianna's line was busy.

I went out into the night. There were no gigantic automobiles waiting to mow me down. There was just the night and the spit of rain and the rhythm of traffic in the city. I followed the rhythm, picked it up and tried to get lost in it, tried to wipe out the persistent image of Meredith Berens in the morgue and the equally persistent image of Alexander Wayne threatening me, ordering me to "call off" the police. As if I had that kind of authority. Or any other kind. Could Wayne really think I carried that much weight with OPD? Not a chance. I'll admit I'm a pretty impressive kind of guy, but even so—not a chance. So why the visit from Wayne? Under his anger, I now decided, there had been a distinct undercurrent of—what? Panic? Desperation? Nobody likes having the cops pry into his affairs, and even priests, Scout leaders, and members of the ASPCA are apt to grow nervous when it happens. But worry is one thing, panic something else again.

Having the cops nosing around had made Alexander Wayne panicky, all right. Panicky enough to try to scare me—or kill me— to get me out of an investigation he didn't know I was probably already out of? Maybe. Panicky enough to want to buy off my client, or former client? Definitely. Panicky enough to waste his breath telling me to call off the cops? Obviously.

Why all the fuss? Because Wayne was afraid the cops might just be able to find something to pin on his sonny-boy.

Or because he was afraid they might find something else.

The car ended up in front of Dianna Castelli's house.

Every light in the place was burning, and it was still early, so I didn't feel bad about dropping in. Given my reason, or excuse, for being there, even Miss Manners would forgive me for not phoning ahead.

She answered the bell almost immediately. She wore a floppy purple-and-yellow sweatshirt with the sleeves pushed back, tight black pants like Laura always wore on *The Dick Van Dyke Show,* and a frazzled expression. "There you are," she said by way of greeting. "Do you know anything about VCRs?"

A little confused, I followed her into the living room, a smallish square space at the front of the house. Lots of woodwork, old and faded wallpaper, fat-slatted, out-of-style venetian blinds, and a large cardboard box, its paper and plastic and Styrofoam innards spread out on the rug amidst a tangle of cables. "Just that I don't understand the VCR mentality," I said. "There's so much junk on TV, I can't find more than a couple hours a week worth watching. What would you want to tape any of it for?"

She fixed me with a look. "There's a lot of junk in bookstores, too. You think people should give up reading?"

"You bite your tongue," I said with fervor.

She laughed. "I think of this as a time-management device. I can watch what I want to *when* I want to, not when some network nitwit thinks I ought to. All the good movies are on after midnight. And by the time I get done zapping the commercials, I can watch an hour show in about forty-five minutes."

"And you in advertising," I chided.

"Public relations. What's that got to do with anything?" She knelt on the oval rug in front of a wall unit that held the TV set. Her slightly spiky hair was a little more relaxed by evening, I noticed, and if her figure was a shade too ample for the tight slacks, she at least had the panache to carry it off. She was engrossed with the mess in front of her. "I got this thing today to replace my old clunker, which went to that big electronics store in the sky. The book says *this* cable"—she held up a length of black coaxial cable—"goes from the wall to the VCR. Then *this* cable goes from the VCR to the TV. But I have a cable converter. So this cable *should* go to the converter box, and *this* one from the box to the TV set. Right?"

"Uh . . ." I said, and invited myself to sit down. "Aren't you even a little curious about why I'm here?"

"Because of my message, and because I've been tying up the phone all night." She bent at the waist, leaning on her arms crossed on her thighs, and stuck her nose into the instruction book. "But when I do *that*," she said to the book, "I don't get any signal on the VCR, just the set."

"What message?"

She didn't look up. "On your machine."

I had been first too shaken, then too distracted, to even look at the answering machine when I got back to Decatur Street.

I said, "I haven't gotten my messages yet. Why don't you just hook this machine up the same way you had the old one hooked up?"

Dianna shook her spike-topped head, still fixed on the book. "The old one wasn't cable-ready. The cable went from the wall to the converter to the VCR to the TV, and I couldn't watch one channel while I taped another. Now I can. Or at least I *should* be able to. Why is it these directions are always written by Japanese high school students?"

"The average Japanese high school student knows more English than the average American student knows Japanese."

"That's supposed to make me feel better?" She looked at me. "Well, if you never got my message, then what *are* you doing here. Not that I mind the company . . ."

I got down on the floor next to her and looked at the instructions. "Then you haven't heard . . ." I said ineffectually.

Dianna sat back on her haunches, the video recorder forgotten, and looked at me for a long moment. "Oh, my God," she breathed.

"I'm afraid so," I said. "The police found her this afternoon." I gave her the story. By the time I was through she was crying gently into her left hand, her face turned away from me.

The world probably is full of people who know just what to say or do in situations like this. I'm not one of them. I sat there mutely for too long a time, flipping aimlessly through the instructions for the video recorder. Finally I wised up enough to lean forward and put my arms around Dianna. She responded by wrapping her arms around me and letting out a new series of sobs and gulps. Then she finished with that and sat back on her heels and wiped her face with her fingers. I offered my handkerchief and she laughed wetly.

"You don't want to do that," she snuffled. "I'll get a Kleenex."

She did, and when she returned ten minutes later it was with a dry, fresh-scrubbed face and a glass in each hand. She gave me one and I tasted it. Scotch.

"I don't know about you," she said, seating herself, "but I need one. If you don't want yours, I'll drink it too."

I got up off the floor and sat on a low-backed sofa under the front window. "I'll drink it," I said. "By the way, your converter box has to be tuned to channel four if you're going to watch a tape, not channel three, because three's in use 'round these parts." I put the instruction booklet on a lamp table to my left.

She attempted a laugh, which emerged as a hiccup. "Da-dammit," she gulped. "E-every time I c-cry . . ."

It's hard not to laugh at someone who has the hiccups. I didn't even try. Soon we were both laughing, although Dianna's was still a little damp. It was the slightly guilty, slightly nervous, slightly relieved laughter of people who are still alive when Death has come near. God knows, there was nothing to laugh about. Unless just being alive is reason enough.

"Ah, G-God," Dianna breathed helplessly when she was through. "Jeez, it was only a w-week ago that Meredith was discussing w-wedding plans with me. Now—Poor, poor Meredith." She shook her head and dabbed at her eyes with the crumpled tissue in her hand.

"Let's talk about those wedding plans," I said.

She snuffled another laugh, wiping tears from her cheeks with the heel of her hand. "I told Meredith, I'm not the one to ask about marriage."

"Been through the wringer, have we?"

"Hasn't everyone?" She exercised the Kleenex some more. Women can get more mileage out of a tissue . . . Me, I get about half of a good honk into one and it disintegrates. "Oh, I haven't been *married*," she said, stressing the word as if it were something distasteful. "But I came real close a couple of years ago."

"What happened? As if it's any of my business."

Dianna smiled sadly. "I guess I'm just too independent. He—this guy I was living with—he was offered a teaching job at Drake, in Des Moines. A good position, the kind of job he'd been hoping for. He wanted me to move there with him and marry him. But I was finally getting the agency on its feet after a few real lean years and—well, like I said, I'm just too independent. I couldn't give up my freedom. What about you? Have you ever been married?"

"Have been and am, on paper at least. My wife and I are sort of separated." Explaining the true nature of our on-and-off marriage was too complicated, and I wasn't altogether sure I understood it myself. "But it's funny. As . . . unorthodox, and sometimes downright shitty, as my marriage has been, I've never viewed it as encroaching on my freedom or independence."

She shrugged. "When you're married and your husband gets transferred to the middle of Iowa, you go. You're not married, you don't go. Or at least you don't *have* to go. You have a choice."

"You *always* have a choice. I mean, in a way I've chosen to be apart from my wife—in that, in order to be with her, I have to follow a lifestyle that is distasteful to me. Neither of my options was especially attractive, but I had a choice and I made it. Life's full of hard decisions, and choices between lesser evils. With or without marriage."

She pursed her lips and cocked her head and gave every indication of wanting to appear to be giving my comments due consideration without actually wanting to consider them at all. "Be that as it may," she said diplomatically, "the fact remains that I'm no expert on weddings or marriages or anything else except maybe the PR business, and I told Meredith as much. Nicely, of course. You don't want to rain on someone's parade when they're as excited as Meredith w-was . . ."

Again with the Kleenex.

I said, "About those impending nuptials . . ."

"But I thought *you* thought Meredith . . . Oh, *I* get it. You think maybe instead of Meredith making up the engagement, Thomas Wayne made up a story about Meredith making up their engagement, don't you?"

"As usual," I said, "I'm not at all sure I know what you just said. What do *you* think?"

She sighed. "My brain's been buzzing ever since you first told me about it. It's hard, you know what I mean." She used the Kleenex again. "On the one hand, while Meredith was kind of a different kid, a little mixed-up, maybe, and not as mature or savvy or what-have-you as a kid her age should have been—blame her mom—I can't make myself believe she was so crazy that she could just go and invent a whole engagement and delude herself into, you know, believing it. I know she was pretty crazy about Thomas, and I could understand someone kind of, you know, *inflating* a relationship in her own mind. But not Meredith. Not like that. But on the other hand, I know Thomas pretty well, too, and I can't believe that *he* would make it up. Still . . ."

I waited a decent interval. "Still . . ." I finally prompted.

"Well . . ." she said, clearly reluctant to commit to what she had begun to say. "It's so far-fetched . . ." She stood and wandered over to the shelving unit against the east wall. It was one of those standard "entertainment centers" you can buy just about anywhere. Room enough for a nineteen-inch television set and a VCR and a compact stereo, plus the necessary records, tapes, and discs to feed the hardware, plus a few books and some photos and the other general dust-collectors you'd expect to find. Dianna flipped on the television set and tuned the cable box to channel four, then shoved a tape into the VCR sitting on the floor, wires and cables running to and from its back like entrails. After a moment the commercial on the tube flipped once and vanished, replaced by the image from the video recorder, "electronically reproduced," as they say at the end of the newscasts.

"I'll be damned," she mumbled, half to herself. "You were right."

"Occasionally it'll happen," I said.

She turned and smiled sadly, then powered down the VCR and tuned the TV to one of the music channels. The volume was turned all the way down, as it had been all along. A very pretty young man with long blond hair and rouged lips appeared to be screaming over the top of an electric guitar that looked like a scimitar. There was a lot of colored smoke. Without sound, it was all pretty comical.

I said, "I read somewhere that these music-video channels are loaded with sex and violence. So I spent an entire evening glued to one once and didn't see much of either."

"People are good at finding what they want to find where they want to find it," Dianna said, returning to her chair, an old-looking wingback shoved into a corner beneath a wall-mounted swing-out reading lamp. She sat with one leg folded beneath her, the other foot dangling a few inches above the floor. She took a breath and straightened her back. "After you were at the agency this morning, I got to thinking. About Thomas, I mean. I still think that your . . . theory or conjecture or what-have-you is all wet, but I was reminded of something. It took me awhile to check it out. When I did, that's when I left word for you to call me."

I nodded.

"I remember hearing something years ago. About Thomas. Now, this is just, you know, hearsay, and I *don't* want it getting back to Thomas that you heard it from me, because *I* don't know whether—"

"For cryin' out loud, Dianna . . ."

"All right, all right." She took a breath and let it go, then took a drink, just a sip, a nervous action. "All right," she repeated. "I sort of remembered something this afternoon, and I had to call a couple of people, a couple of people who know Thomas, to see whether I remembered right. What I remembered was someone a long time ago saying that the reason Thomas never got married, and never gets really serious with a woman, is that he had a girl-friend or a fiancée or whatever a long time ago and she got killed."

I said nothing, but what I was thinking must have been written all over my face in twenty-two-point type.

"I know," Dianna said hastily. "It's too horrible to think about. I mean, it *can't* be. But . . ."

"It's a helluva coincidence," I said gently.

"Coincidences happen," she said after a while.

"That's the trouble with them." I sipped some liquor and thought for a moment. Was *this* what Alexander Wayne didn't want the cops—or me, or anyone else—to discover? "Do you have any details?" I asked Dianna.

She shook her head. "Like I said, I had just about forgotten all about it. But when you were at the office today . . . Well, you know how it is when you sort of remember something but not quite? It's on the tip of your mind, but you don't know if it's real or a part of a dream you had once or if you're remembering it right at all? That's how this was. That's why I didn't say anything then, or until I could talk with a couple of friends."

"And how did you go about this? You didn't say, 'Hey, do you remember anything about Thomas Wayne having a girlfriend who got killed?' Killed how, by the way?"

"Car accident, I guess. And, no, I'm a *little* more discreet than that. I made up a story about having had a conversation with *another* friend. I said the talk came around to car wrecks—I had sort of remembered that Thomas's girlfriend was killed in a crash—and that this friend and I remembered, you know, the basic story, but that we couldn't think who got killed."

It was a pretty good way of going about it, and I said so. Too many people in too many instances, whether accidentally or on purpose, taint responses by the way they phrase their questions. It's the When-Did-You-Stop-Beating-Your-Wife Syndrome. "Do you remember something about Thomas Wayne having a girlfriend who got killed a few years ago?" is likely to produce a positive response, even if the respondent doesn't really remember it. No-body likes to appear uninformed.

I said, "Did either of your friends recall the story in greater detail?"

"No, not really. One of them said she thought it had been a

high school sweetheart. But she wasn't really sure. Both of them pretty much remembered it the same way I did—just one of those stories you hear about people, you know? No real details, no real source. Just a notch or two above a rumor. Later you can't even remember where you heard it or who you heard it from. That's how it is with me, at least, and both of these women I talked to."

"A high school sweetheart. Did the accident occur when Thomas was in high school?"

"Search me."

"That would be . . . what, twenty years ago, twenty-one . . ." I mused. "Was Thomas involved in this accident? As a driver, a passenger, a witness?"

Dianna shrugged. "You already know everything I know. What, you think Thomas killed this girl back then and then repeated the act twenty years later? Sort of a long time between murders, wouldn't you say?"

"A long time between two deaths—the first may not have been murder—that have Thomas Wayne as a common denominator. I would like to know more about the high school sweetheart. It would be interesting to see if there were similarities between her and Meredith."

"Similarities? Like what?"

"Like, did the high school sweetheart expect to marry Thomas Wayne?"

Dianna whistled out a long breath and took a drink and said, "Jesus, Nebraska, doesn't it ever worry you that you think that way?"

"It worries me more that other people think that way, and some of them act on it. Do you know Thomas's father very well?"

"Alexander?" She frowned. "Not very. I've met him is all. Why?—Oh, Christ, Nebraska, you don't think *Alexander* had anything to do with Meredith's . . . with Meredith, do you? He's an old man, for Pete's sake."

"For whoever's sake, he's not that old—I doubt he's sixty-five yet—and it looks to me like he's in pretty good shape."

"But what could he possibly have against Meredith?"

"Thomas," I said. "Specifically, Thomas's 'engagement'—whether or not there ever really was one has become unimportant. What's important is that if Meredith had become more trouble to Thomas than she was worth, it could have been Alexander just as easily as Thomas who decided to take matters into his own hands."

Her look was incredulous, though whether that was owing to what I had said or the mere fact that I had said it was hard to tell.

She said, "That's even crazier than your idea that Thomas killed Meredith. Where'd you come up with a screwy thought like that?"

I told her about the call Alexander Wayne had paid me.

"I admit it's pretty . . . odd," she said when I had finished. "But it doesn't prove anything."

"I agree. But it's enough to make a fella curious, wouldn't you say?"

"Well . . ."

"Here's something else that's curious: A few minutes before Wayne turned up at my door, someone tried to flatten me out with a very large and very unfriendly-looking car."

"Good God," Dianna gasped. "Are you all right?"

"Yes. I went into my Spider-Man act and escaped unharmed. But here's the curious part: Not ten minutes after my near-miss, Wayne shows up, visibly upset, and not only orders me to stay away from his son but also orders me to order the *cops* to stay away. Then he drives away in a car that could—*could*—be the car that I almost got a close-up view of the underside of. Then I come over here and you tell me that Thomas once had a girlfriend who died in an automotive accident of some sort. Like I said, curious."

"But like *I* said, people find what they want to find where they want to find it. Everything you've said could just be coincidence. It doesn't necessarily have anything at all to do with Meredith. *Anyone* could have killed her."

"You're right about the first, wrong about the second. I'll bet money that Meredith was killed by someone she knew, or who knew her, and for a reason. She wasn't robbed; her purse was missing, which may or may not mean anything, but she was wearing a gold ring that no self-respecting robber would have left behind. She wasn't raped. The cops haven't located her car, which indicates one of two things: Either she was attacked at Point A and transferred by her attacker to Point B, which a mugger wouldn't bother with. *Or* she met her killer at Point A and voluntarily rode with him or her to Point B, where she was killed. Plus, Meredith was beaten to death—I'm sorry, but there's no pleasant way to phrase it. It wasn't a case of being hit over the head too hard by a purse-snatcher. It wasn't a case of a mugger getting carried away when his intended victim fought back. It was a case of somebody taking a stick or a bat or a pipe and beating a young woman to death, then concealing the body. Murder. So it couldn't have been just 'anyone' who killed Meredith, Dianna. It was *someone,* someone specific."

By the time I wrapped it up she was crying again. Jennifer, Koosje, Dianna . . . do I have a way with women or what?

chapter

12

The two staircases at the front of my apartment building are open. They are slabs of exposed-aggregate concrete set in shallow iron boxes mounted in an iron frame. That's why it was easy for them to get the jump on me.

I had returned home late, after leaving Dianna Castelli. I had found a parking space in the minuscule lot next to the building, so there was no need to cross the no-man's land that the city maps call Decatur Street, no occasion to dodge careening cars.

I had one foot on the bottom step and the other in midair between that step and the next one up when something—an arm, I guess, I don't know—shot through the opening between the two steps and went around the back of my ankle and pulled forward, sending me backward to sprawl, dazed and bruised and breathless, on the sidewalk in front of the stairs.

And then they were on me.

There were three of them, darkly menacing figures illuminated only slightly by the stray light from the street and the pale yellow lamps on the front of the building. One of them kicked me in the ribs, and not gently. Another aimed at my head but got my shoulder instead. The first of them, having had such good luck with my ribs, aimed another shot, this time at my groin. I got my legs up in time and deflected the kick. Then I kicked back, and sent the off-balance attacker staggering down the five steps that lead to the lower-level apartments, which sit halfway below ground. The attackers had hid in the darkness of the kind of dugout walkway in front of the garden-level apartments.

That left two—the other kicker and the third attacker, who seemed to be holding back for some reason.

The kicker had hold of my left arm, so I rolled to my left, toward him, and put as much of the momentum as I could into a right to his breadbasket. He *whuffed* satisfyingly in the darkness and loosened his grip on my arm. I tightened my grip, however, on one of his arms and rolled back to my right, pulling him down over me, off of the sidewalk and into the mucky yard in front of the building.

I clambered to my feet, breathing hard, and faced the third attacker, who backed up a couple of steps.

But the man I had thrown over was behind me now, and not hurt as badly as I might have hoped—obviously, for I suddenly felt a sledgehammer blow between my shoulder blades, sending me to my knees. I was able to turn just enough to see the attacker, silhouetted against the leaden gray of the night sky, raise his arms, fists interlocked, to deliver another piledriver. I went forward from the knees, flattening myself against the cold, wet pavement, and the man staggered over me.

I rolled onto my back and tried to get up. But the first man, the one I had thrown down the stairs, was back. He landed on me like a ton of bricks, or two hundred pounds of bricks anyway, and my head slammed against the concrete and I saw stars even though it was a cloudy night.

The next thing I knew I was on my feet, sort of, propped between the two men I had tussled with, my back against the rough brickwork of the retaining wall in the long dugout under the stairs. If I let out a shout, one of the garden-level tenants might at least look out his peephole to see what the commotion was. The nearest door was only five or six feet away. But a meaty forearm across my windpipe made the shouting-out proposition difficult at best.

The third man had moved in, now that there was little danger of my harming him. He was a small man, skinny, I would have bet, under the bulk of the oversized raincoat he wore, and several inches shorter than me, though I'm not especially tall. He wore a wide-brimmed hat, but even so I could see his face clearly in the light of the yellow lamp next to the nearby door. His face was long and thin, and his features suggested mixed blood—predominantly black, but also Latin or Indian or even Asian. Thin wisps of dark hair circled his mouth and trailed down his chin in a poor imitation of a goatee. His voice was as wispy as the would-be beard and his smile was a sneer when he said, "I dint think you'd be so feisty . . . Ned."

Ned? *Ned?* Who—

"An' I dint think you'd be so *aj*-eye-ul either, Ned," the little man was saying. *The little man with the big car,* I thought. Thinking was all I could do at the moment, and I was doing it furiously— or trying, too. Most of my brain was on coffee break and the rest of it was doing its imitation of plum pudding.

The little creep smiled into my face for too long a time. I smelled cheap, heavy cologne and whiskey and tobacco and marijuana. I saw the shallow pockmarks that marched from his left cheek across his wide nose and onto his right cheek. And I saw, an instant before he delivered it, the punch he sent into my gut. There wasn't a damn thing I could do about it, thanks to the creep's friends. Luckily, with no weight behind it, the blow wasn't much worse than being hit by a flying marshmallow.

"Now you listen to me, *Ned,*" the creep breathed into my face. "You've annoyed a friend of mine. A very *good* friend. Unnerstan?"

He seemed to expect a reply, so I grunted, which was the best I could do under the circumstances.

"Good," he lisped. "My friends and me, we're here to ask you to quit annoying my friend. Unnerstan? Else nex' time we gonna have to be more . . . per-*sway*-sive." His oily eyes left my face, drifted hazily, even lovingly, to the men on either side of me. Then his right knee shot up between my legs and the dim yellow lighting suddenly went very bright and white. I doubled involuntarily, or tried to—the men holding me were better prepared for the blow than I had been, and they held me. Long enough, at least, to take and throw me to the pavement, hard. I lay there, retching. One of them aimed a kick at my head. This time it connected.

It was a long time before I could get in touch with my brain to get in touch with my arms and legs to see about moving. When we all got together, it was all we could do to get me over onto my back, where I lay looking at the underside of the concrete-and-iron walkway that fronted the second-level apartments. My apartment was on the second level. My door was almost directly overhead. But it might as well have been on Saturn.

I got onto my side and slithered over to the foot of the stairs from the dugout to ground level. I figure they called these lower apartments "garden level" because when you look out your window you're on the same level as the garden. Relying heavily on the handrail I pulled myself into a sitting position on the bottom step. Neither my aching gut nor my aching head seemed convinced that this was at all the thing to do, but the rest of me was convinced that it would rather die in bed than there on the cold, cold ground, and if the longest journey must begin with a single step, I figured, the step I now sat on was it.

Ned.

The delicate little violet had called me Ned, and the only Ned I knew was Ned Brazda, the too-cute pseudonym I had invented when I called on Meredith's friend Jahna Johansen. Too cute by half, I reflected ruefully. When in doubt tell the truth. Or at least learn to lie better. Jahna Johansen hadn't bought my goods. Perhaps she had never been taken in, perhaps it had come unraveled when she looked out her window and saw me in consultation with the cop in front of her building. Didn't matter. It would have been an easy thing for her to get the license plate number from my car as I drove away and turn the number and my description over to her scrawny friend. Whose friends weren't so scrawny.

I pulled myself to my feet and dragged myself all the way up to ground level before I had to rest again, leaning against the railing until the screaming pain in my outraged muscles faded.

I wondered if I had spoiled Jahna's "party." If she had thought I was a cop, or working with the cops, and if she thought we were interested in her and her two-bit prostitution scene, she might have been scared enough to cancel tonight's festivities. I hoped so. There's nothing worse than being invited to a party and feeling too lousy to go.

The thought cheered me up enough that I was able to get up the next flight of stairs and get my front door open and collapse onto my sofa without throwing up even once.

chapter
13

I planned to sleep in. I felt entitled. Someone else had other plans.

"Someone else" came tiptoeing into my room on dainty, little size-twelves that must have been shod in solid concrete. According to the clock at my bedside, it was just a few minutes before eight A.M. With effort, I pulled myself into a sitting position, my back against the sofa back of the pull-out bed, and reached for the .38 that I had left on the bedside table before falling—plummeting, rather—to sleep the night before. I held the gun in my lap, aimed at the doorway.

The figure that hesitated there almost literally filled the doorway. I said, " 'Morning, Tom." It came out a croak.

The big man said, "How come you don't answer your door?"

"Because I didn't want to see anybody. No offense. Take a pew."

"Huhn?"

"Sit."

He looked around. The room isn't large, but it was crowded. The sofa bed, when folded out, does a good job of taking care of most of the available floorspace. There's the desk chair, of course, but to unfold the bed I have to shove the chair all the way forward into the kneehole of the desk and, well, you'd have to be even skinnier than the little creep I'd encountered last night to slip in there. My unannounced guest settled for planting a buttock on the edge of the desk, one foot up on the edge of the bed. I didn't mind. Not enough to muster the energy to complain.

His name was Tom Carra and he was a hood, a foot soldier in the Mob's Omaha corps. Omaha is an offshoot of the Chicago and

Kansas City operations. It's small but profitable. Gambling, drugs, women, a little bit of this, a little bit of that. As the defense budget joke goes, "A million here, a million there, pretty soon you're talking about real money." Three or four years ago I'd been swept up into the middle of a wee bit of a power struggle amongst the Omaha bosses. Tom Carra had enlisted me. It's no immodesty to say that yours truly was the deciding factor in the outcome of that power struggle. And it's no exaggeration to say that if I hadn't acted then the way I did, Tom Carra would today be lurking around on the bed of the Missouri River, not in my bedroom.

"Jesus Christ," the hood said, "what happened to you?"

I looked down. My chest and belly were bare above the sheet. Both were liberally sprinkled with bruises and scrapes, many of which were already turning interesting shades of yellow, green, and blue.

"Pretty, aren't they. Part of a whole collection I started last night. You wouldn't happen to know anything about that, Tommy, would you?"

"Huhn?"

"Shoulda known. You know anyone called Jahna Johansen?"

His eyes went around the room a little before coming back to me. "This is like a joke, right?"

"Yeah, it's *like* a joke, except jokes are funny. Jahna Johansen's some kind of penny-ante hooker. She organizes entertainment for the convention trade."

The big man shook his head. He had heavy, looming features, a dark beard that showed through his skin even at eight in the morning, and smooth olive skin stretched across the craggy, almost lumpy contours of his face. "Must be indie," Carra said sagely. "Too little for the big guys to fuck with."

"So to speak. The girl's got a friend, though, a skinny little runt who could be Prince's stand-in."

"I used to have a dog named Prince."

"I used to have a tennis racquet named Prince. This joker's maybe five-five, five-six. About yea big around. Little bit of fuzz here." I traced around my mouth with the thumb and forefinger of my left hand. "Kind of whispers everything."

Carra was nodding. "Yeah, I know who you mean. Queer little pipsqueak. I don't know his name, though."

"Could you find out?"

"Maybe."

I sighed. "What do I have to do?"

The hood spread his hands. Each palm was the size of a dinner plate. "Hey, just stop by the house some time when you got a minute."

"House? What house?"

He rolled his eyes. "*The* house. The boss's house."

"Tarantino?"

Carra nodded.

Paul Tarantino was in charge of the Omaha operation. I had never met him. He came up from Chicago several months after my involvement with the local kids' ruckus. I had done my bit, and then the Grim Reaper had done his bit, and the upshot was that the torch got passed anyhow. The best laid plans, and like that.

"What's Tarantino want with me?"

Tom Carra shrugged. "I don't get paid to ask questions, Nebraska. The boss sends word he wants to talk to me, I go. I don't ask how come. Then he says do I know a private cop named Nebraska. I says yes. I don't ask how come he wants to know. Then he says I should look you up and invite you—*invite,* he says— to come by the house 'at your convenience.' I don't ask how come he—"

"I think I've got the idea now, Tom, thanks. Tarantino wants to see me and you don't know why."

His hands fanned again. "That's it."

There was no bad blood between me and Tarantino. No blood of any kind, as far as I knew. Except that, in a way, the mobster owed me a favor. Second-hand, you might say. Thanks to me, Tarantino's predecessor, Sal Gunnelli, had died in bed rather than being usurped, thus greasing the way for Tarantino to succeed him peaceably, easily. While it was too much to hope that the man was eternally in my debt, I couldn't imagine Tarantino bearing me any ill will. And I figured my "invitation" would have been far more forceful if Tarantino had something in mind deleterious to my well-being. So what the hell.

"What the hell," I said to Carra. "Tell him I'll be out later this morning."

Carra nodded and made for the day.

"Hang on a minute. You didn't take my lock out, did you?"

The big man smiled and patted a pocket of his sport coat, which jangled like a set of keys. "Would I do a thing like that?"

"Later this morning" turned out to be about as late as you can get and still have morning. I was moving none too rapidly, thanks to the combination of the beating I had taken and the muscles I had exerted trying to avoid said beating. No morning fast-walk for me today. Simply showering, shampooing, and shaving were difficult enough. I managed it with frequent rest stops on the toilet seat cover and the edge of the bathtub when the room started spinning too annoyingly.

I had a couple of cups of coffee and three aspirin for breakfast. I always take aspirins in threes. The theory is, I'm too absent-minded to remember to take two every four hours, but not so absent-minded that I can't get the *average* to work out to two every four hours. Besides, I hurt all over.

I tried calling Donna Berens, to see how she was faring after her little bender the night before, but the line was tied up. Alive, at least, I figured.

Elmo Lincoln called from Chicago. He hadn't had any luck tracing the number from Meredith's Rolodex. And it bugged him. You could hear it in his voice. "Man, whoever's got that number does *not* want you to know about it."

"I don't get it; doesn't the phone company have to keep records of that kind of thing?"

"Sure. But they *don't* have to tell you about it. And believe me, friend, they *aren't*. I've got a good friend in the business office down there; I called him yesterday to have him check it for me. He does that kind of stuff for me all the time. He called back yesterday afternoon and said he couldn't help me. Just like that— 'Sorry, Elmo, can't help you.' I said, 'What do you *mean* you can't help me,' but he'd hung up."

"Funny."

"Tee-*hee*. I've got a couple other things to try, though. I'll get back to you this afternoon."

I told him not to waste any more time on it, but he blew me off. It was a matter of pride. He wasn't about to be done in by seven lousy digits.

I called Kim Banner.

"One of your customers complained to me about you last night," I said.

"As long as it's you and not my boss," Banner said, unruffled. "Something I should worry about, I hope."

"Yeah, I'd go ahead and get my desk cleaned out if I were you." I filled her in on my conversation with Alexander Wayne—if "conversation" is the word.

"The man's gotta be two-thirds loopy," was Banner's assessment of the situation. "He ranted and raved about it to us, too, when we were out there yesterday."

"What's his main problem? In twenty-five words or fewer."

"I half wonder whether *he* doesn't half wonder whether the kid killed her. I call Thomas Wayne a kid even though he's my age, about."

"I call him a kid *because* he's my age, about. What's the official thinking *in re* Mr. Wayne?"

"Which Mr. Wayne?" Banner said coyly.

"Choose one."

"The official thinking is that this investigation has just gotten underway and, so far, has produced no conclusive results."

"Okay. What's the unofficial thinking?"

She sighed, and her breath buzzed heavily in the phone. "The kid—Thomas Wayne—is a hothead. You told us that yourself, and I could see it when we chatted with him. It was all he could do to keep a lid on it. But I don't know if he's *enough* of a hothead, you know? There's a gap between losing your temper and losing your mind. I'm not convinced Wayne has closed that gap."

"Is he alibied?"

"Yes and no. We haven't gotten the coroner's report yet, so we don't know for a fact when she was killed, Sunday night or Monday morning. Sunday night he's accounted for until about eleven-thirty. He was entertaining some out-of-town clients. Took 'em to a game, bought 'em dinner, stayed out late."

"Late for a school night, at least."

"He says he left them about eleven-thirty, and the two we've gotten hold of vouch for that, give or take fifteen, twenty minutes either way. He says he went home and to bed. His father, whom we talked to separately, of course, says *he* hit the hay after the ten o'clock news, read for a while, and fell asleep. He didn't hear Thomas come home. That leaves Thomas unaccounted for between eleven-thirty Sunday night and seven o'clock Monday morning, when he had breakfast with his father before going to work."

"So if Meredith was killed between eleven-thirty P.M. Sunday and seven A.M. Monday . . ."

"Then Thomas Wayne doesn't have an alibi, that's all. Like everyone else in town. It doesn't mean he did anything to have an alibi *for*."

"You're no fun anymore," I said. "I don't suppose either of them's considerate enough to have a record of any kind."

"Not in this burg; we're checking with Lincoln—state and PD. But what's with this 'either of them' business? You don't suspect the father just because he got worked up about us questioning his boy? Hell, his boy got worked up too."

I said, "So far the only one with any kind of motive for killing Meredith Berens is Thomas Wayne . . ."

"Says you."

"You have any other candidates, trot 'em out. Meanwhile, Thomas Wayne: His only reason for getting Meredith out of the picture, as near as we can guess, would be this engagement, whether real or a figment of Meredith's imagination."

"Okay . . ." she said as if she felt it was anything but. We've had similar conversations before, Kim Banner and I. Banner likes to pretend that, as a member of the Omaha Police Division, she is guided by facts and facts alone. Like Joe Friday, she assembles pieces, turning them this way and that until they either fit or must be discarded. Eventually, with dogged determination and a little luck, she pieces together a picture, or enough of one on which to hang a case. She further likes to pretend that a free agent such as myself isn't hindered by the need to stick to demonstrable facts. According to her, I can invent a scenario and then hunt for the facts to fit it. I don't have to worry about the captain, the chief, the DA, the mayor, the public. I just have to satisfy my client. That done, I collect my check and go home, letting someone else worry about the slow-turning mills of justice.

The truth, though, as usual, lies somewhere in between. And in that in-between place, Banner's approach and mine—or, let's say, the official and unofficial approaches—are more similar than different. It is neither a matter of merely assembling "clues" until the truth is revealed, nor a matter of collecting circumstantial evidence to clothe a preconception. It is both. It's taking this piece of evidence and trying to imagine how it came to be; then testing the possibility against that piece of evidence; then revising, discarding, inventing and reinventing as necessary. You need both halves of your brain, the objective and the imaginative, the half that processes cold data and the half that plays "what if." Whether you work in the public or private sector has little to do with it.

"Meredith was being a pest," I went on. "Either because she had gotten hold of this engagement idea and wouldn't let go, or because there had been an engagement that Thomas Wayne now wanted out of . . . or for some other reason that we don't know about."

"I wish I could be a fiction writer," Banner said dreamily.

I ignored her. "For whatever reason, Meredith was at best an embarrassment and at worst a threat to our young up-and-comer. Okay?"

"Sure, why not."

"But that state of affairs could be just as obvious to *Alexander* Wayne as Thomas. See? Maybe you're right—Thomas has a bad temper, but he's no killer. What about his old man?"

Nothing from the other end of the telephone line.

"We both saw *his* temper in action last night," I continued. "He basically offered, through me, to give Donna Berens a blank check to drop the case. Why? Because he's afraid of what the publicity might do to his son? Maybe. Because he's afraid his son might be guilty? Maybe. Because *he's* guilty? Maybe. You see what I'm getting at?"

"Maybe," Banner said flippantly. But not so flippantly that I couldn't tell there were wheels turning under that mop of dirty-blond hair. "Have you discussed Wayne's offer with your client?"

I wasn't the least bit sure I still had a client, but I didn't say anything about that. I merely said I hadn't spoken with Donna Berens yet today, which was perfectly true.

She said, "I'm going to have to talk with her today."

"She'll have a head on her," I said. "Let her have till noon if you want her to be good for anything."

"That's okay. I can take whatsername, Castelli, and the people at Meredith's office this morning yet. Swanson and Murdoch are at Meredith's building right now. Do the mother this afternoon. And I want to talk to that Johansen woman, too."

That made a couple of us.

I remembered the house, one of those big-ass ramblers set way back from the street in one of the more secluded and exclusive pockets of the secluded and exclusive development known as Regency. The yard sloped gently upward and back from the street, although I suppose when you have that much yard you call it "grounds." The house had a very gentle angle to it, subtly suggesting wings that pushed out from the double doors at center. The roof rose high on a steep pitch, the eaves hung low to give the house a shaded, shielded look. The house was a pale gray, a Cape Cod gray, with charcoal trim. A high wall surrounded the yard—grounds—or at least appeared to. At the edges of the lot dense foliage took over. No telling what was in there.

I don't know how the deed was made out, but the house belonged to the Mob.

Sal Gunnelli had lived there when he headed the Omaha operation. That was the one and only time I had been to the house. Now Gunnelli was long gone and the house, with the other perquisites and privileges, had been passed to Gunnelli's successor, Paul Tarantino.

There was a wrought-iron gate that closed off the long curved driveway from the riffraff that might blow in from the street. The gate was electrically operated from the house. The last time I'd been summoned to the place I had had to be admitted. This morning the gate stood open. I couldn't decide whether that was a good sign or not.

I put a few miles on the car by pushing it to the top of the long driveway.

By the time I got the engine shut off and got out of the car and got the door closed, one of the two overgrown doors at the front of the house was open. A man stood at the threshold. It had taken me longer than usual to get out of the car, but not *that* long. I smoothed my tie into my jacket—yeah, I had put on a coat *and* a tie—and glanced around for the surveillance cameras. Unobtrusively, I hoped, though I don't know why I should have cared. I didn't spot any cameras. But it was a safe bet that the man in the doorway didn't spend his days sitting there watching for cars to pull up. There probably was an electric-eye beam across the driveway at the gate. I hobbled toward the man.

"Mr. Nebraska?" I confessed.

"My name's Ballard. I work for Mr. Tarantino."

He was younger than me, and in better shape. Not that he was a bruiser. The average college student is younger than me, and in better shape.

"I'm expected, I see."

"Yes, sir. Mr. Tarantino's inside."

"Inside" had changed. There used to be a wide, open entry, beyond which lay the living room. Now the entry had been closed off, like an airlock between the great outdoors and the inner sanctum. I could see why they didn't worry so much about the gate these days. Security had been moved indoors.

No effort had been made here to hide the surveillance camera, a black Sony CCD Handycam in a corner where two walls met the ceiling. CCD cameras are expensive, but they're good for surveillance or any other application that requires a camera to remain stationary for some time. They use microchips to capture an image, so there are no tubes in which to "burn in" a picture. Also handy if you need some footage of the noonday sun.

Except for the camera and a small crescent-top table, the room was bare. Ballard took something from the table. A hand-held metal detector. He passed it down my right side and up my left, then forward and back. Then he took a little black box, somewhat larger than a pack of cigarettes, from his coat pocket, depressed a button on the box, and waved it in front of me at chest level.

"I do my act without wires," I said.

He smiled politely. Then he put away the black box and pulled out a blue-gray box that had been clipped to the waistband of his pants. It looked like a pocket pager. He worked a stud on the box a few times, holding his hand in such a way that I couldn't see the number of times he worked it or how long he held it each time. After a few seconds the heavy security lock on the door into the house buzzed and Ballard yanked it open for me. It took some yanking, too. I guessed it had a core of solid steel.

I preceded him into the house and he preceded me through it. The place had been done over entirely since my previous visit. I don't know why that should have surprised me, but it did. In Gunnelli's day the place had been sparsely furnished, decorated in a spare, cold fashion that was artificial and uninviting. Then it was a page from a magazine; now it was a house. An expensively outfitted house, to be sure, but a house like the kind people live in. Comfortable furniture and lots of it, thick carpeting, pictures on the walls, junk on shelves and tabletops. Ballard took me into the sunken living room, asked if he could get me anything, and invited me to have a seat while he went in search of his boss. I decided against sitting. I'd only have to get up again when Tarantino showed, and all this up and down was murder on my battered carcass.

Paul Tarantino was younger than he looked on TV, older than he looked in the papers. Call him fifty-five. He was of medium build, about my size, but I'm pleased to report that he carried more of a gut than I did. His hair was dark and thinning, parted low over his left ear and swirled across his forehead and plastered down with hairspray. That always fools 'em. His eyes were dark and deceptively mellow—I say "deceptively" because I noticed, as we spent time together, that they were never still; they darted constantly, observing, appraising. He had a great Roman beak of a nose, with dramatically flared nostrils, and a thin, bloodless gash of a mouth that, with the nose and the dark, darting eyes, gave him something of the look of a bird of prey. Yet his voice was soft, even cultured, and his handshake was no knuckle-buster.

"Mr. Nebraska? Paul Tarantino. Thanks for coming out."

We sat, him in a ladder-backed rocking chair, me—gingerly—on a mushroom-colored sectional.

I said, "I don't get invited here very often, so when it happens I'm . . . curious."

Tarantino crossed his legs and brushed imaginary lint from the topmost knee. He wore designer jeans faded with scientific precision, an expensive dress shirt worn open-collar, cuffs turned back with deliberate casualness over the pushed-back sleeves of a gray cashmere cardigan. Beat-up tassel Loafers with no socks. A heavy gold watch was nestled in the thick dark hair at his left wrist.

"Curious about what?" he wondered quietly.

"I'm a heckuva nice guy, Mr. Tarantino, but the last time I was asked up to de big house it was because I had something that the owner, or resident, perhaps I should say, wanted. This time I have nothing. Nothing, that is, outside of my incomparable charm, good looks, and modesty, and I've *always* had those. Why should you just be getting interested in them now?"

He smiled politely. The guy didn't come off like a gangster. He reminded me of an accountant. Which, I suppose, he was in a way.

"Mr. Nebraska . . ." Tarantino paused and smiled almost shyly. "We're awfully formal this morning. Why don't you call me Paul and I'll call you . . ." He made it a question.

"Nebraska's fine."

The shy smile grew into an uncertain grin. "No first name? What do your friends call you?"

" 'Nebraska,' mostly, outside of a few choice monickers on special occasions. Of course I have a first name, Paul. I'm just not wild about it."

He shrugged in a uniquely Mediterranean way. "Nebraska, you did the previous occupant of this house, Salvatore Gunnelli, a great favor."

"Not exactly," I corrected. "I didn't give him what he wanted. But I also didn't give it to his rival. Al Manzetti. Without it, Crazy Al was stymied. He didn't dare move against Gunnelli. In the end, someone moved against Crazy Al."

Tarantino was nodding. "I know the story. My point is, by not siding with Manzetti, you did Gunnelli a favor. It didn't go unnoticed. I was still in Chicago at the time, but I heard about it there. If you know anything about the history of this organization I work for, you'll know it prizes loyalty and friendship above all. Many things have changed since the early days, but not that. We still need to know where people stand. We need to know which people will do exactly what they say they'll do, whether they're friends of ours or not. *You* did exactly what you told Sal Gunnelli you would do. That counts for something."

I wanted to ask what. In fact, I did ask.

Tarantino smiled. "We've left you alone. For, what, almost five years now? Think about it: you possess some information that could be dangerous to us—"

"I defused most of the danger myself." I was referring to my forcing the resignation of a Mob-backed politician. If I had been foolish enough to have wanted to play touchy-feely with the big kids I wouldn't have insisted on the resignation but rather on a monthly stipend for keeping silent.

"Troublesome, then," Tarantino said equably. "Bothersome. But you had proven as good as your word once; we decided to wait and see if you would continue to be so."

"Did I pass?" I was under no illusion that the set Paul Tarantino ran with would think twice about flattening me like a bug if it suited their purposes. And *wouldn't* think twice about flattening me like a bug if it suited their purposes. The reason they hadn't was easy to figure. Their organization, as Tarantino had called it, existed and exists not so much on loyalty as obligation. Who owes what to whom. They owed me a favor because of what I had done or hadn't done for Tarantino's predecessor years ago. Tarantino admitted that easily. And then immediately pointed out that *I* owed *them* a favor because I had been eating solid food, or any kind of food at all, for these past few years, courtesy of them. Charming crowd.

He spread his hands. "What would you say?"

"No, I mean did I pass *today's* test? You didn't ask me out here just to be neighborly. There's something you want. That you don't seem to be zeroing in on the point tells me there's some sort of test I've been undergoing. How'm I doing?"

Something like annoyance flashed across Tarantino's birdlike features, but it was gone just as quickly. He glanced from me to the open archway that separated the living room from the south wing of the house and back. When he spoke again it was with a slightly raised voice. "All right, Mr. Nebraska." We were back to being formal. "You *have* been . . . tested, as you put it. Whether you've 'passed' or not, I can't say . . ."

He let it hang and glanced toward the archway again.

The man who had been standing around the corner, out of sight, listening in, stepped into the room.

chapter
14

The newcomer was a little older than Tarantino but far slimmer. Slimmer in a way that suggested he had been a big man who, through illness or injury, had lost a great deal of weight which was only slowly coming back on. His shoulders were broad but his long face was pasty and just this side of haggard. He had thick hair that was more gray than black and which he wore combed back and parted high. He moved into the room slowly, almost delicately, and silently. He was in full dress uniform: gray pinstripe suit, high-gloss black wing tips, yellow power-tie, horn-rimmed glasses. Ralph Lauren frames was my guess. He negotiated the single step down into the living room with some noticeable uncertainty, then crossed the room unsmilingly toward us.

Tarantino stood and so did I, albeit reluctantly, my tortured muscles all protesting in unison.

I expected Tarantino to make introductions, but he remained still. There was a subtle but definite shift in the atmosphere of the room. Thirty seconds earlier, or less, Paul Tarantino was clearly in command; now, although there had been no noticeable change in Tarantino's demeanor, power or authority or *droit du seigneur*, or whatever it was had undoubtedly transferred to the newcomer.

And no wonder. I recognized the unhealthy-looking one as Tarantino's boss, and lots of bosses' boss, one of those "reputed Mob leaders" you read so much about and one of the top three bosses in the country. His unrobust appearance he owed to someone having served him five .38-caliber slugs for dessert in one of his favorite restaurants nearly eighteen months ago. The news reports said he wasn't expected to live. The way he looked and moved today, I wondered if he had.

He stopped five feet from where I stood and sized me up with dark, liquid eyes behind slightly tinted lenses. While he did that, I did the same thing to him. Despite his resemblance to the picture on a bottle of iodine, he was a strong man. Not physically, maybe, not now, but with what the books call "inner strength," which is perhaps more important. I realized two other things as well. The first was that there was no point in letting Elmo Lincoln continue to beat his brains out trying to track down that telephone number in Area Code 312. The second was that I was about to meet Meredith Berens's father.

"Michael Berenelli," he said on cue.

He didn't extend his hand and neither did I.

For a long moment it looked like we were going to have a stare-down; then Berenelli turned and glanced at Tarantino. The two men exchanged little half-nods and some kind of unspoken or previously spoken message passed between them. Then Berenelli slowly seated himself at the other end of the sectional on which I had been sitting, at a right angle to my location, and Tarantino silently evaporated from the room.

They called him "Baron Mike"—I suspect these monickers exist more to please reporters than because mobsters are enamored of them—and, meeting him for the first time, I realized that the handle derived not just from his surname but also from his bearing, his carriage. Sick as he was, he still comported himself like a baron or a duke or something. I sat again and waited.

"Now you know why I wanted to meet you." The voice didn't fit the frail frame: It was deep and strong, although a ragged, congested kind of rattle rested on top of it.

"Yes and no," I said. "I know who you are—I don't just mean that I recognize you from your pictures; I know *who* you are. I'm sorry about your daughter. I assumed that's what's brought you to town. But I don't see what it has to do with me." I told the truth when I told him I was sorry about Meredith. Not for his sake; for hers. A man like Michael Berenelli deserves whatever he gets, but Meredith Berens was an innocent.

"My daughter . . ." the Baron said ruminatively, as if he was hearing the word for the first time and trying it out on his tongue. "Someone I never knew. Her mother . . . Her mother and I sep-arated when she was very young. You know this?"

His eyes had been resting unfocused on a heavy glass ashtray on the coffee table that sat between us, diagonally. They came to my face when he asked the question. I nodded.

"They moved back here," he continued in a kind of monotone, as if delivering a synopsis he had rehearsed too often. "I tried to keep in touch, I wanted to, but Donna was very good at shielding Meredith from me. She turned the girl against me, filled her daughter with her own hatred for me." His shoulders went up and down in a mechanical imitation of a shrug. "Eventually I stopped trying. It seemed better for everyone. I almost forgot I even had a daughter." The black eyes bored into me from behind their glass walls. "Almost."

It was as I had guessed. Quite a few months earlier, from out of the blue, Meredith had called her father. "Of course, the first thing I think is that something has happened to her mother," Berenelli said. "But no, she's just calling to talk. To talk. After so many years . . ." So they talked. And talked, and talked. The call grew into many calls, into an exchange of letters, into Meredith visiting Wilmette. She had never known her father, and she had known her mother perhaps too well. Now she was making up for lost time, or trying to—blissfully ignorant, as are we all, of how finite our time really is.

"She was such a little girl when her mother took her away," Berenelli was saying. "Now she was all grown-up. Grown-up and pretty." The eyes swiveled to my face. "She was a very pretty girl," he said, not argumentatively but informatively.

I agreed. But the picture in my mind had been taken in the morgue.

The Baron sighed. "And so, after so many years—a little girl's whole lifetime—I had my daughter back. My little girl. Someone had taken her away from me, but she had come back. On her own, because she *wanted* to come back." He turned his face from me, suddenly interested in a three-panel print on the south wall. "Now someone has taken her away from me again, and this time she will never come back. Do you have any idea how that feels?"

I didn't, of course, so I kept silent.

"I understand Donna hired you to look for Meredith," Berenelli said, as if switching gears. "That was a bad idea." He looked at me expressionlessly. "Nothing personal, you understand, but it should have been kept . . . internal. She should have called me. If she didn't want to talk to me, she should have called Paul." He cocked his head toward the archway through which Tarantino had disappeared at the beginning of the audience. Then he gave me a look I didn't get, a half-amused, half-knowing kind of look. "But I guess you've shown you can be trusted."

"That's what Mrs. Berens, or Berenelli, I guess—"

"Berens," he said with some distaste. "She had it changed after the divorce."

"—said. That's what *everyone* says. I didn't understand her then and I don't understand you now. How does she know me? How do you, or Tarantino, except second- or third-hand?"

The mobster smiled. Either that or he grimaced in pain. It was hard to tell. "She didn't tell you?" he said. "Well, she wouldn't, that one. Too worried about her 'image.' She always was. How would it look, what would people say. Her *image,* her daughter's image—what good does any of it do anyone now? What people think, who cares? What people *do,* that's all that's important." He had worked himself up a little; now he calmed himself with an obvious effort. "Before Donna's name was Berens, it was Berenelli. You know that now. And before it was Berenelli it was Gunnelli. When I first met her she was Donna Maria Gunnelli, straight out of school, a cute little Italian stringbean with big brown eyes and the shiniest, blackest hair you've ever seen."

"Not to mention an old man who just happened to be running this town for the boys back in Chicago."

The Baron shrugged.

Much was clear now. Why Donna Berens had been so elusive on the subject of her ex-husband, why she had been coy about how she knew me, about the "favor" I had done her "friend" years ago, why the telephone number on Meredith's Rolodex had had no name against it, why pages were missing from her diary, why the man who answered it when I called—not Berenelli—had been so unhelpful, why Elmo Lincoln couldn't track down the number's owner. Many questions remained—near the top of the list, who killed Meredith Berens and why—but many had been answered.

Berenelli was still talking. ". . . people in my organization who could have handled it, and should have. But since she saw fit to turn it over to an outsider . . ." He shrugged fatalistically. "I want you to continue your investigation."

"There's nothing to continue," I pointed out. "My job was to find Meredith. I found her."

"Now your job is to find her killer."

I had seen that one coming from way up in the stands. "I may already have a client," I said. "Your former wife."

"I thought you said your investigation was over."

"Last night she asked me to help her. I'm uncertain what she meant, and I haven't spoken with her today. Until I know what kind of help she wants, or whether she still wants it, it'd be unethical for me to take on another client connected with the same investigation. Plus, as I seem to always be telling people, the police are experts at this sort of thing. They have the resources, both in manpower and facilities. Me, I just have these clean-cut good looks, an eleven-year-old Chevrolet, and a bottom-of-the-line telephone-answering machine. Plus, you yourself must have resources that are pretty impressive. You've as good as said so yourself. Surely your people . . ."

Berenelli raised one hand. The shirt cuff around his wrist was too big. "You're right, you're right. About everything. But you must understand . . ." he paused, allowing himself a meager, cadaverous smile ". . . the police and I, we don't have a great deal of fondness for one another."

"Even so—"

"I want this sonofabitch for myself!" He didn't shout, he didn't even really raise his voice, but he cut me off with a sudden vehemence that was as good as a shout, as effective at shutting me up. "*I* want him," he continued more easily. "I. For *me*. Not for some white-livered judge, some overpriced defense lawyer, some bleeding-heart jury. For *me*." He tapped his sunken chest, hard, with a forefinger. It thudded emptily.

The sick man got to his feet. He had to pull his legs to one side and roll onto one hip and lift himself by using his arms on the back of the sectional, but he got to his feet and moved with shuffling, uncertain steps to the French doors at the far end of the room. Beyond the doors was a patio that had been covered and enclosed since my last visit there. Beyond the patio the yard, or grounds, if you like, stretched halfway to Wyoming. Berenelli looked off into that distance.

"Word has gone out," he said after some time. "Word has gone out that the *bastard* who did this is to be found. But there are other matters, matters of business, that must be handled. I can't afford to devote one hundred percent of my people's resources to

a . . . a *personal* matter. It wouldn't be right. It wouldn't be wise."
He half-turned, his hands clasped behind him, and glanced at me.
"It could be dangerous, you understand? There are people—rivals—who do nothing but wait for the moment that I am distracted." He turned to the doors again. "Salvatore Gunnelli had
many friends. They will want justice for his granddaughter's murderer. Still, however . . . business is business."

The Baron moved away from the French doors and circled the
room haltingly. I wished he'd go and sit down again. His moving
around made me nervous. I was afraid he was going to take a
tumble. He didn't, though, and ultimately wound up standing behind me, his hands resting on the back of the sectional, one on
either side of my shoulders.

"As far as your current client is concerned," he said, "you will
hear from her later today. She will either instruct you to continue
your work for her, with your assignment now being to find Meredith's murderer, or she will terminate her agreement with you
and pay you, in full, in cash, immediately. In which case you will
be free to accept my offer of employment."

I remembered what Donna Berens had told me last night: *When
he beat me up he always made sure the bruises didn't show.*

I said, "Must be nice to be so sure of one's persuasive skills."

Berenelli said nothing for a long time. I couldn't see his face,
even if I could have read what was going on behind those dark
eyes. "It's easy to be persuasive when you narrow a person's choices
before you present them," he said slowly, instructively. "Donna
will be given a choice. In or out. If she chooses to remain in, she
will follow my instructions. I have let her have her way for too
many years. Twice it cost me my daughter. Now I have *my* way."

The ball was in my court. About the last place I wanted it. There
are two outfits that I make a point of never playing games with.
One of them is the Mob. The other is the IRS. I try to stay out
of their respective paths for one reason: Either of them can flatten
you flatter than you ever thought a person could be flattened. It
doesn't pay to be cute with either of them.

It occurred to me that I hadn't had a vacation in a long time.
Maybe now would be a good time for one. As I had told Dianna
Castelli, you make choices. I could choose not to be involved in
what had all the markings of a full-blown vendetta in the making.
Couldn't I? Sure. But then everything would be even between me
and the mob—Paul Tarantino had made that pretty clear—and

the next time I found myself painted into a corner with them . . . well, time would tell.

On the other hand, if I strung along with Michael Berenelli I would have not only the Omaha people in my debt but also one of the Chicago, and therefore national, big shots. That didn't sound like such a bad idea, for a guy in my line.

Then, too, there was the picture of Meredith Berens. Not the one I carried in my pocket, the one I carried in my head, the one of her bruised and shattered and lifeless on a slab. The picture would stay with me for a long time. Maybe it would never go away, maybe it would join all the other pictures up there in the dark, cold attic of my mind, always there, ever-present. But maybe I could stand to look at it more if I knew I had at least tried to do something about it.

I looked at Michael Berenelli, who had returned to his place on the sectional. He was looking at me.

I didn't like the man. I didn't like what he did for a living. Not that I was all that keen on what *I* did for a living, either, but at least I didn't make my miserable salary on the misery and degradation of other people. Or if I did—for when do people turn to someone like me except when they're miserable—at least I wasn't the cause. And not only did I not put women on the streets, or take and sell dirty pictures of runaway girls and boys, or feed on people's compulsions and addictions, or skim money from the tops of countless otherwise reputable undertakings, I also didn't whine about it when someone did something shitty to me and mine.

No, I didn't like Berenelli. I wouldn't have liked him if he had been a florist or a traffic cop or a high school principal. I didn't like his type. I didn't like his veneer of civility, the cloak of decency that he put on and took off like his expensive suit whenever it was convenient. I would rather he had been a thug. I wouldn't have liked him any better, but I would have had more respect for him.

I said, "If I have any luck identifying this maniac, I'll have to tell the police."

Berenelli said, "Everyone does what he has to do. Do you have anyone in mind? Suspects?"

The answer was yes but I said no. I had seen how these people work, and I didn't want either or both of the Waynes found in a lonely ditch somewhere with bullet holes in the backs of their heads.

I recalled my meeting, years ago, with Salvatore Gunnelli in that same house. Out on the back patio. I had a stack of blue pictures, blackmail photos, that Gunnelli wanted to buy. I wasn't selling. He wanted to buy my assurance that I wouldn't sell them to his rival, Al Manzetti. I wasn't selling *anything,* I told him. But he pressed a thousand-dollar note on me and I was too gutless, or greedy, to refuse it. I made a big deal of keeping the "filthy" lucre separate from my nice, clean, hard-earned lucre, and blew the wad on a horse the first chance I got. I swiped the idea from a Ross Macdonald novel, I think. Now I had at least tacitly agreed to take on a job for a man who was far worse than Sal Gunnelli ever hoped to be. I must have mellowed in my old age. Or maybe I'd just grown less naive.

Of course, Gunnelli wanted me to do something that was patently and obviously *wrong* and which would have injured an innocent girl. Now, in this instance, the innocent girl had already been injured, beyond all redemption, and there was nothing inherently wrong with what the Baron was asking me to do. Just with what he wanted to do if I succeeded. That didn't make Berenelli's money any cleaner than the money I wouldn't sully myself with years ago. But if I've grown less naive, I've come to realize dirty money is all around. The tentacles of organized crime, to say nothing of the unorganized and disorganized varieties, are all around us. That's not to say, What the hell, I'm getting mine. It's just to say, Don't be such a Boy Scout all the time. Like it or not, we all traffic with the criminal world on some level, to some degree. You buy a stick of furniture that's delivered by men whose union is controlled by organized crime. You buy a "gray market" camera or computer. You shop at a market whose supplier is a front for the Mob. We won't even *talk* about the little dime bag of recreational goodies you buy from your friendly neighborhood dealer, who's only a step or two removed from the you-know-what. If that much.

Cynicism. The beginning of apathy. But Swift—Jonathan, not Tom—said, "Vision is the art of seeing things invisible." As I've gotten a little older, I hope I've gotten a little smarter. I hope I can see some of those things invisible. Not so that I can avoid them, necessarily. Not so that I can embrace them, either. Just so I can see them.

I could see Michael Berenelli plenty clear. I could see what he wanted. He wanted me to find his daughter's killer, sure; but he also wanted some of his minions to keep an eye on me. That's why he didn't fuss when I said I'd turn Meredith's killer over to the badges if I found him. He figured that when I found him *he'd* find him too, and there'd be no time for the cops to get involved.

Things invisible.

I'd have to keep my eyes skinned.

chapter

15

She had a head the size of a beach ball and her eyes were dull and her lips were parted in a way that suggested they didn't have much feeling to them. She had made a half-hearted swipe at getting the dark hair arranged properly, but it wasn't good enough. She wore no makeup, but that was only part of the reason she looked so pale. The rest of the reason was that she was still suffering from the effects of too much liquor taken too fast on an empty stomach, to say nothing of the event that had caused her to attack the liquor in the first place.

Which also explained why she was still in her robe, a white terry number with aqua stripes, even though it was well past noon.

I said, "Good afternoon, Donna. How're you doing today?" An idiotic expression—*how are you doing?*—but, like the rest of the population, I find that it fairly leaps from the tongue before I can do anything about it.

She mumble-grumbled something and shut the door behind me and shuffled into the kitchen. I ditched my sport coat in a chair and followed. Now that I knew her parentage, I recognized Donna Berens's décor as being remarkably similar to that of Paul Tarantino's house back when Sal Gunnelli lived there. Cold and empty. In the kitchen, Donna had a tall white pot on the table in front of her, a big mug from which a thin thread of steam rolled lazily, an unopened newspaper, and an untouched slice of black toast on which a pat of margarine slowly melted.

"Coffee," she mumbled, with a distracted wave toward the white pot. Then she went back to concentrating on the contents of her mug.

I opened a couple of cupboards until I found where the rest of the mugs were kept, took one down, figured out how the pouring arrangement on the thermal pot worked, made the transfer, and leaned against the counter. Sitting was okay, as far as my aching muscles were concerned, and standing was okay, and lying down was okay, but the activity involved in going from one position to another was NG.

"Have you eaten anything?"

She gave me a look. "Please," she said sourly.

"It'll help. So will aspirin, and lots to drink."

She grunted. I pushed off, went into the bathroom, and rifled the medicine cabinet. She had a plastic bottle of regular-strength— whatever "regular strength" was—Tylenol Caplets on the lower shelf. Weren't the Caplets one of the families in *Romeo and Juliet*? According to the bottle, I wasn't supposed to use the product if the foil inner seal was broken, but it didn't tell me how I was supposed to get the medication out without breaking the foil seal. I shook out three Caplets and ate them, then shook out two for my patient. Then I went back to the kitchen and poured a tall glass of water and put it and the painkillers in front of Donna.

"Here," I said. "The pain-reliever hospitals use most. Because they can get it the cheapest."

She looked at the pills, looked at me, then, fatalistically, took them one at a time, following each with a tentative sip of water. "How come you're so good to me," she said sarcastically.

I glanced at my wristwatch. "Any time now you'll be having company. The police. They told me they'd give you until after noon, but they have questions that must be asked. It won't be easy, probably, and you'll have to be in some kind of shape to take it."

Donna nodded and sipped some more water. "What kind of questions? Didn't we take care of everything at the . . . yesterday?"

"Yesterday was to satisfy the bureaucrats. Today the cops will want to know everything about Meredith. What she was like, whom she knew, whether anyone had anything against her—the whole nine yards." I paused. "They'll have questions about you, too, Donna. They'll need to know about you and your relationship with Meredith, and they'll need to know about the rest of Meredith's family, too. They won't be put off as easily as I was, either. In fact, they won't be put off at all."

She said nothing, having gone back to inspecting her coffee. I said, "I met your husband today."

I had hoped for some kind of reaction, but she would accommodate me only to the extent of glancing at me and saying, "Ex-husband" before returning to her inspection.

"He wants to hire me to look for Meredith's killer."

Nothing.

"I said I couldn't commit until I had spoken with you. Last night you said you wanted my help. But I don't know what you m—"

"Do what he wants," Donna said in a weary monotone. She looked at me, her face matching her voice, and I realized that there was more to her current state than shock and a hangover.

"Then you've talked with him already."

She moved her mouth into something that you might have called a smile. "I listened. *He* talked. I—" The smile vanished. "Listen, just do what he wants, okay?"

I said, "You're in the hot seat. I can tell Berenelli I'm not interested, I don't want to get involved. That takes you off the hook."

She grunted a laugh. "He'll think I had something to do with your decision. No, it's better in the long run, for *both* of us, if you just go along with him."

I shrugged. "All right."

"The arrangements have all been made. One of his . . . people came by a while ago with some money I'm supposed to give to you. An advance or a retainer or whatever you call it."

"You already paid me a retainer, and the meter's still running."

"That was for me; this is for him. I'm supposed to use some of the money to pay you what I already owe you and the rest of it to get you going on what *he* wants. You're supposed to give me a receipt. If you need more, for expenses or anything, you're supposed to call me. Everything, all the transactions, will be between you and me. That keeps *him* clean. There's no connection to you."

"Except *you*. Donna, I can understand why you didn't want to come out and tell me that Meredith's father and grandfather both worked for the Mob. But you understand that you can't keep that from the police, don't you? They may already know who your father was."

She bobbed her head toward one shoulder in a tired, defeated who-cares gesture.

"Try to eat some of that toast." I looked at my watch again. The cops, probably Kim Banner herself, would be on the doorstep any minute now, or maybe any hour now. You never know with those guys. Sometimes they seem to be everywhere at once, sometimes they seem to have disappeared entirely. *Seem* to have. "I gather they leaned on Thomas Wayne pretty hard last night," I said, as if Donna Berens had been keeping right up there with my thoughts.

"Why not," she said lifelessly. "He killed her, didn't he?"

"What do you know about Wayne?"

"Nothing." She drank some coffee, made a face, and drank some more. "I never heard of him until you told me about him last night."

"Never? Meredith never mentioned him to you? You never met him?"

"Didn't we already go through all this?"

"And you'll have to go through it all again with the police. What about Thomas's father?"

"What about him?"

"Alexander Wayne. Does the name mean anything?"

"Not to me."

"Your daughter never talked about him either?"

She said nothing, which I took to mean that she didn't think it was worth saying anything.

"What about someone named Jahna Johansen?"

"What about him?"

"Her. Never mind." More to myself than to Donna I said, "It's funny Meredith wouldn't have mentioned Thomas to you. If she was planning on marrying him."

"That's what you say *he* says. I don't believe it."

She meant she didn't believe the engagement story. She was sticking by her guns, holding fast to her belief that she and her daughter had had a close relationship and that the girl told her everything that was going on in her life. Obviously not so. Obviously there was much in Meredith's young and short life that she kept hidden from various parties. But the engagement, or at least Meredith's belief that there was an engagement, was fact. Dianna Castelli and Steve Lehman and Thomas Wayne all agreed on that one point: Meredith had talked about an engagement.

Which, as always, brought things around to Thomas Wayne.

If Meredith had a secret life, then so too did Wayne. A secret past, more accurately. Alexander Wayne's attitude and actions the night before pointed in that direction. They pointed at something hidden that he wanted kept hidden. What? That Thomas once had a girlfriend who was killed in some kind of automobile accident? If in fact it was an accident. All of my nice theories about Alexander Wayne having as much motive as his son for wanting Meredith Berens out of the way might work just as well on the other girl's death, if the other girl's death wasn't accidental.

Too many ifs.

I didn't figure I could stroll into the Wayne house and invite Alexander to tell me a little more about himself. Thomas might be more workable, if I could doctor up a way to make his quick temper work to my advantage. And Alexander wasn't entirely out of the equation either. I just had to figure out how to play things.

When I left Donna Berens the police hadn't yet shown themselves, which was all right with me. When I asked her if she wanted me to hang around until they did and hold her hand after they did she said no, which was even more all right with me.

The afternoon was cool and blustery and gray. The sky was a solid gray, no clouds, that hung so close that you kept feeling the impulse to duck. No precipitation, not yet, at any rate, and the puddles that remained on the pavement were vanishing fast in the breeze.

I put some miles on the car, which was about the last thing it needed, but which helped make me as sure as I could get about whether or not I was being tailed. More private-eye talk. I wasn't, as far as I could tell.

When I felt reasonably safe, I made what was getting to be a habitual pilgrimage to the building that contained Midlands Realty and Development Corporation, in virtual certainty that young Wayne would not be in. I was not disappointed. I made up a story about having an appointment with him for that hour, an appointment made last night "at the house," to explain why the efficient young thing behind the reception desk had no knowledge of it. She looked through an appointment register the size of a ledger book and, can you believe it, announced that my name appeared not at all for today or any other day this week, nor had Wayne mentioned it to her this morning.

I was not amused.

Frowning, she said she would check Wayne's personal appointment book if I would wait there a moment. I agreed. She went away and came back and said there was nothing about an appointment with me on his desk calendar either. I made what I felt was an appropriate comment about "this Mickey Mouse outfit" and left. I had what I wanted. I had read it upside-down in the big appointment book when the secretary took off for Wayne's office. The book was upside-down, I mean, not me, but I could nevertheless decipher the entry for Wayne's current location as well as his appointments for the rest of the afternoon.

It was one of those big, shiny new office buildings that they don't seem to be able to get filled. It had been up for a couple of years now, looming over Maple from one of the curvy streets west of Ninetieth, and it still had the big banner across the Maple Street side, near the top of the building, telling you where to call for rental information.

One thing: It was easy to find a parking space in the asphalt lot alongside the building. Which I did after driving around the neighborhood with an eye peeled for a car or cars that seemed to be keeping the same pointless route as me. There were none.

I went in and wandered around. The high-ceilinged lobby was occupied by a Thai restaurant that had a nice open-air look to it and which explained why they weren't having a lot of luck moving the "choice office and retail space" the lobby card spoke of: Who could get any work done in a building that smelled of cooking food all morning and cooling grease all afternoon?

The lobby card referred potential renters to a suite on the mezzanine that hung over the restaurant on three sides. A renter I wasn't, but Suite M-100 seemed as good a place as any to start.

I went up and went in.

A middle-aged woman who had shoved too much of herself into too little navy-and-red knit dress sat behind a bleached-oak desk just inside the suite's double doors. There was enough thick maroon carpet and textured beige walls and artfully neutral artwork to suggest that the failure to fill the building hadn't yet driven the management to anything so desperate as belt-tightening. "Can I help you," the woman said in a routine monotone that suggested that helping me was the furthest thing from her mind.

I said, "You can tell me why places like this always install double doors but end up locking one of them, usually the one someone is most likely to try opening first."

She looked up from the papers on her desk. "I beg your pardon?"

"Skip it. I need to see Thomas Wayne. Is he here?"

"Yes, but he's in a meeting with Mr. D'Agosto . . ." She glanced to her left, and so did I, toward a bleached-oak door that bore a skinny vertical window and a plastic-wood sign that read CONFERENCE ROOM.

"This is important," I said. "Would you mind getting him?"

"I can't interrupt them!" She managed to almost appear shocked by the suggestion.

I hurt all over and I was tired and crabby and I had spent the day dancing minuets with mobsters and their ex-wives and I didn't feel like dancing anymore and, besides, every so often a guy just feels like being an asshole.

"Fine," I said, and crossed to the door.

Her reflexes were lousy, and I was into the conference room before she could stop me. I'll give her credit: She didn't try making excuses to her boss. When she saw she was too late she stopped and stood there in the doorway behind me, awaiting instructions.

There were four men and two women in the room, all of whom looked up in varying degrees of surprise, one of whom got over it fast and replaced it with a look of extreme vexation and came to his feet.

"Goddammit, Nebraska, what's the big idea?"

"We need to talk, Wayne. Miss Whatserface here said she couldn't interrupt you, so I had to do it myself. These nice people will excuse you . . ."

"Like hell," he said heatedly. "Call my office and make an appointment."

There was a vacant chair not four feet from me. I went and made it unvacant. It hurt, but it was good theater. "As far as I'm concerned these nice people can hear what I have to say. That is, unless *you* mind. I need to discuss a rumor I heard about you. Something about an old girlfriend . . ." I let it trail.

It took him maybe three seconds to catch the allusion. When he did he tried to stare me down. Bad move. He had no way of knowing he was facing off with the stare-down king of Harrison Elementary. He folded after about twenty seconds, mumbled excuses to the befuddled audience, and headed for the door. I stood up.

"Thanks for the use of the hall," I said, and followed Wayne.

He was waiting for me outside of the suite, at the rail of the mezzanine.

"Jesus Christ, Nebraska, have you lost your *mind?* Those are important clients in there, important people—"

"Meredith Berens was an important person, too, Wayne. As far as I'm concerned she still is. As far as some other people are concerned, too."

He sighed with heavy anger. "The police," he said. "I've already been put through the wringer by them, Nebraska. I answered their questions, I told them everything I knew. I sure as *hell* don't have to go through it again for your benefit. If you want to—"

"Not just the police," I said mysteriously. "Tell me about this girlfriend of yours who got killed. Not Meredith; the *other* one."

Wayne's eye widened for an instant, then narrowed to dangerous slits. "You son of a bitch," he hissed. "I don't know what the hell you're talking about."

"Bullshit. You gave yourself away inside, there." I jerked my head toward the half-useless double doors behind us. "Try again."

He had a slim leather attaché with him, which he now balanced on the flat steel rail, crossing his arms on the case and looking down on the Asian restaurant workers cleaning up after the noon crowd and readying the place for the evening clientele. "Fuck," he sighed. Then he looked at me sideways, head down, shoulders hunched. "You really are a son of a bitch, you know that?"

"I have it on the best authority."

I like to blame what followed on my physical state, which at the moment was far from good, but I'm not sure I'd have seen it coming even if I had been one hundred percent. "It" was Thomas Wayne's attaché, which one second was resting flat on the rail in front of him and the next second was in my sternum, corner-first. The wind went out of me the way the wind goes out of a balloon when it gets too close to the business end of a hatpin, pain spidered from the center of me all the way out, and I doubled over, slamming into the railing.

The shape I was in, there was no chance of catching Wayne, who was doing his impression of a rabbit in retreat. I didn't even bother.

*   *   *

If I were Thomas Wayne, my office is the last place I would go. Of course, *if* I were Thomas Wayne, I would figure that the good-looking but slow-witted private investigator to whom I'd just given the banana peel would figure that the office is the last place he'd go if he were me, so I'd go there.

Fortunately, most of the world doesn't think like me. I skipped Midlands Realty and Development—I'd seen enough of those offices already anyway—and found the house that Thomas Wayne shared with his father, or vice versa. It was a nice big two-story plantation-ish place on a gentle hill of a lot out west of Boys Town. You know the kind of place I mean—four big columns across the front holding up a balcony to which there's no access, shading a concrete slab on which sit two or three pieces of white metal furniture designed by someone who never sat down. The place was slate blue with white trim, and it was deserted. At least, no one answered the bell. I went around the side of the house and peered through a flyspecked window into the garage. No cars.

I tried the bell again and then sat in my car and listened to the radio long enough to convince myself that Wayne—either Wayne—wasn't going to put in an appearance any time soon. I hit the steering wheel in frustration and self-anger—what was one more bruise?—and jammed the car into gear.

I had better luck on my next stop: Jahna Johansen was home. I put a finger over the lens of the fisheye peephole-viewer in her door and leaned on the bell, so she either had to ignore the bell or open the door to see who was calling. She opened the door.

"Fuller Brush man," I said.

She didn't believe me, or she already had all the brushes she could use. Anyhow, she tried to close the door but I expected it and leaned in at the same time she did, only harder. She stumbled back into her apartment and I stepped inside.

"Oh," I said, "did you want this closed?" I slammed the door shut.

"What do you want, you son of a bitch," she snarled. It didn't work, the snarl. Not with her high-pitched girlish voice.

"Why do people keep calling me that today, I wonder."

"Fuck off."

"Gee, nobody ever *'splained* it like that before. Get away from that phone, blondie, I'm not in the mood."

She looked at me and drifted away from the telephone that rested on a parsons table between two armchairs, but drifted back and ended up in one of the chairs.

"What're you so steamed up about, Ned?"

"Not bad," I said, "but too late. The light, conversational tone, I mean. You should have tried it first, before 'you son of a bitch' and 'fuck off.' Now it lacks sincerity."

"Screw you."

"See? *That's* sincere. You also shouldn't have told your boyfriend the name I gave you, since obviously you knew I had pulled it out of thin air. Your friend couldn't resist using it when he and his pals were stomping on me last night. When he called me Ned I knew who had sicced him on me. Though not why. I mean, where did I drop the cake?"

"I don't know what you're talking about." She was good. She didn't look away or look down or blink or blush or anything; she just lied right into my face, and even at that she didn't frost over with the hard, unblinking stare of inexperienced liars. Her gaze was forthright and open and, yes, honest.

"I keep running into that today, too. Did you think I was joshing you about the goddamn phone?" Her fingers had been doing the walking toward the instrument, so I snatched it off the table and unplugged the cord from the base of it and set it back down, throwing the cord on the carpet. "Now we won't be interrupted while you tell me your friend's name."

She looked away from me and crossed both her arms and her legs.

"Fine," I said. There was a cheap Jefferson secretary against the wall by the door. I went to it and lowered the writing surface and started in on the four little drawers.

"Hey!" Jahna Johansen belted out.

I got lucky on the second drawer, before the woman was on me. I pushed her and she sat down on the floor and I inspected my find, a little address book with a gray fake-leather cover. Its flimsy pages bore some conventional name-address-and-phone number entries, but mostly telephone numbers with nothing more than initials against them.

"Gimme that, you bastard!" the woman bellowed.

"Eventually." I slipped the book into my jacket pocket. "I figure I just have to go through this book line by line, number by number, until I find the man I'm looking for. I just hope you're smart enough to not have any of your clients in here, because of course I'm going to tell everyone I call exactly how I got his number."

She closed her eyes, hard, and balled her fists, hard, and seemed to be holding her breath. I opened the door.

"God*damn* it," she said in a burst of air. "Shit." She looked at me. "If I tell you his name will you give me the book?"

"No. If you tell me his name and where I can find him and you don't tell him about this little tête-à-tête and he turns out to be the one I want . . . *then* I'll give you the book."

Her eyes became slits. Yesterday I had thought Jahna Johansen a pretty woman, maybe even a beautiful one. Not today.

I said, "And you can start it all off by telling me what tipped you to me. Professional curiosity."

Jahna considered it, her eyes in motion, trying to find the hidden trap. There wasn't any, but untrustworthy people can't trust anybody.

"You said you got my address out of the phone book," she finally said. "I'm not in the phone book. Then I saw you out front talking to that cop."

It's always the little things that'll trip you up. For want of a shoe, and so on.

"Fair enough," I said. "You're off to a good start, Jahna. Don't lose your momentum."

The eyes were still restless in their slitted sockets. This time they were looking for the way out. There wasn't one. She said, "How do I know I can trust you?"

"I don't know," I said. "How?"

Jahna Johansen rolled up onto hands and knees and pulled herself heavily onto the sofa. "Shit," she repeated, scanning the room, as if an alternative lay there forgotten. Then her eyes came back to me. "His name's Aurelio," she said reluctantly.

chapter
16

When Thomas Wayne came home late that afternoon I was waiting for him. He jockeyed his ugly little BMW into the wide driveway as the overhead garage door swung upward automatically. He paused for the door. Then he goosed the gas pedal and bumped the sawed-off car inside.

Between the pausing and the bumping, I got my Impala peeled away from the curb across the street and into the driveway, and when Wayne put his car in the garage I nosed in after him, right on his tail, the front end of my car jutting eighteen inches into the garage, in case he got the bright idea to hit the garage-door closer button in his car and shut me out.

But Wayne was fresh out of bright ideas. He staggered out of the BMW and fixed me with a malevolent red-eyed stare and climbed over our bumpers without a word, and without bothering to close the door on his car. I did it for him, and followed him through the side door into the house, since he had thoughtfully left that door standing wide, too.

The side door opened to a small utility room containing washer, dryer, half-bath, and a coat closet. Beyond that was an airy eat-in kitchen done in pale blues and yellows. Thomas Wayne sat at a large round table under a low-hanging ceiling lamp in front of a picture window that looked out upon the backyard, or would have if the translucent curtain liners hadn't been pulled. His suit jacket lay in a heap on a sideboard behind the table. His tie was loosened and his collar was open and his left hand was wrapped around a green bottle of beer. He lifted the bottle in a sarcastic toast when I entered the room.

"Welcome, detective," he said with drunken, too-precise diction. "There's more where this came from." He jerked his head to indicate the yellow side-by-side refrigerator in a corner of the room.

I had had worse offers. I got the beer, Moosehead, got the cap off, and propped myself in a right angle of the kitchen counters. The beer was cold and flavorful. Most mass-market beers not only taste alike, but they taste like water. I like something with a little character to it. Increasingly that means paying a premium for imported beers or paying a premium for domestic beers from microbreweries, and good luck finding them at your local liquor mart.

I said, "Before we were so rudely interrupted . . ."

Wayne laughed. It wasn't an amused laugh, of course, but a half-drunk, half-mad cackle. He swigged a mouthful of beer and swallowed it, belching silently. "That's good," he said. "Almost funny."

"That means so much, coming from you. What was the big idea sucker-punching me and taking off like that?"

He shrugged. "I didn't feel like talking to you."

"I guess *not*." I took down some beer. "Didn't it occur to you that you were merely delaying the inevitable? Or did you really think I would give up and go home?"

He looked away from me and at his bottle, whose label he began stripping away with a thumbnail. "There's always hope," he mumbled.

I studied him for a minute, gauging the wind, sizing up the audience. That afternoon I had come at him hard. That was partly my mood, partly my strategy. Soften him up. Now, though, Wayne had done his own softening up, using grain alcohol, and I suspected the hard-boiled routine would be no more successful now than it had been earlier, except I would beware of flying briefcases.

"Believe it or not, Thomas, I'm trying to do you a favor."

His red eyes moved under heavy brows from the bottle to my face and back again just as quickly and his brown mustache twitched. "Thanks," he said tonelessly.

"You're welcome. See, a girl has been killed. And there are questions that have to be answered."

"I answered them. I don't have to talk to you."

"No, but I'm not the only one interested in the answers. The next people who come around with questions, they won't be as professional as the cops or as pleasant as me."

He needed half a minute or so for that to penetrate. Then he looked at me. "What the hell does *that* mean? What 'next people'?"

I drank slowly. I had his attention, now I wanted to hold it. When I finished swallowing I said, "Do you know who Meredith's father is?"

Wayne sighed dramatically, flapped his arms, and crossed them. "We've been through all this, haven't we?"

I ignored it. "The name Berens is a contracted and Anglicized version of the name Berenelli. Meredith's father's name is Michael Berenelli."

"Rooty-toot-toot for him."

"If the name Michael Berenelli doesn't mean anything to you, I suggest you stop by the public library sometime when you're sober and look him up in *The Reader's Guide* or *The New York Times Index*. He'll be in there. There'll be lots of references. And cross-references to organized crime."

It had the desired effect, even if the audience was two-thirds drunk. Wayne's mouth opened and closed again and his eyes widened enough for me to see just how bloodshot they really were, which made my own eyes tear.

"Meredith's old man is one of the top crime bosses in Chicago, which makes him one of the top bosses in the country. He and his friends, and he has a *lot* of friends, are real eager to find out who beat up his daughter."

A minute or so later Wayne found words, but even so the best he could do was, "You're kidding."

"About which part? Michael Berenelli being a Mob chief? Go look it up. Berenelli and his friends wanting the hide, or other anatomical parts, of whoever killed his kid? What do you think?"

Whatever he thought, he took quite a while thinking it. That was okay with me. Most people do a better job of scaring themselves than you or I could ever hope to do. I sipped at my beer and listened to the refrigerator hum and let the seconds pile up on each other. Finally Wayne said, shakily, "I didn't have anything to do with Meredith's death. You *have* to believe me . . ."

"Not really," I said casually. "And even if I do believe you, Berenelli and friends aren't liable to accept it on my say-so alone."

"Oh, Christ." He crossed his arms on the dining table and rested his forehead against them.

Nice work, Ace, I told myself. You got a drunk on the ropes. Now for some fun.

I said, "Okay, Thomas. If you didn't do in Meredith, then who?"

"I don't know," he said to the table.

"Who else would have a motive?"

"I don't know," he repeated. Then he raised his head an inch. "What do you mean, who *else?*"

"You've got a motive, Thomas. We've been over that ground, and I'm sure the police took you over it again. The question is whether that motive was sufficient. You say not. Okay. So give me an alternative. Who else?"

"I don't *know.*" He came upright and pounded the table hard enough to upset the beer bottle. It danced and he made a grab at it, but his reflexes were dulled by the liquor I suspected he had been putting down all afternoon, and all he managed to do was knock the bottle off the table and onto the floor. It bounced once on the linoleum and rolled toward me, dribbling a trail of juice as it came. I reached down and picked up the bottle and set it on the counter. Not as smooth, or as painless, as I make it sound, which only goes to prove what a perfect guest I really am.

"How the hell would I know?" Wayne was continuing. "I didn't even know what her real name was, or who her father was, or even that she *had* a father."

"Everyone has a father, Thomas. It's a prerequisite."

"You know what I mean. I didn't know that much about her—you know, her past or whatever. I don't know who might have had it in for her. And anyhow, why's everyone so certain it was murder? Couldn't it just as easily have been an accident?"

There were half a dozen reasons, already discussed, that said no. But I didn't bother illuminating them for Wayne. Instead I said, "Sure. It could have been an accident. It could be that you and Meredith met somewhere Sunday night—"

"Wait a minute . . ."

"—to discuss your . . . difference of opinion. About this famous engagement."

"There was no enga—"

"You said *tomato* and Meredith said *tomahto* and things got hot."

"You're a goddamn liar!"

"And you hit her. We've seen your temper."

We saw it again. Drunk or no, he came up fast, fast enough to upset the chair he had been sitting on, and covered half the distance between us. He'd have covered the other half, but I had his beer bottle from the countertop, holding it like a truncheon. He saw it and hesitated.

"I'm not in the greatest shape," I admitted, "but I'm sober."

Wayne took my meaning, snorted a curse at me, burped, and returned to his chair, righted it, and sat.

"You hit her," I repeated, replacing the bottle where it would be near to hand. "You miscalculated—you hit her too hard. She was dead. You panicked. This would be even worse for your career than the maybe/maybe-not engagement, especially if you envisioned a career outside of the private sector." I took a sip of beer to give him time to protest. He didn't take advantage of it. "Rattled, you decided to try and make it look like Meredith had been the victim of a mugger. You beat up the body, hid it, ditched her car somewhere. Then you came home and went to bed and went to work the next day like nothing happened."

The thing was full of holes big enough to steer an ocean liner through, but Thomas Wayne wouldn't know and I didn't care. I was just making a hook and seeing if he would put himself on it.

"Anyone can understand an accident," I said avuncularly. "Covering it up afterward, well, you'll have to pay the piper for that, but believe me, a charge of manslaughter or whatever they may bargain down to is a lot smoother than first-degree murder, which is what they're looking to pin on you. That's assuming you last long enough to end up in the lap of justice."

He closed his eyes and slunk down in the chair and rested his head against its high back. "I told you," he said dully, "the last time I saw Meredith was a week ago Monday."

"Uh-huh," I said noncommittally.

"It's the goddamn *truth*."

"The truth is, you stick with that line and you'll swing. Come clean and you might have something resembling a chance."

He opened his eyes. "What, the only way I can avoid burning for something I didn't do is to confess to something *else* I didn't do? What kind of witch-hunt is this? Besides, do you expect me to believe that whatsisname, Meredith's father—"

"Berenelli."

"—that you're going to tell him I killed his daughter by accident and he's going to say, 'oh, all right,' and that'll be the end of it? Jesus Christ, man, the way you tell it I'm as good as dead already. Why should I confess to something I didn't do?"

He was good.

I said, "Berenelli doesn't know about you. But he will; the connection between you and Meredith is there, it's real, and it's only a matter of time before his people find it."

"I thought *you* were his people."

"You flatter me. Or you insult me; I'm not sure which. I'm still working for Donna Berens, but her interests are the same as her ex-husband's. Namely, identifying Meredith's killer. The police and I both require something that we call evidence; for Berenelli and his people, circumstantial evidence will do just fine. And in that regard, Thomas, you're the man of the moment."

"Great. Is there any beer left?"

I checked. There was. I gave him one.

"Let's say you didn't kill Meredith."

"That's what I've *been* saying."

"Berenelli's going to see it the same way I outlined the other day, and he's not going to bother about investigating further. That's why you've got to help me do the investigating *first*. Give me something I can give Berenelli to take the heat off of you. Understand?"

"I'm drunk," he said sourly, "not stupid. But what can I tell you? The only thing that'd help me is to be able to prove I couldn't have killed her, and I can't. Not unless the coroner's report comes in saying that Meredith died before eleven-thirty or twelve Sunday night. 'Cause after that I'm unaccounted-for, I think is how the cops put it."

"I know all that."

"And from the way they were going at me last night, I think *they* think that's not going to happen. I think they expect the coroner to say she died later than that. And then they're going to charge me." He sighed mightily. "Maybe I won't post bail. At least I'll be safe in jail."

"What's the matter with you, didn't you ever watch *The Untouchables*? The only way you'll *really* be safe is if a more likely candidate emerges."

"Like who?"

We weren't to that point yet.

I said, "Shortly before you gave me a bellyful of briefcase, I said I wanted to talk to you about a girlfriend you had who had been killed. I understand it was some kind of automobile-related accident."

Wayne said nothing.

I sighed. "To someone who doesn't share my passion for trying to see all sides of a story, it might look like you're in the habit of running around bumping off your girlfriends."

"It was a long time ago," he said tonelessly.

"There's no statute of limitations on murder. That's something else you would know if you'd watched *The Untouchables*."

"It was just a dumb accident," he said. "A hundred years ago. I was in high school—we both were. Her name was Stacy, Stacy Eitrem. We were—She was my girlfriend. And one night our senior year she was walking home from school. She had stayed late for something and it was autumn, so it was pretty dark already by the time she went home. Maybe that had something to do with it. Anyhow, this car jumped a stop sign—this is what they figured out later—and hit her and killed her instantly. They never found the car or the driver."

"Were you close?"

He shrugged. "Yeah."

"Where were you when she was killed?"

His mouth went tight and his hands, which had been wrapped loosely around the bottle in front of him, tightened. "School," he said through his teeth. "I had wrestling practice."

"Where did you go to high school?"

Seconds passed before he answered. Too many seconds. "Lincoln."

"Guess again," I said. "Your old man told me you two moved to Lincoln twelve years ago. So unless you were, what, about twenty-seven when you finished high school . . ."

He said nothing.

"Don't burst a blood vessel thinking about it," I advised. "People leave a trail. I go over to Lincoln and snoop around, credit applications, bank references, and so on, and that tells me your previous address—addresses, even, depending on how frequently you moved, since banks don't trust you if you've been at your current locale less than six months or a year. That takes me back to Indiana, where your dad says you were before Lincoln. I repeat the process there, and that takes me somewhere else. Your dad says you've been all over the Midwest. Eventually, Thomas, I find out where your family's tent was pitched when the obstetrician slapped you on the butt. All it takes is time and money. Money's no problem for me, since it's no problem for my client. Time's no problem, either. For me, that is. For you . . . well, Berenelli's going to get itchy, and when he gets itchy, friend, he may just scratch *you*." God, I love that kind of talk!

Wayne's arms were still on the table, his hands still encircling the bottle. Now he fanned his hands, exposing his palms in a gesture of defeat. "All right, all right, all right. We lived in Sioux Falls, South Dakota, until I was eighteen. Then we were in Mankato, Minnesota, for not quite two years. Then Dubuque, Iowa, for a year. Then Evansville, Indiana, for about three years. Then Lincoln. Then here. Happy?"

"Ecstatic. What ever happened to your mother?"

That earned me an if-looks-could-kill look, but all he said was, "You like to jump around a lot."

"It's the only exercise I get. Your mother?"

He got up, suddenly though not so suddenly as the last time, and came over toward me. I was braced, but he gave me a look that said Get out of my way, so I got out of his way and he opened a top cupboard that I had been blocking, took down a dimpled blue tumbler, and filled it with water from the tap.

"She died," he said.

"I know. When?"

He emptied the glass and refilled it and took it to the table. "When I was about two."

"What from?"

He looked at me. There was nothing in the red eyes. No emotion, I mean. None of the anger, the hatred, that had been there mere minutes ago. Nothing. And the voice matched. "Cerebral hemorrhage," he said. "I guess she'd had a headache the night before. Next morning she just didn't get up." He studied me frankly. Something had come back into his eyes, not anger exactly, just a kind of peeved look. "What's it got to do with anything?"

Time for the plunge.

"Sunday night, the night Meredith was killed, what was your father doing while you were out entertaining your clients?"

The corners of his mouth went down. "I don't know." His voice was tight, constrained. "He told me the police asked him that. I supposed they would have to. I suppose you would, too. But I don't know. He says he was home all afternoon and evening, reading, watching television. I suppose he was. I'm *sure* he was. It's what he usually does on Sunday. Why would he lie?"

Both of us knew that that one didn't deserve an answer.

"What about—what, twenty or twenty-one years ago? The night your friend Stacy Eitrem was killed? Where was your father that night?"

Wayne frowned in apparent confusion. "I don't understand . . ."

"All right, let's do a paint-by-numbers. Let's talk about your motive for wanting Meredith out of the way."

"I have *told* you, I didn—"

"You have told me you didn't kill her. I heard you. Did you hear *me* tell *you* that you nevertheless have a motive? Right. Either you were engaged or you weren't. If you were, you might have decided it was a bad move and wanted out, but Meredith may not have been graceful about it. You're a visible young man, Mr. Wayne, and you may have hopes of becoming still more visible. You wouldn't want a stink. Same goes if there wasn't an engagement, but Meredith acted as if there was. That situation may even be worse, because it puts you in the position of having to choose between calling a young woman a liar, and possibly a mentally unbalanced one, or being branded a liar yourself. Those are good motives for a man with great expectations."

I gave it a minute to absorb.

"Or the *father* of a man with great expectations."

The look he gave me, while murderous, also suggested that he had seen where I was going and got there a little ahead of me. "You're reaching," he said with venom.

"Not very far. Last night your father paid me a visit. I don't know whether you know that or not." His face said not. "He tried to bully me off the investigation, he tried to enlist me as bag man for paying off my client to drop the investigation. The first didn't work and I didn't even suggest the second to my client. She's got access to more money than your father could ever hope to touch. Anyhow, my point is that your father made a heartfelt speech about you. 'Everything I've ever done has been for him,' that's what he told me. He didn't specify the 'everything' part. Perhaps it included taking care of one or two young women who for one reason or another were bad choices for his boy?"

"That's pathetic."

"I agree. Stacy Eitrem. Did you plan to marry her?"

It came at him out of left field, which is as I intended.

"I—I don't know. I don't know. We were just kids . . ."

"Plenty of 'kids' get married right out of high school. Was that your plan?"

"I don't know . . ."

"But you *had* discussed it?"

"I don't *know*. Maybe. Just to talk about it . . ."

"The night she was killed. Where was your father?"

He looked at me. The confusion in his eyes, I thought, was real. "I don't know," he said softly.

"Does anybody?"

"He was at home when I got home from practice," he said lamely.

"That doesn't mean anything," I said. "When did you find out about your friend?"

"Later. Later that night. Nine or ten, I suppose."

"How? The police?"

"No. One of the kids from school . . . her dad was an ambulance driver . . ."

"Was there an investigation?"

He shrugged. "I suppose so. I suppose they must have looked for the car. No one ever told me. They never caught anyone, though."

"Did your father know you and Stacy had contemplated marriage?"

He shook his head. "We were just kids," he repeated, as if that meant something. "We weren't serious."

That didn't mean someone else hadn't been.

"According to the coroner, death occurred no earlier than one A.M. Monday morning."

" 'One A.M. Monday morning' is redundant," I said. " 'A.M.' means 'morning.' "

"Damn," Kim Banner said. "And I always try so hard to talk good when I'm around you." We were at a booth in the side dining room at Caniglia's, the original one, on Seventh Street in the old

Italian neighborhood. We had each made a drink disappear and were working more slowly on second rounds while we waited for our dinners.

"That leaves Thomas Wayne on the hook, then," I observed.

"I thought your current theory was that his father killed Meredith."

"The beauty of my theories is that they cover all contingencies. Every time I adjust it to suit the father it fits the son, too, and vice versa." I had told her about my late-afternoon meeting with Wayne *fils*. The high points, at any rate. "Thomas appeared alternately outraged and confused when I was troweling suspicion onto his father, but that doesn't necessarily indicate Thomas's innocence. I mean, he could be grade-A U.S.D.A.-certified guilty and still be stunned that I was heaping the blame on his old man."

"Well, let's see how this fits into your picture: According to the coroner, Meredith was three months pregnant."

I rated it worth a low whistle, and gave it same. "I wonder if Thomas Wayne knew."

"Yeah," Banner drawled over the lip of her glass. "I wonder, too. Tomorrow I'll find out."

"She didn't tell Dianna Castelli," I mused, "or Dianna certainly would have told me. I wonder what that means."

"The Castelli woman didn't mention it to me, either, when I talked to her this morning. Neither did the mother."

"What a shock that is," I deadpanned. "But Dianna Castelli . . . Meredith told her things that she didn't tell her mother. That she was seeing Wayne, that she was engaged to him . . ."

"Maybe-engaged," Banner corrected.

"Maybe-engaged. Maybe *engaged*," I said. "Maybe this was her ace in the hole. If Meredith got pregnant on purpose—"

"Do I have to listen to this kind of sexist crap just because you're buying?"

"Who said anything about me buying? Meredith could have seen her pregnancy as a way of turning her fantasy nuptials into real ones. Thomas could have really panicked. Dumping Meredith, that could be bumpy. Dumping Meredith and an infant . . . Naturally, it works just as well with Alexander Wayne stepping into the role of murderer."

Salads came.

"Not quite," Banner said around a Club cracker. "With Thomas in the lead, you have to assume two things, the first being that Meredith told him about the pregnancy. Which we don't know. With Alexander in the lead, you have to really stretch. Why would she tell Alexander and not Thomas? Or, having told Thomas, why would she tell Alexander?"

"Why wouldn't *Thomas* tell Alexander? He was in trouble and knew it. Maybe he turned to his father to bail him out. Maybe his father had bailed him out of trouble once before, about twenty years ago. And maybe his father bailed him out again this time. What's the other assumption I have to make?"

"Hmm? Oh—" She chewed a mouthful of rabbit food and swallowed. "That Thomas was the father. I checked into that Johansen woman. She's well known to the vice detail. A real pa-harty gal, like the old song used to go."

"Does she work for anybody?" I already knew the answer, I was pretty sure, but it sounded like the kind of question I should ask.

"Sort of. A penny-ante lowlife named Aurelio Ramos. Sort of a pimp, sort of a partner. Between them, Ramos and Johansen line up a fair amount of 'entertainment,' mostly but not exclusively for the visiting-businessmen trade. If your Meredith was a pa-harty gal too, and it looks like she was, at least pa-hart time, then that widens the field considerably."

I speared a black olive and ate it. "The field of *candidates*," I agreed after a space. "It still leaves Thomas Wayne as Meredith's . . . what would you say? Father of Choice?"

"For God's sake," Banner said. She raked a hand through her short blond hair, which is always a sign of some internal churning. "What year does *your* calendar say this is? Meredith 'gets pregnant,' 'on purpose,' to force her beloved to make her 'an honest woman' so she can have a nice house and an automatic dishwasher and two-point-five kids, is *that* how you have it figured? I think you've perfected the reverse gear on your time machine, professor; now why don't you return to the *twentieth* century?"

I didn't blame her for being hot. The scenario was pretty well imbued with those sexist, man-stalking overtones—enough so to make me a little uncomfortable about it, too. But while we can adopt the fashionable and socially accepted liberal, enlightened attitude, it's a big mistake to think that everyone else on the planet has too.

Putting down my fork I said slowly, "There are still people in the latter half of the twentieth century who think that black men only want white women and that Jews control all the money and that adolescent boys can 'turn into' homosexuals by looking at certain books and that you come out of a Vietnamese restaurant with the impulse to chase cars. I do not hold those beliefs, but I know people who do, and dearly. I also know people who believe that a woman's place is in the home with the automatic dishwasher and the two-point-five kids. Some of those people are women. I do not know Meredith Berens's personality well enough to determine what she may or may not have believed, thought, or done. I doubt whether *anybody* knew her that well. She was a complicated and probably unstable personality. She showed only minute facets of that personality to the various people in her life, different facets based on . . . based on I don't know what. What she wanted a given individual to see her for, I suppose. If she told anybody she was pregnant, it was probably the person who would be most inclined to deny having been told—Thomas Wayne. Given that, all I can do is make guesses. Believe me, Banner, I wish to Christ that Meredith was here so that she could tell us herself what went through her head."

"Yeah. Well, that makes two of us," Banner said tightly. Her salad plate was empty and she set it to one side, picking up her water glass. "All right, as long as we're guessing, try this: Meredith is sleeping around on a quasi-professional basis. For all we know, she was moonlighting on her moonlighting—putting together her own action unbeknownst to Jahna Johansen. That's where she was Sunday night, with a client. But it goes wrong. The john gets pissed. He wants something she's not prepared to deliver, or he's a freak who gets off on beating up women. Anyhow, they tangle. He kills her and hides the body. If he's an out-of-towner, and even if he isn't, the odds of finding him are a bazillion-to-one against."

Dinner came. Mostaccioli for me, petite filet for Banner.

"It explains why she wasn't robbed," Banner continued when the waitress had departed.

"Where's her purse?"

"She dropped it during the beating, or left it in the car. The john took it and got rid of it."

"The car?"

"He used that to drive her to Fontenelle Forest and dump the body. By the way, they were able to get a tire impression, but it's pretty poor and not much use until we have a tire to compare it with. Anyhow, when he was through he ditched the car, probably making sure to leave behind nothing that could lead anyone to him."

"Did a good job, too. That car's been missing since Sunday."

She scowled. "You've got an imagination," she said. "I've seen you use it. Use it now. There are probably only about nine hundred and ninety-nine places in town where you can park a car for days on end and have it attract no attention whatsoever. The airport. A hotel ramp. An apartment building parking lot. A hospital. A private garage—"

"I get the idea."

"And if you want to be *really* clever, you drive it to another town and ditch it and take a plane or a bus back. If you're from out of town, you don't even have to do that. You just disappear."

"You're just a ray of sunshine."

"It's the least I can do, considering this fine dinner you've bought me."

I started to protest, but thought better of it. The meal would go down as expenses. And my expenses were being picked up, ultimately, by Baron Mike Berenelli. Banner would choke on her baked potato if she knew. Maybe someday I would tell her. For now, my knowing was enough.

I raised my glass. "Enjoy," I said.

chapter 17

While I waited for Aurelio Ramos to show his weasely little face, I flipped idly through Jahna Johansen's address book, aided by the glove compartment light. The night was moonless and the wind was up and the car rocked a little, now and then, when the breeze got particularly insistent. I was parked along the curb across the street and two or three doors up from the address the Johansen woman had given me as Aurelio's. It was a sagging little clapboard house whose uneven roof hung low over the yard. The yard had no lawn, but it had an older Buick Electra that could easily have been the car that nearly flattened me across Decatur Street. Aurelio Ramos's block was full of other houses like his, houses with missing windows replaced with plywood or cardboard, houses with junk cars sitting out front, houses with garbage stacked on the porches and spilling out into the yard. It was a sad and decrepit neighborhood full of sad and decrepit houses. The residents were the poor and the elderly, and the elderly poor. There was much desperation; it was palpable. Desperation was not all bad; where there was no desperation, there was apathy.

I looked at Ramos's house. It was a minuscule firetrap composed of two boxes, a larger one whose pitched roof ran north and south and a smaller one, butted up against the front of the first box. A slab of concrete along the front of the larger box constituted the porch or stoop; the front door sat at the join of the two boxes. I figured the larger box was big enough for a living room and a kitchen; the smaller would hold a bedroom and a bathroom. Certainly no room for much more than that. There were three windows visible in front: a picture window, which didn't suit the house and which was covered by a heavy drape or blanket that allowed only a sliver of light to escape on one side; a semicircular window in the front door; and a darkened bedroom window on the other side of the door from the picture window. Tattered curtains hung in this window.

What's sad about houses like this one is that they don't begin as sad little houses. When this place was built, forty or fifty years ago, it was someone's dream house. Some young couple, the ink still fresh on their marriage certificate, moved in there when the house was shiny and cute and the tiny lawn out front was green and well-tended and every house up and down the block was the same way. Dad went to work in the morning and mom stayed home and looked after a kid or two, and after a few years when things were better they all moved to a bigger house and a better neighborhood, and the people who moved in here after them didn't have as much or didn't care as much. And the cycle, the downward spiral, began.

The cycle wasn't finished yet. But it didn't look like it had much further to go to hit bottom.

I put the book away and closed the glove compartment door. The book hadn't been too fascinating. It wasn't as if Jahna Johansen was one of those fashion-model types of call girls with a little black book full of the names of socially and economically and politically prominent men. She was two-bit, strictly third-class. The book, as I've said, was filled mostly with initials and numbers. I could have made some guesses at some of the initials—and, in fact, a few of them and one or two telephone numbers struck chords in my mind—and I could have tracked down most if not all of the numbers if I was so inclined. But I wasn't. I wanted a rematch with Aurelio Ramos, one in which he didn't have his goons to help him, and Jahna's book was simply my insurance that I would have my way without her tipping my hand.

The front door of the house opened and voices spilled out into the night. I sat up.

Ramos's two friends stepped out onto the concrete patch. They looked around, trying too hard to look cool and tough. They wore hats with wide brims, canted at rakish angles. One of them wore a long, oversized green coat that reached down almost to his ankles and which was tied around his waist with a sash. It was hard to tell his racial heritage. He looked white, but there was something

Latin around the eyes. His companion was black, although light-skinned. He wore a baggy, shiny double-breasted suit and red high-tops. A moment after they stepped out a girl joined them, a slim black girl with straight blond hair that may or may not have been a wig. She wore a plastic raincoat, open, and a dark, shiny mini-dress.

A minute or so later Aurelio emerged. He too wore a floppy black hat, but his was pushed back on his head. He had an overcoat draped over his shoulders, a white scarf draped over that. Under the overcoat he appeared to be wearing a dark suit with a ruffled shirt, no tie.

They climbed into the Buick—Aurelio first, into the back seat, followed by the woman; the two goons up front—and took off like they had somewhere to go.

Me too.

We went clear the hell across town, practically to Millard, and ended up in one of those shiny, too-perfect suburban strip-malls near 120th and Q. By then I had half-guessed where we were headed: The Queue, which billed itself as "a civilized eating and drinking emporium," whatever the heck that meant, and which would be gone and replaced by a liquidation center inside of six months. At the moment, however, it was the latest "in" spot.

I was a little old for the place, judging by the look of the young-sters filtering in and out on their way to and from cars to engage in their various vices, but at least I was up to the dress code, which leaned toward the upscale.

They nicked me for a cover charge at the door, and I paid without complaining—more of Michael Berenelli's money, I figured, al-though the nature of my mission was personal—but the cover was taken under false pretenses. I don't mind so much when its purpose is to underwrite live music, but when all you get for your five bucks is a pimply-faced kid spinning records while lights flash and the fishnet-stockinged waitresses go by with overpriced, watered-down drinks . . . Well, I was glad it wasn't my money.

The main room, the drinking and dancing room, was done in dark green and brass and mirrors. Music blared from a dozen speakers hung at ceiling level around the room. Each was the size of a small African nation. There was a big U-shaped bar with low-backed stools; lots of small, long-legged tables with the same stools;

and, in a back corner, a kind of alcove, very intimate, with very low tables and very low overstuffed chairs and couches.

It was there that Aurelio Ramos and company were seating themselves as I entered.

The place had as many video monitors as stereo speakers, also hung from the ceilings. Some of the monitors showed the DJ at "work" in his glass booth next to the dance floor. Some of the monitors, inexplicably, showed the people on the dance floor, which you could have seen "live" by merely turning your head. And some of them showed random, ever-changing images—clips from old movies, old cartoons, old commercials. Odd, and oddly hypnotic.

I found a stool at the bar, from which I could keep an eye not only on the monitors and dancers but also, incidentally, on the Ramos party, shouted a drink order at the bartender, forked over so much money that the bartender had to have a friend help him cart it over to the cash register, and settled in.

It was to be a long wait. I didn't mind. The music was okay, if too loud, and my ordering neat bourbons made it tough for the bartender to water them down, and the waitresses weren't too hard to take. They wore high-necked jackets reminiscent of the ones bellhops always wear in the old movies and, between the bottoms of their jackets and the tops of their high-heeled shoes, not much else besides legs. As I said, I didn't mind the wait. I nursed two bourbons, almost enough liquor to fill a bathroom Dixie cup, and kept half an eye on Aurelio Ramos while letting the remaining half an eye alternate among the action on the dance floor and the shenanigans of the disk jockey and the legs of the waitresses. I consulted Jahna Johansen's little book once. Something about it stuck in my craw, but I couldn't think what and now was not the time to puzzle it out.

Thus passed ninety minutes, give or take. Their waitress had made four trips to the Ramos table, her tray filled each time. I figured I wouldn't have long to wait and I was right. Aurelio stood and said something to the black girl sitting next to him. She nodded. The guy in the double-breasted suit stood, too, and followed Ramos as they picked through the tables and the people, heading toward the front of the room.

I was ten steps ahead of them.

When you entered The Queue's tiled lobby, you had two choices:

You could bear left, to the disco, or continue forward fifteen feet to where a tuxedoed maître d' would feed you dinner if he liked your looks. Across from the maître d' there was a little alcove partly shielded by a pale gray wall that stopped ten inches shy of the ceiling. You didn't have to be much of a detective to guess what was through that alcove. You also didn't have to be much of a detective to guess where, after three or four drinks, Aurelio Ramos and his double-breasted buddy were headed.

I was there first, and took up a position in the stall nearest the door.

The self-closing door to the restroom opened and there were footsteps on the mosaic tile, and low, echoing comments between Aurelio and his friend. I gave them half a minute, kicked the flush lever on the toilet, and stepped out of the stall.

The setup was good. Not perfect—perfect would have had Double-Breast in one of the stalls and Aurelio alone at the urinals—but good. Aurelio was indeed in place, taking care of business, while Double-Breast stood with his back against the opposite wall, arms crossed, legs spread in an unmistakable imitation of a bodyguard. Aurelio Ramos had a delusion about himself, and the delusion was that he was important enough to need protection. This one night, he was right.

Double-Breast glanced at me desultorily, glanced away without interest, then, a spark of recognition igniting in his head, glanced back.

He spent too much time glancing, and he was positioned all wrong. Between his first look in my direction and his second I covered the short distance between us and brought my right knee up between his obligingly spread legs, and hard. He doubled up, naturally, and I brought my fist up under his chin, also hard. His head went back and cracked the tiles on the wall and he collapsed like a South American government.

The event filled no more than ten seconds, perhaps as few as five.

Ramos looked over his shoulder. There was no concern in his pretty little face, just mild curiosity. Getting a look at me moving toward him changed that. But he was not in the best of positions, standing there with his tool in his hand, *in medias res,* so to speak. He didn't know what to do first.

I did. I put a foot in the small of his back and pushed. He fell forward with a guttural cry, grabbing the plumbing for support with his free hand. Trying not to fall in, he kind of spun around on the tile, still hanging on to the fixture. I had to dance back a couple of steps to avoid getting my shoes wet. Then I moved in and grabbed Aurelio by the lapels and slammed him against the metal wall of the stall that was just right of the urinals. He yelled, or tried to. It emerged a strangled squeak.

"Remember me, sweetie?" I said into his face. In the hard, white light of the restroom his features appeared more strongly Hispanic than they had last night, although not exclusively so.

He gulped.

"We didn't get much of a chance to talk last night, Aurelio, on account of your friends. Now it's just you and me."

He gulped again. The light, long whiskers on his chin and lip vibrated. "Now wait a minnit, man—"

"Shut *up*. You got to talk last time. Now you *listen*. I know who you are and where you live and what you do. I even know when you go to take a goddamn *leak*, Aurelio—"

He tried to break away but I slammed him against the wall again.

"Stand still," I growled. "And listen. You seem to think you're something, some kind of big shot, some kind of important man. You're not. You're nothing. Your hired muscle is nothing. And from what I can see"—I glanced pointedly at his exposed privates—"you're just a boy, not a man."

He moved to cover himself but I slammed him again.

The restroom door opened and a fat kid with wet-curly hair came in, caught sight of the unconscious man on the floor and Aurelio and me against the wall, and stopped dead.

"We're full up, kid," I said and he beat it.

I turned back to Aurelio. "Now here's the arrangement, boy. You're going to forget me. You're going to forget who I am and where I live and how you know me. You're going to forget everything about me except my face. And you'd *better* remember this face, boy, because the next time you see it is gonna be the last time you see it. Understand? I don't like fucking around with third-rate losers like you. It's a waste of time. So stay the hell away from me. I don't care if we're in a goddamn K Mart, you see me and you'd better get the fuck out of there before I see you. Got it?"

I was putting it on thick, of course. The idea was to catch him

with his guard down, or rather *knock* his guard down, show him
how flimsy and transparent it really was, shock him and reduce
him psychologically, then hit him hard with the message. Although
I doubt he had ever thought of it in such terms, it's exactly what
Ramos had tried to do to me. His big mistake was using his goons—
although he lacked the physical resources to have handled the job
himself. But anyone can be beaten up when he's ganged up on.
There's no shame in that, no psychological stripping. I had done
the opposite: I had single-handedly torn through Ramos's line of
defense like wet tissue—it was almost laughable, of course, but
he hadn't thought so—and gotten to him. I had manhandled him
and insulted him and reduced him, and there was nothing he could
do about it. Unless I missed my guess badly, Aurelio Ramos *would*
run in the other direction if he caught sight of me at the other end
of a supermarket aisle.

As if concurring, he nodded with quick, jerky bobs of his head.

I pulled him away from the metal wall and hurled him against
it again. "I can't hear a *nod,* Aurelio!"

"All right," he blubbered. "I *got* it."

I let him go, straightened myself up, smoothed his lapels, flounced
the ruffles on his shirt front. He was sniffling, trying to keep the
panic in check, trying not to cry or do anything else that would
qualify as uncool. It was too late for that, standing there with his
dick hanging out. "Good," I said calmly. "As long as we understand each other."

Ramos sniffled once or twice and started to zip his pants. As
soon as he had both hands occupied I grabbed him again and spun
him around and took him by the back of his jacket collar and
pulled him toward the urinals and stuck his head into the one he
had been using. He let out a cry and I drove my right knee into
his ribs.

"You forgot to *flush*, Aurelio," I said, taking care of it for him.
Then I let him go and he fell onto the floor, wiping water and piss
out of his face. I moved to the sinks and smoothed my hair in the
mirrors above them. "Can't stand a guy who doesn't flush when
he's done," I said to the reflection.

I paused out in the parking lot, lounging near the Radio Shack
window two doors down along the mall. I didn't think it too likely
that Aurelio Ramos would pull himself together, pull his double-

breasted bodyguard together, collect the other bully-boy and come
after me. I considered it more likely that he and Double-Breast
would compose themselves as well as possible in the john and
return to their table, saying nothing, ever, to their comrade or
anyone else. Maybe later tonight the girl would wonder why Ramos
couldn't get it up. Maybe she wouldn't. Gift horse, and so on.

Still, a jittery fellow like me likes to make sure. If they were
going to come, they were going to come within ten minutes. No
more. I could afford to blow ten minutes.

Radio Shack had computers on sale. For the eleventieth time I
indulged my fantasy that electronics was the key to converting my
writing income from embarrassingly low to embarrassingly high.
To an extent it probably was true. I'm the world's worst typist,
and the amount of time, effort, and paper I devote to producing
clean, final drafts, particularly of any manuscript longer than about
thirty pages, could be put to better use. Especially where my novels
were concerned—I had the guts to refer to "novels," plural, even
though to date there was one completed and one on apparently
permanent hold—it would be nice, when finished, to simply push
a button and produce a clean manuscript instead of facing the
mind- and finger-numbing chore of having to *type* the damn thing
in a form that could be deciphered by a human being or even an
editor.

I looked at the price on the card in front of the display. Not
bad. Then I squinted out the fine print and saw that the figure
didn't include a monitor, a printer, or, more than likely, the cord
you needed to plug the machine into the wall.

We live in a wonderful age.

Seven minutes went by with no sign of the Ramos party. I was
in the clear, but I decided to stick to the full ten minutes. I wandered past The Queue's front doors and loitered down by Twenty-
Four-Hour Martinizing—I don't know about you, but *I've* never
been able to get anything out of those people in an hour—and
watched my minute hand creep around the dial.

My hand went back to Jahna Johansen's book, in a side pocket
of my sport coat. Something about it kept gnawing at the back of
my brain like a forgotten appointment. I tried to switch off the
conscious part of my mind and flip through the little book on
autopilot, hoping for my subconscious, a gestalt, or The Force to
kick in.

It did. I stopped the backward riffle of pages and thumbed forward slowly, a page at a time, to see what had caught my eye without my mind being aware of it.

A telephone number. One of dozens in that book; one of a half-dozen or so that were unidentified even by a pair of initials, suggesting that Jahna was well familiar with the number and its owner.

I went into my pants pocket and got out my card case and went through the contents. Like standing around in front of the dry cleaners, it was an unnecessary maneuver.

"Sorry about your beauty sleep," I said curtly. "Maybe you can catch up at the office tomorrow."

Steve Lehman pawed self-consciously at his tousled red hair, which at the moment looked a lot like Stan Laurel's coiffure. He wore pale yellow pajamas with blue windowpane checks, a blue cotton robe, and a squinty, scrunched-up look that indicated he had been deep in the arms of Morpheus when I came pounding on the door of his apartment. It was, after all, well past midnight. But my apology was far from sincere.

"Well, what's the matter," Lehman grumbled sleepily, flopping on a sofa that was too big for the room. "Is it about Meredith?"

"Not exactly. It's about you. It's about this." I spun the little address book through the air and into his lap. He picked it up and went through the pages.

"What is it?"

"It's an address book. It belongs to a woman named Jahna Johansen. Know her?"

"Nope." He went on flipping through the book.

On TV, liars give themselves away with obliging flickers of their eyes, or even more unsubtle reactions. In real life people are less cooperative. Not that the planet's teeming with poker faces, but there are enough of them to keep an investigator interested.

"Well, that's odd." I had gone into my pocket and pulled out Lehman's business card, on which he had jotted his home number. "She's got your number in the book," I said. "Ninth or tenth page from the back, if you're interested."

He wasn't, not enough to check. He put the book on a yellow plastic table near the end of the sofa and said, "So?"

"I had hoped for better," I admitted. "Shall I put on a pot of coffee?"

He nipped at a fingernail, or what was left of it, but the gesture wasn't significant. "Look, Nebraska, I'm in sales. I meet people all over the place. I go to every ribbon-cutting, every open house, every Chamber deal I can manage. I talk with people and I trade business cards, and et cetera, and I basically try to meet as many people as I can. But I can't remember *everybody* I meet. What difference does it make anyway?"

"Now *that's* more like it," I said. I retrieved the book. "The thing is, Steve, that this has your *home* number in it, not your number at Castelli and Company." I displayed his business card. "When I went through this book, something stuck. This. Your home number."

Lehman plucked a TV remote-control box from the yellow table and fiddled with it. Again, the gesture didn't necessarily mean anything. He was a nervous kid. "I probably exchanged phone numbers with a girl at some party or reception or something," he said. "What'd you say her name was?"

"Jahna Johansen." I spelled it. "She's a hooker."

He looked at me. "So?"

I had to laugh. "This is good. I like this. No embellishment, not much invention, just damn the torpedos. You probably could sell escalators to Eskimos, or however the expression goes. The problem, Steverino, is I'm not buying. Meredith Berens is dead—I'm sure you've had that news flash by now. It was not a pleasant death, if any of them are. She was beaten to death. By a man. Probably a man who knew her. You're a big, strong kid . . ."

"Hold on a minute—"

"Just an aside. It turns out that Meredith was several months pregnant—"

"Wow. Really?"

"Yes, really. Nobody knows who the father is—except, of course, Meredith, and maybe the father—and nobody knows whether her pregnancy had anything to do with her death—except maybe those two people again—but you and I both know you had a little-bitty thing for Meredith, and I can't help but wonder if you weren't being modest when you told me about how you struck out with her."

Lehman said nothing. He lounged there shaking his head sadly, a you-poor-dumb-sap smile on his face.

"There's more," I said. "Jahna Johansen's a hooker. I told you that. What I didn't mention is her game. She organizes events, 'parties,' as she calls them, mainly for visiting businessmen. Food, liquor, and girls. Meredith Berens was one of the girls."

"You're joking!"

He wasn't good enough. The reaction, the wide eyes, the dropped jaw, the heavy inflection—too much.

I smiled. I could afford to. I said, "Let's consider a scenario. I've been doing a fair amount of that lately, and to less than appreciative audiences, but everyone needs a hobby. Let's imagine a sharp, young salesman. We'll say he has red hair, maybe getting a little thin on top."

Lehman stroked his scalp self-consciously.

"Let's say the salesman, through his contacts, ends up at a soirée hosted by Jahna Johansen. Also at the event is Meredith Berens, but not as a guest. She's working. Our hero scores with her, not that that's much of an accomplishment under the circumstances. The situation is ripe for subtle and unsubtle pressures, blackmail, even, and it cuts both ways. Our hero can make life tough for Meredith, she can make life tough for him. Peaceful coexistence, that's the ticket. Compromise. Accommodation. The question is, how much compromise and what kind of accommodation? And who did how much of which? Was there an imbalance? And did someone end up dead on account of it?"

He ignored me. It was more refreshing than the standard angry denials, but bad strategy. You can protest too little as easily as too much. Surely my creative thinking deserved some kind of response.

I said, "You might as well talk to me, Steve. Thanks to this"— I waggled the book in the air—"I can absolutely guarantee that Jahna Johansen will be astonishingly cooperative with me. Or the cops."

Lehman dinked with the remote control some more. Then he tossed it down on the table and lay back on the sofa and crossed his arms tightly across his chest and inspected the ceiling.

"I didn't kill her," he said tightly. "I never hurt her."

"That's the end of the story," I said. "Maybe. Let's have the beginning."

It was about as I had guessed. A potential client from out of town knew about the Johansen woman's "parties." He had been to one or two, since his work brought him through town fairly frequently. He took Lehman to one, ten or twelve months ago. After that, Lehman was a frequent, if irregular guest. Sometimes he'd bring clients or prospective clients, sometimes he came solo for recreation only.

Eventually, inevitably, his schedule and Meredith's overlapped.

Lehman had pursued Meredith for months, with no success. Now he had her in a spot where she literally could not say no, not only because not saying no was what she was there for, but also because Lehman could queer her "real" life. But if Meredith was caught, so was her captor, for she could do him just as much damage as he could do her.

An uneasy truce was reached—uneasy because, outside of the unreal world of Jahna's "parties," Meredith paid Steve Lehman no more attention then she had before. Despite the hold he had over her, there wasn't much he could do about it because of the hold *she* had over *him*. He began to attend Jahna's parties even more frequently. Meredith wasn't always there, but often enough to make it worth his while. If Lehman was to be believed, his attendance hadn't coincided with Meredith's for almost two months. That ruled him out as the baby's father. Since I had fudged on details when I told him how far along Meredith's pregnancy had been, I could be reasonably sure that he hadn't plucked the two-month statement out of the air to get him off the fatherhood hook. But that didn't mean he hadn't invented the time span in order to distance himself from Meredith's murder.

I said, "Sunday. You were where?"

He thought about it. "Here, mostly. What time Sunday?"

I shook my head. "You go first."

He sighed and continued his examination of the ceiling. "I went out to lunch with some friends of mine around eleven. I suppose that lasted until two, two-thirty. Then I went to Westroads and did some shopping. I probably got home around four, four-thirty. I cleaned up this place a little, did some dishes, did my laundry, cleaned the bathroom, and et cetera. Then I got a carry-out pizza and watched TV until eleven or twelve, then I went to bed."

"Anybody come over?"

"Nope."

"Anybody call? You call anybody?"

He chewed a fingernail. "Nope."

"What you're telling me is that you were here, at home, alone all Sunday evening and night until you went to work Monday morning and there's no one who can back you up?"

"I didn't think I'd *need* anyone to back me up. I was just hanging around my apartment, you know, minding my own business. I didn't know I'd need an alibi."

That was reasonable, cuss it. In the movies, it always looks bad when the suspect can't account for his whereabouts at the time of the murder. But actually it's a rare suspect who can and one who can bears watching all the more. Hell, *I* didn't have an alibi for Sunday night.

Finding out whether Jahna had held one of her parties Sunday night, and whether Meredith or Steve Lehman or both had attended, would be easier than writing a bum check. But whatever answers I got wouldn't prove anything in any direction. Except for Jahna Johansen, there wasn't a strong connection between Lehman and Meredith. He may have wanted a less professional relationship with her, but that didn't strike me as a strong motive for his bludgeoning the girl to death. Not only that, Lehman himself didn't strike me as the violent type. You can't tell by looking, of course, just as you can't make the mistake of thinking that someone who displays a quick and even violent temper is *ipso facto* a killer. But Lehman as Meredith's killer . . . The casting just wasn't right. His attitudes and reactions and demeanor weren't right. His motives weren't right. When I pushed him to the wall, he confessed. Maybe it was a snow job—we mustn't forget I was dealing with a salesman, and a PR-slash-advertising salesman at that—a good way of throwing me off the scent. But I didn't think so.

On my short list of the three most likely contenders, Steve Lehman was a distant third.

I moved toward the door, stopped, and looked back at him. He had sat up on the couch, surprised that the interview was apparently over. He didn't know what to make of things, and it showed in his face. I recognized the look. I see it often enough in the bathroom mirror.

chapter

18

I was up before the sun, which was no trick since the sun decided not to put in an appearance that day. It rained most of the morning, a steady though light rain with enough wind behind it to make an umbrella pointless. The dampness penetrated everything, saturating it with a coldness inappropriate to September. It would warm up again, of course. We can always count on some good blisterers into October. But this served as a good warning of the inevitable.

My muscles were still stiff and sore, the area around my slowly healing bullet wound especially so, but a long, hot shower helped.

I called Elmo Lincoln and told him to forget about the telephone number I had put him onto the day before yesterday. He insisted that it was only a matter of time before he tracked it down. I assured him I knew that to be so, but that the case had taken a different direction and the Chicago angle was no longer important. It was true, to a large extent. Just as it was true that I was afraid Elmo's continued investigation might put him in some peril. Elmo didn't buy my excuse, not one hundred percent, but what could he do? Pursuing it on his own would be a complete waste of time, as opposed to the utter waste of time his efforts had been so far. He was at that swing point where you half want to tough it out and continue till the end and you half want to drop it and move on to something else. Ultimately, he took the only course open to him. I told him I'd send him a bottle of twelve-year-old Scotch. He said make it a case. That was our joke: Elmo was a recovering alcoholic, and the only Scotch he'd allow himself near came on a tape dispenser.

I called Donna Berens and told her I would be out of town for a day, maybe two. She didn't ask where I was going or why, and her tone of voice suggested that these things and many others were far beneath her concern. The only thing she wanted to know was what she should tell her ex-husband if he asked her where I was. I suggested she try the truth: that I'd told her I was going out of town but I didn't say where or why.

I called Dianna Castelli and told her the same thing. Unlike Meredith's mother, she was extremely interested in the details. I told her because I felt that someone should know, but I also told her to keep it under her hat.

"It's about that girl, isn't it?" she said anxiously. "Thomas's girlfriend, the one who got killed. You think he killed her. You think he killed Meredith."

"Let's just say I'm working a cold trail," I said.

I was on the highway by noon.

The rain followed me the entire distance. Or perhaps I followed it. In any event the windshield wipers got a good workout, and so for that matter did the rest of my old Impala. I don't run it on the highway as much as I should, letting it get good and warmed up. I threw a bottle of Gumout into the tank when I gassed up before leaving the Big O, and by the time I hit Missouri Valley, half an hour up I-29, I could feel the engine loosen up as it worked out the coke and crap and found the "groove" at which it could cruise with a minimum of gas-pedal help from me. On that old car the groove is at about sixty-three miles per hour. With the speed limit on rural Interstates raised to sixty-five, I could actually drive at a legal velocity for the first time in more than a decade.

There are more boring drives—I-80 across Iowa and I-94 across North Dakota, to name two that I've driven—but that stretch of I-29 is a definite contender. Every so often there's a curve you have to negotiate, so the steering wheel isn't exactly in a locked position. Now and then you pass a tree or a particularly fascinating billboard, but mostly the scenery is farmland, a very flat terrain that must have thrilled pioneer farmers to no end the first time they came upon it but hasn't exactly wowed anyone since. I have to admit, at the height of the growing season, on a cloudless July afternoon, it can be quite a sight. This wasn't July, however, and the afternoon was anything but cloudless, and there wasn't much to look at except gray fields awaiting drier weather and the harvest, the road in front of me, and the southbound lane to my left.

Barring the sudden appearance of a deer, a dog, or a wide load on a flatbed, there's no reason for the speedometer needle to move to the left from the time you leave Omaha until the time you arrive in Sioux City, Iowa, some ninety minutes later. Mine didn't. North of Sioux City I pulled into a truck stop where I ate lunch and got gas, and filled up the car as long as I was there. The rain had passed through by then, leaving gray skies and wet pavement and a blustery chill in its wake.

For a brief stretch, as the Interstate slices through Sioux City, you run parallel to the Missouri River. It's quite wide at that point. Today it was the color of a slug and about as ambitious.

The last ninety minutes of the ride are through farmland again. There is a bit of a roll to the land here, as if it couldn't decide, eons ago when the decisions were being made, whether it wanted to be prairie or plain, and settled for an amalgamation. The Interstate will take you all the way north, if you like, through South Dakota and through North Dakota and right up to the Canada border, where it meets up with Canada's Highway 75 and shoots straight into Winnipeg. I've always told myself I'll do that someday, climb behind the wheel and roll on north into Canada, which isn't all that far away but which to date hasn't been blessed with my presence. But today wasn't the day. For one thing, the needle on my old gas-hog was drifting down into the quarter-tank zone again. For another, I had reached my destination.

One hundred thousand people live in and around Sioux Falls, which gives it roughly one-seventh of South Dakota's population. It is the region's shopping, entertainment, and medical center, sitting as it does where Iowa, Minnesota, and South Dakota meet, and only sixty miles or so from the northern Nebraska border. You see a lot of different license plates, in other words, and the town's always full of people who don't know where they're going.

I was one of them. It had been a good five or six years since circumstances had brought me that far north, and my hazy recollection of the streets was completely inadequate. The town had sprawled to the southwest, past I-29, which previously formed the western edge of the city but now appeared to merely bisect it. I took the Interstate to Twelfth Street, which I dimly remembered as a fairly straight, if long, shot into downtown. It was three-fourteen in the afternoon and the traffic was nice. Another five years, I figured, and it could be almost as zooey as Omaha's. Communities, like people, must have goals.

Twelfth Street took me where I wanted to go. The old high school was right where I had left it on my last trip through, at Twelfth and Main. Parking was as much fun as it always is around a downtown high school; the fact that I had come on the scene just as the inmates were being released didn't help any. I found a meter two blocks away and fed it some coins and got my exercise for the day.

The school was and is an ancient four-story structure that fills virtually all of the city block on which it stands. Washington Senior High School. Most of the building is constructed of the pinkish-gray, or grayish-pink, quartzite indigenous to the region, although some of it, an older portion of the building, I suspect, is of a darker, almost black stone. The tall, wide windows were partly filled in with newer, more energy-efficient panes that spoiled the looks of the place only a little. Other than that, the joint looked much as it must have fifty years ago. In size and atmosphere, if not looks, it reminded me of my alma mater, Central, in downtown Omaha. They don't build 'em like that anymore. I say that with regret.

A kid directed me to the office, just down the hall from the main doors. The wide corridor was dimly lighted and echoed with the noise of escaping students. I checked in, like a good citizen, and told only a medium-sized lie concerning my reason for being there. I gave my true name—none of this Ned Brazda shit, no matter what Travis McGee has to say—and said I was there to research one of their alumni. But, and here's where the medium-sized lie comes in, I told them I was a free-lance writer from Omaha preparing a feature for *Omaha Now!* magazine. It's a gag I've pulled so often that I'm not even ashamed of it anymore. *Omaha Now!* is a city magazine I've written for now and then. It's no better or any worse than the other Omaha city magazines that have come and gone, or most other city rags, for that matter, and it has the advantage of being run by an editor who will back me up on just about any outlandish story I care to tell. If I told you I was doing a story for *Omaha Now!* on the sexually therapeutic value of guano-extract enemas and you called the magazine to see if a writer with the unlikely name of Nebraska had been assigned such a story, the editor would say yes to both questions. If he assumes anything, I think, he assumes I'm doing background on a story that I may or may not pitch at him. Or he just doesn't want to be bothered, and figures going along with the gag is the fastest way to get you off the phone. Whatever his reasons, it makes a good, convincing cover.

The man I tried it out on, one of the vice principals, couldn't have been more accommodating. He suggested I try the school library, where they had a selection of yearbooks going back to when the first high school students climbed out of the primordial soup, and gave me directions that got me lost only once and not severely.

The library was a big, airy, high-ceilinged room with thin carpeting and heavy furniture and not too many students hanging around to work after school. I would have been disappointed at anything else. I tried the free-lance writer bit again, on one of the librarians, and it worked again. She steered me to back editions of *The Warrior* yearbook.

I had neglected to pin Thomas Wayne down on the exact dates of his high school career, but it didn't matter seriously. He was thirty-nine, I knew, so, assuming he was neither astonishingly brilliant nor astonishingly dense—neither of which conditions he had given me any indication of—he would have graduated high school when he was about eighteen, twenty-one years ago. I found and grabbed three books, for twenty, twenty-one, twenty-two years back, and had at the mug shots.

No luck.

I went back to the oldest volume and tried again.

The photographs were arranged by class, of which there were only three since the local district was on a three-and-three system— seventh, eighth, and ninth grades comprising junior high, tenth, eleventh, and twelfth making the senior high. Even so, there were a lot of pictures, the school being big, and each volume was noticeably fatter than the last, indicating an increasing student population. I moved through the books more slowly, scrutinizing the Ws for each of the three classes in each of the ten books.

Still no luck.

"Son of a bitch," I breathed to myself. Luckily there were no students nearby. They would never have heard such language, and I would hate for their first exposure to vulgarity to be from me.

It looked like the bastard had sucked me in. And I should have known. Sioux Falls, South Dakota. It sounds like the kind of town Clark Kent grew up in.

I closed the latest volume, stood up, and leaned over the mezzanine rail. No matter how old you get, you still always feel like spitting when you do that, don't you?

Why would Thomas Wayne have lied to me? To throw me off the scent, sure, but to what end? It wasn't as if he could disappear on me. The police would have other ideas. And it wasn't as if he could obscure his past forever. As I had told him yesterday, people leave a trail whether they want to or not. The most he could do would be delay me. What would be the point?

I went back to my table and idly flipped open the topmost book. There was an index in the back. Two, in fact: faculty and students. Naturally! The official mug shots aren't the only pictures in a high school yearbook. There are the requisite building-the-float and falling-asleep-in-class and acting-sober-at-the-dance shots, too. If Thomas Wayne had avoided the portrait photographer for three years running—unlikely—maybe he had been inadvertently caught in the act of being himself, as Alan Funt used to say. Or maybe there was a listing of "not pictured" students.

There was. He wasn't in any of them.

Nor was he in the student index.

Okay, maybe Wayne was older or younger than thirty-nine. You could put it past me: The older I get, the harder it is for me to judge people's ages, especially if they are younger. I had only Alexander Wayne's say-so for his son's age. I couldn't see why he would have lied about it, especially since he'd provided me that information before he decided he didn't like me. Still, I had subsequently decided Wayne was untrustworthy . . .

I went for the yearbooks from eighteen, nineteen, twenty-three, twenty-four, and twenty-five years back. Thomas Wayne couldn't have been much younger than me, and if I had to guess—as, apparently, I did—I would have guessed that he was a couple-three years older.

But I guessed wrong on all counts. No Thomas Wayne in those books either.

I was at the point where I had to decide whether to chuck it or go through still more yearbooks. Then, on a hunch, I quit looking for Thomas Wayne and started looking for Stacy Eitrem.

Shazam.

I found her in the twenty-one-year-old volume, the one that *should* have featured Thomas Wayne's senior picture. The picture of the Eitrem girl wasn't the kind of formal portrait that seniors usually go for. It had the assembly-line look of the pictures snapped by the photographers who come to the building and set up on the auditorium stage and process nine hundred kids an hour. I guessed that this was a rerun of Stacy Eitrem's junior-year shot, that she had been killed before she ever sat for her senior-year picture. The yearbook staff dolled up this leftover, though. They gave her a page to herself, blowing up the photo to twice the size of everybody else's and printing it in the middle of an otherwise black page, with a brief, sincere little eulogy reversed-out beneath it. She had been a pretty girl, blond, with an oval face and black-rimmed cateye glasses like girls wore two decades ago. She wore her hair high on top, long on the sides, curving out into stiff-looking wings over either shoulder. She had been active in drama, band, and chorus, the book said, and was the president of the Spanish Club.

I tried again for Thomas Wayne—the button's always there the third time you look for it—but still no luck.

Then I went through the whole damn book page by page, picture by picture. Wayne had definitely said he and Stacy Eitrem had been in high school together. He had definitely said she had been killed "our senior year." If she was there he should have been too. But he wasn't.

Odd. If Wayne had been blowing smoke, where did the Stacy Eitrem story come from? If he had been telling the truth, then where was his picture? Odd, odd, odd.

Something even odder: Going through that book page by page, I came across one of those inevitable "candid" shots. Some kids cutting up in what appeared to be a math room, from the half-unfocused scribblings on the chalkboard, clowning for the camera. In the distance, near the board, also not well-focused, the teacher smiled tolerantly. The smile was familiar.

So was the name, when I went back to the faculty index and looked for it.

Alexander Wayne.

He was twenty-some years younger, twenty-some years thinner, and his hair was twenty-some years darker, but he was definitely "the" Alexander Wayne. Somewhat stunned, I checked all of my books for him; he was in every volume up to that one, the twenty-one-year-old book. The one carrying Stacy Eitrem's obituary. After that year, no more Alexander Wayne on the faculty.

The library, which had not been jam-packed, was virtually deserted now. It was past four-thirty, and I doubted they stayed open later than five. I stacked my yearbooks on the returns cart and hunted down the librarian.

She was helpful, but no help. Having been on staff only nine years, she didn't have the vaguest idea who Alexander Wayne was. I asked whether there was anyone on staff who might have known Wayne, some long-hitter I could get in touch with. She thought about it. A tall, pimply-faced kid behind the counter, who had been checking in books and checking out our conversation, which was not confidential, said, "What about Mrs. Kjellsen?"

The librarian looked from him to me. She was a sawed-off thing, narrow in the shoulders and wide at the hips, with graying dark hair and a serious expression and a soft, measured voice perfectly suited to a library. "There's a thought," she said. "Vera Kjellsen. She retired last year after forty years with the district, most of them here. She taught civics."

I didn't care if she taught small engines. "Do you know where I can reach her?"

The librarian went behind the counter and pulled out a saddle-stitched booklet with a pink cover. The school district phone book. She flipped through from the back, stopped on a page, and said, "You're in luck. A lot of our retired teachers move away. But Mrs. Kjellsen still lives in town, according to this." She spun the book around the counter, holding her place with a short-nailed forefinger, so I could copy the address and telephone number.

There was a pay phone in a closet by the office. I sank a quarter into it, called Vera Kjellsen, used the magazine-article dodge, and got invited over.

Mrs. Kjellsen was a wizened, emaciated wisp of a woman with bad posture, almost transparently white hair, and bright pale-blue eyes that danced in a lively fashion behind the thick lenses of her eyeglasses. She was the type of person who doesn't so much die as disappear. Frail as she was, though, her voice was clear and so was her mind, and I guessed it would be quite a while before she disappeared.

She lived in a one-bedroom apartment on the west side of town, as tiny and friendly and just-so as she was. There was a pot of coffee on the stove and a plate of frozen cookies that she gave a shot of microwaves, and then we situated ourselves in a living room that overlooked the five o'clock traffic on Forty-first Street.

"I remember Alexander Wayne," she said in response to my question. "Not very well, I'm afraid, but I remember him. Why did you say you were interested in him?"

I repeated the line I had told her on the phone, a variation on the theme I had sung for the vice principal and the school librarian. "Alexander Wayne built a very successful commercial real estate business down in Omaha. He's more or less retired now, and his son is running the show. I'm doing research for a possible magazine article about them—you know, father and son build a business empire in America's heartland, that type thing."

Vera Kjellsen nodded, and I got the uncomfortable feeling that I was being graded. "What," I said quickly, "can you tell me about Alexander Wayne back then?"

"Well, he was one hell of a good-looking man." She giggled. "When you called me, I went into the back room there and looked in the old yearbooks. I remembered Alexander as a good-looking man—we used to talk about it, the women teachers—but I had forgotten how good-looking. Other than that . . ." She turned one thin, clawlike hand. "He was a friendly man. And funny—he always had a joke or a funny comment of some sort. I think he got along with everybody. I don't remember any run-ins. Mostly, I guess, he just did his job, like the rest of us."

"Did you know him socially?"

"No, not really. My husband and I didn't really see much of any of the other teachers on what you would call a social basis. He was in insurance, my husband, and somehow most of our friends were insurance people or people he met through his work. We'd see Alexander at the faculty Christmas party, of course, but that was about it."

"Was he a good teacher?"

"I'm sure he was. I don't remember him being otherwise, and that's the kind of thing that sticks with you—the ones who had trouble managing a class or who had other kinds of problems. He must have been."

"Do you know why he got out of teaching and left town?"

She giggled. It was a girlish giggle, not fitting at all the wrinkled old woman it came from. "Do you have any idea what kind of money a schoolteacher in this state earned twenty years ago? Or today, for that matter? By nearly every yardstick, we're the lowest paid teachers in the country. People like to point out that we get three months off during the summer, but they conveniently forget that it's without pay. Well, anyhow, now you know what union I belong to. My guess is that Alexander Wayne reached a point where he had to, or wanted to, make some money for a change. A lot of teachers are forced to make that kind of decision, and not just in this district. Especially the men, for some reason. I suppose there's more pressure on them to be successful, to make money. Alexander always seemed like a bright fellow; I'm not surprised he's been successful in business. Real estate, did you say?"

I nodded. "He never told you his reasons for leaving?"

She shook her white head. "I don't think he told anybody. If he did, I never heard about it, and that would be unusual. Sooner or later you hear *everything*."

Sooner or later *you* would hear everything, I silently amended. Not that I felt Vera Kjellsen was a gossip or a busybody. Certainly no worse than anyone else. I just had the feeling that she liked to know what was going on, and that she kept her eyes and ears operating all the time. And there's nothing wrong with that. I'm much the same way myself.

Switching gears, I said, "I understand there was a girl, a student at the high school, who was killed in a hit-and-run accident. It apparently happened that last year that Alexander Wayne was on the staff . . ."

"Really?" She thought a moment. "I remember the girl, of course—she was a student of mine, a beautiful girl. And I remember the accident. It was horrible. But I didn't remember it being Alexander's last year. Of course there's no reason to link the two in my mind. There's no connection."

It might have been a question, though she put no question mark at the end of it and neither did I. If it was, I ignored it.

"Was there anything suspicious about the girl's death?"

"Suspicious?" She acted like she had never heard the word before. "I wouldn't say suspicious. Tragic, yes. She was walking home from school when she was struck and killed, killed instantly, by a car that had jumped a stop sign. There's nothing suspicious in that."

Maybe. "The driver was never found? No one was ever charged with the crime?"

Mrs. Kjellsen was shaking her head. "They never had a clue. It was such a shame . . ."

I said, "The girl, Stacy Eitrem—"

"Yes, that was the name."

"—had a boyfriend. Another student at the high school. He was Alexander Wayne's son, Thomas . . ."

Vera Kjellsen frowned. It was a bad idea for her to do that. Her face, which was deeply lined anyway and crisscrossed with a network of pale blue veins under her almost colorless skin, became an ugly voodoo mask when she frowned. "You're mistaken," she said with finality. "Alexander Wayne never had a son, not when he was here, at least. He didn't have any kids at all. He wasn't even married."

My turn to frown. "Are you sure, Mrs. Kjellsen? I was told—"

"You were told wrong. Alexander Wayne was the most eligible bachelor in the building. I can remember the unmarried women teachers—and even some of the married ones, too, if you want to know the truth—talking about him."

"In what way?"

She giggled again. "The gist of it was that they wouldn't mind ending his bachelor days for him."

I sipped some coffee. It was a good excuse to be silent for a moment and do my award-winning impersonation of a man trying to think. No Thomas Wayne in the school yearbooks for the time he should have been there. I find his father instead. But according to someone who knew him, the father didn't have a son at that time. And if Alexander Wayne had started his family after leaving Sioux Falls, his son, Thomas, would be twenty or more years younger than in fact he was. Adoption? Both Waynes clearly referred to Thomas's mother and Alexander's wife having passed away when the boy was very young. Could Vera Kjellsen be mistaken? She sounded awfully certain, but I know plenty of people who never sound more sure of themselves than when they're dead wrong. You probably do, too. I mean, you probably know people like that. Maybe she had Wayne confused with someone else, or maybe she just didn't realize that Wayne had a teenage son in the same school where he worked. If Wayne's wife had died when the boy was small, and he never remarried, perhaps Vera Kjellsen and other teachers in the building mistakenly assumed he had never been married at all.

None of which explained why Thomas Wayne appeared to be the little-student-who-isn't-there throughout his supposed high school years.

I wasn't the only one in the room who had been using the brief coffee break to do some thinking. Vera Kjellsen's face was still worked into a frown. "You know," she said slowly in her clear, somewhat brittle voice, "I do remember that poor Stacy had a boyfriend. He wasn't a student of mine, but I seem to remember the two of them together, her and her young man. What was his name?" She was talking to herself, to her memories, not to me. "Dark-haired boy, nice-looking . . . Thomas? Is that right?" She looked toward me, not at me. "But not Wayne. Thomas . . . Thomas . . . Cox? No, not Cox. Thomas . . . Cott. Yes, that's it." Her eyes, which had rested unseeing on my face, now came into focus and she was speaking to me, not the room. "Tommy Cott," she said with certainty. "He seemed like a nice boy. It was too bad. I think he dropped out shortly after, you know, Stacy . . . Probably a combination of things. Stacy, poor grades, and —well, I understand his family life wasn't the greatest."

"I thought he wasn't a student of yours."

Mrs. Kjellsen smiled tolerantly. "I didn't have him in a class, and I didn't know him very well, but I knew him—I knew who he was. Not only was he Stacy's boyfriend, but he was part of the theater crew and I was an assistant drama coach for a few years there. Besides, I told you, sooner or later you hear everything. I understood Tommy's father was nowhere to be found and his mother had . . . something of a drinking problem. You see it happen, in cases like that—the student simply loses interest, loses focus, runs out of steam. Too bad, too . . . he only had a few months till graduation . . ."

I said, "Mrs. Kjellsen, you said something about having yearbooks in the other room . . ."

She was on my wavelength. A minute later she was back with one of the volumes I had been perusing at the school library. It was the twenty-one-year-old book again, and she had it open to the senior-class pictures. It required no more than a glance to see that the face above the name Thomas Cott was remarkably similar to the face that currently went around attached to a man who called himself Thomas Wayne.

chapter
19

Sudden focus: Thomas Wayne, né Cott. People don't up and disappear and change their names for a lark. Not even teenage people. They have reasons, usually compelling reasons.

Killing someone would qualify.

I didn't understand the connection between Tommy Cott and his soon-to-be "father," however. Vera Kjellsen confirmed that Wayne had been the Cott boy's math teacher. I've known a lot of really dedicated teachers over the years, but I don't think any of them would have gone on the lam with me just to keep me company. There had to be a stronger bond—complicity or something else but something just as powerful.

I wondered what ever became of Tommy Cott's mother, and so did Vera Kjellsen. "I never met the woman," she said, leafing through a telephone directory that had sat under the instrument on an end table. "I knew her by reputation, though, from a story of her coming to conferences so drunk she could hardly stand and so abusive they finally had to call the police." She peered into the book, then closed it and returned it to its place. "No Cott in there that sounds like it could be her," she pronounced. "Of course, she may have moved away . . ."

"Or she may be dead, or she may have remarried and changed her name, or she may just not have a phone." I fell silent. I doubted whether the school itself would maintain twenty-year-old records, but there was a bare possibility that the local school district office would. It would at least give me a place to start looking. When you're working a cold, cold trail, you take anything you can get.

"I beg your pardon?" I said to Vera Kjellsen, because I had been thinking so loud that I didn't hear what she had said.

"I said, I remember where they *used* to live, Tommy and his mother, if that's any help. I used to give rides home to some of the drama students after the productions. One night I gave Tommy Cott a lift. I remember the house because it wasn't really a house at all. It was more of a . . . almost a garage."

That's exactly what it was. Vera Kjellsen gave me precise directions and I found it without a single wrong turn. It was a two-story, rectangular, concrete-block structure, slathered with pink paint, as Mrs. Kjellsen had remembered. It sat in a kind of valley or hollow not far from the cataract that gave the town its name, the falls of the Big Sioux River. In fact, I fancied I could hear the low and lazy rumble of water as I sat in my car across from the place. It was not a residential neighborhood. There was a metal-recycling operation across the street and a gas station further down the gentle hill, a cafe and a truck lines and a factory or plant or something beyond that. The state pen wasn't too far away, either, as I recalled, just over the rise to the north. The pink building hadn't been intended as a residence, either, or at least not exclusively so. It looked like it had begun life, forty or fifty years earlier, as a service station with an apartment on the top floor. The lower level still featured two overhead doors facing the pocked street, one of normal height and one tall enough to admit a medium-sized truck. A slab of concrete in the barren yard probably marked the spot that once had been taken up by gas pumps. It was in about the right location with regard to the building.

But no commerce was carried on there these days. A rusted-out, cannibalized, thirty-year-old Chevy pickup, dark green and bulbous, lay in the weeds alongside the joint. In the crumbling, weed-sprouting driveway, a fifteen-year-old Ford wagon in not much better shape stood waiting. The front end looked as if it had had an argument some time ago with a power pole. The car lost. Litter and garbage, cans and bottles and old papers, were strewn everywhere, the latter flapping damply in the steady breeze that came from the direction of the river. The weather here was similar to that down south, but chillier and windier.

I let up on the brake pedal and the car rolled down the hill forty feet. Then I pulled the wheel and circled the car around against the opposite curb, in front of the pink building.

A long, steep set of wooden stairs on the east face of the building led up to a small landing and the apartment's front door—only door, unless there was an exit through the garage bays below.

I locked the car and climbed the stairs.

The door at the top of the shaky stairs had an opening for a window, but the opening was currently covered with a piece of unpainted plywood, nailed on from inside. There was no bell. I rapped on the plywood. After a while the door was opened by a slovenly woman in a dirty, red T-shirt and tattered blue jeans. She had matted, gray hair and dirty, gray skin, and rolls of fat, and her huge, sagging breasts jiggled under the T-shirt when she fought the door open. The sour stench that escaped from the apartment, and her, strongly suggested that it had been many weeks since either had been anywhere near anything that might accidentally have cleaned them. She stared at me blearily. "Whattya wan'?"

"Mrs. Cott?"

"Whattya wan'?" she said again, and belched.

"Are you Mrs. Cott?"

She looked at me as if just noticing me. "Martha Cott," she said drunkenly. "Whattya *wan'*?"

"I want to talk to you about your son, Thomas . . ."

Again she stared. Then she looked away and teetered. "Got no son," she mumbled. "Go 'way."

Martha Cott went to slam the door on me but she was too lit. She lost her balance and instead of slamming the door she ended up on her keester inside the apartment, looking confused, as if she wondered how she'd got there.

I said, "I know you have a son, Mrs. Cott. I know his name is Thomas, and that he dropped out of Washington Senior High School twenty or twenty-one years ago, after his girlfriend was killed in a hit-and-run acci—"

"Who the fuck are you?" the woman bellowed. She rolled onto her side—she didn't really have a side, being mostly round, but she rolled onto what should have been her side and struggled to her feet. A litany of half-intelligible verbiage, much of it obscene, dribbled from her. "Who the fuck're you," again, and, "Wha're you doin' here," and, "Whattya wan'," and some more that I didn't catch, a senseless, drunken stream of consciousness that Martha Cott probably didn't even know she was spewing. In time, and with much effort and no little huffing and puffing, she got to her feet and teetered farther into the small apartment, making her unsteady way to a couch whose age was showing, not to mention its stuffing and springs.

Going in there was the last thing I wanted to do, but there

seemed few options. I took in some fresh air—there was no telling when I'd get more—and entered, leaving the door as it stood, open.

The grotesque woman had seated, or sprawled herself on the couch. Breathless, she sat for a moment, her back to me, lost in her own drunken reverie. More unintelligible talk leaked out of her. I couldn't make sense of it, but it seemed to be a kind of lament. The last word she spoke sounded like "Tommy," but it may have been "thirsty," because as soon as she had spoken it she put a grubby hand around the neck of a bottle of cheap bourbon and took care of what remained of the contents. It seemed to surprise her that the bottle was now empty. She looked around the room, as if trying to determine where the liquor had gone. The room was small and square and was both kitchen and living room. The furniture, what there was of it, was old and in bad shape. A banged-up console TV guarded one corner of the room. The carpet was stained and threadbare, worn clear through to the padding near the door, and probably accounted for much of the stench. Plates with the remains of long-gone meals and dirty glasses and beer cans and empty bags and bottles and wrappers were everywhere.

The drunk woman's search eventually brought her to me. She looked at me—I was standing just inside the doorway, where the oxygen content of the atmosphere seemed higher—then looked out the open door, then looked back. I was afraid she was going to tell me to close the door. Instead she said, "I'm thirsty," and looked out the door again.

I took her meaning, and I was glad of the chance to get out of that place. I went down the rickety stairs and down the hill and across the street to the cafe. They had a "lounge" there, as they called it, and an off-sale license. I bought a fifth of Jack Daniel's. I knew the good stuff would be wasted on Martha Cott, who wouldn't have cared if I stopped at the gas station next door and brought her back a bottle of Heet, but there was the chance I might be called upon to drink too, and I have more respect for my innards, especially when I'm on expenses.

I needn't have worried. Bearing gifts as I was, I was welcomed back a bit more cordially, but no effort was made to invite me to partake. Still, I noticed, Martha Cott had changed her top, to a lime-green polyester shirt with long sleeves and white top-stitching, and had somehow managed to coax a comb through her greasy, knotted hair. The effect was negligible and did nothing for the foul odor of the dirty little apartment. Still, I suppose I should have appreciated the effort. She even had a glass for herself, a slightly used twelve-ounce glass with the Peanuts kids on it.

I let her get a couple of swallows down her. Then I said, "Mrs. Cott, I'm a detective. I need to ask you about your son."

"Tommy," she wailed softly.

"Yes. Where is he? What happened to him after he left school?"

"Dead," she spat with that odd, quiet belligerence that only a drunk can manage. The hair on my neck went up. But then I remembered that "Tommy" wasn't dead—Tommy Cott might have been, but he had been reincarnated as Thomas Wayne—and then she said, "Never had no son."

I sighed, inwardly at least. I had tried getting information out of chronic, terminal boozers before. Usually it was a waste of time. No one makes very much sense when he's drunk, but the hardcore incurable alcoholic makes no sense ever, drunk or sober, because he's never sober. The stuff has corroded his brain and his mind and blurred forever the distinction between fantasy and reality, if in fact there is any kind of reality for them, to the point where it's no use your trying to separate truth from fiction in what they tell you, because there's no difference to them.

Still, a guy likes to be a sport, and I had a powerful itch to try to get at the connection between the boy and his erstwhile teacher. As if speaking to a child, I said, "Now, Mrs. Cott, you know that's not right. You have a son. Tommy. Remember?"

She was on the couch again, the bottle in one hand, propped on her fat thigh, the glass in her other hand, resting on the other fat thigh. She craned her neck to look at me.

"Tommy," I said.

"Tommy."

"What happened to Tommy?"

She had to think, and that required liquor.

"Dead," she finally decided.

"How did Tommy die?"

That took more liquor.

"Dead," was her answer.

"Yes, but *how* did Tommy die?"

"Tommy," she said again, and started blubbering.

At that moment a door at the other end of the room opened and a tall, broad man loped into the four-foot-long corridor at the back of the living room-slash-kitchen. He was an Indian with long black hair parted in the middle and pulled back behind his head. He wore a dirty athletic-style undershirt that did a lousy job of covering his pot belly, blue jeans, no shoes or socks. He regarded me without interest and ducked through a doorway at a right angle to the one he'd just come through. The latter looked like a cramped bedroom, the former I supposed to be a bathroom. The guess turned out to be right: I heard running water, as the novelists euphemistically put it, a second later.

The woman had forgotten what she was crying about and was entertaining herself again with the Jack Daniel's. I felt like I was in one of those episodes of *The Twilight Zone,* you know, where someone keeps wandering around bumping into people who don't act at all the way people should act, and then at the end you find out it's because they're all department store mannequins come to life or something.

"Mrs. Cott," I said, making an effort to hang onto my nerves because I figured one of us should. "When did Tommy die?"

She looked at me and smiled. "Cheers," she said. It sounded like *jeers.*

The Indian came out of the bathroom. He walked into the room with a slow, long-legged, easy gait, popped open the fridge and liberated a can of Pabst, and went back down the hall and into the bedroom, closing the door. If he gave us so much as a glance, he did it when I blinked.

I looked down at the drunken woman and decided to try another tack. "Mrs. Cott, Tommy had a teacher, in high school, a math teacher. Mrs. Cott, are you listening to me?" She looked up, in increments, a silly, distracted little smile on her face. "Tommy had a high school teacher. His name was Alexander Wayne—"

Vera Kjellsen was reasonably sure that Tommy Cott had had Wayne for a teacher, and I was reasonably sure that Vera Kjellsen was right, but Martha Cott seemed to have some objections. She yowled as if I had dropped something hot on her and threw her glass against the nearest wall, where it shattered into atoms and left a dark spot on the wall, and emitted a string of obscenities that would make Eddie Murphy blush. Among the tamest were, "Tha' sonofabitch," and "Tha' stinkin' cocksucker," and sandwiched in there were, "Tha' fucker killed my boy! Tha' fucker killed my Tommy!"

She went to blubbering again, and wailing, and kicking up a fuss that even two or three applications of alcohol from the bottle couldn't fix. I tried to calm her. I didn't go over and put my arms around her or anything so unhygienic as that, but I did sort of say, "Now, now, Mrs. Cott, calm down," and like that, but it didn't seem to help. Just the opposite, in fact. She seemed to get more and more worked up, going so far as to haul herself off the sofa and waddle around the room, yelling in her confused, nonsensical way, knocking things over, swearing and crying over her Tommy and insisting that I leave.

It sounded like an idea to me, and I was in fact trying to get past her and over to the door without, you know, actually *touching* her, when the back room's door opened and the Indian came out and took care of the problem. He grabbed me with one hand and grabbed the door with the other, opened the latter and threw the former into the great outdoors. I stumbled over the threshold and slammed into the wooden railing around the landing. The staircase affair was so decrepit that I was afraid my momentum would take the whole thing out, just peel it away from the side of the building and fall, taking me with it, to the ground a story below. But it didn't.

No time for a sigh of relief, though. The big man grabbed me again before I had a chance to get either my breath or my footing. This time he flung me down the stairs. I tumbled down about half of them before I managed to grab hold of the railing and bump to a stop. The stairs were very hard and I was very sore, though not as sore as I would feel after the new bruises got a few hours to settle in.

I got to my feet and, with as much dignity as possible, went down the rest of the stairs and across the yard and into my car. Where I sat and probed for broken bones and contemplated my next move.

It was past six. I had hoped to wrap up whatever it was I had intended to accomplish here in a single afternoon and head back to Omaha, but that was premature. I still wanted to know more about Tommy Cott aka Thomas Wayne, and the forces that brought him and his "father" together. Murder, or . . . ? I was strongly convinced that that relationship was at the heart of the matter, the most significant of the many things invisible in these two men's lives, and the key to the murder of Meredith Berens.

It suddenly hit me that I may have been engaging in my favorite sport, conclusion-hopping, when I assumed that Wayne and Wayne were not father and son. Couldn't it have just as easily been that Tommy was the illegitimate son of Alexander Wayne and Martha Cott? The "Mrs." in front of her name may have been purely decorative, then, and the old man who had taken a powder may have been fictitious.

The idea required a little massaging, since the woman was thoroughly repulsive. But perhaps she hadn't been nearly forty years ago and, hell, *someone* fathered the kid, presumably in the traditional manner.

Was it Alexander Wayne? That would explain a lot.

Now I definitely had to stay over, in order to check birth records when the county courthouse opened in the morning. Luckily for me and my 50,000-mile tires, which had over 60,000 miles on them, Sioux Falls was the county seat. I even knew, from previous visits, where the courthouse was. The record might or might not reveal anything of importance, of course, but it would have to be checked.

I looked back at the block building, dirty-pink against a dirty-gray sky, and briefly considered my chances of getting anywhere with Martha Cott on the subject of the elder Wayne. It was my mention of him that had set her off. Presumably because he took her son away. How would she know that, though, unless Wayne was the boy's father. I mean, it didn't seem like the sort of thing you'd tell a comparative stranger—"Hello, Mrs. Cott, I'll be taking your son to live with me now." It definitely didn't seem like the sort of thing you'd tell your mother. But it would be a reasonable guess, if your kid disappeared, that he had gone to be with his father. A reasonable guess, that is, unless you were Donna Berens, in which case you couldn't possibly consider the notion.

I turned away from the building and started the engine. There was nothing more to be learned there, unless I wanted to wait until Martha Cott had gone through an intensive detox program. And then see what, if anything, was left of her mind and her memory.

I put the car in gear and pulled away.

Towns change so much in so short a time, especially when they are fast-developing communities like this one. The city had boomed in the past decade, in no small measure owing to the arrival of several credit-card operations drawn by the state's liberal usury laws and nonexistent corporate-income tax. The medical profession had been doing its share, too—the three drives I had taken across town just this afternoon showed that. The two major hospitals had sprawled and spawned innumerable "specialty" practices, one on every corner by the look of it. Great stuff for the Chamber of Commerce handouts. New people come in, and new businesses, and new buildings go up while old ones come down. The population becomes increasingly mobile. And none of it makes it any easier to pick up a twenty-year-old trail.

Well, no one at the Acme Mail-Order School of Private Detection and Locksmithing ever said it would be easy. As long as I was here, I figured, I had better put my time to good use.

With some small work, I would probably be able to find out where Alexander Wayne had resided when he lived here. There may be a neighbor, a landlord, somebody who would remember him from the old days. I didn't know what I would say to such a person, exactly, but then I seldom did. In instances like this, you mainly follow your nose and see where it leads you.

Vera Kjellsen's directions to Martha Cott's home had taken me past a Holiday Inn downtown. Within walking distance of the Minnehaha County Courthouse, as it happened, which was a bonus. I found my way back and checked in for the night. I had had the foresight, for once, to throw socks, underwear, a clean shirt, deodorant, toothbrush and toothpaste, and shaving necessities into a battered canvas gym bag, anticipating the overnighter, so I was fairly well set. When I got situated in the hotel I went across the street to an army surplus store I had passed on the way in, and bought a pair of corduroys to replace the chinos I had torn on my way down Martha Cott's stairs. Then I went back to my room and showered and dressed, and came down for dinner alongside the indoor pool, where I basked in the rejuvenating vapor of chlorine and overheated pool water. After the Cott place, it was like breathing lilacs on a spring morning.

Across the street from the hotel in the other direction was a public library. I hiked over there after dinner and, with the help of some ancient city directories and a not at all ancient librarian, found Alexander Wayne's address from the time when the Beatles dominated the pop charts. The *first* time, I mean.

There are two four-year private colleges in the burg. Given the population, that's pretty amazing, almost as amazing as the fact that they are practically next door to each other. Nestled more or less between the two campuses, on a wide and tree-lined street, I found a small white bungalow with red decorative shutters that, according to the literature, had been Alexander Wayne's home up until about twenty-one years ago.

I started with the house across the street. Across-the-street neighbors usually have a better view of what's going on than next-door neighbors. You ask next-door neighbors what they heard, across-the-street neighbors what they saw.

The across-the-street neighbors hadn't seen anything, because they had lived there only three years. They didn't know the where-abouts of the previous residents, and they didn't know how long those people had lived there either.

I tried the houses on either side of the across-the-street neighbors and had just as much luck.

The neighbor to the north of Alexander Wayne's old house wasn't home. The neighbor to the south was. He was a small, bald-headed man in his late sixties. He had lived there since for-ever and he remembered Alexander Wayne, but he didn't re-member anything special about him. The man, whose name was Hohm, and his wife hadn't been close to Alexander beyond their shared lot-line. Wayne lived alone and minded his own business and kept his yard mowed in the summer and his walk shoveled in the winter, and that was all Mr. Hohm cared about. He didn't know why Wayne had moved away; he didn't much care. One day a for-sale sign went up in the yard and another day a moving van showed up out front and yet another day the for-sale sign went down and another moving van came and the Hohms had new neighbors.

I don't know exactly what it was I wanted. Something to clear the haze surrounding the relationship between Alexander Wayne and Tommy Cott—or between Wayne and Tommy's mother. One or the other being a frequent guest of Wayne would have helped. Or something that would in some fashion pertain to Stacy Eitrem's death, since I couldn't help but believe that that killing was some-how connected to the more recent murder. I had my guesses about it all, but it's always nice to have something substantial to upholster your guesses with.

Giving up on the old neighborhood, I found my way back to

the hotel and tried Dianna Castelli's number. No answer. It was about eight-thirty P.M., but I tried the agency anyway. You know these entrepreneurs. Same story there, however.

I had bought a newspaper and a couple of paperback novels earlier in the hotel gift shop. The local paper filled all of twelve minutes of my time, including the used-car ads. I tried Dianna again.

She was in, and out of breath. "I just got in and ran to answer the phone. The whole day's been like that—running to catch up. Are you back in town?"

I told her no and gave her my current location. She asked how things were coming and I gave her a *TV Guide*-style account of my afternoon.

"So Thomas Wayne isn't Thomas Wayne, and Alexander Wayne isn't his father," she said in wonderment when I had finished. "But Thomas's mother—that woman. Why did she tell you her son was dead?"

"I suppose he *is* dead, as far as she's concerned, and has been for twenty years. As for saying Alexander Wayne killed him, well, I guess he did kill Tommy Cott when he took him away and turned him into his own son, Thomas Wayne."

"Well, no *wonder* Alexander tried to keep you from looking into his past. I mean, it doesn't sound like he legally adopted Thomas or anything; he just took him away and they lived together as father and son."

"You watch too much *Dallas,*" I chided her. "Alexander, for all we know, could be Thomas's biological father. And whether he is or not, he didn't swipe Thomas out of his crib, and no one's going to come and take his almost-forty-year-old son away from him. Thomas was eighteen, presumably, or at least legally old enough to make most of his own decisions. Having met his mother, I doubt it was a very hard choice at all. After all these years, that secret's hardly worth keeping, especially looking into the teeth of a murder investigation, as they are. No, there's something else here, something that Alexander Wayne tried actively to keep me clear of, by threat, and Thomas Wayne passively, by fudging on the details of his parentage."

"You still think Thomas killed that girl." She had stopped saying it accusingly, at least, and now had begun to render it as a mere statement.

"I don't know. I think it's funny that Thomas's—Tommy's—girlfriend is killed and they never find the killer and then Thomas disappears and turns up twenty years later with a different name and, P.S., a girlfriend who's been killed. 'Funny' isn't the word. Try 'frightening.' "

"You're scaring me, Nebraska."

"That's why I switched to 'frightening.' As near as I can see, though, you don't have anything to worry about, unless you plan to start dating Thomas."

"I don't think so. What's next?"

I told her I planned to try to poke into Alexander's background more tomorrow—new day, fresh start—and that I expected to be back in the big city late afternoon or early evening. "I'll call you when I get in," I said. "If it's not too late, maybe we'll grab something to eat."

"I'd like that," she said. Then we hemmed and hawed a bit, trying to figure out how to end a conversation that had taken on a new and personal tone. We finally came to the conclusion that "good night" suited the purpose, so we both used it and got off the line.

Dianna Castelli was a little, shall we say, larger than life for my tastes. She was perhaps a little too loud, a little too outlandish in her style of dress, a little too everything. But I liked her. I liked the way she cared about her employees, the way she tried to protect Steve Lehman from mean old me, the way she cried for Meredith Berens. I still hoped that I could patch things up with Koosje, and I realized that, given the event that had driven the wedge between me and Koosje, starting a new relationship, however innocent, with another woman wasn't perhaps the swellest idea I had ever had. But I'm one of these wacky guys who likes female companionship, whether platonic, as with Kim Banner, or romantic, as with Koosje Van der Beek. Koosje would sort things out based on whatever criteria she used to sort out such things. In the meantime, I didn't intend to pursue the monastic life.

I spent some time with the TV, reinforcing my opinion that VCRs aren't worth owning. Nothing wrong with the technology, but it presumes that there's something on the airwaves worth capturing, and there sure as heck wasn't tonight. They pumped ten channels into the hotel, and all it meant was that there were ten

channels' worth of dreck instead of the usual three or four. I take
that back: There was a good movie on HBO. I had already seen
it, and recently.

Likewise, the first of the two paperbacks I had bought downstairs
was no good. Maybe that's not fair to say, since I didn't last beyond
page thirty-eight. It seems the guy who wrote it was afraid of the
word *says* and any of its common synonyms. So no one in the
book—up to page thirty-eight, at least—*said* anything. They *quipped*
and *retorted* and *enthused* like crazy, but they never *said*. Maybe
I'm too close to it, what with pretending to be a writer and all,
but that kind of stuff drives me loopy.

So, as I *said*, I called it quits after a couple of chapters. Luckily,
I had hedged my bet on the unknown quantity with a Nero Wolfe
novel. I'm neither an authority on nor a particularly avid en-
thusiast of the Wolfe books, but I've probably read a dozen of
them or more over the ages and I've never been disappointed
by one.

Wolfe and Goodwin took me up to the point where it began to
be an effort to keep my eyes on the page. I turned off the set
and the lights and put my head on the pillow and thought lazily
about the case. My case, not Nero Wolfe's. Investigations have a
peculiar way of changing not just shape but also direction on
you. Sort of like those calculus problems, where you're trying to
figure something out while the values are changing. Alexander
Wayne, the former math teacher, would be good at that. In this
instance, a missing-person hunt turned into a homicide turned into
another homicide turned into another, different kind of missing-
person hunt turned into . . . what? I wasn't there yet. There was
a light at the end of the tunnel, but I couldn't yet tell what it
illuminated.

The facts were these: Tommy Cott was Martha Cott's kid. Alexander Wayne had been Tommy Cott's high school math teacher.
Stacy Eitrem, Tommy's girlfriend, had been killed and the killer
was never found. Tommy Cott disappeared shortly afterward. So
did Alexander Wayne. Two decades later Wayne turns up in the
Big O with an adult son, Thomas, who coincidentally used to be
Tommy Cott. Thomas's girlfriend, or fiancée, if you like that version better, gets killed. And neither Thomas nor his father, or
"father," if you like *that* version better, is setting any records as
far as cooperating in the investigation is concerned.

It floated across my mind in that lazy half-second between waking and sleep that I could simply present the facts to Michael Berenelli and let him worry about what to do with them. *He* sure wouldn't lose any sleep trying to figure out exactly what the hell was going on. But then I didn't lose much sleep over it either.

chapter

20

In the dream, my high school math teacher was trying to kill me because I wouldn't take his Advanced Calculus course. In real life, any math teacher would be more inclined to kill me because I *had* taken his class, but in the dream, as in the way of dreams, it made perfect sense, as if math teachers routinely use the threat of death to fill empty seats in their classrooms. The math teacher definitely was my high school instructor, but in the dream he had the face of Michael Berenelli. He was shooting at me from rooftops with an elephant gun. I wouldn't know an elephant gun if I surprised one in my pajamas, but in the dream it was an elephant gun. When shooting me didn't work, he tried to run me down in a big Buick. I ran down some steps at the side of a pink block building and ducked through a steel door and hid in some kind of boiler room. It was hot and dark. Although the door had been unlocked when I entered and I had done nothing to change that status, it now was locked somehow, and Berenelli, on the other side of it, was pounding, pounding, and yelling my name.

The soft rapping at my hotel-room door didn't qualify as pounding, and the hushed voice from the other side was hardly a yell, although it was pronouncing my name. "Mr. Nebraska?" It was a woman's voice, soft and low, almost a whisper with no more extra volume than was necessary to push it through the door. "It's the assistant manager."

Numbly, stupid with sleep, I staggered out of bed and into my new pants and over to the door, wondering why she hadn't just used the phone.

The answer was immediately clear when I opened the door. It

was no assistant manager. Unless, that is, Dianna Castelli had taken a moonlighting job nearly 200 miles away from home base. I started to say something brilliantly witty, or as brilliantly witty as I can be at two A.M., but something in Dianna's face stopped me. There was a tightness around the throat. Her eyes were wide and her nostrils were flared and she seemed to be breathing a little hard. Excitement. Or fear. Or both.

The door swung inward a little more and she kind of half-stumbled into the room and then the man she had been with in the hallway, who had cautiously stayed out of peephole range, entered, preceded by a Colt .45 automatic.

I instinctively backed away from it. And came fully awake.

"I'm surprised," I said. "And then again I'm not surprised. If you catch my drift."

"Shut up," said Alexander Wayne.

He closed the door and I turned my attention to Dianna. She appeared to be on the verge of going into shock, and I didn't wonder. The past three hours, in the middle of the night in a car with an armed man who has killed before, must have been a nightmare with no end in sight.

There still was no end in sight.

I said, "Brave heart, Dianna."

She looked at me as if for the first time. "Nebraska," she said throatily. "He made me tell. I didn't want to. He had a gun . . ."

"So I see," I said. "Don't worry, Dianna. It's all right."

"Do you really think so?" Alexander Wayne said. He asked as if he was curious—there was nothing gloating or superior or melodramatic about it. In fact, there was none of the Jolly Charlie *bonhomie* that he had tried to affect even when he came to scare me off of the investigation the other evening. He was simply asking a question.

"Sure," I said with both a casualness and a conviction that I didn't feel. "You're painted into a corner, Wayne. I think you must know that. Why else did you bring Dianna all this way? You know the game is up, you knew it when you forced her to tell you where I was, but you couldn't admit it to yourself. You brought her here, at gunpoint, because doing so allowed you to postpone having to make a decision about her."

He shook his big, white head. "Use your head, Nebraska. I would have killed her when she told me where you were, except

I couldn't trust her. She had already lied to me. When I called her late this evening and said I needed to get in touch with you but couldn't seem to locate you, she lied. She said she didn't know where you were or what you were doing. I knew she was lying. The way you talked about her the other night, I knew you would have told her. So I went to her house and I convinced her to talk." He waved the heavy weapon slightly. "But I didn't trust her. I couldn't very well leave her there to call the police, to warn you. And I couldn't kill her, not then, since I didn't know whether she was just a good liar. Most women are."

"And people call me a sexist," I said low. "Be that as it may, this is the end of the line, Wayne. You can't go on protecting your son—we'll continue that fiction, since, after twenty years, it's probably as good as true. I won't say he's pathological, that's not for me to determine, but two murders in two decades isn't evidence of normal, well-adjusted behavior, plus it's frowned on by Miss Manners and other authorities. When he killed Stacy Eitrem you took him away, away from a bad life and a bad situation. You thought you were doing the right thing. Maybe the law will look at it that way. But now . . . there's nothing right about this, not any of it. You have to see that. Put down the gun and let's get some help for him, for Christ's sake, before another girl makes the fatal mistake of falling for him."

The older man said nothing, which bothered me a lot. The silent seconds dragged into a full minute. Then he spoke. "Finish dressing," he told me.

We took Wayne's car. I drove. Dianna sat in front with me. Wayne sat in the back, in the far right corner where I couldn't see him in the rear-view mirror but from where I could feel his eyes, and the gun, on me constantly. He gave directions and I followed them. The streets were virtually deserted, the houses and businesses we passed were black and silent. The wind was up and there was a pale silver moon but no stars and the sky had the heavy, sweetish smell of impending rain.

It looked like we were going to Martha Cott's house. Apparently Wayne was going to burn all the bridges—Dianna, me, and the Cott woman. It wouldn't end the investigation, but it might give him and Thomas enough time to disappear, as they had done before, and reemerge elsewhere.

Wayne couldn't know about Martha Cott's boyfriend, the Indian who had lifted me like a sack of dog chow and thrown me down the front stairs. The Indian would throw a wrench into Wayne's plans, I figured. Prayed, if you prefer. I would have to be doubly watchful, wait for the exact moment and act.

Dianna, whether from desperation or just nerves, had picked up on the line I had fed Wayne back at the hotel and was prattling on in a way that would have been pretty annoying if I hadn't been thinking too hard to pay much attention. I got the gist of it, however. She was echoing the opinion that covering up for Thomas, to the point of killing us, wasn't helping him any, that things had gone too far to be stopped by our deaths, that Wayne was only making things worse for himself and Thomas, that Thomas may not have been responsible for his actions but Wayne surely was.

"Save your breath," I told Dianna gently. "Although in a few more minutes you won't be needing it anyhow. It isn't Thomas who needs help. It's Alexander. He's the one with the sickness." And that was the only way it made sense, now. The problem all along had been that whatever theory I concocted to indicate Thomas Wayne's guilt could also be hung on Alexander Wayne with few if any alterations. Thomas had struck me as the more logical candidate for the available slot, with his father acting as accessory. But when I portrayed Thomas as being a brick or two shy a load, and when Dianna had picked up the refrain, Alexander had failed to rise to the bait. He didn't defend his son, nor did he tell us to shut up. I'd read a lot of detective novels, and this just wasn't the way it was supposed to go. If Alexander knew that Thomas was sick, you would expect him to want to help his son, and I don't mean help him in his career as a killer. If he wouldn't admit to himself that his boy was off the beam, you wouldn't expect him to stand around like a park statue while comparative strangers said he was.

The conclusion was that my conclusion was wrong. And that left only Alexander Wayne to carry the banner.

To Dianna I said, "Alexander's the one who killed Stacy Eitrem. That's the name of Thomas's old girlfriend. And then he took Thomas away from his mother, which was in the way of doing him a favor, and the two of them, masquerading as father and son, kicked around the Midwest for twenty years or so, eventually ending up in our little hamlet. I'm assuming," I said, raising my voice for the benefit of the invisible man in the back seat, "that you didn't leave a trail of corpses everywhere you went. I'm guessing that, after Stacy Eitrem, Thomas was smart enough to keep women at arm's length, for their own good. No telling when his 'father' would decide that one of them was getting too close, and bump her off. By the way, you aren't Thomas's natural father, are you?"

There was no sound from the back. I could have been talking to myself, for all I knew.

"Of course not," I said. "Then the sonny-and-pappy bit was a convenient way to defuse any speculation about what two unrelated men were doing living under the same roof."

A dry chuckle came from the darkness behind me. "That's not a very enlightened attitude, Nebraska."

"No? Well, the sixties weren't a very enlightened time, I'm afraid. Much more of a stigma attached to, uh, the love that dare not speak its name. Especially given the twenty-year age gap, and that one of the consenting adults was barely an adult."

Dianna was a step or two behind us. "Did he kill Meredith?" she wanted to know.

"Oh, *hell* yes," I said. "Meredith had the bad luck to fantasize that she was engaged to Thomas. That wouldn't do." It had to have been a fantasy: Knowing, or even just suspecting, that Alexander had done in Stacy Eitrem, Thomas wouldn't put another woman in that kind of danger. Unfortunately for Meredith Berens, she didn't know any of this history. She put herself in danger, and Thomas's efforts were insufficient to shake her off before it was too late. I went on: "You'd have to ask our friend whether he was motivated by a concern for Thomas's future or plain old jealousy."

She didn't ask, and Wayne didn't volunteer.

We had threaded through the empty downtown streets and under a low railroad trestle and were taking the long incline that intersected with the street that the Cott house fronted. But before we got that far up the hill, Wayne instructed me to turn off onto a narrow road that led down into a semi-wooded valley. There was a wooden sign along the drive, momentarily illuminated by our headlights as I made the turn: FALLS OF THE BIG SIOUX RIVER.

"My guess is that he called Meredith and arranged to meet her someplace. As father of the prospective groom, any excuse would do. The hit-and-run trick would have been better, smoother, but it wouldn't have been as easy to arrange with Meredith Berens as with Stacy Eitrem. The Eitrem girl walked to and from school, and Alexander either knew her route or learned it without trouble. Meredith, if she's like everyone else in this part of the country, drove everywhere. Anyhow, they met and he killed her and stashed her car somewhere." For Wayne's benefit, I added, "He must be pretty unsure of himself, and of Thomas, if he has to keep killing anyone who has any real feelings for his 'son.' "

"Thomas loves me and I love him," said the voice from the backseat. "He's my son."

"You know what? After all these years that's probably true. It may have started as a masquerade, a way to keep people from wondering or talking or being too inquisitive, but I suspect you're right: Now Thomas *is* your son, and like anybody's son he's bound to leave you and lead his own life."

"This will do."

I thought he was referring to my yakkety-yak, but he meant I could park the car. I did.

We were off of the road and partly hidden from it by a big jungle of scruffy, untamed trees and bushes. The moon provided the only light, and it was liquid and cold. When I shut off the engine I could hear the loud swish and swirl and rumble of water tumbling over rock.

"The woman and I will get out first," Wayne said.

He was pretty good, good enough, at least, to see that Dianna was too scared to try to pull anything. He held the gun aimed at the base of her neck, eight inches back, and synchronized his getting out of the car with hers, so that there was only an interval of a quarter of a second when the post between the front and rear doors blocked his aim.

I sat still with my hands on the wheel.

Wayne marched Dianna around the back of the car and to the driver's side. He stood well away from the doors, Dianna still in his sights. "Now you."

I got out of the car.

Wayne had brought something with him from the backseat: a heavy pole, like a closet clothes-pole, eighteen inches long and two or two-and-a-half inches in diameter. He carried it loosely in his left hand. It was not the pole he had beaten Meredith Berens with. That one would be long gone. This one was fresh and new and gleamed white in the moonlight.

"Does Thomas know?" I challenged Wayne. "Does he know you've killed the only two people who have ever become close to him, just so that you can maintain your influence over him? I wonder if that's why he tried so desperately to end things with Meredith—if he suspected her affection for him could have fatal consequences."

"The bitch was crazy," Wayne said conversationally. "Thomas didn't have any interest in her, or anyone, for that matter. All she wanted was to get her hooks into my boy."

"You'd know all about that," I agreed. "You hooked him but good. Cut him off from the only real life he'd ever known—a crappy life, okay, but *his*—took him away, gave him a new identity, remolded him in your own image . . ."

"Enough," Wayne said. He sounded tired, not angry. "Over there."

I found myself wishing that Thomas Wayne had been the killer. I knew from experience that I could provoke him easily, and with far greater success than I was having with his father. If Dianna had not been along, I had seen a couple of openings where I probably could have taken the gun away from Wayne. He was larger and heavier than me, but I was younger and, presumably, in better shape. I probably would have tried it, in any event, but Wayne cagily kept Dianna between me and him—and, more significantly, the gun—at all times. That may have struck him as another good reason for hauling her along, and I would have had to agree with him, based on how things were going so far. And he seemed impervious to any attempts to sting him, goad him into reacting rather than acting, into making the mistake, giving me the opening. He was imperturbable, damn him, and he was guiding us to the water's edge.

We were moving upriver, toward the high point of the falls. The water wasn't particularly high, since the season hadn't been uncommonly wet, and the falls themselves were nothing too dramatic—no Niagara—but the rush of water over them was swift, and you didn't need a great deal of imagination to guess what would happen when the energy inherent in that rush slammed a human body against the outcroppings of rock that glistened in the moonlight.

The noise of the falls would be sufficient to muffle the sound of two gunshots.

We moved past the viewpoints roped off for the public and onto the rocks. They appeared to be the same pink quartzite that half the buildings in town were constructed of. They were worn smooth by the glaciers that deposited them there and the water that had flowed over them for centuries without number before the river narrowed to its current bed. They were slippery from the mists kicked up by the waterfall. Dianna slipped once and almost fell. I slipped and went down on one knee, hard. Alexander Wayne, cuss him, was as sure-footed as a mountain goat.

We reached the highest point, a triangular ledge poking out into the water. It was as far as you could go and still be dry. Two bodies pushed into the river from there would be swept over the cataracts—down a short drop and over a shelf of rock and then down a longer drop and into the lower river—ending up broken and battered and God knows where. Wayne's plan was transparent. The pole had made it so. A blow or two to kill us or at least render us incapable of resistance, then he would tip our bodies into the river, to be swept over the falls. The deaths might well appear accidental, then, the injuries from the pole indistinguishable from the injuries from the rocks in the water.

It only remained to be seen what Wayne intended to do with the one of us while he took care of the other. I assumed he had a plan.

"I'm surprised Martha Cott isn't with us," I said. I risked a glance over my shoulder. "Or do you have other plans for her?"

"What would be the point," Wayne said. I knew what he meant. "This is where we part company."

I looked at him again. We were at the very tip of the triangular ledge, where the point disappeared into the black-silver water. He was behind us—too far behind us for my liking—with the gun. He pointed it at me and set the pole on the ground, kicking it toward me and then stepping away from it. Out of range.

"Pick it up," he said.

"Phooey on that noise," I said.

He jerked the automatic.

"I'm ahead of you, Wayne," I said with a nonchalance that I didn't feel. "I'm supposed to take the stick and give Dianna a couple of good whacks. Then you'll use the stick on me. No bullets.

Nothing to trace back to you. Not a bad plan, although I would certainly put up a fight the minute you put the gun away to bludgeon me. We won't know how that would turn out, though, because I'm not cooperating. You have a contingency plan?"

It was the gun. "I'll use this if I have to," he said.

"It looks like you have to. *If* you're a good enough marksman in this light."

"I am. If I have to be." I didn't doubt it. And with the sky and the moon behind us, we were good targets.

When I had slipped and fallen farther downstream, it was because a loose, flat rock had twisted underfoot. When I had gone down, it was to palm the rock, which was larger than my hand and about two inches thick, but which I hoped would go unnoticed in the tricky light. It had. For all the good it had done me, since Alexander Wayne had given me no opening. But now Dianna Castelli did. Wayne barely had his last words out when she let out a cry, the sound of a night's worth of tension and fear escaping, and turned and sprang at him.

It was a damn fool thing to do, but she was doing it and it was the first opportunity to come along. I whirled.

Wayne had the gun up but Dianna slammed into him and the shot that leaped from the weapon disappeared into the night, whining against a rock somewhere as it escaped.

I moved in and shoved Dianna out of the way and brained Wayne with my rock. Tried to, anyhow. For a big man he moved fast. The stone took him in the collarbone and a low groan escaped him as something under the fleshy skin gave. But in a movement that almost mirrored mine, he brought the gun to the side of my head and pulled the trigger.

The sound of the shot was so loud that I could hardly hear it: My ear sort of filled up and all that came through was a high-pitched kind of feedback. The flash was blinding even through my closed eyelids. I felt warmth on my face, pleasant at first but then, in an instant, too hot, and there was a hotter, searing pain along the left side of my head, above the deaf ear. I was lucky, if you want to call it that, that Wayne had had neither time nor room to take aim, and that, when he brought the gun up, the butt had clipped me on the cheek. The angle of the slug was up and away from me. Two degrees the other direction would have taken it through my empty skull.

As it was, though, the shot stunned me and blinded me and deafened me. It carved a shallow gutter in my scalp over my left ear and took the very tip of the ear with it when it went. And, through some strange physical reaction that Isaac Newton would have understood, the shot at my head took my feet out from under me and I went down, backward, into the cold black water.

chapter

21

Some part of my brain, the one one-hundredth that was neither numb with shock nor frozen with panic, registered the sound of another gunshot. By the sound of it, it had been fired on Venus.

The water behind me was not deep. It was cold, and unbreathable, but not deep. The ledge on which I had been standing was in fact part of one long shelf of rock that dipped down into the water and then jutted up again thirty feet out. Where I fell, then, the water was no more than two feet deep. But it was moving fast and the stone beneath me was smooth and slippery with moss or algae or some other aquatic vegetation, and I barely had time to cough out a choking mouthful of water and suck in a strangled breath of air before I was swept off the shelf and down toward the falls.

The water shoved me toward the nearer bank and into a cropping of stone rising two or three feet above the foaming surface. Blindly, instinctively, I clawed at it. It was as smooth as glass, as slippery as ice. The water pulled me down, beneath the surface, and slammed me into a submerged rock formation. By luck rather than by skill I pushed away from it with my legs, propelling myself away from it and upward. That's where the luck part came in: I couldn't tell up from a 1966 Pontiac Catalina at that point.

I grabbed some air before the water took over again and flung me over the first drop.

This was the short one—maybe six feet from top to bottom. I went over easily enough, and the water itself provided some cushioning when I landed on the ledge below. Enough of my brain was working that I knew this would be a good stopping-off point, if I could manage it. The next drop was the killer.

WILLIAM J. REYNOLDS

I got to my feet, sort of, and scrabbled for the bank, sort of—slipping and gasping and sobbing for breath. The footing was too smooth and slippery and the water was too insistent and I was too tired, too tired . . .

I was eight feet from terra firma and I wasn't going to make it.

Below the higher fall, I had noticed on our way up, jagged, broken rocks lay in testament to the destructive power of the water. Even if I survived the drop, I wouldn't survive landing on those rocks. Not in any shape that would make me glad to have survived, at any rate.

I was seven feet from terra firma and I wasn't going to make it.

The water simultaneously tugged at me, urging me over the brink, and impeded my pitiful progress toward the bank. My lungs were screaming for air, my muscles, which had hardly recovered from my beating the other night and my tumble down the stairs that evening, were throbbing in agony, and I was shivering almost convulsively from the effects of the cold water and mortal dread. The only thing that didn't hurt, ironically, was my head. It felt six times its usual size, puffy and soft-hard the way your lip does when you have a mouthful of Novocain, but it didn't hurt.

I was six feet from terra firma and I wasn't going to make it.

In fact, I didn't make it. I stepped on something slimy and both feet went out from under me as if I was on icy pavement, and that was all the invitation the water needed. I went down on my back and it rolled me over the edge.

There was a piece of wood, a weathered old four-by-four, wedged between the rock that formed the outside wall of the falls and an anvil-shaped formation that protruded from the shorter drop. Someone had thrown it in, or it had fallen in upstream, the current carrying it until luck took over and jammed it between the rocks there. When I had realized that I couldn't make it to dry land, seconds before it became reality, I set my sights on that four-by-four. As the water rolled me over the edge I grabbed at it and caught it with one hand and threw the other arm around it, squeezing it tight in the crook of my arm.

With a kind of squeal against the rocks, the four-by-four slipped.

Slipped three inches, maybe, and held. I wrapped my other arm around it and, after a couple of attempts, got my right leg hooked over it as well. I hung there like a sloth from a tree branch, dripping, working on getting my breath back.

It all sounds pretty heroic, huh? Batman, the Man from U.N.C.L.E. and Sergeant Preston all rolled into one handsome package. Guess again. The moment Alexander Wayne's gun went off my brain went to Fort Lauderdale for spring break, leaving my body to muddle through the best it could on instinct alone. That was just as well. Rational thought would insist that I couldn't survive the waterfall, so why bother? Instinct, not knowing from rational thought, was only interested in keeping me alive and worked reflexively to that end. Once it saw that the danger had momentarily passed, my brain hopped back into the driver's seat and started pushing buttons and pulling levers again.

A week later, maybe two, the signals reached the appropriate outposts, and my body, which had sort of thought its job was done when I glommed onto the four-by-four, went back to work. Slowly, very slowly, and painfully, I worked my way down the four-by-four to the wall it was jammed against. There were toe-holds there. I found them and climbed five or six feet to the top of the wall, which turned out to be a thick, short column whose top was at the same level as the ground, good old Ma Earth, some ten feet over. The column must have once been connected to the mainland, but the vagaries of erosion had separated them.

I went down the column on the far side and carefully tested the waters at the base of the stone. It was calm here, sheltered in a kind of miniature bay between the column and a low, wide outcropping a few feet downstream. But that wasn't what I was checking. I wanted to see if there was firm footing between the column and the wall that led up to the ground. There was. The column and the wall shared a floor of stone only two or two and a half feet underwater. I waded toward the wall slowly, an inch at a time, lest the floor suddenly disappear beneath me. It didn't, and I reached the craggy wall and started up it. My shoes were wet and slippery and the toe-holds were wet and slippery and I nearly slid down the face of the wall once, but I made it to the top and rolled away from the edge, onto the gritty, dirty rocks and the sparse, coarse grasses that grew up between the fissures, and was never so glad of anything in my life.

Eventually I rolled up onto my knees and vomited up the remains of my supper. The heavy smell of chlorine from the swimming pool at the hotel hung in my nostrils.

Feeling better now, but still pretty shaky, I stumbled away from the water and across a paved parking area and across a playing field and into some thick bushes. I had no way of knowing how long my swim had taken. Anywhere from five minutes to a fortnight, I figured. Alexander Wayne may have been long gone by now, or he may have been hanging around, looking to see where my carcass ended up, waiting to finish me off if the roiling waters of the Big Sioux hadn't taken care of me. If he was still loitering there, I wanted any confrontation to be at my instigation. I was in no shape to be on the defensive.

I made my way back upstream, where the drama had begun, sticking close to the bushes. Not only did that reduce the odds of my being spotted against the night sky, but it gave me a place to duck into and disappear if I *was* spotted.

I didn't have to worry. I reached the spot where I had parked Wayne's car. It was gone. He may have driven farther down river to see where I ended up. It didn't matter. He wasn't there, and he wasn't up by where I had fallen in.

He wasn't, but Dianna was. I saw her before I reached her, saw her prone shape on the triangular ledge, pale in the moonlight. The scenario was obvious. I had gone over the edge and been written off as dead. Wayne, shaken after our struggle, dropped Dianna with a single shot, the one I had heard after hitting the water. He hadn't bothered to tip her body into the water. He hadn't bothered with anything, except running.

I came up to her. One leg hung over the edge of the rock formation, dipping playfully into the water. I smoothed her pale hair, dampened by the mists of the falls, away from her face. The bullet had struck her high in the chest. I hoped she had died instantly.

I lifted her and carried her onto the grass eight or ten feet back.

I put her on her back, looking at the nonexistent stars, and lay down beside her. I wanted to rest. I wanted to go to sleep and wake up in the morning in my queen-sized bed at the Holiday Inn City Centre, between the stiff, heavy sheets, and find that this night had all been a dream. A nightmare.

Well, it had been that. A nightmare. One that I lived through and Dianna Castelli did not. I pulled myself to my feet and looked down at her. You'd have thought she was sleeping. One leg was straight and one leg was bent a little, one arm lay a little to one side and the other was draped across her stomach. Her face was turned to one side, her lips were parted and her eyes were closed. You'd have thought she was sleeping, except for the bullet wound that stained the front of her sweater black-red in the moonlight and which showed slightly above the sweater's scoop neck.

The hotel wasn't far from the falls. Maybe a mile, maybe more. I was almost there before I knew that's where I was headed. The streets were deserted. Between the falls and the hotel I spotted only one moving car, a white police cruiser. The cop must not have seen me or he surely would have stopped to investigate a bloodied, soaking-wet man limping along the city streets at three, three-thirty in the morning.

I'm guessing the time. My wristwatch had taken a licking, all right, but it hadn't kept on ticking.

The parking ramp at the hotel could be accessed from the street, without going through the lobby, so that's what I did. I got in my car and headed toward the Interstate.

How long between the time I fell into the water and the time I heard the gunshot? Minutes. Five? Six at the outside? How long between the gunshot and the time I came upon Dianna? Twenty minutes? Half an hour? Impossible to say. Let's call it thirty to forty minutes between the time Wayne killed Dianna and the time I found her. Another twenty to thirty minutes for me to stagger to my car. Ten minutes for me to thread through town and onto I-29.

At best, if Wayne had dawdled, wasting time, looking for me, he had an hour's head start. At worst, if he had hit the road immediately and my time estimates were off—for all I know, I could have hung on that four-by-four for ten or fifteen minutes— he had a couple of hours on me.

Part of my brain said it didn't make any difference. Where was Wayne going to go except back to Omaha? Things had gone wrong for him tonight, and so he might have to disappear, but he would not have planned for them to go wrong so he wouldn't be ready to disappear immediately. He would have to go home first and make quick arrangements before he could amscray.

I hoped.

I hoped real hard, because if I was wrong then Wayne was already out of my reach. He could have taken I-29 north, to Canada, rather than south to Nebraska, and if he had, he was gone;

if he had headed anywhere other than Omaha, he was gone. I-90, which intersects with 29 near Sioux Falls, could take him west across South Dakota and into Wyoming or east across Minnesota and into Wisconsin. From I-90, or I-29 if he chose that route, he could link up with interstates or other major and secondary highways that, with no effort, could take him into Minneapolis-St. Paul, Des Moines, Madison, Chicago. He could be in any of them before noon. You can't deal with that, with the "anywhere factor." He could be going anywhere, and you can't be everywhere. So you toss a coin and make the decision to be not everywhere but in one good place.

Omaha.

He would be observing the speed limit. He couldn't afford to be picked up and ticketed. Once I was clear of the city and its double-nickel speed regulation, I nosed the needle on the speedometer to seventy miles an hour. When I looked down a little while later I was surprised to see it was at seventy-five. I left it there until I hit the Iowa border. Iowa cops are reputed to take their speed laws seriously. I dropped to a prudent sixty-nine miles an hour until the tangle of ramps at Sioux City slowed me down to fifty-five again. I had to put gas in the car at Sioux City—it's a wonder the truck-stop attendant didn't call the cops on me, but, come to think of it, I didn't look much worse than he did—and once I cleared the city I inched back up to sixty-nine again.

I had the heater on in the car and my clothes were drying in that stiff, uncomfortable way wet clothes have of drying on you. And, of course, my back and my butt and the backs of my legs weren't drying at all, thanks to my vinyl car seats. My head was pounding steadily and my body was exhilarating in all kinds of aches and pains it had never before experienced and, in all, it was the longest drive of my life.

Shortly after six, with the sun painting the bottoms of the gray eastern clouds pink, I turned off onto I-680, "the Nebraska side," as interstate aficionados have it. I-29 continues south through Iowa, through Council Bluffs, at which point you can get off and onto 480 into eastern Omaha. I-680 takes you into Nebraska, around the north side of town, and down the west side. It was the fastest route to the Waynes' place.

Alexander Wayne's car was in the driveway.

I pulled in behind it and let the bumpers kiss. He wasn't going anywhere, not in that car, not unless he could coax it up over mine.

I fished the gun out of my glove compartment, checked the cylinder, and got out and moved toward the house.

The sun was up. The sky was heavy with clouds—honest-to-goodness clouds, not the solid grayness that had hung there for days on end—but the light found an occasional gap to peer through kind of sidewaysish. Despite the clouds, the world had that hard, unreal look that the morning sun gives things.

The Waynes' overhead door was down but the front door was open. That bothered me. I tightened my hand on the gun and moved laterally up the stoop, trying to stay out of the range of the big window in the storm door.

I came up even with the door and waited. Nothing happened.

I peeked around and looked through the screen over the window. There was a wide, short entryway that led from the front door past the kitchen and into the living room. From there, only the very end of the living room could be seen. But what I could see of it was a disaster. Furniture was tipped, breakables were broken, junk was scattered everywhere.

Raising my weapon, I tried the storm door. It was unlocked. It swung open easily, soundlessly, and I went in.

The kitchen was to my left, the dining room beyond it, the living room, which also was accessible via the entryway, beyond that. I paused near the open doorway to the kitchen, brought the gun up in both hands, took a breath, and peeked around the corner.

Neat as a pin.

I stepped onto the linoleum. After being soaked and dried improperly, my shoes squeaked on the hard floor. But I needed only three long steps to cover the distance to the pocket doors separating kitchen and dining room. The doors were parted six inches. I glanced through into the formal dining room. It, too, looked like a page from a magazine.

Liking the silence of carpeting better than the kitchen's linoleum or the dining room's parquet, I slipped out and back into the entryway and padded softly to where the entryway turned into the living room in one direction and a long hallway to the bedrooms in another. It was there that the carnage began. But that was only the beginning. I glided around the corner into the big room. It had high white walls and a vaulted ceiling and tall windows on the southern exposure. The carpet was thick and powder blue, blue, that is, where it wasn't stained purple-red with blood.

I took a breath and held it and let it out again. It was a good thing my stomach was empty.

The room was a disaster. I've said that already, but it bears repeating. Except for the big sofa near the windows, there wasn't a stick of furniture in its proper place. Most of it was knocked over, much of it was broken. Books, photographs, little mementos and all the bits and pieces of this and that which people are apt to collect and display—strewn and shattered.

In the center of the room was Alexander Wayne. He was on the floor, on his knees, cradling the body of his son. Thomas Wayne, Tommy Cott, was bound hand and foot. His ankles were tied with yellow nylon cord and his wrists were tied with the same cord, another short length of which attached his wrists to his ankles. A white cloth had been twisted into a thick gag and stuffed between his teeth and tied around the back of his head but someone, presumably Alexander, had removed the gag and pulled it out of his mouth, down around his chin.

The younger man lay in the older man's arms, his head flopped grotesquely to one side. His forehead was a mass of bloodied, torn gristle. A goodly portion of the back of his head was missing.

Not "missing," exactly. Just not where it should have been. Where it was was on the walls and the furniture and all over the carpeting. It's the effect you achieve when you tie someone the way Thomas Wayne had been tied and you put a pistol against his skull and you pull the trigger. What they call execution-style.

Thomas Wayne had been executed, in a big way, and I didn't have the slightest doubt in my mind who had taken care of it. Not Michael Berenelli, of course; he wouldn't be found within six hundred miles of this place. Not even Paul Tarantino. Someone much, much further down the list—but someone who could be trusted, nevertheless, to handle the job and keep it to himself—had pulled the trigger, but on the Baron's orders. I didn't know whether his people simply accumulated the same circumstantial evidence as I had and deduced Thomas's guilt from that, or whether one of them had followed me yesterday despite my precautions and reached the same conclusion. It didn't much matter and I didn't much care. Thomas Wayne may have been innocent of the murders of Stacy Eitrem and Meredith Berens, but he surely knew or strongly suspected that his father had been guilty—his evasiveness indicated that much—and consequently shared in that guilt. Shared responsibility for the deaths of Stacy Eitrem and Meredith Berens and Dianna Castelli. I had no tears for him.

Alexander Wayne looked up at me. From the look on his face, the look in his eyes, he may not have recognized me. Probably didn't. He had been there for some time like that, judging from the way blood had soaked into his jacket and trousers.

"My son," he said. "My son is hurt."

I said nothing.

He looked back at the younger man's ruined face. "Who did this to you, Thomas," he moaned. "Who would do this to you? My son . . ."

Martha Cott had been right. Prescient, but right. Alexander Wayne had killed her son. Not directly, and not quickly, but certainly.

I said, "The man who did this may have drawn the erroneous conclusion that Thomas killed his daughter. Or perhaps he meant to have you killed last night but, you being unavailable, settled on this instead. A son for a daughter. Either way, Wayne, the man responsible for Thomas's death is in this room with me."

He looked at me again, bewildered, and only then seemed to recognize me. His face hardened and his lips pulled away from his teeth in a hideous parody of a grin. "You bastard," he said, his voice a growl. "This is your fault."

He moved then, going for his gun. After so many years in this business, you get to where you can judge intent just from the movement, the set of the body, the look in the eye. But the gun must have been in a pocket in the side of the jacket that was under Thomas. He couldn't draw it without letting go of Thomas, and he wouldn't let go of Thomas.

Anyway, long before he could have gotten to the gun I had mine up and aimed at his head.

He looked at me, and the death's-head grin was back. "Go ahead," he said hoarsely. "I don't care."

I could have done it. Pulled the trigger and ditched the gun and let the cops speculate about why one of the corpses had been tied up and shot in the back of the head and the other had been shot from the front, untied, and each from a different gun. It would be little enough in return for what he had put Dianna through last night, and me, and for Dianna's murder, and Meredith Berens's, and Stacy Eitrem's.

"Go on," he repeated. "I don't care."

I lowered the gun and uncocked it.

"I do. I care about Meredith Berens and Dianna Castelli and Stacy Eitrem, the ones you killed and the one you tried to kill— me. And I even care about your 'son,' who was in many ways your biggest victim. Caring like that means it would be real easy to honor your request. Too easy. Even pleasurable. But, corny as it sounds, I also care about being able to look myself in the mirror in the morning and distinguish myself from people like you. And I care that Meredith's father is one of the biggest Mob bosses in the country, and that he'd be disappointed to find out he'd whacked the wrong man and I didn't give him a chance to set it straight."

I pocketed the gun and turned to leave, pausing where the living room met the entryway.

"Good-bye, Mr. Wayne," I said to the big white-haired man, who hadn't budged from his position on the carpet. "I doubt we'll be seeing each other again."